THE STARLESS KING

LUCY TEMPEST

THE STARLESS KING
INTO THE NETHER COURT, BOOK ONE
Copyright © 2022 by Lucy Tempest
Cover Art Copyright © 2022 by Lucy Tempest
Maps by: Folke Mueller
Edited by: Belle Manuel
ISBN (Paperback) : 978-1-949554-20-5
ISBN (Ebook): 978-1-949554-19-9
Published in 2022 by Starkindler Ink
Sign up to my VIP Mailing List at www.lucytempest.com/newsletter
Contact at lucytempestauthor@gmail.com

STARKINDLER INK

In the death-chamber for a moment Death,
Shamed by the presence of that living Might,
Blushed to annihilation, and the breath
Revisited those lips, and Life's pale light
Flashed through those limbs, so late her dear delight.
'Leave me not wild and drear and comfortless,
As silent lightning leaves the starless night!
Leave me not!' cried Urania: her distress
Roused Death: Death rose and smiled, and met her vain caress.

Percy Bysshe Shelley, *Adonais*

Nexia
Ericura
The Forbidden Ocean
Eglantine
Arbore
Campania
Orestia
Acronisi
Crisotemia
Lorthos
Cloacina
Pythia
Deep
Galatia
Granaria
Galantis
Lower
Meropis
Lycopolis

AIR-FOLK OCEAN
THLAND
OMS
ORCAGE
CANTABRIA
YI
TRAMONTANE
OPONA
THE ZORY
URSANE
ART
LYONESSE
BUYAN
DRAGONHEAD ISLES
UPPER CAMPANIA
ALMASKHAM
IACOOT
SILVER SEA
ISLES OF ZAFIR
CAHRAMAN
SUNSTONE
SILENT OCEAN

NIGHTMARE REALM
RIVER OF DREAMS
RIVER OF AGONY
THE COLISEUM
QUICKSILVER LAKE
THE SPIRAL OF SUFFERING
RIVER OF W
THE VOID CHASM
PRIMORD
BLOODST

E DREAMFIELDS
MAZE OF MADNESS
RIVER OF MEMORY
TRIMORPHIUM
NASIA
PSYCHEPOLIS
SMOKE QUARTZ HEADQUARTERS
GLASS HALLS
THE LIFETIME LIBRARY
ATE
TERS
ED SHORE

*To my mother, grandmother and aunt, without you this book would not
have seen the light of day.*

DRAMATIS PERSONAE

MORTALS:

CORALIA SPICA Heir to the Granary, Demigod daughter of its Mistress

CHLOË MARAINO Her maternal cousin

CASSIA GRANTURCO Their cousin, animal caretaker

CERELIA SPICA Mistress of the Granary, Cora's mother

LYSSA Maenad companion of Theoneus

RHOXANE Sorcerer-priestess of Eglaia

AETHUSA Princess of the Summer Court, faerie granddaughter of Lyceus

PERILLA Dryad groundskeeper of Almagera

GODS:

ADAMANTUS God of the Underworld

POLYOPE Goddess of Dark Magic and Nocturnal Mysteries

LYCEUS God of the Sun

EGLAIA Goddess of Beauty and Desire

ALMAGERA Queen of Heaven, Goddess of Fertility and Health

<h1 style="text-align:center">DRAMATIS PERSONAE</h1>

TELEPHASSA Goddess of the Moon

MACHAIUS God of War and the Forge

FORMETA Goddess of Bloodshed

THEONEUS God of Inebriation and Madness

ARISTAGNË Goddess of the Unseen Deep

THE HORNED GOD

You kissed his mouth with mouths of flame:
you made the horned god your own:
You stood behind him on his throne:
you called him by his secret name.

Oscar Wilde, *The Sphinx*

A MEETING WITH DEATH

For a thousand nights, I had wandered these misty paths, compelled by a dark and inexorable lure. And every night, my roaming had been in vain.

But tonight would be different. Tonight, I was determined to meet what called to me, what awaited me at the end.

Dusky light permeated the lifeless spaces as I trudged farther than I'd ever gone before. Clouds of fog retreated to unveil what I always saw. Namely nothing, for as far as I could see as I crossed damp meadows and descended steep hills.

Then I finally reached sprawling, silvery fields. I couldn't tell whether the stalks were wheat, barley or corn. A difference I of all people should know blindfolded, by smell alone.

But there were no scents, or sounds for that matter. No grass crunched beneath my bare feet, no insects or lizards fled my footfalls. All I could hear was running water, of what sounded like a nearby river.

Suddenly, musical notes like harmonizing bells pierced the air around me. They emitted from the stalks that gave me no resistance like in my fields, rained no dust or parasites as they parted themselves to make my way. Once on the other end, the whimsical tune became an eerie moan, overwhelming my senses. And that was before I saw what lay before me.

A vivid purple river divided a lilac-grey clearing from a maze of twisted black trees. And I just knew it. Beyond those woods was what I had been looking for for years.

Drawing in a bolstering breath, I took longer, faster strides, heartbeat rising with a mixture of dread and anticipation. After so long, I was so close at last.

...but close to what?

I never knew what I was searching for, only that I needed to find it. It was an inexplicable urge that had sunk its talons into me over three years ago, tugging me out of my bed each night. A compulsion stronger than the climbing madness of hunger or the siren song of sleep after a day of grueling grunt-work.

My pace stuttered to a stop by the riverbank.

Not much intimidated me, but something about the eye-watering vibrancy of the coursing amethyst waters had me wrestling with hesitation.

Some part of me knew what this was, and what it meant, but it had been shoved to the very back of my mind. But I was not one to ignore my instincts. If something unsettled or, somehow, scared me, my subconscious had to have an excellent reason as to why.

This wild-goose-chase had strung me along for far too long, and I ought to stop before I became another figure in folkloric tragedy. After all I'd witnessed and survived, and with all I aspired to, I always thought I was meant for one of two deaths: a peaceful one after decades of fulfilling duty, or a spectacular one in a star-shattering blaze of glory.

If I met a pointless end at the hands of an insignificant river nymph with a penchant for drowning people, it would be awfully embarrassing.

Measuring the risk, I eyed what lay across the glaring, roiling current. Towering black trees tore from the iron-grey ground, their branches like contorted limbs with clawed fingers, ending in leaves like knife-sharp spades. Beneath them sprouted flowers, familiar yet strange. Glassy, ghostly, and glowing, their light accentuated their silvery stems ending in spikes of pale, palm-sized blooms, with dark lines bisecting their six petals.

A hum accompanied their intensifying glow, like the sizzling of a reddening coal, persistent, rhythmic, and hypnotic.

The haze sliding over my focus shattered when a call echoed beyond the woods, sparking a rush of goosebumps that raised my every hair.

Curiosity overpowered my unease, and reawakened my determination. This was the call, the mystery that had long gnawed at my mind, and answers lay within reach, and with that someone who could explain it all.

Whoever it was, and whatever they intended, I could handle it. I'd gutted man-eating lamias and strangled equally-monstrous ghouls without hesitation. Nothing could phase me, or would keep me from my goal now.

Steeling myself, jaw locked on grinding teeth, I waded into the bone-chilling, sour-smelling and borderline-acidic water.

The call echoed in my ears, my mind again, compelling me to run against that waist-high current eager to wash me away into oblivion.

Luminous liquid sluicing off me, I finally struggled out of the river at the edge of the woods. Panting, the heat of my breath became vapor in the deepening cold, joining the mist that blurred my view.

That call rumbled through me again. It yanked on the hooks it had sunk within me years ago. I staggered forwards, as if my feet had a mind of their own.

River water dried into dew drops on my skin, intensifying my shivers as I passed the first row of twisted black trees. Their tops reached for each other, the gnarled fingers of witches long-corrupted by their dark magic. Beneath them, neat paths split the flower beds, and a whistling wind rustled their swathes, eliciting crystalline tinkling. Their soothing symphony along with the mystical glow of the giant blooms spread warmth to my frozen extremities.

Every step I took left something spawning in my wake, grass, sprouts, wildflowers and mushrooms. Their distraction had me looking back as I forged deeper into the woods. It wasn't until I faced forward again that I saw what blocked my path.

Draped in rippling shadows, the terrifying form of a massive man towered stark in the distance, his stag's skull and antlers silhouetted against a green-glowing background.

I knew him.

All who glimpsed him attempted to flee his approach, to avoid his grasp at all costs, desperate to continue their lives.

But there was nowhere to run from what came for us all— man, beast, and plant alike.

Except, I didn't want to run. An irrational, irresistible attraction to the spectral figure that obstructed my path beckoned me now as it had for so long.

I approached, breathless and brave, and called back, unsure in what language, or if I had even spoken out loud.

He gazed right at me, a dazzling, dreadful violet glow blasting from the cavernous sockets of his bare, inhuman skull. Air clogged like a fist in my throat.

Here was what I had been desperately searching for all these years, and there was no point in escape, neither was there a desire to.

I had come to him. Willingly. Yearningly.

Instead of reaping my soul from where he stood, he approached with a rustle of murky robes. His momentum halted within a leaping distance, only for his macabre head to tilt at me.

"You can see me?" His low yet magnified voice reverberated around and within me, filling the skipped beats of my over- worked heart.

Yet no part of me, no matter how rational, wanted to run. I just edged closer, mouth dry and tongue heavy, enslaved by excitement.

His question only registered upon repeat, curious rather than sinister. "You can see me?"

"I can see *only* you," I heard myself say, voice a thick, hungry rasp.

He was silent for so long I thought he wouldn't talk again, would disappear.

I was about to rush towards him, not knowing what I'd do when I reached him, when he spoke again. "Who are you?"

"That's what I should be asking you," I whispered, heart-strings tightening with agitation, and loosening with anticipation. "Are you what's been waiting for me?"

"Not waiting." His fathomless timbre thrummed through my joints, skittered spasms in my core. "I've been searching for you, across realms and eras."

If my heart were a seed, that was what it needed to sprout, the tendrils of unforeseen joy intertwining among my ribs.

What I'd been longing to find had been searching for me as well.

Rationality dictated I ask why, that I heed the wariness that insisted I keep as far away from him as possible.

But his hold over me was far greater, as if I had leaped off a cliff and was hurtling towards the sea. The narrower the distance between us got, the more powerful his already relentless lure became. And I knew one thing for certain.

I was on the cusp and plunging into the depths of the unknown.

Despite having no human features, I could read his rapt intensity. As I set foot after another closer, the purple light emitting from the eternity of his bottomless sockets flashed, his prodigious form expanding.

"You do not fear me," he said slowly, words spaced with disbelief.

Riveted by the power of my own attraction even more than his influence, I breathed. "No."

"You should."

"Telling me how I should or shouldn't behave has never ended well for anyone."

His grim head shifted upward as if in surprise. "Is that so?"

As if marionette strings were stitched under my cheeks, my lips pulled back in a devious grin, no reservations about flashing my teeth at the dark entity before me.

Instead of exhibiting signs of offense at my provocation, I could only feel his fascination as he said, "When are you?"

Not "*Where are you*," not even the "What *are you?*" I had gotten my fair share of. When.

Instead of demanding an explanation for his unusual question, I echoed him. "When are *you?*"

"I have no use for time, when I am so far from the heavens and their light." Before I could make heads or tails of that, he persisted, "What year is it where you are?"

"It's the last quarter of eighteen-hundred-and-twelve," I blurted, spurred by his urgency.

"Which calendar?" he stressed.

"Imperial Campanian."

He seemed to ponder the information for a long, still moment.

My heart almost uprooted itself when he moved abruptly, reaching out an ominous hand, flesh pale and nails sharp and dark, commanding, inexorable. "Come with me."

Air escaped my lips in a heated rush of anxiety and excitement. But there was no hesitation as I mirrored him, reaching eagerly back.

The moment our fingertips touched, the world was overturned.

A LINGERING WHISPER

I stumbled back with a startled gasp, stunned eyes darting around.

It slowly sank in that I was no longer in the dark, misty woods, but staring at a poplar forest in the early morning light.

I'd sleepwalked again.

The worst part about this habit was it never felt like I was asleep. Especially this time.

Disoriented, I remained in my spot, waiting for the experience to fade into haziness as those before it always did. It only solidified.

Unlike all the previous instances that ended in futility, and warranted no preservation in my mind, this encounter only got more vivid. And while I only had elusive realizations while experiencing it, now the surge of context painted everything in clarity.

I'd finally met what had been luring me on my nightly wanderings for years. It had turned out to be the entity widely-feared as Death himself.

But why would I dream of him in that form, what was euphemistically dubbed the Horned God by those who dreaded his attention? The antlered depiction was born a mere thousand years ago, in the younger kingdoms stretching from Arbore north of my region, to Opona in the far northeast. The Campanian and Orestian forms were far older, and what I would envision if I dreamt up an encounter with the Lord of the Dead.

Unless, it wasn't a dream...

"Cora?"

The shout shattered my bewildered musings. I turned on numb legs to find a middle-aged man I vaguely recognized. He was riding closer on a chestnut horse, with another horseman behind him.

"Cora, is that you?"

"It is...Xanthus?"

He smiled brightly, pleased that I'd gotten his name right. I somehow always differentiated between the tens of thousands I'd seen across the Folkshore.

"What are you doing here?"

Realizing I was standing in the middle of nowhere, barefoot in a soaking nightgown and hair, I fired the first thing that came to me. "Surprise inspection."

"Your mother wants the poplars inspected?" The younger horseman had joined us, his son Baileus. If my still-jostled mind recalled correctly, they both oversaw the white-grape vineyards south of Crisotemia—

I'd sleepwalked clear across the city.

"Cora?"

"Hmm? Oh, not exactly—" Struggling to reconcile that I'd trudged for dozens of miles, I dropped my gaze as I searched for a reasonable explanation. There was a line of mismatched growths—a cluster of daisies, lumps of long grass, and patches of wood sorrel—breaking the ground along my footprints. But it was the handful of death caps that gave me an idea.

I kicked at the mushrooms. "There have been complaints of parasitic mushroom infestations, all deadly. Needed to see for myself, and to be sure no one falsified their reports."

Not waiting to see if my explanation satisfied them, I started walking back.

They trotted after me, insisting on escorting me on one of their mares. I only accepted because the sun declared it was past seven o'clock. I'd already missed work, and the fastest way back was a horse—if I didn't want everyone to see me running as fast as one.

At the edge of town, I thanked them and promised a visit to their winery soon, then took a carriage bound for the city-center of Greater Crisotemia.

Still-damp head against the window, I stared at the scenes whipping past us; golden wheat, corn and barley fields swaying in the early morning breeze, each expanse punctuated with hand-fuls of cork oak trees. All sprawled beneath the hilltop settle-ments of those who oversaw these parts of our lands. And I'd walked through all that unaware.

Groaning with frustration at being unable to trust my mind or memory, I rubbed at my temples and closed my eyes. Each time I arose to wander like the living-dead, I always ended up wandering farther. This was the longest distance I'd ever put between myself and the Big House in Quartacollina.

At Olivetree Bridge, I hopped off. "Anything you need before you go, Pietro?"

He grinned. People were always delighted when you called them by name. They felt seen, known.

"Actually, I was hoping to pick up some chestnuts."

"Their harvest time is close, but not yet. I will send you some pistachios instead."

As he spluttered in surprised thanks, I waved him off, and made my way down my usual path, one I could, and *did*, walk in my sleep.

It was too easy to get sucked back into the eerie vision. That had to be what it was, not a dream, but not real either.

But the biggest mystery wasn't why I had seen Death in the

form feared by foreigners, or even that I'd been seeking him at all. It was how long I had been.

People who felt or saw him did so once, and it was him who sought them. Then they either lost someone or their lives. The lucky few who lost neither, remained forever traumatized by the encounter, until he came for them at a later date anyway.

I'd never heard of anything like my own years-long experience, or of people seeking him when they didn't want to die.

Yet, it hadn't felt like an omen. Hadn't even felt like his doing. He'd been as surprised to see me, even confused, when Death knew all those he came for. Then he'd asked who and *when* I was.

So maybe he'd been checking if I were on his list of souls?

If that was the case, and he came for me for real, I was going to cave his skull in and hang his antlers on my wall. I was not leaving this world any time soon.

Then why did I reach for his hand? And so eagerly?

I shook my head like a wet dog, trying to rattle off the treacherous memories. They only clung like tentacles around my brain, their rows of suckers siphoning me back to relive the dark caress of his lure, the dreadful delight of his touch.

Wishing for any distraction, I invited the heavens to pummel my body, or the earth to blister my feet. But the sky was clear and the sun's heat was not in the stones beneath my bare soles yet. So I tried to occupy myself with something positive as I crossed the half-moon bridge; the picturesque views I loved so much.

Across our longest river, the Aphtonia, and atop the endless levels of our seven green hills, the stone-brick farmhouses were layered like the tiers of a cake, encased by semi-paved roads and the thick, rounded heads of evergreen oaks. While the more modern villas were like vivid frosting, boasting manicured paths bordered by explosions of flowers, and teeming teardrop-shaped juniper trees. The crown jewel, of course, was my family's residence.

An age-old stone-and-cement villa, it spread over a platform encircled by our endless hectares of groves. Dubbed the Big House, it had been built by our ancestors at this vantage point, to oversee our land for miles upon miles. Ancient yet well-maintained, sprawling yet functional, it presided over the whole valley.

Soon, I was ascending the spiraling path leading to my home, each level to the conical peak designating a level of responsibility of its dwellers. I lived at the top with my mother, Cerelia, the one who held the ultimate authority as Mistress of the Granary. Luckily everyone on every level was too busy rushing around getting things ready for tonight. Only a few spared my more-disheveled-than-usual state a confused or curious glance.

The higher I climbed, the cooler and more humid the weather became, a herald of the arrival of autumn, what we would celebrate with tonight's full moon. Comforted by the idea at last, I breathed in the damp earth and wet wood, the crisp air exhaled by the surrounding trees carrying their distinctive scents and bird chatter. Everything seemed to be welcoming me home.

That thought fractured when I remembered the actual welcome I'd encountered at home. The only family I was likely to find at this hour were my useless aunt and her filthy-rich husband, emphasis on filthy. The last thing I needed was to be nagged by Junia or ordered around by Tertullian.

They had long worn out their welcome, and I was anything but tolerant to start with. One more broken glass or dirty dish littering our house, and I was chasing them back to Lycopolis on Cassia's nutty, squirrel-eating horse. I was going to bite their heads off anyway, the moment I saw either of them.

But the Fates saw fit to spare them from my worsening mood. The first to intercept me was my cousin, the only one from that family I wanted to see.

Chloë, all gangly limbs and golden hair, came rushing out in a smudged shirt, her brown pants held up by suspenders stuffed into riding boots. Whenever she visited, she couldn't wait to get out of her city frocks and into my "casual style" as she called it.

"I've been looking all over for you!" She rushed to meet me, with an exquisite smile between welcoming and worried, pigtails flying behind her. "Cassia said you were supposed to meet her at the stables, but you were nowhere to be found. Where were you?"

"Long story."

She watched me expectantly, looking pointedly at my still-soggy nightgown.

I only bypassed her into the shade of the patio, and pet some of the prowling cats that kept us free of pests. Judging by the yelling coming from inside, Junia had picked a fight with her and my mother's cousin, Cassia's mother. Sylviana had the lungs of an opera singer, a shorter temper than my own, and even less patience for the iffiness of the city-bred.

"How long have they been at it now?"

"About a half-hour. Erasmus did something quite deranged." Chloë sighed, following me up the external steps that led directly to my window. I would rather avoid her parents right now, not to mention that ear-splitting row.

"What did your monster-brat of a brother do now?"

She remained quiet.

I paused to shoot down a suspicious glance. "Well?"

Her color deepened in mortification. "Kicked one of the cats."

Fury roared in my chest. *I'm going to kill him.*

"Not if Sylviana gets to him first. She's swearing she'll spank him with a cleaver."

"Only a cleaver? If he touches a cat or a dog, or any animal *ever* again, I'm punting him into Mount Fulgera."

Chloë stifled a snort. "Isn't that volcano on Lorthos? You'd really make that journey just to teach him a lesson?"

"It won't be a lesson, but a favor. To you. With Papa's

Precious Heir gone, you'll get all that warthog's money and his estate."

"Not unless I marry a richer man, I won't."

There it was, the bane of Chloë's existence. The mistake of her mother's life that she, for some brain-dead reason, wanted her daughter to recreate. Running off with an oligarch to the cities and becoming a miserable, and powerless, housewife.

While my mother and I were in charge of everything that grew in Granaria, whether farmed or otherwise, and our relatives, the Granturcos, oversaw all that roamed the lands. Sylviana and her daughters managed the natural, while her husband Renatus and their sons kept track of the supernatural. That was, among attempts by the wild Cassia and Citronella to cuddle wildcats, and the idiot Illarion and Macion to chase nymphs. Those siblings had a death wish.

But the point was, had Junia remained here, like generations of Spica women before her, she would have married a man from a known and trusted family, who respected, and feared, my mother. He would have had to be a good husband lest he suffer the consequences.

The last man to mistreat one of us was Cassia's grandfather. My grandmother had him made into a living scarecrow.

Crucifixion was a sentence of the past, falling out of favor with the collapse of the Campanian Empire, but she brought it back this once to make a ruling. Abuse a Spica woman and pay with your life. The bastard was bolted to his house posts, burning in a sun more merciless than he'd been, and suffering agony worse than the wife he'd beat almost to death, as carrion birds pecked his flesh clean off his bones while he still lived.

But such abuse had been one more reason each Mistress of the Granary continued refusing marriage, and claiming her heir was fathered by a minor god. That was what the last seven generations of our family women had done, and what I would do in turn.

Once I climbed into my room with Chloë in tow, I peeled

out of my nightgown and dressed for work, in one of my identical beige burlap pants, white linen long-sleeved shirts and brown suspenders. She sat on the edge of my rock-hard mattress with one of our indoor cats.

My three-legged wonder Terzia, a splotchy calico who was missing the tip of her right ear and her left paw, preferred my firm furniture to any other part of the house. She was the only one who'd seen me rise from my bed every night, and sleep-climb out that window. I wondered what she thought I was doing before she sigh-purred and went back to sleep herself.

"You said it was a long story," Chloë reminded me as I braided my hair. "Best start now."

It should have been a simple story to tell, but I found myself oddly speechless.

How did I explain this without sounding delirious? Or worse, delusional?

"It's not important."

She scowled at me, bringing our family resemblance to the forefront. Save for the difference in size and hues, we were nearly identical, bearing the face of our grandmother Cornelia.

Besides that, we also had her golden hair, even if mine was frizzy, wavy and in all the shades of a wheat field, while hers was straight and silky like spun gold. Mine also fell to my elbows, a length more convenient for keeping it out of my way in braids. It was either that, or chop it off completely. While Chloë could afford to keep hers in a more fashionable length, and right now the ends of her gilded pigtails brushed her collarbones.

But Cornelia had passed down more traits to me than anyone else. Not only her long weaver's hands and the archetypal, chiseled Campanian nose, but her puzzling bone structure, somewhere between ferocious and feminine. I had her wide, firm jaw, a matching set of sharp cheekbones, and a prominent brow that cast shadow over my too-large, prominent eyes. "Green as a venomous toad," the most pleasing insult I'd ever gotten.

For a long while as I grew up, snide remarks about how off-putting my resting face was had gotten to me. But once I realized the effortless intimidation my heavy-lidded glower and full, snarling lips earned me from such people, I grew to appreciate it.

Anyone who judged others based on their looks was not worth knowing anyway.

But while Chloë almost had my face, just with hazel-green eyes and a smaller layout, it was still soft and approachable. I couldn't quite explain how.

And she was still waiting for my story.

Sighing as I led the way back out the window, I recounted my unsettling adventure to her.

"You sleepwalk?" she squawked, aghast, as we hit the ground. "Since when? And why?"

"If I knew why, I would have put a stop to it." I tightened my suspenders over my shoulders and started running downhill.

She chased after me, spluttering, "Couldn't you just lock your door and window before you sleep?"

Stupid questions always stoked my impatience, and earned spits of sarcasm or outright condescension. But those usually involved work or the politics surrounding it. Chloë was only concerned, not to mention a favorite of mine. I would do anything for her, the least of which let her get away with what got others chewed out.

Still needing to channel my aggression, I stomped even harder as I said, "Sleepwalkers aren't toddlers, Chloë. I've heard of them doing complex things from cooking to having debates, so locks won't do much."

"Use sturdy ones, like those on cellar doors?" she suggested hopefully. I only gave her a disbelieving look out the corner of my eye, and she groaned. "You'd just break it, wouldn't you? But with what?"

Another stupid question. The obvious answer would be with any instrument from my toolbox. Not that I'd need any. My hands would suffice.

But I wasn't mentioning that. I always tried not to stand out more than I already did. And I didn't want even her demanding a demonstration. The only things I was planning on breaking today were walnuts against the feast table.

Our speedy scramble to the bottom slowed down as soon as we saw our cousin Cassia atop her trusty mahogany-brown steed Aethon. She watched us approach with hands on hips and mouth tugged to the side in displeasure.

Between the three of us, Cassia was the shortest and with the stockiest build. Her hair was chestnut and her mossy-green eyes were also the darkest among us. Features-wise, she resembled both of us.

Though photographs were still a novelty, my mother had one framed in her office from last summer, with us standing in order of height. Even in grainy black-and-white, Cornelia Spica's face had undeniably been stamped onto each of us.

We also had her complexion that weathered our harshest sun, and tanned easily and evenly. Good thing for me as I worked the fields, and for Cassia who spent most of her time training and riding horses, both the earth- and sky-bound kinds. Chloë only needed the sun-kissed skin to bring out her coloring. According to her mother, this should land her a richer husband.

As we came to a stop before Cassia, her wide-brimmed straw hat did nothing to obscure her glower. "Of all the days for you to sleep in, you chose this one?"

"She didn't! She was—" I cut Chloë off with a swift jab to her side.

Cassia's brows shot up. "You know you just made me more curious, right?"

I kicked into a run, calling over my shoulder, "Yeah, have fun guessing!"

They soon caught up with me, both of them now on the horse.

"Race you to the barns," Cassia yelled over the galloping noises, a taunting grin in her voice. "If you lose, you have to tell me everything."

I looked up, meeting her gaze head-on with my own challenge. "And if I win?"

"I'll babysit one of your city boys all night."

That would take keeping one of them out of trouble off my hands. If my own relatives were a stifling presence, then the Character-Building Program that had the wealthy funneling their intolerable sons to our land for a few months of "hard work" and "simple living" was smothering me.

"Just one?" I yelled back.

Cassia smirked. "I can't exactly juggle them."

That was exactly what I'd been doing all summer. I'd lost count how many rich boys I'd been corralling into mucking out the stables, or forcing into the thousand other hard-labor chores around. And it killed me that I couldn't backhand or deck them as they deserved, when they always did a lousy job. We were being paid very handsomely to entertain their parents' fantasy of toughening up their boys. We needed to supplement our exports' income to construct new buildings throughout the farmlands, and luxury accommodations to further encourage tourism.

So, along with my endless responsibilities, I had to shepherd those overgrown brats, without roughing them up—too much.

But the absolute worst had been the two from our neighboring kingdoms, since I wasn't supposed to smack them around at all.

Arbore had granted me the memorable encounter with its crown prince, Leander. That one had harassed me until I threatened to run him through with a hayfork. I ended up knocking him down on his ass with a single head-butt.

Now Orestia had sent us someone even worse, some member of their extended royal family. If I were a cow, then Erthamos was my gadfly. And I couldn't squash him without causing "another international incident."

But Cassia's bet could be just what I needed. She wasn't the heir around here, and her actions wouldn't cause a diplomatic crisis. She could flatten Erthamos for me. After an evening with him, I was sure she would.

I grinned up at her. "Fine. But I'm picking the one you'll be stuck with."

I didn't give her the chance to argue before I bolted down the short-grass slope towards the citrus groves, the shortcut I needed to reach the barns faster than she could.

A faraway shout of, "Cheater!" made me chuckle. Cassia Granturco had no one to blame but herself. She knew me well enough to realize I didn't make bets unless I knew I'd win.

But midway through the groves, I realized there was something amiss. There should be people gathering the ripe fruits at this time of day. I'd seen no one so far.

Foreboding gripped me even before I heard the distressed voices. Then I saw the milling crowd, their baskets discarded, hundreds of limes and lemons littering the ground

Heart hammering in my throat, I barely slowed down as I pushed through the unyielding bodies. "What's going on? What are you looking at?"

The only response I got from the ashen-faced people was them stepping aside, unveiling the macabre scene they had stumbled upon.

A young, blonde woman lay half-sunken in the soil, opaque-green eyes wide open, rib cage caved in, and chest cavity full of mushrooms.

Mushrooms like the one that had grown along my footsteps.

MURDERS IN THE FAMILY

This wasn't the first time I'd seen a dead body, human or otherwise.

Neither was this my first encounter with ungraceful death. In fact, I'd never witnessed the clean dignity afforded to those who died in their beds, peacefully passing from dream to his brother, the unending sleep.

I'd known nothing but messy or violent ends.

Apart from that, I was desensitized to all sorts of morbid things. My mother had made sure of that. She'd sent me roaming the Folkshore for years to get acquainted with the world I'd take on once I succeeded her, to learn its secrets and savageries.

But way before that, she'd drilled the harsh realities of nature into me, and that my job was to nurture everything that grew, until time came for it to nourish others. Mourning anything or anyone had no place in the circle of life, or the state of the world.

In the farms and fields, I'd been exposed to death long before I was old enough to grasp its concept. And in my years of travel and trials, I'd seen everything, from carcasses left to reek and writhe with maggots under the summer sun, to battlefields littered with guts, gore and gruesome death, to lamias mid-feast, elbows deep in their still-spasming victims.

Yet this was the first time I'd seen a corpse like this. Something had literally crushed her to death, then scooped out her ruptured heart. The sight of the deadly fungi growing out where it used to be covered my bones in painful frost, and pummeled my throat with a geyser of nausea. It was the first time I was thankful my stomach was empty.

Shock and horror notwithstanding, my ingrained training kicked in. I was born and bred to take over, to solve problems and make decisions. I stopped the men who'd started digging the body out of its semi-grave, sent some for the guards and medics, then examined the scene. I had to have a detailed report for my mother.

From the lack of maggots, she'd been dead less than two days. But strangely, there was no evidence of struggle, no spatter of blood when she'd been eviscerated, and no tracks other than her own. I knew of nothing, natural or supernatural, that could kill so violently yet so cleanly, let alone attack and retreat without a trace.

By the time I committed every detail to memory, the guards and medics arrived, and Chloë and Cassia finally caught up with me.

"Who is—who was she?" Chloë asked in a small, stricken voice, clutching my arm as if to hide behind me from the brunt of the ghastly scene.

It would have been another stupid question if Chloë didn't know I remembered everyone I ever came across.

"Theodosia." I gritted out the name, harsh and clipped. I'd seen her only once, but recognized her on sight. "She's a relative of ours. A third cousin."

In another situation, this would be when I griped about how many branches the Spica family tree had, or made a crack about strong resemblances despite the distance between said branches. But as I stared at Theodosia's lolling head as they extracted her from the earth, it felt as if I was looking at my own lifeless face, or worse, Chloë's or Cassia's.

A spike of paranoia fizzed within me, as if the contractions of my heart carbonated the blood it pumped. The vision of vicious antlers and a sharp-nailed hand flashed behind my eyelids as I slowly blinked, and that compelling voice echoed in my ears again.

Come with me.

Had this been some kind of omen, after all? Had he appeared to Theodosia, too, before she was killed? And now that I'd seen him, would I or someone close to me follow?

"What do you think did this to her?" Chloë whispered, as if afraid Theodosia would hear her discussing her death.

"We should ask my father," Cassia said, haunted yet furious gaze following the medics as they loaded the body onto their cart. "He keeps track of everything that could possibly do this. Then once he identifies the miscreant, and the celebrations are over, we'll hunt it down. Whatever it is, I'm going to rip its heart out."

The same violent sentiment echoed within my constricted chest. But I somehow knew this would be beyond Renatus' expertise.

Something intelligent had done this, not any of the creatures he catalogued and whose populations he controlled.

Out loud, I only said, "Good idea. You go to your father, I'll alert my mother."

With a grim nod, Cassia leaped back onto her horse, and galloped away towards the celebration site, where her father was in charge of decorations.

Chloë scampered to fall into step with my longer strides as I followed the guards and medics to the urban end of eastern Crisotemia. I could feel her eyes on me.

"What?"

"I think you should take off," she said, unfazed by my crankiness, eyes glittering with unshed tears. "Go back for a nap, and I'll tell Cerelia."

"What makes you think I'd want to do that?"

Agitation only intensified in her large eyes. "Because though I thought it impossible, you seem—shaken."

I stared down into her reddened eyes, and realized this was disturbing her almost as much as seeing Theodosia's mutilated body.

Plastering on a smirk for her benefit, I snorted dismissively, giving her a light shove. "If only you knew the things I've seen, you'd know it would take a lot more than that to shake me."

She sighed as she leaped onto the paved ground that heralded leaving behind the rural areas. "Come on, Cora. It's me."

"What about you?" I evaded as I adjusted my footfalls over the lumpy, worn-down cobblestones. They were uneven from countless carriage wheels and hooves, along with a few mild earthquakes belched our way from the islands of Orestia.

"I know you don't like people to know you have feelings," she grumbled. "But unlike everyone you need to keep in line, I know you. You don't need to keep up this facade with me."

Irritation scraped at my facial muscles, making me itch to frown. I knew she was attempting to comfort me, but the last thing I could do now was loosen the reins of my control. I was no use to anyone if worry caught me by the ankles and dragged me in its muddy tracks.

I huffed. "That's sweet, Chloë, really, but again, I don't scare that easily."

"I'm not saying you're scared, just upset."

The outstretched hand of Death threw itself back to the forefront of my mind. But the only thing that upset me at the memory was that I couldn't hold on to his hand, that I only got that fleeting, fate-changing touch.

"I'm not upset, I'm frustrated." Mainly with myself and my inexplicable urges. "Today was supposed to be fun, but now something crushed Theodosia's chest like an eggshell and sucked out her insides, and I have to tell my mother, who'll tell *her* mother, who'll be devastated, and instead of celebrating life, we'll have a funeral and—"

I heaved in a painful inhalation. It felt like the shredding icicles of Oponan winter air, that rare experience even my sturdiness couldn't stomach.

I kicked a stone in my path with a growl, and Chloë grimaced at the sound my bare toe made connecting with it. "What do you have against shoes?"

I turned a foot up to show her that my dirt-stained sole was callus-free. My skin had no need for them. "Shoes are for the weak."

She threw her hands up. "Here we go!"

"And where are we going?"

"Back to where you pretend nothing's wrong, and your only feelings are grouchiness, aggression and sarcasm."

"Sarcasm isn't a feeling."

She let out an owl-like screech that made my lips twitch in spite of everything. "Don't correct me while I'm trying to connect with you."

I goggled at her. "Why would you want to connect over being upset of all things?"

"Because I want you to feel better, of course!"

"I don't care about "feeling" better or anything else. As long as tonight goes as planned, with nothing accidentally catching on fire, no pegasus raining dung on the audience—and no more bodies turning up."

I didn't add that I no longer cared how tonight went, either. Whatever had destroyed Theodosia was still out there, and all I wanted was to find it, and watch the light leave its eyes as I tore its rotting heart out.

Shaking away another irresistible and inadvisable urge, since I couldn't walk out on my duties tonight, and I had a dozen chores awaiting me right now, I picked up speed again. The sooner I told mother, and got this night over with, the sooner I could hunt that monster down.

Chloë almost ran to keep up with me. "Talk to me, please!"

"If you don't drop it, I'll make you eat every apple core from next week's harvest until you get cyanide poisoning."

"I will, right after you eat all the poppy heads in the south and actually sleep in your bed instead of on your feet." She bumped her shoulder against my arm, barely jostling me. "You know, before your Foreign Death lures you off a cliff next time."

I glowered down at her. "You're joining your brother in the volcano."

She waved me away. "Cassia and one of her flying horses will save me."

Before I could retort, she put a hand on my shoulder, forcing me to meet her beseeching eyes. And I realized what this was all about.

Inwardly calling myself every kind of unfeeling moron, I mirrored her grounding hold on me. "Nothing's going to get you, Chloë. I wouldn't let that happen, you know that, right?"

She winced. "That's exactly why I want you to confide in me. You're always worrying about everything and everyone in the Granary. You need someone to worry about you."

"You certainly don't need to. I mean, look at me." I gestured at my size and expression, what always made everyone give me a wide berth. Apart from that, I'd killed monsters with my bare hands.

"Yes, I need to. Being big and strong and tough as nails doesn't mean you're invincible, or that you should try to be. You at least need someone to let your guard down around. You're my cousin and I love you, and that someone should be me!"

It was hard not to surrender to her offer of comfort, because she was right. She was not among those I needed to intimidate into respecting me, or to advertise my fearlessness to.

Exhaling tiredly, I leaned over to brush a kiss on her forehead. "You don't know what you're in for. If you get sick of my complaining, just remember you asked for it."

She beamed up at me, triumphant.

And for the remainder of our trek to the Grand Temple of Eurycrius, where my mother would be by now, I gave her what made her feel better—a venting act, complete with going off on tangents for authenticity's sake.

It was hard, *very* hard, to ramble, even in pretense. Saying little and showing even less was what I was taught since childhood. It had been drilled into me that I must have an iron grip on myself at all times, or I would lose my hold on this land.

Women in positions of power were already few and far in between, and we had to act like an idealized man to garner respect and allegiance. For the seven generations of Mistresses of the Granary before me, any softness associated with our femininity had to be buried deep for us to be formidable and fearsome, and to snuff out any murmurings contesting our matrilineal succession.

That was needed now more than ever with the divine-parentage excuse wearing thin. I would be facing the harshest opposition to continue holding the reins of the region that fed the world.

That was another reason Chloë's father's presence here infuriated me. After twenty-five years of considering us all peasants below his regard, Tertullian Maraino had suddenly decided to visit his wife's homeland—with his manure-heap of an heir in tow. Since he'd arrived, he'd been questioning, not just who had fathered me, but if the people would genuinely choose a woman over a man to lead them, if given the choice.

That foul, flabby maggot fancied he could swindle my land out from under me in favor of his son, considering that Erasmus had as strong a claim as I did. Stronger even, based on what dangled between his legs.

It was a shame neither father nor son ventured out of the Big House, and refused all attempts to take them exploring the farmland. An unfortunate accident would have locked them up in the pigpen, and they would have been taken care of. Pigs would eat even their own, and wouldn't have had any qualms feasting on those rancid creatures. It would have been another major favor for Chloë, and the rest of the Folkshore.

But if they truly challenged me for my position, I wouldn't care about making their deaths seem accidental. I would run them through, in a stack, and pin them to the side of the Big House they were trying to take over. That would be the ultimate warning for any other would-be usurpers.

Chloë poked me, fingernails kept functionally short and neat, unlike her mother, Lady of the Garish Talons. "You're doing it again."

"Doing what?"

She scrunched up her face, mimicking my ferocious frown. "Thinking of something upsetting."

"Says who?"

"Says your face. It makes all the grouchy, aggressive, sarcastic things you think too obvious. So you might as well tell me the details."

Fondness inverted the tug at my lips into an unwilling smile. "You've heard it once, you've heard it a thousand times."

She mimed taking down notes. "One more time won't hurt. Go on."

Giving in, I threw an arm around her shoulders, tension loosening as I rehashed my dismal view of her family through the last stretch to our destination.

If the Horned God's visionary visit did spell my doom, the only one from that side of the family I wanted to succeed me was Chloë. Unlike her uppity mother, she had always enjoyed being here, never shied away from the grunt-work, or showed any disgust of the animals or what came with them. She loved it here, and land couldn't be nurtured without love.

But land also needed a backbone as hard as it was. And after years of her parents and city society reducing her to a walking womb to birth the heirs of whatever weasel her father chose, Chloë's confidence had been damaged, and her self-worth had shrunk.

Once my mother retired, I would fix that. I would twist enough arms to render equal primogeniture into actual law, so females would inherit like males. Hopefully in time to help Chloë and our generation. If not, then certainly the next one.

I was still giving her an earful as we reached the Great Temple. A white-marble edifice atop a platform that held it high above the city's skyline, the House of the Head God was so enormous it made people climbing its steps seem like ants. It further boasted its importance with elaborate architecture, its domes gilded and beveled and its columns etched and soaring. The extravagance reached its peak in the pure-gold spire that ended in his symbol, the lightning-bolt, as the apex of its weathervane.

This was where we always ushered in an equinox, to give thanks for the climate of the previous season had it been good, or lodge our complaints had it not been, and pray to him for a clement weather for the next season.

Not that it felt like an equinox now. The weather had been strangely stagnant the past weeks. The temperature hadn't dipped in the slightest, and the spectacular storms that always marked the end of summer hadn't come to pass. Among the theories floating around to explain the unprecedented conditions were murmurings that Eurycrius was withholding Autumn until we made more substantial offerings.

Whatever it was, I had enough mysteries as it was. For now, I needed to find my mother, get the horrific news off my chest, and rush back to my chores.

Taking in a bolstering breath, I sprinted up the endless steps, leaving a chagrined Chloë far behind.

Soon, barely breathing faster, I reached the gigantic vestibule. It was centered by a thirty-foot-tall seated statue of Eurycrius atop a ten-foot-high pedestal, bolt in hand, stern face with its wind-blown curls and paternal beard surveying all from the heavens.

I streaked over the endless mosaic tiles that formed the image of roiling clouds split by a jagged bolt of destruction—only to stumble midway.

Heart almost uprooting itself, I came to a shuddering halt, gaping at the gruesome sight.

Another blonde woman. One I also recognized at once, and not because of my infallible memory. Because I knew her well. Not only was she my second cousin, but we were friends.

We'd gathered grapes together just a week ago. She'd made me laugh all through, skipping around, hilariously mimicking our elders.

Now the vivacious Prunella was still and silent forever. And this image would replace all I'd ever had of her. Dead and draped at the feet of a ruthless god's effigy. And where her big, kind heart once beat, a dark pit yawned.

A CONSPIRACY OF CORPSES

All the blood fled to my feet, leaving my head light and my legs leaden.

I still walked towards Prunella's body, my approach the lifeless shamble of a mindless revenant dragging its feet towards the necromancer that had interrupted its eternal rest.

But there would be no raising Prunella. Like Theodosia, she had been utterly destroyed.

She would never run through the fields again, or kiss Matteo behind the barns, or have children or grow old. I would never crack up over her impression of myself, or hear that unique way her r trilled when she sing-sang Cora. So much life, so much potential, demolished.

To make it even worse, the way she was arranged, where people placed offerings and knelt in prayer, had a sacrificial vibe that intensified the sickening swirl in my gut.

It was as if she was what we'd burn tonight at the bonfire.

I stopped a few meters away from the raised altar, stood swaying. From this perspective the statue's neck and beard were overlapped by Prunella's protruding ribs. Their jagged, meatless ends seemed to reach up to Eurycrius' face like sharp claws, as if about to maul him. As I wished they could.

But there was no touching the gods. And she, and everyone else were just helpless pawns and sacrifices in their cruel, pointless schemes.

The heat of the sun and exertion, and the warmth of Chloë's concern dissipated in the coldness of the vast temple, allowing the chill of horror to sink back in my bones, just as the implications did in my mind.

Prunella hadn't been left to rot in the woods like Theodosia, her corpse fuel for fungi. She had been brought here. Not in mourning by someone who loved her, but as a message to all who laid eyes on her, including the stone gaze of the one who looked down on us all.

This wasn't a prayer or an offering, this was a point being made. Almost as if her presence was meant to complete the scene of the Sky God on his throne, making it seem he was staring down at her to the exclusion of all else. As if *this* was all that had his attention now.

The question was, what was this? What did this?

No, not what. Who.

The certainty made my blood boil again, burning everything away but fury.

The brutal urge to fight made me grab the arm of whoever dared to touch my shoulder. Before I twisted it out of its socket, ferociousness evaporated at the sight of my mother.

In her flowing, burnt-orange gown, with her greying cascade of brown hair crowned by a circlet of bronze oak leaves, she embodied the spirit of autumn. She always felt like the land incarnate to me.

But instead of the laughter-lines that framed her striking face at home, or the furrows of weathering the sun and elements in the fields, the tension of crow's feet now gripped her countenance. An apt effect now, since those grouped in a murder.

She squeezed my arm, unknown agitation staining her moss-green eyes. "What brings you here, Cora? Why aren't you at work?"

"I came to report a death—a murder." I quickly, haltingly, told her about Theodosia, before forcing my gaze back at the altar. "I only came to find Prunella—killed in the same..."

I choked on the rest, and her face crumpled for a moment.

Then she steeled her expression, pulled herself taller. The top of her head only reached my chin, but as always, she felt larger-than-life.

I wanted to tell her what Chloë had told me, that she didn't have to be Cerelia Spica now, our leader, the one responsible for everyone and everything on this land. Not around me. That she could give herself permission to experience the pain and rage in the safety of our bond.

But she gestured behind me, and it was only then I realized who the imposing stance and expression were for.

A group of people were solemnly approaching us and the grisly scene from the temple's entrance. My eyes first flew to Chloë at the back, my teeth grinding at how terrified she looked. I had no more than a second to meet her gaze, to try to renew my pledge before the others eclipsed her—the priest of Eurycrius, and probably all the mayors and governors of the surrounding towns and cities.

But my gaze clung to only one person; a woman in a floor-length, midnight gown, with her face obscured in a sheer, same-colored veil.

I'd heard of those priestesses who emulated their faceless goddess. She was also nameless. Maybe because of how little she mattered out here, or because it was blasphemy to speak her name. Her cults were relegated to cities where witches and those entranced by their dark arts huddled in secret congregations, making people's imaginations run wild about their practices in their goddess' service, from peddling curses, to sacrificing goats —and people.

I'd seen a statue of hers in Orestia, in a rundown temple that overlooked the Deep Red Sea. She had six arms like an insect, but no head, which must have been knocked off ages prior. A pitiable state for a goddess that had, seemingly, once been so important that ruins of her temples were found from the coast of the Forbidden Ocean all the way to the Silent Ocean's.

But though any information I had of her nature and that of her worship was hearsay, I somehow knew her priestess being here was worse news than what I had come to deliver.

"What's going on?" I asked my mother, turning my back to the approaching group. "Why are these people here?"

She hardened her square jaw, exhaling. "They've come to report similar crimes, not only in our other cities, but in other countries. Yet it was only when there were too many victims within each given region that the authorities began to notice a pattern."

"What pattern?" I asked, trying not to rush to any conclusions.

A flicker of panic crossed her eyes before she suppressed it. "That they were all exceptional. Strong, beautiful, in perfect health, like..."

"Like you," interjected a new voice cheerfully.

Or not so new. That was the voice of one of the last people I wanted to see. Erthamos.

As all the others held back at a respectful distance, he was the one who barged between us, with Chloë in tow. He'd been doing that for the past weeks, his nebulous royal status affording him access to the dinners my mother and her main underlings arranged, to discuss work and other aspects of life in our domain. He always chose a seat across from myself and Chloë, his invasive gaze putting a stopper to our giddy gossip, like he was an olive lodged in our throats.

But I would unload him on Cassia tonight. She'd make him regret ever setting foot in our region.

My aversion to him resurged ten-fold when he laid a hand on Chloë's shoulder. Any other time she would have slipped out of his reach, but he was taking advantage of her stunned state.

"These murders started in Opona in the far northeast,"

Erthamos said, not even attempting to hide his excitement. The sick bastard. Those idle-rich seemed to find entertainment in the macabre misfortunes of others. "They've been zigzagging all over the Folkshore since mid-summer. And now they've reached your region."

"How do you know so much about this?" I growled, fists clenched, imagining pulping his smarmy face. He peered up at me, those reptilian blue-grey eyes twinkling, as if daring me to do it. But I still vividly remembered my mother's lectures, and the trouble with Arbore after I head-butted Leander. That made me look away from the temptation of his patrician nose. "And why are we just hearing about this now?"

"If I may," interrupted the soft voice of the priestess. She approached me with a rustle of her layered skirts and a tinkle of her many bracelets. "As Mistress Cerelia said, the murders didn't seem to have a pattern at first, with the victims being men, women and even children. That's why all those equipped to suspect one, like officers of law or practitioners of magic, were thrown off. But we at the Sisters of the Silver Circle now believe that this is a ritualistic search."

Sisters of the Silver Circle. Any other time I would have scoffed, *Say that five times fast.*

But for the life of me, I couldn't find something more appropriate to say.

"Silver Circle? Is that a moon goddess thing?" Chloë asked, edging away from Erthamos. I was silently thanking her for saving me the effort when his fingers tightened on her shoulder. I suppressed a snarl, promising myself the future pleasure of shattering them one by one. Looking uncomfortable, she still added, "Is that why you're here? For the Harvest Moon?"

"If they are, then they are blaspheming against Telephassa." Erthamos swung toward the priestess, all but spitting at her. "Your monster goddess is down in the Underworld and has been for eons. What are the lot of you still clinging to her for? What are you doing here? Don't you have better things to do—like butchering and eating babies?"

"This is just rude!" Chloë exclaimed as she dipped her shoulder out of his grasp, giving him no chance to recapture her. "And Telephassa doesn't have a monopoly on the moon."

"Careful, you don't want to offend her," Erthamos warned as she skittered to our side. "Defend those Cisterns of the Slaughter Suckers and she might leave you to them to feast on."

"We do not partake in human sacrifice or cannibalism," the priestess said calmly. "But we are familiar with those particular methods of divination."

Divination. That word plucked a vague chord within me, made me step forward to face her. "You said earlier that this was a search?"

It was my mother who answered, sneaking a glance at her hidden face that I couldn't fathom, and I doubted anyone else noticed. "Sister Laia suspects that might be the point of this method of murder. That one victim's heart is being used to pinpoint the next one."

"You mean those victims are somehow connected?" I said, bile rising again in my throat. "But how, when they were from all across the Folkshore?"

"Yeah, and let's not forget about the hearts, what we all know black magic cults love to eat," Erthamos sneered as he approached Chloë again. "This could all be the Cisterns' doing, and now they're coming forward with information to throw suspicion off themselves."

I blocked his path, looking down at him with a warning glower. "What are you doing here again? Shouldn't you be back at the stables, miserably failing at mounting a horse like the other rich brats?"

The glee left his eyes, but his mouth twisted in a hateful smirk. "You really should be more careful how you address me, Carlotta, considering I could be saving your life."

I bared my teeth at him, expanding my chest to accentuate

my size, and his disadvantage. "What in the bottomless hell-pit are you talking about? You couldn't save someone drowning in an inch of water."

"*Cora.*" My mother's command stressing my name was an admonition for us both. But it was the unprecedented vulnerability in her gaze that silenced me. "Erthamos was the one who found this last victim. Along with all the reports our esteemed mayors and governors brought me this morning, there has been an alarming change in pattern. Before the murders reached our region in the past few days, as Sister Laia mentioned, the victims only had their perfect conditions in common. But since they reached the Granary, all the victims shared more than that. And that's why Erthamos has deduced that you and Chloë are in danger. Regretfully, I believe he is right."

"Take it from me, he's incapable of being right..."

Her hand pressed my back, hard. I resisted her, wanting to show that insolent rodent what it felt like to be touched without consent, here and now. But her tense touch over my *acanthomatia* had been her shorthand for *shut up* since I was four. It had been then she'd branded me with the symbol of Consus, the protector of the grain, and my supposed divine father. According to his cult, it conferred his protection of the fields against pests and disease to me, and acted as a conduit of his power from me to the fields.

I never thought that ugly, puckered, thorns-encircled eye had any effect, but she always insisted it had a role in my sturdiness, since every injury before and since had healed in record time. And right now, she believed we were in danger.

This time, I believed her. I already suspected as much, anyway.

"Why us?" Chloë squeaked.

"Because both new victims, and I suspect all the others in our region, resemble us," I answered, wanting to be the one who spelled it out for her.

"The murderer has been solely picking off young, blonde

women who look like you," Sister Laia said, as if translating what I said more bluntly.

I could swear she looked me straight in the eye as she said *you,* so emphatically. As if she meant only me.

Chloë blanched, looking ready to spray out the liquified remains of her breakfast.

I rubbed her back soothingly and returned my gaze to my mother. "We must warn and guard every girl who answers the basic traits of the victims."

"Maybe not every blonde girl in the region is in danger," Sister Laia persisted, and I got the impression she knew more than she was letting on. "From the identities of the victims so far, they all belonged to your extended family."

"You could be right," I mumbled, my empty stomach starting to gnaw itself. "But you could also be wrong. We can't gamble the lives of all those girls based on a theory."

My mother nodded. "We will provide protection for them all."

Sister Laia inclined her head in concession. "As you see fit, Mistress Cerelia. But I would suggest fortifying your measures for your family."

I frowned at her. "You really think only our family members are in danger, don't you?"

She shook her veiled head. "Not Cassia. She isn't a blonde, and doesn't resemble you as much as those who have been killed did."

There was that *you,* again. She *did* mean only me.

"And when they come for you two, they'd probably take you out in one go, since you seem attached at the hip," Erthamos said snidely, gesturing between me and Chloë. "You would benefit from a separation."

As if I'd let Chloë out of my sight after this vile vermin's manhandling demonstration.

Baring my teeth at him in a silent snarl that said, *"Over your dead body!"* I turned to my mother. "What now? Is tonight cancelled?"

She shook her head, a weary cast conquering her indomitable act. "We can't afford to anger the gods further, or worry people even more. Guards will be patrolling all night, and Sister Laia and her associates are here to offer their services. The killer has to be caught tonight."

"Guess I better keep an eye on these two for you, Mistress Cerelia," Erthamos said, all but leering at Chloë.

Before I could show him who needed protection among us, my mother thanked him and that was that.

As I promised myself vicious vengeance on that leech, Chloë's parents descended on us. They'd heard the news, and insisted she was safest with them, and away from me.

Abandoning her to them was only marginally better than leaving her with him. But at least, she'd be safe stuffed between them. Even if they were treating her like an investment they couldn't afford to lose.

Sighing, I walked back from seeing them out of the temple to find Sister Laia and Erthamos gone. I hoped I'd never see either of them again, if not for the same reason.

My mother was supervising the medics in removing Prunella's body, and conferring with her mayors and governors, but urgently gestured for me to wait for her. She wasn't letting me out of her sight, either.

Unable to remain among the echoes of horror and loss, I rushed past the altar, still seeing Prunella's gruesome offering in my mind's eye, and delved deeper into the temple.

I'd always meant to explore a specific section, and since I had time to kill, so to speak, it might as well be now.

It was where they gathered lesser gods that didn't have their own cults, or were too abstract. Those were grouped under the roof of more powerful gods they were connected to. Like the spirits of rivers and lakes venerated in a sea god's temple.

Here, it was the embodiments of time. They were revered in

mosaic paintings—on the ground, beneath Eurycrius' feet and those of his priests and worshippers.

The ones that caught my eye weren't the hours—personified as women in ancient garb with every shade of hair, and depicted around a sundial—but the seasons. Having far more detail, they were represented around the image of the sun nestling into the crescent moon.

The tableaus went clockwise, starting with Summer; a woman standing in a field, holding a bundle of wheat. Everything about her and her surroundings was golden, vibrant and bright. In the framing curve above her was Lyceus, the Sun God, in his chariot, dragging his celestial charge across the sky.

Autumn was the same woman, descending into a woodsier setting, with piles of fallen bronze and copper leaves, and Telephassa, the Moon Goddess, riding overhead with the moon in tow.

Winter was the pastoral figure of Death as the reaper, in a black robe with a scythe. But instead of being confined to his frame like the others, one boney hand reached up, penetrating the dishwater-grays and bruise-purples of his surroundings to claw into the sun-drenched vitality of Spring. He was reaching for the now-younger woman, who was oblivious to the dark entity about to drag her down by the ankle to his domain.

Just like he'd done to Theodosia and Prunella.

And even if I'd gone to him willingly, he'd almost done the same to me in my vision.

From the horrific developments, and everyone's predictions, that might yet come to pass.

But as I walked away from the disturbing scene, one thought echoed in my mind,

This could all be because of me.

It was too much of a coincidence to see the Horned God in a dream that wasn't a dream, then find out my lookalikes were being murdered. He had said he'd been searching for me, but didn't know who I was. All these girls could have died because they resembled me. And what? When they turned out to be the wrong person, he took their hearts to read, for a hint at how to find me?

Only—that didn't make sense. As far as I knew, Death didn't actually kill. And he had to have the person on his list before he visited them. And then, he'd asked where and when I was. Up until this morning, when I'd told him, he hadn't been able to locate me, so couldn't have had anything to do with those girls' deaths for days now.

But most of all, I didn't feel he wanted to reap my soul.

If he didn't, and I wasn't on his list, why had he been searching for me? And even if it hadn't been him behind all this, he still had sway over who died, right? So, if I sleepwalked to him again, could I bargain with him for Chloë's, Cassia's and my other lookalikes' lives?

I had heard of many instances when people made deals with Death. But in all the different versions and myths surrounding him, Death and the Maiden was ubiquitous across all cultures. So maybe I could be the one to charm him in this story? Even if it had always struck me as the strangest concept of all?

For what could Death possibly want with a mortal woman?

Except now nothing seemed implausible anymore. Not after my day had begun with Death reaching for me, followed by ritualistic murders of my lookalikes.

It was anyone's guess how that day would end.

I would take anything, as long as it didn't in another murder.

5

THE HARVEST MOON

In any given situation, I aspired to be the most prepared. Being experienced and desensitized, I always kept a level head and acted. Anything else could come later.

But the line between readiness and agitation had begun to blur as Lyceus painted the sky in sunset shades of rose and coral, and darkened the clouds to indigo.

Chloë had been right. Nothing had ever shaken me like this.

Before, no matter how stressful the experience or dire the danger, I could always remain detached. Whether I was snapping ghouls' necks in caverns, or chasing away raiders attacking my caravan, or leading a revolution against a magical despot in a hosting country, none of it had ever been personal.

None of it had been because of me.

That shrouded priestess had practically stated that belief. Death telling he'd been searching for me supported it. My relatives could end up mutilated and discarded just for resembling me.

Yet it made no sense why. Why those who looked like me would be targeted. Why I wasn't targeted first. Why I would be targeted at all.

Sure, I was hated by many, wished gone by more, but it still didn't add up. Even when I formulated theories—why anyone would be doing this, to intimidate me or send me a message or something even more far-fetched—the bigger picture, of those being killed across the Folkshore, demolished them

I was at a total loss, and it was something I'd never experienced.

And I'd also never experienced such rage and anguish. I couldn't bear to think of the girls who'd been murdered, or the horror and agony they must have suffered.

Now, while their families mourned in private, and I waited for the culprit to attack again, the Harvest Moon celebrations went off without a hitch.

It hurt to see the festive scene with the tables full of people eating and drinking around lit bonfires and beneath dangling effigies. But the Autumn equinox and its rituals were too vital to our region, they had to take precedence. Even something as terrible as a murder spree had to be hushed up, left until tomorrow to be dealt with.

Unfortunately for me, instead of patrolling with the guards, and finding heads to bash in or necks to snap, I was "at risk". No amount of arguing got me involved in the preventative efforts. Or out of having Erthamos tail me and Chloë. My mother straight out ordered me to stay put, and to accept his infuriating presence.

He had glued himself to Chloë's side as we sat around a table at the foot of Starset Hill, waiting for Cassia's pegasus show to begin, and sampling the food brought to our table. And not only was I forced not to haul him away from her, I had to act as my mother's heir, and entertain the visiting dignitaries.

I was in danger of roughing those up, too. Even if they were heirs like me.

But unlike me, they had titles. Our seaside neighbors in mountainous Orestia had maintained their monarchies post the collapse of the Campanian Empire. Lower Campania, on the other hand, had fractured into dozens of city-states packed with oligarchs, merchant-princes and lord-governors—save for our region.

Granaria, as dubbed by our ancestors, was the most fertile land on the continent, and every other region depended on our exports, from wheat, legumes and produce, to meats and dairy products, to seasonings and wines. The other kingdoms were known for more frivolous exports, like the flowers that majorly came from Arbore to our north, and the rare spices from Cahraman across the Deep Red Sea. And while we also had massive fisheries along our coastal regions, we left seafood exports to the kingdoms who had nothing else to contribute.

Speaking of seafood, I could do with some shellfish to smash right now. Something to channel the murderous irritation Erthamos stoked within me as he laid it on thick with Chloë. Pity she was too trained in civility to scare him off, and scar him for life, like I always did to overprivileged creeps.

At least, Grand Duke Acastus had given up on charming me without me causing another diplomatic crisis. He'd intimated he found me as dull as I was large, and left to wine and dine Thalia, who'd been trying to catch his eye. Knowing her and her ambitions, she'd probably convince him to marry her by the end of the evening.

Sighing in exasperation, I eyed the mishmash of cuisines prepared in honor of our foreign guests; a delicious display that ranged from our pastas and risottos, to Armorican roasts and pies, to Orestian dolma and spanakopita.

Yet, for the first time in my life, my omnipresent appetite was nowhere to be found. I was only eating for fuel. Being unable to enjoy one of my favorite pastimes while being side-lined made everything seem even worse.

"Curse my mother's orders," I grumbled around my crammed mouth.

"Since when did orders stop you?" Chloë leaned away from Erthamos and into me, her own mouth half-full.

I sought out my mother, a beacon in her ceremonial garb, a

loose gown in gradations of ripening lemons, her cloak the same but in autumnal shades. The symbol of her position, the circlet of bronze oak leaves held up her piled hair, baring the greying temples. Like every year for as long as I remembered, she remained the image of the Summer Maiden from that mosaic depiction as she became one with Autumn.

Judging by how stiffly she held herself and her sunflower staff, she was expecting the worst, and for the first time in my memory, she seemed—terrified.

"Since I don't want to stress my mother even more," I finally answered, swallowing hard, and scanning the table for the next thing to stuff myself with.

Chloë suggested a few items she'd enjoyed, but the scent of the olive oil cake had begun to tickle my nose when a canon boomed through the air, announcing Cassia's aerial show.

Welcomed by cheers and applause, the flying horses and their riders zoomed high above us, with Cassia at the forefront of the formation.

As always, she started with a jaw-dropping stunt, somersaulting with her winged, spotted mare to a chorus of whoops as the rest flanked her like a squadron of enormous birds.

The wonder of that sight never failed to enthrall me. It now unlatched the anchors of frustration and dread, and filled me all over again with awe and pride.

The pegasi were a majestic breed, once broadly militarized until they were abandoned on the battlefields of a collapsed empire. Unlike the swords and chariots left to rust under the southern sun, relics of an era distant enough to be romanticized, the pegasi were living treasures. Thankfully, when they were repurposed, it was people like Cassia who took the reins.

Instead of an instrument of war, and always in danger of being shot out of the sky and plummeting to their and their riders' deaths, they became prized companions. When put to work, it was either in sport or emergencies. Now the beating of their giant wings was not the herald of strife and danger, but the signal of joy and relief.

Caught in Cassia's breathtaking choreography, I almost jumped out of my skin when something landed on my shoulder.

Fists up, I jumped out of my chair, knocking it down. Aggression fizzled out the moment I realized it was my mother, her face ashen and eyes bulging.

"Where's your cousin?"

My gaze slammed around, my every nerve loosening with nauseating alarm.

It had gotten dark, everyone's attention was focused on the festivities—and Chloë had vanished.

So had Erthamos.

Fury erupting within me like a keg of explosives, I swung around, searching for the gleam of his peculiar silver hair in the firelight.

He was nowhere to be found. But I'd been preoccupied for a mere minute. He couldn't have gone far with her. That bastard must have dragged her into the nearest grove, under cover of the crowds' noise.

Barely registering what else my mother said, I snatched a lantern off the table, and exploded towards the trees.

Dismay tinged my rage when I realized this was where I'd seen my very first human corpse, its twisted form being fed on by butterflies. A sight more horrific than gut-clawing lamiae, a grim lesson that even the most ethereal beings had their macabre sides.

And this maggot had dragged Chloë away from my protection when an unknown monster was on the loose and targeting her. If anything happened to her...

Unable to complete that thought, I hurtled past the fir trees. A hundred feet in, I stumbled on an upturned cart and shovel, just as a shrill scream rang through the darkness.

My muscles spasmed like I had fallen through a glacier, the fright freezing my blood flow.

Chloë!

Snatching the shovel up, I stampeded deeper into the woods.

I didn't care how much trouble harming him would cause us. I would *destroy* him. I would grind his flesh into pig-feed, and his bones into fertilizer for sickly trees, make use of him in death when he'd provided none in life.

But sound traveled here. The closest direction a sound came from could be the farthest.

Weighing the risk of being wrong, I decided to heed my instincts, my experience, followed the farthest echoes, into the darkest reaches of the woods.

After a few minutes, I was sure I was approaching Chloë's voice. She was sobbing. I poured on the speed until I was close enough to see them.

He had his back to me, and Chloe was draped over a fallen log, her leg twisted in an unnatural angle, and her arms raised to hold him off. Then I made out what she was saying.

"...just please—please don't kill me!"

I froze to the spot, outside the patch of moonlight that encased them.

Kill her? The worst I feared from that slimy miscreant was that he'd force himself on her, so her father would in turn be forced to marry her off to him. He wouldn't get her any other way. Tertullian wanted to trade her hand for money not a title.

So why would Chloë fear, not that he would get her killed, but would kill her himself?

It seemed Erthamos himself considered this ridiculous, as he scoffed, "Kill you? You think I would go to all this trouble, just to kill you?"

"If you won't kill me, now you've shown me what you really are, then what do you want?"

Even trembling with fear, Chloë still kept her head. She was making him talk, no doubt buying time until I came to her rescue. In another circumstance, I'd be proud.

"Oh, I have big plans for you." Erthamos advanced on her

slowly, dry branches cracking loudly beneath his feet, his hair undulating in a breeze I couldn't feel. "My hunch about this place, this family, paid off. I just had to stick around long enough to make sure. There was no way that ogre was your father, and your mother fits the profile of his lovers, not to mention that their luxury could only come from a god's favor to his bastards. And I was right. Now I finally get to keep one of you!"

"Wh-what are you talking about?" Chloë moaned, clearly in severe pain. I added pulverizing every bone in both his legs to his punishments.

He laughed, cold and ugly. "I'm talking about picking off all the obvious ones, the pretty nymph-like blondes with their time-less beauty and grace. Those were shots in the dark in the search for you. But that worked in my favor, for the misdirection." He gripped the front of her dress, raising her roughly to shove his face into hers. "Your keepers did me a favor by sheltering you from unworthy eyes, my sweet calf."

That was it. I'd heard enough damning proof. Now I'd end him, like he'd ended Theodosia and Prunella and all the others.

But I had to be careful. The way he'd murdered all those girls suggested he had to have magic at his disposal. I had to take him by surprise, give him no chance to hurl a spell my way—before I split him in two.

Putting down the lantern, I approached, shovel gripped in both hands, bare feet soundless on the dirt.

Dangling in his hold, Chloë seemed about to pass out as she choked, "You're not making any sense..."

"None of them had that spark, that godly glow..."

The woods blurred around me as I exploded in a run that ended in a flying leap. Right on top of him, roaring, I brought the shovel down with all my strength.

Upon contact with his head, the blade bent out of shape and snapped off its socket, and the shaft shattered into a thousand splinters.

The aftershocks of the collision reverberated through my

arms, my whole body, stunning me stiff. And that was before, without turning around, Erthamos' head rotated to face me, inhuman eyes flashing with pale-blue light.

The moment he saw me, a sudden windstorm pummeled me, carrying his delighted cackles through the air like the howls of a hurricane.

"It's *you!*"

UP IN THE AIR

Erthamos' grin grew into a horrific gash that linked his lips to his ears.

The rest of his human disguise melted in the rising wind as he turned around, seeping off him like colors washed away in a stream.

"It has been you all along!" Lightning crackled through the cracks between his shark-like teeth, his guffaw the war-drums of thunder, rattling my ribs. "I should have known it would be you, my burly beauty."

In shock's chokehold, I could only bolt for the shovel's blade, and the lantern. But before I could splash him with the latter's oil, then throw it at him, hoping he'd catch fire, his gale tore it from my hand and smashed it against a tree, dozens of feet away.

He approached lazily, the faint moonlight filtering through the thick treetops going through him as if he was made of tinted glass.

"But you hid so well, I mistook you for that flimsy cousin you kept clasped to your bosom. It must have been her proximity to you that misled me." The storm within his face brightened to a painful intensity. "Thank you for exposing yourself before I committed the unspeakable mistake of claiming her!"

My answer was to hurl the blade of the shovel at his head like a missile.

Had he been solid, it would have lodged into his forehead, slicing his brain in half. As it was, it sailed right through his insubstantial head.

"Darling, I know you've been itching for a fight, but I'm going to give you something better. A chase!"

With a wave of his hand, the now-unconscious Chloë rose in the air, folding on herself like a wet rug. I hurtled to grab her, only to be knocked back with a brutal gust of wind.

I hit the forest floor with a loud thud that broke something beneath me and punched the air out of my lungs, just as my head rebounded with a smack.

Struggling to clear my darkening vision, I scrambled up as he left the ground with Chloë in his arms, the outlines of his silver-blue hair and loose clothes billowing in the wind he generated.

"Wait," I shouted, not expecting he would. But he stopped rising, see-through head tilted in anticipation. Struggling not to give in to the ill-advised urge to attack him again, I got to my feet. "If you narrowed down who you were looking for, and it wasn't to kill them, why did you kill the others?"

"Ah, you're not as clever as I thought, after all. Good. I like them big and dumb."

I would have attacked him again, no matter how pointless it was, if it weren't for Chloë.

"It's others who eliminated your lookalikes, my big, dumb farmgirl." He guffawed, his light blinding me with each thunderous rumble of glee. "They were hoping one of them is the one they need dead. You. But I beat them to you, and I have such big plans for you." He winked one of those flashing eyes at me. "Now—catch me, Carlotta."

Then as if to taunt me, and to show me exactly where he was heading, he rose slowly in the air until he cleared the trees, then flew west.

I exploded into a run, realizations blaring in my head.

He must be some kind of weather spirit. He'd created this Orestian royalty persona—since there were too many of them, and we couldn't know them all—to blend among our visitors, to search for what those others had left a trail of bodies in their wake to find. Me. The shift in victims to only those who resembled me *had* been on my account, after all,

But this wasn't the time for me to give in to guilt, or to overthink anything. I was at my best when I acted on instinct, when I focused on one thing to the exclusion of all else. Getting Chloë back was the target at the end of my narrowed scope. I might not have magic, but what I had in spades was stubbornness.

It would take a lot worse than some weather spirit to get the best of me!

But how was I going to battle the wind?

I'd find a way. I was going to snuff him out, and bring back Chloe, if it was the last thing I did. Before I found her discarded, chest concave and crawling with what fed on her death.

Barreling out of the woods, I streaked towards the clearing where Cassia and her team were grooming their pegasi after the end of their show.

Cassia came running towards me, windblown hair still all over. I only yelled an abbreviated explanation of the situation as I flew past her to her pegasus, Pardalus, giving her no chance to object or ask anything as I mounted the spotted mare.

Reins gripped tight, knees steeled against my mount's flanks, I yelled. "If I don't come back, tell my mother to make you her heir!"

Cassia's shout as she ran after me waving her arms was swallowed by the flap of giant wings, as with a forceful kick Pardalus launched us into the air.

Ascension was a brutal fight against the unyielding air currents and gravity, felt like an inverse swan-dive. It dried out my eyes to cinders, almost ruptured my ear drums, and tore through my hair and clothes until they cut at my skin.

My mother had always said exposure begot acclimation. But

the pressure kept mounting, giving way to lightheadedness, dimming my vision. I wasn't like Cassia who had always longed to sprout wings of her own, and weathered flight as well as any creature born with them. I was a creature of the earth. I'd been airborne a handful of times only to gain the experience, and none had gone beyond grazing the tree-tops.

Bent flat on the mare's back, I struggled to keep my tearing eyes open, hearing nothing over the din of wind and wings but my booming heart. And against my better judgment, I looked down.

My land shrunk beneath me, its topography and population mere shapes and pinpricks. The sketch of a master cartographer —and a sickening sight that threatened to tip me off my steed.

If vomiting was on the horizon, I was saving that spray of acidic bile for Erthamos.

After reaching a height beyond which I knew I couldn't breathe, I steered Pardalus westward, to chase Erthamos' crackling blue light in the distance.

The flight seemed to go on forever, with him constantly receding, until I feared I would freeze to death, and Pardalus would plummet from the sky in exhaustion.

Just as I thought I'd be forced to give up, relief flooded its warmth into my icy chest as we approached the mountain peak where Erthamos had just disappeared. It had sculpted-out-of-rock towers, spiraling paths, arched windows—and the soaring doorway the spirit had entered through.

Wings pulled in, the pegasus shot through the entrance and I wasted no time in dismounting and continuing my pursuit, ignoring every disoriented slip and stumble, and the agony of blood rushing back to my frozen extremities.

The opulence reminded me of the last mountaintop palace I'd visited in Cahraman. Only I wasn't here to laugh at the pettiness of elite women, or watch how the unusual antics and ingenious lies of my shifty new friend panned out. While Ada remained on her mountain to become the future Queen of

Cahraman, I was here, chasing after a malevolent spirit made of storms.

Following his draft, my bare footfalls slapped on pebbled floors, and echoed off curved stone walls whose corners were cut into sculptures that balanced the ceiling over their heads.

I recognized some, even if they were corroded and missing key features. Almagera, Queen of Heaven, our most important fertility goddess, ever-pregnant, with child in one arm and scepter in another. The moon goddess, Telephassa, who we were meant to be celebrating tonight, her head crowned with a cow-horns-like crescent.

At the giant double-doors at the end of the hall stood the most mysterious deity, Orcus, God of the Underworld. Not how I'd seen him in my vision, but in his middle-aged, bearded form, all weathered save for his signifiers; a skull gripped in one hand, and his two-pronged staff in the other.

Ear to the door, I listened for sounds of struggle, but none came from Chloë. She must still be out. I only heard Erthamos' howling wind, felt it mocking me. He knew I'd followed him. He'd made sure to lure me here.

I had no idea what I was going to do once I barged in. Throw her over my shoulder and run back to the pegasus? Would I even make it far before he swept past me and blocked my way with a wall of wind? What would I do then?

Exhaling my frustration, I dared another look at the weather-worn form of Orcus. "You don't have any advice on how to kill this thing, do you?"

No response, of course. I was on my own here.

"Since you're no help, I don't think you'll mind if I help myself, right?"

Even knowing he was a frayed and inferior simulation of the god, I still winced with a pang of misgiving as I broke the bident from his hold, taking a few fingers off with it.

Then I rounded on the door. On the third slam of my

smarting shoulder, it burst open, hurling me through with my unopposed momentum.

Skidding on my side on the roughened floor, I took in my surroundings at a glance even as I heaved up to my feet.

The room was vast, with more sculptures all around the periphery, between tall, shuttered windows. They were all of Erthamos this time. And he was nowhere to be found. The only light came from the fireplace, its roaring flames casting Chloë in an eerie, red glow as she lay on her face like a rag doll.

"I was hoping you'd make it."

A loud slam shut the doors behind me and I swung around, falling into a defensive stance, prongs pointed in his direction, for all the good they'd do.

Erthamos, still translucent, but looking mostly human again, approached me with open arms and that punchable smile. "You know, most people take it in stride when someone they know is carried off by a god."

My mind stalled at that statement.

That being of weather and whims, that had us locked in this room, was a *god*? A figure of pompous speech, or for real?

"They don't even think of attempting a rescue." He started to circle me, ogling my breasts and buttocks, making me feel he could see through my practical and obscuring field clothes. I'd decked men for less. "It's an honor to most, a blessing to all, to be chosen by me."

Holding back from attempting to stab him until I learned more, I growled, "And just who are you?"

Offense marred his faded face. "I'm Erthamos, the West Wind."

So, a minor god, but a god nonetheless. Not that it changed anything.

I met his crackling eyes. "So you lured me here. How clever of you. What do you want with us now?"

He glanced over my shoulder with disinterest. "Her, I will

dispose of, but *you...*" He leaned in too close, rank with humidity, colors deepening as he leered at me. "...you, I will make my consort." He threw his head back and cackled in delight. "While my competitors have been killing the rest, I only wanted to make use of one of you. You, with your lineage, will be of the most use to me."

He spoke with the enthusiasm of a butcher choosing a fattened calf, or a predator salivating over the most succulent quarry.

But I wasn't cattle, or prey. And I'd heard enough.

He meant to kill Chloë. And to own me.

Without warning, I struck. Orcus' stone bident broke upon impact with his form, the pieces scattering through him. Then I truly threw caution to the wind. Or rather, at him.

My first collided with his face, not feeling flesh and bone, but a resistant force that was knocked aside by my strength all the same.

For a second, he mirrored my amazement. I took the chance to land another hit to his jaw, feeling like I was plowing into his very substance.

He staggered, and I followed it up with a kick into his chest. This time, he toppled over.

He slammed to the ground with an explosive gust that almost blew me off my feet, but I struggled against the blast, and pounced on him. Straddling his semi-substantial body, I rained blows on his head, my fists distorting his face and skull, and making him vibrate with pain as he started solidifying.

This was working! I was hurting a god, would overpower him—

A deafening bellow erupted throughout the room, almost bursting my head.

"THAT'S ENOUGH!"

A cyclone roared out of nowhere, throwing me off him. It attempted to batter my attempts to rise, but I managed to resist, to get to my feet. Now I knew what to expect, I fought against his storm, using the pebbled floor's traction, watching alarm flare in his eyes.

A vicious grin tugged at my lips as he stumbled back at my advance. "Once I get my hands on you again, I'm taking you apart..."

I choked, coughed. The current had reversed, and air was fleeing my lungs. In seconds, breathlessness started igniting, like my chest was being infested with hot sand.

Vision darkened at the edges as the invisible stranglehold tightened. I couldn't stay upright, crashed to my knees, strength and drive siphoning out with my breath.

"Not so tough now, are you?" he taunted as he came to loom above me, hair whipping in his own wind.

Wildfire numbness swarmed me, until movement remained only in my fingers.

I curled all but one.

"I think it will take a few more asphyxiations before you finally break," he sneered down at me, his manic malice reverberations of thunder in my constricting chest. "But you better learn to behave fast, or I'll compromise and rip out one of your lungs."

I should pretend to surrender, then take him down when he least expects it...

No. That would save only me. He would kill Chloë as soon as he incapacitated me.

Maybe if I incensed him enough, as I always did most men, I'd make him respond like one, try to subdue me physically. In a fight, I felt certain I could best him.

"I will—never—behave..." I spat.

"That's what you think. I will train you, by withholding your very breath. Mark my words, the day will come when you will never stop begging for my suffocation."

"I...will never stop...trying to rip...your putrid essence out... you literally spineless worm..."

He took a few rash steps towards me. Yes, yes.

Just as I thought he'd come within reach, and I'd grab and

pummel whatever he was made of into pulp, he stopped, a sinister frown marring his fading-again face.

"You're valuable only if you submit."

"I would rather die."

His face contorted again, until it settled into that shark's grin. "So be it."

This time, his vortex ripped every last wisp of air from my lungs, so forcefully, I felt I would crumple.

In less than a minute, there was no fight left in me. I felt my burning lungs collapsing, and my darkening eyes about to burst out of my straining skull. He would keep up the pressure until they did.

I'd gambled, and I'd lost. But as my heart flailed on its last beats, I knew I couldn't have done anything else.

Reveling in my defeat and agony, his sadistic howls rang over the suctioning gale about to rip my soul out, and—

—two sharp spikes burst through his chest.

Abruptly, the siphoning halted, and I flopped onto the floor, thrashing and swallowing air in shearing gulps.

Erthamos had solidified, blue-grey eyes shocked and lifeless as he hung off the ends of a silvery, two-pronged staff like a dead fish.

Struggling to keep my swimming vision afloat, I managed to hold my pounding head up to eye the new monstrosity.

In a floor-length cloak the deepest purple of eternity, holding the staff that had pierced the very wind, stood the Horned God.

Like in my vision, he tilted his skeletal head at me, sockets glowing a deathly violet as his fathomless voice reverberated in my bones.

"You're an inexplicably hard woman to find."

DEATH HIMSELF

Thoughts bleeding at the speed of a severed artery, I stared at the figure looming over me.

I might have never been choked before, but I knew the side effects of asphyxiation included hallucinations. This had to be another dream, a dying one, and I'd summoned the entity I'd been longing to meet for years in my last moments. And I'd imagined him taking revenge on my killer.

"I'm dead, aren't I?" I coughed, words feeling like dragging a bristly rope out of my throat. Which was strange, to feel anything in death.

"I did only feel you when you were on the verge of death. But you are still very much alive."

That made me bolt up sitting. "I am?"

For answer, he flicked Erthamos' body off the prongs of his staff like a rotten piece of meat off a fork.

The wind god landed with a nauseating *thump* beside me.

Then just like in my vision, the Horned God extended his hand to me.

I swallowed the precious air rather than breathing it.

Whatever good it did me, unlike in my vision, I decided to remain defiant and not reach back.

Helping myself up, I rose on unsteady, swollen legs. Every inch of exposed skin had taken on the bruised hue of suffocation, my chest felt filled with glass, and pain spiked in my head with every movement.

I swayed, but did my best to square my shoulders and grit my jaw. I was still unable to stare back into the unrelenting depths of his sockets. Avoiding them, I glared down at Erthamos' body. If I could, I would have spit on it.

"Is he dead?"

"Indisposed." He breezed closer with a whisper of his cloak and a whiff of something vaguely metallic yet intensely pleasing. My heart tangled tighter in its strings with his every step. "But the wind is a resilient element. He will recover, faster than I would like."

Asphyxiated mind still struggling, I fixated past his skeletal head and on Chloë.

All of this had happened because Erthamos had mistaken her for me. He'd taken her knowing I'd willingly follow him into his environment to save her. He had lured me here, and had brought me to my knees, not by overpowering my strength, but by exploiting a weakness I hadn't anticipated.

I'd been helpless, utterly, for the first time in my life.

That scared me far more than the embodiment of death, who had, in turn, taken out Erthamos like he was nothing.

Compared to Orcus, Lord of the Dead, a minor god like Erthamos was nothing.

What did that make me?

Far less than nothing, of course.

Exhaling raggedly, I gestured at the gold blood that stained his bident. "What's he going to do when he wakes up?"

The Horned God inclined his macabre head at me. "I would need to know more of the situation before hazarding a guess. Why was the West Wind suffocating you, and how did you come to be here?"

I choked out a scrambled account of the spree of murders of my and Chloë's lookalikes, Erthamos' abduction of her, my pursuit, and our fight.

His sockets flashed a deeper purple that felt like he was weighing my words, before he said, "Then I expect he will be too overcome with shame at being bested by a mortal."

"I didn't best him. He almost killed me."

"According to your account, only by being underhanded, and after you almost defeated him. I would expect him to keep this incident a secret—and to come after you again."

"Then he will finish the job of killing me," I groaned.

"I doubt that, or that he would have truly killed you, not if he considers you valuable."

A sarcastic huff escaped my still-burning chest. "Oh, he would have killed me all right, if you hadn't impaled him like a trout. Strange of you to underestimate the unbridled vanity and wrath of fellow gods."

"I have no fellow gods."

There was no vanity or wrath in *that* statement. He calmly, cerebrally knew no god was on his level, that he had nothing in common with any of them.

Death was unlike anything. He was the end of everything.

And I was standing here, having a conversation with him, in the bedroom of the wind god he'd stabbed for me. The vile narcissist I hadn't seen the last of.

Of course he would come after me again.

And if not him, others would. Even if he kept our encounter a secret, if he had worked out my identity, it was a matter of time before the others who'd been killing my lookalikes did, too. My home would be the first place they'd look for me. My mother and family would be guarding me, and when they defended me, they'd die with me.

"Why is this happening? *What is going on?*" I wheezed, hating how vulnerable I sounded, but my throat was raw, my lungs shriveled. As if any amount of posturing mattered to everyone's worst nightmare.

Everyone but my own, it seemed.

His silence was nerve-wracking. It felt as if he was examining me, trying to fathom what I was, and unable to make up his mind.

When he seemed to come to a decision, he reached out a hand to me again.

But this time it wasn't a helping hand. It felt like it had in my vision.

His next words proved it. "Come with me, and I'll tell you what I know."

That serene offer, spoken in that sonorous voice I wished I could listen to forever, almost stopped my heart.

I stared at his large, elegant hand and the urge to grab it overwhelmed me.

But this was no vision. If I took his hand now, he *would* take me with him.

Staggering a step back, putting a breath between us so I could think, I still stared at his proffered hand, only then noticing the wide, gold rings on each finger of his marble-pale palm. As for his gleaming, dark, talon-like nails, I couldn't tell where they began on his fingers.

Unlike Erthamos and most representations of gods, he didn't hide his inhuman traits. And it somehow made him more appealing to me.

Of their own volition, my eyes dragged up his form, the experience of being close to someone much taller than me alien, yet gratifying. At his chest, I caught the golden glint of a medallion and the sheen of indigo silk from underneath his cloak, its material indescribable, felt—*alive*. Its smoky folds practically breathed as he moved. His very outline felt like a cigar-burn in the canvas of existence, distorting the scene around him in a swirl of dark deliverance.

Finally, I reached the head—the antlered skull with its ghastly grin on permanent display. Past the length of incisors, I was sucked into the dark depths of his sockets, falling into those amethyst lights that pulsated like long-dead stars.

"Who are you?" I rasped, not knowing why I said that.

"I should be asking you that," he said, echoing what I'd said to him before, a hint of something like irritation breezing through the endless depths of his voice.

"You know who I am, you've been looking for me."

Just as I said that, my lethargic mind reached the conclusion it had been inching towards.

Death had lured me from my bed in a waking dream this morning, and within the day, he had found me, right before a god ripped the air from my lungs. He had been an omen, after all.

As if reading my rising agitation, he raised a hand. "Not for the purpose others have."

"Then what is your purpose?"

He went still again, as if uncertain. Could Death suffer indecision like other beings?

Making up his mind, it seemed, he curled his fingers, beckoning me in pure command. "We'll see. Now, come."

And I knew. Though he appeared to give me a choice, I had none.

This was Death Incarnate, inevitable, immutable, and nothing escaped him.

But at least, I'd ask questions. I'd never gone into anything blind. Now I needed to know the terms of my surrender, and to glimpse my destination before I delved further past the veil that separated mortals from their deities.

"Coming with you doesn't entail dying, right?" I rasped.

"The living can enter my domain under certain conditions, mostly at my behest."

"What about Chloë?"

"She comes, too."

"And both of us will *remain* alive?"

At his nod, any traces of primal panic dissipated. For I believed him. Death had no reason to lie when he could do whatever he willed.

And then, while I might not have a choice, I did have something to gain. If he had information to give me, something I could use to end this terrible situation, I had to have it. And perhaps, if I could endear myself to him, I might be able to flee his domain with Chloë later.

I looked up into his ghastly visage as he waited for me to yield, and slipped back into the state when I'd first encountered him, fueled by curiosity and the magnetic pull towards him. Back to the unexpected moment when the spectral figure in the dark forest had asked, *"Who are you?"*

"Coralia Spica," I found myself saying. "Of the Granary."

Intrigue flashed in the gloom of his sockets. "Coralia, like the folk-song."

If it weren't for the smothering tension, and my surprise that Death knew that song, that reference would have made me groan and curse my grandmother.

"Cora," I corrected.

He inclined his head, conceding my preference. "Cora."

The way he said my name felt like a balm spreading in my still-aching chest.

Which was beyond strange. Not even the terminally ill or injured welcomed Death calling their name.

Mouth painfully dry, like my gums were about to rip with the next lift of my lips, I prompted, "And you are?"

"I'm sure you have a name or two you refer to me by."

"Orcus and Lucros are the ones I've heard the most. But I want to know what *you* call yourself."

His stillness deepened, and I felt a shift in his gaze despite the morbid blankness of his skull. Almost like he was surprised, just as he was when he had first glimpsed me in our dream-tinged encounter.

"Adamantus."

I lurched. The way he said *his* name. His *voice*. Up to this point, it had held that dreamy vibe of a lulling harp. Now, it struck a different chord, the dark, lonely thrum of a bass.

"I never heard that one, anywhere," I rasped, licking tingling lips. "How come no one uses it?"

"Because you're the first to ask for it."

I stared at him for what felt like an hour, an eternity.

Then I did what I did so easily, so eagerly this morning. Just with one difference.

His outstretched hand had fallen to his side. It was I who reached out and took it.

I was struck by how hard and cold it was, like I was touching a living sculpture on a chilly autumn morning. My tanned hand with its short, dirty fingernails was a harsh contrast against his immaculateness. A word never used in the same sentence as me.

Before I realized how he did it, he was throwing Chloë over his shoulder as if she was a napping toddler. Breaking my grip so it was his fingers that wrapped over mine, he rugged me closer even as he struck the floor with his bident.

A swirling vortex yawned open, its unsteady outline distorting the stone like his own did the fabric of this realm.

Tense with awe, I peered down into the dark depths as one step of a spiraling staircase emerged after the other with the sharp, slicing sound of a sword being unsheathed.

His first step down was like a knell of doom, deafening me to all other noises, including my own labored breathing and booming heart.

"Whatever you do, don't try to run."

"Or you'll do what?"

"Nothing. No use in rescuing what wants to be lost."

The implication that there was plenty down there that could end me, and that he would leave me to my fate if I attempted escaping, was a clear warning. A warning I would have to disregard if I ever wanted to go home.

"I'll be on my best behavior," I mumbled.

"Somehow, I doubt that's something you're capable of."

And he pulled me in after him.

One unsteady step after the other, I followed the Lord of the Dead into his domain, where he reigned eternal over worlds unseen, and terrors untold.

THE BLOODSTAINED SHORE

Many an ancient hero had ventured into the Underworld to find someone or something.

I'd never put much stock into those tales, as every culture's version had conflicting takes on what it looked like, or what lived there.

Now I was about to see it for myself.

But instead of sneaking in to save someone, I was being led by the one to defy. My soul to save was here with me, draped over his shoulder like a child asleep on the walk home.

Since I couldn't snatch her and make a run for it, I unlatched my eyes from Chloë's limp form and glanced over my shoulder. I found the steps fading in succession like a trail of smoke.

That shattered any possibility of running back up. I'd need to scout for another way out. There had to be one, without him and his bident. After seeing what he'd done to another god, stealing it was not an option. It was never one, anyway.

Looking ahead and down again, I skipped several steps and heartbeats. The ball of my bare foot hit the smooth, unidentifiable material hard, just as the light above fled the shrinking portal.

Darkness draped us for a strangely calming moment. Then,

like lanterns fueled by the blue hour, radiance hummed to life. Crystal stalks growing from the walls emitted a cool tone, pinpricks of a milky violet, like the sky at moonset.

Our descent continued, and the scene morphed. As if cracking open a shell, the craggy, crystal-filled casing all around us was pulled apart, to unveil an edgeless location. I hopped off the final five steps at once to match his longer, relentless stride and landed on a jarring sensation.

Beneath my curling toes, a dark beach stretched for as far as my strained eyes could perceive, its sea only within earshot.

Adamantus released my hand. The loss of his cool grip made my forearm pulsate with a strange ache. What my joints had felt in colder lands when I left the heated interior for the blinding blizzards.

"Stay close." His voice was a surrounding sound, as if emitted by his very domain. I could feel its vibration in my every cell.

Fighting to keep my teeth apart and heart out of my throat, I followed, my focus split between the damp sand sinking beneath my feet, and the thorny antlers crowning the skull that bafflingly grew out of his pale neck.

I'd known from his hands that he wasn't a skeleton like some cultures depicted him. That combination of smooth flesh and inhuman bone had me clenching my fists in anticipation. Of what exactly? What the rest of him would look and feel like? Or was it trepidation? Of the things he ruled over being even worse?

I'd dealt with many inhuman or superhuman beings, tending to react to the former with the sharpest thing within reach, and the latter depending on their behavior. But satyrs, nymphs, fairies, centaurs and shapeshifters were familiar, part animal, turning into or behaving like one. Creatures that were one with nature in a way I understood, and always longed to be.

But I'd left the natural far behind when I challenged a god, and took another's hand.

Trying not to choke on my still-burning breath, my attention moved from Adamantus' back, down to the path he was making for me.

Footprints in the sand had always been an adventure to me, something to follow and concoct stories around. But his made my nails dig into my palm. The expanse beneath us was a gradient of bruises, from blue-black to wine-purple, with flecks of glittering white. But where his weight dug the layer beneath, it was blood-red.

That gory effect didn't seem to be stemming from him, like his outline's distortion. I tested the theory, dragging my toes through the sand, only to recreate the torn side of a dying bull. And the sensation of wading in its seeping life.

We were walking across a literally bloody beach!

Shuddering hard at the realization, I blinked as the water I'd been hearing suddenly showed itself, the steady, frothing shoreline as red as our footprints.

It was like when a whale washed ashore, covered in gaping wounds from battling what lurked in the deep, and bled out further as people scavenged it, its violent death dyeing the water, its shattered bone littering the beach, and its fleshy remains rotting into the sand.

Strangely, it didn't reek of rot here, but smelled of something I knew but couldn't articulate. The air after a lightning-strike, copper melting, blood burning...

"What is this place?" I whispered, as if afraid to disturb whatever lurked here. Laughable, when I had no reservations with Death Himself.

"Primordial Waters and its Bloodstained Shores," he said, calm as the tide rushing to our feet. "A remnant from when the world was still being formed."

I stumbled, the sensation of air leaving my lungs under pressure assailing me again. I truly hadn't been expecting a response, let alone one that hit like a punch between the brows.

I was walking where it all began. Way before the titans

reigned, and people still lived in caves and spoke languages lost to the winds.

Still trying to wrap my mind around the concept, a pale barge emerged through the distant fog, moving faster than anything its size ought to. The bow approaching us curved up into a sharp point, while the stern, where its navigator stood, was flat and blunt.

A demonic gondolier. That was the only description for the spindly, shadowy figure that brought the boat to a stop before us. Back hunched, face hidden in his hood, he was deathly silent, no sign of movement from his chest. His hands were the only visible part of his shrouded form, textureless and translucent, as if made of unblemished glass.

After setting Chloë inside, Adamantus waited with an offered hand. I ignored him and clambered up into the vessel unaided, scrambling to sit beside Chloë. I gathered her to me, hoping to comfort her with my presence in sleep, even as the boat's strangely familiar material pressed against my own body.

Adamantus only walked through it, like he were a ghost, and sat facing the ferryman. "To Blackglass Hall."

Obeying at once, the ferryman dug his pole into the bloodied shore and turned us further into the spine-chilling expanse.

Out from the dim distance rose a stark gate, standing as high as the mountains on its sides, that seemed to have been leveled to make way for its intrusion. It seemed to share the boat's pale material, with alternating sharp ends slotted together like gargantuan fingers. As we approached, its proportions became overpowering, making me feel like a speck of sand. Thoughts stuttering, blood curdling, I knew what I was looking at.

The Gates of the Underworld.

Adamantus suddenly stood, and threw his arms out. Blinding blue flames burst out in ever-expanding curves, a firestorm of unimaginable power, wrenching the Gates apart. The waters became towering waves that sloshed into the barge, electrifying the sensations beneath my feet, sparking recognition.

Bone. We were sitting in a hollowed-out, gigantic rib, and the Gates we were passing through looked like the jaws of some ancient and unnamable behemoth.

I held Chloë with shivering arms, trying to use her presence to fuel my depleting stamina. I could only be thankful she was blissfully unaware as the mind-shattering jaws snapped shut behind us with a scraping screech that almost sheared my flesh off my bones.

It would remain a folktale to her, how souls entered this place the living only dared mention with reverent euphemisms and abject terror. She would be spared having this horrific memory of sailing past the point of no return.

Into the Nether Court.

Yet, I didn't have the luxury of resignation. Remaining here wasn't an option. No matter how impossible the odds of escape seemed, I would somehow find a way home.

9

BLACKGLASS HALL

Past the Gates, all my resolutions fled as our sanguinary path emptied with a bone-rattling crash into a great, snaking river.

The splashing waters drenched me, spraying into the mouth I opened on an involuntary cry. Frantically spitting and wiping at my lips, my mind flooded with a dozen horrific side-effects of swallowing primordial water.

Then I noticed we were no longer sailing in those. The waves had turned from simmering and bloodstained to salty and luminescent-white. Their intense light illuminated the obsidian cave-like surroundings, reflecting off the smooth walls and bringing out the arcane patterns hewn into them. And all around echoed wails I couldn't trace.

The miserable cries trailed through the sharp, cool air, piercing even my thick skin and infecting me with an overpowering weepiness.

It wasn't saltwater that led us in, that I tasted. It was tears. This had to be the River of Woe, where every drop shed in grief gathered to carry the mourners' departed souls to their destination.

How much had I contributed to these waters when my

grandmother left us? Would I be able to see her soul? If I did, would I be tempted to be like every idiot that tried to escape from this place with their loved ones? My jaw twitched with the urge to know where she was.

As I considered what Death would do to me for even asking, other barges manifested ahead and behind our own, each with its own identical ferryman, a spindly hooded figure brandishing a browning-bone pole.

This was how many cities in Lower Campania started depicting Adamantus in the last centuries, especially in winter equinox festivals. I had to wonder if this confused image of the Grim Reaper had been brought back by sufferers of near-death experiences.

Souls packed the barges, faded, see-through and emitting a faint glow en masse. My heart clenched as I wondered how many of the newcomers were from the mutilated girls across my region, that Sister Laia had compared to Theodosia and Prunella? Those murdered in this ritualistic search for me?

As I pondered the macabre thoughts, we entered a wider space, unveiling something above us akin to a dawn-lit sky.

Beneath what felt like a permanent blue hour emerged outlines and shadowy shapes of wilderness, and on varying levels of hilly elevations rose—*buildings?*

As we sailed in deeper, there was no doubt anymore. Buildings did crowd the hills, with towers and spires rising from their countless roofs and balconies and windows adorning their facades. They stood out like gathering crowds against a mishmash landscape of fields, forests, plains and deserts of unthinkable hues and textures, the closer ones shimmering in the verdant brightness of the water—what I realized was no longer the River of Woe.

The transition had been so smooth I hadn't noticed as the tears had emptied into the new river's emerald hues, which kept growing more intense as we crossed the chthonic lands.

After navigating a grand curve, we sailed near sounds of a

roaring waterfall, then arrived at a crystalline stairway that steadily darkened as it climbed up the side of soaring towers that seemed hewn from obsidian.

With the same ghost-like ease, Adamantus disembarked with Chloë, before turning, extending an undeterred hand out for me. This time, with the reality of being here weighing me down, I let him help me onto the platform.

I managed to keep up with his floating yet unhurried ascent, probably for my benefit.

Halfway up, unexpected sounds of life met us, just before three metallic hounds rushed down, coming to circle me with agitated, suspicious sniffs.

Gaping down at them, I was hypnotized by the way the light shifted over their polished bodies, and the fact that they were truly made of metal.

The silver hellhound had the form of a wolf, growling in intimidation, showing off its glinting, razor-like fangs. The platinum one was the image of a sleek watchdog, with its erect ears larger and slim tail whipping. The smallest was shaggy and golden, the model of a hunting retriever, floppy ears and calmer demeanor included.

Fascinated, I reached for the silver wolf and his loud growl pounded on my eardrums, making me snap back my hand.

I'd faced down men, animals and monsters alike at their worst temperament, but my fortitude had yet to replenish itself. There was no use steeling myself against a harder metal, anyway.

"Argentus!" Adamantus reprimanded, and the heat in the wolf's territorial snarls were snuffed out in a swift turn of his head, angling his majestic profile sheepishly towards his master.

The sleek, platinum watchdog rushed to sniff at Chloë's dangling form, and the remnants of my aggression were fanned.

Before I could push it away, a thunderous snap of Adamantus' fingers stopped us both in our tracks. "Platinus, behave."

Cowed into ignoring the anomalies their master had brought, Argentus and Plantinus beat the golden one to his side.

Adamantus greeted each with an ear-aching scrape of his diamond-hard nails along their metallic heads. "Cressida, lead the way to the chambers."

As sharp and swift as an arrow, the golden hellhound bolted off the stairway and down a pathway to the right, leading us to an area spread in black-glass floors.

The whole space was drenched in a soft light that accentuated columned corners, nacre doors, and dark crystal sculptures that marked the beginning and end of every section. I documented our path for a way back, until we approached a fountain frothing with a liquid that looked like moonlight mingling through dark clouds.

"What is that?" I asked, tempted by its bittersweet aroma and the crystal jug on the basin's lip.

"Nightwine. I don't recommend you sample it yet."

That made me want to try it even more. "Why not?"

He craned his skeletal head over his shoulder, presenting me with its sinister side snarl. "At your current state, you'd be too tempted to drink enough to ensure you never leave here again."

Thirst almost overpowering me, I bit over the split in my lower lip, tasting the coppery tang of blood to ground myself. "Would you even let me leave?"

His chuckle rumbled through the glassy walls, making them hum like struck crystal. "You're welcome to leave anytime you want."

I leveled him with a disbelieving stare. "Really?"

"Yes." He turned, continued gliding away. "If you can find your way out."

Why was I not surprised?

Before I could ask something else, maybe glean any information from his answers, he was suddenly dozens of feet away, forcing me to run after him.

After a while or going down similar areas, we passed by a balcony that stretched across huge, circular arches. But I couldn't see what it overlooked, only heard both running and falling water.

Just as I wished I could take a look, the floor disappeared beneath my feet.

My heart almost catapulted out of my mouth before I realized it had only turned transparent, baring the rushing river beneath.

Was this in answer to my wish? Was this place sentient, not to mention cooperative? Or was it his doing? And how had the river come up so high?

Before I could ask, he disappeared, too, around a corner.

I rushed to catch up with him, only to come to a gigantic, open-air platform beneath a twilit sky. The water that flowed beneath the floor was gushing over the edge to thunder down between enormous pearl columns.

Confused, I approached the edge in a heavy shuffle. Hugging the right column, its smoothness threatening to unbalance me into the jade-green cascade, I peered down.

From its vapor-filled basin far below, the river we'd sailed through flowed into maze-like canals, winding through a city that sprawled with a blend of classical and early modern architecture.

Were there people *living* down there? More importantly, how was there a sky here?

But what did any of this matter? I wasn't here to sight-see.

Shaking myself, I pushed off the column and turned to Adamantus. I saw him nowhere.

Heart booming in my head, it didn't occur to me to call him as I rushed to the nearest door. It nestled within a wall of a thousand shades of purple, as if it was carved from a solid block of amethyst. The door was circular and its pale violet surface rippled and fumed like a brewing elixir.

Instead of a doorknob, its handle was a golden snake biting its tail. I reached for it, and it came to life beneath my fingertips, flashing its emerald eyes at me with a hiss.

Taken aback, I tore away, and crashed into a wall behind me.

I realized I'd bumped into Adamantus only when I felt his gaze burning into the back of my head.

Whirling around to face him, it was the sensations of his unyielding hardness still tingling in my spine, more than anything else, that crashed me back to reality.

I was deep in the Underworld, facing the overwhelming visage of its king.

And Chloë was gone.

"Where is she?" I rasped, voice a shrill whisper.

Adamantus pointed his bident to the door behind him, across from where I stood. "Being tended to by underlings. They will do the same for you once they're done."

"I want to see her."

Not taking his bottomless gaze off me, making me sweat until my scalp was drenched, he waved a hand. The center of the circular door faded to fog, unveiling what lay beyond.

Chloë, half-awake, undressed and in a large, marble bathtub, was being washed by a pair of sallow nymphs. Was their kind the population of the settlement below?

The scene blinked out as the opaqueness returned, leaving me less tense, but my fists still balled. "You said you will tell me what you know about my situation."

"I have more pressing matters to attend to. Once I am done, I will summon you to have an audience with myself and another deity."

"But I want to know now."

His eyes flashed, indigo stars throbbing with dire warning. "You will wait."

"And do what?"

"Remain in your room, make use of what will be provided for you." He took one step closer, making me swallow air. "You will only use or consume what you're given, nothing else. Understood?"

The ingrained inclination to spit in the face of danger crackled within my chest.

But what would that achieve? He wasn't a monster, but Death Manifest, and I was in his domain. Defying him would just send me back to that Gate, as a soul this time.

Where would that leave, not just Chloë, but my family, my land? My mother?

Still, being given a quiet moment to myself wasn't the reprieve I needed. I had to come out of this disaster of a day with an answer. It was the only reason I'd agreed to take his hand.

"Enter," he ordered, advancing on me as he waved the door that almost bit me open.

I walked backwards into the room, and watched the door fuse shut after him, leaving the hounds outside.

It was brighter within the spacious chamber, due to an abundance of mounted lamps. It also boasted a color scheme in hues of green, rather than purple and obsidian like the rest of the edifice I'd seen so far. And there were no windows.

Not a good sign.

If he wouldn't discuss the more gruesome issues now, then I'd try to find out more about what had been luring me nightly from my bed for years.

Unable to meet his simmering sockets, I focused on the hand I had senselessly longed to take in the dream. The very hand that had led me to this moment.

"Was it really you?"

"In which event or tale?" he said monotonously. "I am a stock character in many a fable, and the easiest answer to the unexplained."

"In my dream," I emphasized.

The grip on his bident loosened, the shift of his hard knuckles under his pale skin mirroring my chest opening up, making it easier to breathe deeper somehow.

"How much do you remember?" he rumbled through his perpetually menacing teeth.

My grandmother had taught me it was best to respond with vagueness. The reaction *that* elicited would give me an impression on the person, and let them fill in the gaps for themselves.

Whether what stared me down counted as a person or not didn't matter. There were enough stories of deities reacting like people would, none more infamous than Eglaia, the goddess of beauty and desire, spitefully smiting her daughter-in-law when she failed to control the upstart mortal.

I might be an upstart mortal, but since I couldn't head-butt him for answers, I needed to be aggravating yet careful. Anything to give me a smidge of power at this moment.

I forced my lips up and apart, baring my aching teeth and their dry gums in my best goading grin. "I remember."

Many a man had had a fire lit under his ass by my mere presence. My height, my unkempt condition, even the low register my tone nestled comfortably in, enraged them, and that was before they tried to prove themselves by striking against me, and ending up humiliated.

Yet, Adamantus' only response was a vibration that expanded his smokey outline, like an ink-blot staining a lush painting.

"Rest," he ordered. "We'll have much to discuss when I'm done."

The moment the breathing shadows of his cloak swallowed him whole, I reached my limit and collapsed where I stood on my knees.

But I couldn't afford to surrender to depletion. If he was as preoccupied as he'd claimed, then I had time to search for a way out. According to him, I could leave if I found one. Once I got answers, I needed to be ready for a swift escape. And I would be.

Most figures in history or mythology, alleged to have ventured in and out of the Underworld, weren't ingenious or virtuous by any means, only determined.

Luckily, determination was one of my defining traits.

10

A GLIMPSE OF MADNESS

Determination had done nothing for me so far.

Leaving the room was turning out to be even harder than it initially appeared.

And it wasn't on account of the magical door, or the metallic hellhounds posted outside it, but because of the wall-to-wall luxury I was ensconced in.

As wide as an entire floor back home, the room felt like miles of polished, pastel-green stone, with furniture that grew out of the seamless tiles, the likes of which I'd never seen in any earthly court, every piece made of silver, mother-of-pearl, crystal and emerald.

But it was the bed, with its treacherous appeal, that truly tested my resolve.

Unlike my own bed, and any in the foreign places I'd slept in, it had no posts, curtains or nets—all needless as there were no windows or insects. It was also unprecedented in that it was spacious enough to dwarf me. Apart from that, everything about it was fit for a goddess queen, its materials luxury incarnate, its upholstery and embroidery sublime. With every element in all greens, from mint to malachite, it felt like a field of luxury and comfort.

I could almost hear it calling to me, could do nothing but imagine how good it would feel to rest my aching body on its softness, and close my burning eyes. Maybe if I took a nap first...

No.

I didn't have the guarantee of another chance like this, when I was left to my own devices. I'd rest after I explored my options, and concocted a possible escape plan.

With that resolution made, I dragged myself from the floor, and went in search of a way out of this room that bypassed the probably poisonous door and its metallic guard hounds.

Through an adjacent door, I found an indulgent bathroom that also cajoled delaying my mission. Like the bedroom furniture, the sinks and enormous tub grew out from the floor, their taps gold and multifaceted crystal, while silver cabinets held a dizzying array of bath-soap and perfume bottles. But like the bed, it was the steaming water that constantly poured from gaps in the jade walls that almost made me buckle.

As it sparkled hypnotically, I raised my gaze to escape its temptation, only to find the source of the dreamy light; a thin glass orb hovering overhead. It was filled with pale fire like a miniature sun, the closest to daylight this place would ever see.

It was a good thing I looked up, otherwise I wouldn't have noticed the window.

Mounted high over the tub, it was a circle big enough to maybe accommodate me, and sealed with emerald glass.

But the chairs were fused to the floor, the lamps fastened to the walls, and the bottles too fragile to be of any use. I had no other option but my fist.

Thanking the fates that I'd disregarded my mother's suggestion to wear a dress for the festivities, I leaped off the edge of the tub, grabbed onto the sill. Pulling myself up, I brought one knee after the other, until both were lodged against the curved sides.

My limbs shook with exhaustion, and my abdominal muscles and lower back were lit aflame. Never did I think I'd envy insects for their anatomy, but it no doubt made walking on walls effortless. No matter the strain, I had to maintain my beetle-like crouch, because I knew once I fell into the tub, I was not getting back up.

Breathing deep and ragged, I squeezed into the interior of the window. Bracing against its slippery sides, I risked pulling back one arm. Praying to every god I could name, I slammed my fist against the green glass.

Both pain and relief flooded me at the instantaneous crack, spiderwebbing out from the center like a monochrome mosaic. I punched the weakened spot three more times until the entire pane resembled a snowflake. Then it shattered, raining shards around me and outside.

Not caring if I'd sustained any cuts, I scrambled to squeeze through the opening, knowing what I'd find below from the rumble that blared as soon as the window broke. The waterfall I'd stared down a short while ago.

Knowing I had no choice, I tumbled with the thundering cascade, hurtling towards the perspiring depths, coated in a spray of pale green, until I hit the roiling surface with a smarting splash.

The river was deep enough as I'd hoped, providing a safer landing than any I'd feared, its flow immediately carrying me beyond the roar of the crashing water.

In between gasps, I half heartedly swam, letting the river sweep me away from the obsidian tower, and further down the twilit valley. I'd be content to remain this way, but the cool waters threatened to soothe me into drowsiness. I had to remain alert, always moving and searching for a place to climb out.

Under different circumstances, I might have taken a good look at the intriguing settlements that bordered the river, and what moved around them. But even had I tried, I wouldn't have been able to glean anything about this place as the current quickened and my attention began to slip.

Fumes rose from the green waves, the water itself eerily

bright in the darker areas it swept me through. It carried a biting scent similar to peppermint and alcohol, making me gag, like invisible fingers had hooked into my nostrils and throat.

Cold burned my skin as the fumes thickened into shapes that blasted into my mind with a chorus of screams. Scenes played out before me, too vivid to confuse for anything but final moments, plenty too brutal to process.

Ghostly hands reached out of the waves, piling onto my shoulders, reaching for my throat, grabbing at my wrists as I thrashed in panic. Their weight on me grew, dipping my face beneath the surface long enough for me to swallow a gulp that chilled my mouth and shot up my sinuses and behind my eyes.

Memories that weren't my own tore into my mind, infecting it with their unending desperation. In a frenzy, I fought against the vicious current and the drowning specters until I burst through the surface.

I didn't know how long it was before I finally dragged myself out and onto the riverbank.

Gasping and shuddering, I flopped like a drenched rag onto a smooth surface that seemed cut from volcanic rock, and polished to perfection.

What had I just crawled out of? What was that river made of, and why did it implant these foreign feelings in my head? They combined with my own emotions, had tears I hadn't known before or since my grandmother died welling like acid behind my eyes. I rubbed at them shakily, pressing my throbbing knuckles to my temples, as if I'd squeeze the invasive phantasms out.

Minutes of measured breathing eventually calmed me enough to sit up and take in my latest surroundings. It was a grand hallway hewn from a cave the burning-green river bisected. The false sky had been replaced by a domed ceiling covered in endless rows of pale, sharp protrusions, too uniform to be stalactites.

Pushing up to unsteady feet, I started my exploration, leaving behind the river at the first opportunity.

I headed down a quieter space lit by crystalline lamps that revealed that the walls and the ground bordering them had the same countless projections. Whatever demons had carved out these halls and polished the floors, probably couldn't break those off. While they varied from my height to a couple of feet tall, with their bases wide and ends tapering, they were too smooth to be stalagmites, either. Those grew only upwards, anyway.

Soon the lamps petered out, and darkness deepened, but I found many bronze lanterns hanging off hooks—twenty feet above me.

I had just climbed down the protrusions with one, when movement echoed ahead.

While it put me on edge, I needed to investigate it. I might be able to follow whatever it was out of this place, so I can chart a path back to the Bone Gates without another encounter with that sinister river. It was also partly morbid curiosity, what had always been one of my strongest instincts, even if it went against the priority of survival. But I had yet to meet an unpleasant surprise I couldn't handle.

With that thought firmly in mind, I continued through the enormous tunnel that kept widening until it could hold towers within it. But the protrusions that filled it grew smaller, sharper and more plentiful, becoming arranged in continuous rings that only left a path on the ground clear.

As unfamiliar as this pattern was, it reminded me of something that eluded me, yet made my grip on the lantern tighten.

The sounds now echoed towards me, those of footfalls. Not the lope of the metallic hounds or the scuttle of any other creatures. Most sounded like my own feet, but the loudest were slower, steadily tapping an eerie tempo.

Pausing for a long breath that whistled through my pursed lips, my mind streaked for a way to avoid a head-on interception.

Suddenly, I could decipher the approaching footsteps were

coming from the left. It was only then I noticed the large gaps in the walls ahead. I adjusted my path accordingly, entering the opening on the right.

But the change in trajectory did nothing to mute the stomps. Their echoes sounded even sharper, closer, just as a sour stench punched my nose.

It grew more pungent as I ventured further in, my lantern shining on the endless protrusions. It smelled almost like bile, but far worse than any vomit I'd ever been coated in. The acidic miasma seemed ingrained in the walls, increasing in nauseating intensity, until I nearly walked headfirst into a blockade.

But it wasn't a dead end, only an intersection, with another choice between going left or right. Just as I debated retracing my steps, the footsteps grew heavier and a flurry of hushed voices permeated the air around me, darting in different directions. Or coming from them. I couldn't quite tell.

I caught two words coming from the left, a gleeful whisper tracing the shell of my ear.

"Come here!"

A burst of fright sent me hurtling down the right path again, gulps of the foul, acidic atmosphere bombarding my lungs. Airy, echoey giggles only pursued me as I made sharp turn after another at every diversion, each making me twist further into an unknown direction.

I could feel something breathing down my neck and in both my ears, hear its feet ambling closer in a triple beat that outpaced my pulse, before grating chimes that rankled with every step joined in. Arrows clattering in a quiver, keys jangling on a ring, or even claws, longer than Adamantus', scurrying across the hard floor...

Split by a wall, another fork forced me down a new path. One whose mounted torches burst to life as I rushed past them, their light weak and foxfire-green, like the glowing gills of the mush-rooms I foraged in dark groves.

"Don't run away. Just come here," called a trio of smooth, delighted rasps that scraped my eardrums. *"Come to me..."*

Against all caution, I looked over my shoulder and glimpsed what pursued me.

The eye-watering *thing* that stalked my steps rotated at a dizzying speed. All I could perceive were countless, flailing arms, extending and retracting, its central form sprouting eyeballs like boils that expanded until they burst.

It was just for a second, but I had seen enough.

I couldn't even begin to guess what it was, but just a flash of its form in the corner of my eye had imbued me with an uncontrollable, demented terror.

But no matter how hard I ran, I felt its presence bearing down on me.

Then a whisper came too close, blowing air on my nape, almost uprooting every hair on my skin.

"I have you now."

Screaming, I swung the lantern at it with all my strength. It zoomed through the air and shattered against one of its appendages, drenching it in oil—even as my violent momentum made me slip and ram against the sharp protrusions.

Side pulsating with pain, relief burst in my straining chest as fire spread over that thing. But I still didn't dare look directly at it in the flames' unsteady light. Keeping my gaze averted, I pushed against the nearest projection to steady myself. Then I felt its consistency, heard the thing still giggling and shuffling closer—and realization crashed on me.

Running faster and in random directions was pointless. Fighting was as useless. That thing would remain right behind me, for not even fire bothered it. Its trilling chorus of amusement stated a fact, that once this stopped being fun, it would simply catch me...

...because I was trapped in a maze of giant teeth!

That was what the protrusions covering the ceiling and walls were. It was like being inside the gullet of a mythical deep-sea monstrosity. I couldn't even begin to guess what those teeth belonged to, or what was pursuing me in such high spirits.

Stiff with dread, I fought the blinding urge to continue my futile escape until I collapsed. Just as the Horned God had intimated would happen if I ran, I was about to die. But I refused to do so as prey.

Forcing myself to face the horror that hunted me, I screamed so loud I felt my vocal cords tearing, expelling the stress this insane day had wrought, and my rage at such a pointless end.

The abomination advanced on me, arms writhing in an amorphous mass of fused bodies, eyes bubbling all over it like a boiling pot. Legs in arachnid configuration scurried towards me, changing formation and number as more appendages shot out and melted off.

Unable to tear my burning eyes away, I watched the mind-fracturing atrocity as it morphed, shuddered, further breaking off into gnarls of limbs. The rest of the mass sprouted maws that cackled and drove red-hot needles of agony in my scalp and pokers of madness into my brain. The longer I stared the further they were pushed in.

Parts of me convulsed, my teeth chattered and I cried uncontrollably as the bottomless terror sank in, torching my insides like I had swallowed molten iron.

What was I looking at? *What was I looking at?*

"You stopped running," it said with delight, voices cacophonous and suffocating. *"They never stop running."*

Its form suddenly split into a dozen offshoots, each of their fists bursting into flame, flash after flash kindling a wildfire through me.

Tears, snot, and drool oozed out of my burning orifices. My head snapped in violent jolts, wringing cracks from bone and spreading stabs into my spine like a virulent outbreak.

My seizure came to an abrupt halt as the centermost figure burst forwards. A starburst of precise shapes took on clear proportions around it as my senseless legs collapsed beneath my twitching weight. I fell in heavy slowness, like cold honey trailing off a spoon.

Once the mass approaching me solidified, the speed of my collapse returned to normal and my head whacked off the ground.

If my scalp was on fire before, now it had ruptured and my skull had been crushed like an egg. Pain shot to excruciating heights, ripping screams from my slobbering jaw. Senselessness crept up past my waist, claiming my twitching arms and gurgling chest.

Something too thick to be tears oozed from my eyes as I helplessly gazed up at it.

At them.

The incomprehensible mass had split into twelve torch-bearers escorting their enormous host, a vaguely familiar monstrosity with three bodies fused back to back, and three faces that grinned down at me, mouths horrific crescents in the dimness.

The middle body reached long arms down for me, before one voice gasped, "Is that what I think it is?"

The three-way exclamations of surprise was the last thing I sensed before blood filled my eyes and darkness claimed me.

THE THREE-FACED GODDESS

Death loomed over me.

Every living thing would panic, weep, beg for their lives. I only breathed a sigh of relief as a haze melted off my vision, leaving a frosted blur encircling his antlered skull. I would have reached out a hand to caress it if I could.

But soreness weighed me down. All I could do was roll my head and stare up at him.

His fathomless voice reverberated around me, its vibration wholly welcome in the hollow of my chest.

The sentiment it transmitted wasn't.

"Are you out of your grass-fed mind?"

I blinked, eyelashes heavy with a crust that sprinkled granules into my eyes. "What?"

He gripped my arms to force me to sit upright. It was so sudden, the room spun and dizziness flooded into my aching head.

"I told you not to leave your quarters."

"That you did," I slurred, heavy head lolling back on a rubbery neck.

One steadying grip left my arm in favor of my jaw, forcing me to face him. "Do you have any idea what you could have gotten yourself into?"

"Do you?"

His hold tightened, sharp nails threatening to slice into my flesh.

It was confounding how mortal revulsion towards his visage locked horns with my innate fascination for its dark and unearthly allure. The embodiment of death and decay held my face in his cold, clawed hand, and could crush my skull like a grape if he felt like it. I only nestled my face into his palm and hummed in contentment.

A crackling hiss emanated from him, like I had just fed a furnace.

I whimpered when he withdrew his hand.

"I told you to stay put for a reason."

"Don't remember you giving me any."

"I gave you a command. But you didn't even consider heeding it, did you? When not even gods dare thwart me. Yet you did, and had the added temerity to vandalize your guest quarters."

"It's your fault, for posting that magical menagerie at my door."

A storm crackled within those eye sockets that had seen eternity.

Instead of responding as any being, mortal or immortal, should—with pants-wetting fear—I found myself mirroring his head's sinister grin and leaning closer, wanting to get siphoned into the depths of those sockets, to see what unspeakable things powered their violet light.

He reached for me again, gripping me by the neck this time. "From now on, you will do exactly what I tell you."

"Or else what?" I taunted with lightheaded glee, grinning when he didn't specify a threat. "Thought so. Here's a warning of my own—people who tell me what to do don't tend to fare well."

"I am not 'people.'"

My grin grew, cheek muscles stiff, teeth about to grind

together. "Like one could forget, with you looking the way you do."

"You seem forgetful enough." His grip slid to my nape as he leaned closer, fingertips moving in repetitive motions on my jaw, pressing on its hinges in a way that made it slacken. Though he had no eyes, I could swear he was gazing at my opening lips.

Thoughtlessly riding the wave of instinct, I gripped his other hand. The cut gems of his rings were warmer than his flesh beneath my palm. That was if it were, in fact, flesh.

It may have been my imagination, but I heard a sharp intake of breath.

Did he breathe?

To test that theory, I stroked my hand further up his arm, grazing the decorative detail of his coat sleeve, an exquisite embroidery in gleaming, deepest night, stopping at his biceps to dig in my nails. Or attempting to. Impossible to squeeze steel.

Somehow, he allowed this. And seemed to exhale.

Giddy with the discovery, the triumph, I snaked one hand after another to his shoulders.

Continuing to alternate the pressure on my bones and muscles, he warningly scraped the sharp tip of one nail across my cheekbone and along the thin skin beneath my eye. That slight friction sparked through my core before splitting towards my legs, making my toes curl.

"Do you have a death wish?" Adamantus murmured, a puzzled note in his thrilling voice. "Is that why you are this way with me?"

Testing the waters further, I moved my hands up from his shoulders to feel the base of his skull. Another graze over my eyes sent wet heat pooling between my legs. Yet, he still let me.

Here he was, the gruesome embodiment of what everything from insects to dragons fled, in all his terrible glory, within my reach. At my disposal.

"What do you look like under all this?" I mumbled, rubbing

my thighs together, engrossed in exploring the infinite power beneath my fingers.

"What makes you think there is anything else beneath?"

At the strange inflection in his mutter, blurry memories skimmed the surface of my soupy consciousness. Of all the sculptures protruding from courthouses, the statues that presided over cemeteries, and the figurines on the altars of those who dealt with death—butchers, morticians, doctors and soldiers. None bore this version of Death pervasive in cultures that didn't dare depict him, or even speak his name. Those representations, like the other Campanian gods, showed him as a man.

There had to be a reason for that, for ours was one of the oldest cultures and among the few that could still read the language of our ancestors. Gods were depicted under different names in many lands, but they were always basically the same. Except for him. He'd been both man and horned beast. I'd never known where the inspiration for the latter came from, until now.

"No," I breathed heavily, mirroring his touch with both my hands now, holding that macabre jaw. "I don't have a death wish."

"Then why are you defying me?"

"If you wanted us dead, you'd have done it the second you arrived at Erthamos'," I said. "You need us for the same reason he did."

"I told you I didn't."

My fingers were now all over his cold, smooth skull, exploring with reverent preoccupation. "You didn't tell me what your reason was."

"Had you been patient, I would have." His hold softened, stroking more than kneading my cheeks, like the sensation of my skin was as pleasurable as silk.

"Patience is only worth a damn if it's for a known result, otherwise it's being a dupe, or a sitting duck."

Adamantus made a sound, like a lion's purr, that made my

legs spasm. "Impressive, maintaining this attitude in the face of danger."

"Are you a danger to me?" I wrapped my hands around the bases of his antlers.

"I will be, if you do something like this again."

I pulled on his antlers, bringing his head down, shoving my face up into his. "Then don't keep me waiting again, filling the gaps in for myself, and I'd have no need to wind up in a maze of teeth and—"

In an instant, the drowsy haze that lulled me was scorched away, consumed by the intensity of the brain-branding memories that flashed behind my eyes.

Jerking against his grip, stress bubbled back like a hearth fire had roared to life inside me.

"What was that—*thing?*" I choked.

Releasing me abruptly, he moved away, antlers slipping out of my grasp. "So, you do remember."

It seemed he didn't need any further elaboration, but I needed a lot of it.

Swinging stiff legs off a table draped in silver satin, I took in where I was. An octagonal room half-surrounded in windows with pearlescent-slate shutters in a honeycomb design of inter-twining circles. The bound curtains bordering them were a gunmetal velvet overlaid with platinum patterns reminiscent of the Late Imperial period of Lower Campania. The lush carpet matched them, while the luxurious if sparse furniture blooming from the walls or floors was every shade of argent and midnight.

The same twilight of the sky I'd almost drowned under poured through the gaps in the shutters, further filling the room with cold tones, reminding me of the absence of the sun.

It had to be another day back home. My mother would be worried sick. And there was nothing I could do about it.

Fully roused, I slipped off the table on unsteady feet, faced Adamantus with narrowed eyes. "What is this place? And what was that thing I saw?"

"We are in the Trimorphium," he said, as if this explained everything, holding out his hand for me. "And what you saw is waiting to meet you. We will address this situation."

Mere seconds ago, I would have taken his hand with both of mine and continued the sensory exploration that had enthralled me. Now I was wide awake, my impulses were in check, and I was back to finding the situation suspect, if not enraging.

I scowled up at him. "*It* wants to meet me?"

He withdrew his hand when I didn't take it, waved it at the door. It swung open to reveal steep stairs beyond. "Yes, you are by far the most interesting idiot to wander straight into the bowels of the old world."

"What do you mean bowels?" He only turned and floated downward, making me stumble to follow, yelling after him, "And what were those teeth?"

He didn't answer, picking up speed, forcing me to focus on not slipping over the glass steps. They were also almost perpendicular, descending for what felt like a mile, the height of the tower we were in. *And* my feet tingled each time they swirled with light under my weight, like cream the instant it landed in tea.

As soon as I got the hang of navigating them without fear of tumbling down and barreling into him, I hissed, "You didn't answer my questions."

"Are you sure you want to know the answers?" he intoned without looking back.

"Would I ask if I didn't?"

"With that attitude, it's a wonder you remained alive long enough for me to find you."

"You found me? Didn't you say you wouldn't come after me if I ran?"

He made no answer this time, or said anything else until the flight ended in an immense corridor, where the buzzing effect of the stairs amplified.

As I pondered his statement, our every step created a starburst on the glistening, inky floor, an arresting pattern that shot ahead of us, as if leading the way.

At the far end of the hallway, the hounds met us at a marble and silver doorway bordered by wooden statues holding torches. The memory of my horrific encounter with the real thing made me shiver.

But while I had no visual of the other torch-bearers, those sculptures were of masked women, their ears pointed like fey, fauns and nymphs. Curiously, they had looked different from a distance. As we came closer, they had altered, looming larger on their pedestals, their wooden skin taking on the sallow hue of freshly-pressed olive oil, faintly smiling lips becoming navy, while their hair darkened to juniper, tightly arranged like horns, emphasizing the crescentic outline of their heads. Or the hair was supposed to be wrapped around such horns.

As Adamantus stopped before them, I stood on tiptoe to peer at their stark-white lacquered masks—and the torches burst to life.

Lurching back with a gasp, my hand flew up to my head, the agony the similar flames had caused me shooting in my scalp again. It was only then I registered it wasn't burnt to a crisp. In fact, my hair wasn't even singed.

Seemed the burning hadn't been real. I was somehow certain everything else had been.

Refusing to appear rattled, I gazed down at the hounds who were sniffing around me.

As soon as I met his gaze, the lupine Argentus barked at me angrily, before being smacked by the slimmer Platinus. With them at each other's throats, the golden Cressida panted up at me with soulful eyes, shaggy fur literally spun gold and gleaming the firelight.

Finding her friendly enough, I bent to pet her. She shoved her head into my palm, tail wagging enthusiastically, making my love of animals surge, soothing me, grounding me.

Scratching behind her metallic ears and cooing praises and endearments to her, I glanced up to find Adamantus watching us.

"What?"

His sockets flared at my snap, yet his voice was calm as he said, "You do realize she's not a real dog."

I straightened up, still petting her. "Sure acts like one. Where did they come from?"

He faced forward, avoiding my gaze. "I made them."

Made them? He could do something like that?

Out loud, I only asked, "Why?"

"To see if I could." He raised a hand to the torch-bearers. "Take us to Polyope."

The snapping of wood tore through the hall and my nerves as the sculptures came to life, stepping off their pedestals to bow their heads at him.

Alarm bursting in my chest, I couldn't help staggering two steps back.

It had been them!

But Adamantus wasn't giving me time to come to terms with this discovery, striding after them through the doorway with his dogs after him.

Heart booming in my throat, I could do nothing but follow as the animated torch-bearers led us through an even vaster hall bordered by soaring columns and spread in circular tiles.

Inlaid with interlocking geometric designs, everything resembled the tower's window-shutters motifs, just more complex and extravagant. The color scheme was also the same, if more vivid, in shades between sapphire and pearl, every surface semi-translucent and unearthly in the light of their torches and the lanterns that hovered in the air.

It all reminded me of the architecture of Cahraman, but on a *much* grander scale, when I'd thought Sunstone Palace had been the ultimate in immoderate luxury and artistry. My stunned gaze slammed around, new details revealing themselves as colors shifted, and patterns changed proportions and angles with a mathematical precision to make any engineer or architect weep.

After I got acclimated to the larger elements, I started noticing the smaller, and even more interesting ones. What most fascinated me were the blue-opal altars surrounded by floating black candles that smelled like squid ink, and cut-crystal vials and tumblers filled with what looked like living elixirs.

The more I looked around, the more it felt like I was in the opulent backroom of an exclusive apothecary, just on a divine scale.

Then everything paled in comparison to the devices that looked like the center exhibit of a supernatural astronomical museum. Framed within arches opening to the Underworld's pseudo-sky and proportioned for dragons to fly through, the instruments seemed made of solid titanium and gold, in sizes for a god to use. I could only recognize the astrolabes, telescopes, and the hourglasses filled with what appeared to be condensed light—or time.

But the most mind-boggling item of all was the hovering model of celestial bodies that Adamantus came to a stop below. Orbs of varying sizes, that seemed made of garnet, jade, turquoise, topaz and other gemstones, slowly rotated, satellites in the orbit of the pulsating golden globe in the center.

I could see the royals and elites with skyward interests going to war to obtain just one of those magical planetary facsimiles for their great observatories.

What I *couldn't* see was what use a god detached from the heavens had for all this?

"I'd tell you to close your mouth before anything flew in," Adamantus said as I approached him, gaping up. "But we have no little insects here."

"But you have big ones?"

He made a sound between that deep purr and a huff of amusement. Whatever it was, it shot straight to my loins. "There are things lurking within this realm that you couldn't begin to imagine in your worst nightmares."

I waved him away. "Oh, I've been introduced to a few horrors and abominations already. In fact, you're taking me to meet the one that almost fried my mind. Very considerate of you. Remind me to repay the favor sometime."

Though it was impossible with his skeletal face, I could swear he smirked at me.

Before I gave in to the temptation to perform another hands-on investigation, fully present this time, he gestured behind me.

I turned to find the torch-bearers standing in a circle, the floor before them turning into a dark pool, like a lake glinting under a crescent moon.

Then, as one, they stepped in, disappearing in a soundless plunge.

"After you," he offered.

Wary, I tested the pool with a toe.

The pool didn't allow hesitance, pulling me in faster than I could shout.

Next blink, completely dry, my heart was almost knocking me off the feet I swayed on, in a smaller, less grandiose chamber. It had curving walls spread in cabinets and shelves filled with eclectic personal items that ranged from antique books to fili-gree silverware to mosaic wine bottles. At the very back was a staircase that was unmistakably made of bone, harvested from a whale or something of comparative size.

The torch-bearers fanned around the stairs, standing on cere-mony as—*it* descended.

I'd glimpsed this entity right before I'd lost consciousness in the maze, then awoke to Adamantus, hoping it had been a grue-some nightmare. Seeing it again in clear lighting, without the harrowing escape, the maddening hallucinations and the lethal agony, was beyond bizarre.

Nine feet tall, skin like moonstone and hair like a nighttime river, stood three identical women fused back-to-back. One faced us and the others looked to the side, giving the illusion of one body bearing three heads and a sickening amount of limbs.

Gaping at her with my throat closing, I expected her to move like a crab. Instead, it was an even stranger and disturbing method of motion, the front-facing body moving forward while those flanking it side-stepped.

"Glad to see I didn't break you," all three heads greeted in grating, gleeful voices. "Not being a vacant, slobbering shell, like all those who see my true form, is an undeniable portent."

"A portent of what?" Adamantus demanded, deep and intense.

The three heads were thrown back on discordant cackles. "That she could be the answer the Fates have put forward to all our problems."

12

DEMISE OF THE DEMIGODS

There was only so much I could take in a single day.

It was one thing to meet the fabled form of the Horned God, popular in art across the centuries, and another to see *her*. For I recognized her now. The discarded deity of those who dealt in dark magic and had every depraved action known to man attributed to them. The goddess of the priestess who'd come to tell us of the trail of broken bodies, and the unholy search that had led to Chloë and I becoming unwilling guests in the Nether Court.

Though she was no longer in the mind-warping configurations she'd inflicted on me in the maze, what evidently drove anyone who laid eyes on her insane with terror, she was still horrific.

No wonder people desecrated her temples, banned her name, and destroyed her effigies.

"Unless our unlucky encounter did cause some lasting damage." She sounded girlishly excited as she looked at Adamantus. "Did she become mute?"

He tapped his bident against the floor, shaking the whole room and almost knocking me off my feet. "Polyope, pull yourself together."

"Why should I, when you haven't?"

"I'm not the walking night-terror at the moment," he snapped.

With a sigh, Polyope simplified before my eyes, shrinking at least two feet as the excess bodies retreated within the central form. She ended up as a single body draped in a sleeveless peplos that slit up one thigh and seemed made of night, leaving her much more palatable, and marginally less frightening.

"Has she been like this since you took her?" This time only one eerily cheery voice exited her midnight-blue lips as she addressed Adamantus, strangely pretty face scrunched in a pout. "Did I overestimate the malleability of her nerves?"

"She's been talking non-stop since she regained consciousness," Adamantus said, sockets flashing, almost singeing me. "Among other things."

My cheeks did burn as I remembered those other things. Against all odds, the urge to resume them persisted.

"Marvelous!" She clapped excitedly as she approached me. "Come here."

The dreadful memory of her saying the same thing in the maze drenched me.

"Stay away from me," I wheezed.

She tutted. "Don't be that way. I need a better look at you. He took you before I could examine you properly."

"No!" I shook my head vigorously. "I won't let you poke and prod me. I'm only here to know what's going on. Tell me now, or I'm leaving."

My shaky bravado was beyond pathetic, and the two monsters before me knew it.

She sighed again and waved her hands. Expecting the worst, I grabbed for the unyielding barricade of Adamantus' body, half-hiding behind him.

But instead of making my brain bleed out of my ears this time, she only made furniture rise from the twilight-hued floor.

She dropped into a huge, ornate throne that seemed carved from one gigantic black pearl. "Impatient little beast, isn't she?"

"Only one of her many confounding traits." His skeletal face seemed duly baffled as he extricated his shifting cloak from my spastic grip, before he swept down into the wing-backed armchair adjacent to her.

She chuckled, too-sharp, glowing-white teeth on display. "Indeed. I never imagined the day would come when a mortal sought you for protection, of all things."

It was only then I realized that was what I'd done.

I'd literally sought refuge in Death.

Head spinning, I collapsed beside his hounds, who'd piled onto the long, black-leather couch across from their macabre master and our even worse hostess. I set my hands onto the golden hound, grounding myself by petting her.

A round, moonstone table rose from the floor, bearing delicate glassware with steaming deep-sapphire tea. Polyope leaned over to offer me a cup, and I just stared from it to her until she sat back.

Her displeased expression turned into an elated grin so fast, it jogged my brain. "You threw a lantern at me, set me on fire. And when I cornered you, you turned to face me, screaming with all the ferocity I've heard so much about."

I gaped at her. "You've heard of me?"

She only brought the cup to her smirking lips.

Adamantus aimed his inanimate stare at me. I could swear he was frowning. "You said Erthamos told you he didn't want to kill you like the others, because he had plans for you. Did he specify what those were?"

"He wanted to...to marry Chloë," I said, dragging details from my still-scrambled mind. "Then changed his mind after I attacked him to save her, said he'd make *me* his consort." Daring a glance her way as she loudly sipped her tea, I found her slouched in her throne. "One of your Silver Sisters said that all the murders across the Folkshore were divinations, that they were searching for something."

Dragging another noisy slurp, she huffed. "For your kind of course."

"What do you mean my kind?"

Polyope gave me a mocking stare. "You know what, dear."

"I don't!"

She wiggled inky eyebrows at me. "Really? You don't know why the West Wind wanted you, and why others are being slaughtered all across your realm, all perfect specimens, like you? You don't know what you all are?"

"Demigods!" It suddenly hit me as hard as only a fact could. Everything, from my mother's lifelong claims about my lineage, to Erthamos intending to make use of it, solidified the conclusion. "Someone is killing those thought to be demigods! And I'm on their list because they believed my mother's claims of my divine heritage."

Polyope gave a scraping snort. "They're not claims, and you know it. No need to be coy now, dear."

"Y-you mean you think I'm really a demigod?"

"I prefer the word demigoddess."

She *did* believe I was one. This ancient goddess from the age of the titans. And if she did, then I *was* one? My mother had told the truth all my life?

With everything that had happened in the last day, it would explain everything...

My frantic realizations fractured as an ominous rumble swarmed me with gooseflesh and liquid heat, tearing my gaze back to Adamantus.

"But unlike other semi-divines, you've proven impossible to locate," he said, a chilling inflection in his voice, bident rolling between his fingers as if he was contemplating the next victim he'd impale. The way he looked at me, I felt it might be me. "The culprits have been having no difficulty finding the others across the mortal realm. But once they reached your region to look for you, the divination proved ineffective. They had to rely on word-of-mouth, eliminating anyone who shared your basic traits in hope of one being you." The glow in his sockets suddenly turned into flame. "But Erthamos proved more cunning somehow, narrowed down the search better than anyone else. And he intended to—make use of you."

"But he *still* confused that flimsy little girl my nymphs are tending to for you," Polyope added derisively, before glowering at me. "Until you exposed yourself, that is. What were you thinking, pitting yourself against a god."

I shook my spinning head. "I thought he was a weather spirit when I did."

"Did it deter you when you found out what he truly is?" she probed.

"Uhh...no," I said, wondering if this counted as blasphemy.

"You claimed you almost bested him before he resorted to suffocating you," Adamantus said, deep and gravely. "How did you do that?"

I turned my gaze to him, wincing. "I—uh, broke your effigy to use its bident as a weapon. When it shattered, I resorted to my fists and almost beat him, so he suffocated me—until you skewered him."

His sockets flashed before he turned them to Polyope, who only giggled and made a "there you go" gesture at him.

"But why are those people murdering demigods?" I asked, everything making even less sense.

His bottomless gaze held mine.

"You said you'll tell me what you know!"

Still, he said nothing. He was going to renege on his word. I'd come here, and might stay here, for nothing.

Before I succumbed to the suicidal urge to attack him, Polyope moved, setting one hand on his arm. Something passed between them I couldn't begin to understand.

Withdrawing his arm from beneath her touch, he finally

spoke, as if against his better judgment. "You know it's not people who've been killing your kind."

I nodded shakily. "Yeah, it must be other creatures, from that untraceable, and unprecedented method of murder."

"I wouldn't call gods creatures."

That was the final pull at my wits, sending them scattering like a string of pearls.

I howled like a lunatic.

They watched me in entertained and aggravated silence respectively.

When I was almost suffocating again, I gasped, "You're saying the culprits are *gods*?"

His antlered head continued to glare at me.

"But—why?" I wheezed, thoughts streaking with the reasons gods have been known to kill humans. For this specific situation, I found only one possible explanation. It still boggled my mind. "They're threatened by mortals? By me?"

"Don't act so incredulous, dear, it doesn't suit you." Polyope leaned back in her throne, throwing one long, marble-hued leg over its side, showing her moonstone-studded sandal and her clawed, black toenails. "Anyway, mortal history has been shaped by those claiming to be children of gods, or even favored by them. And what happens in the mortal realm has always had a greater impact on the divine one, rather than the other way around. Not to mention the semi-divine becoming deified isn't a thing of the past. In fact, we recently got two new gods."

I goggled at her. "How recent?"

She elongated her nails to examine them. "Just before the murder spree began."

"Maybe *they're* behind this, then? To stop more demigods from being deified?"

"It is one or more older and more important gods, and you..."

Adamantus' growl stopped abruptly as he whipped a glance at Polyope. It was as if she'd told him something I hadn't heard.

After a long, fraught moment, he sat back, seemingly less tense. I looked between them, waiting for some elaboration.

When none came, I asked, "How are you certain of that?"

"The newcomers have no stake in the current conflict," he said, the bite in his voice gone. "There are at least two camps. There are sides I cannot fathom yet, but the clear ones are the side that wants to obliterate the population of divine descendants, and now the other that wants to use them."

"But use us how? What could Erthamos have gained by making me his 'consort?'"

Adamantus gave an elegant shrug of his smoke-shrouded shoulders. "He must have hoped a demigod bride, one who would manifest great power upon deification, could help secure his place in the pantheon as a major god."

Polyope swung her leg and giggled. "If you're bold enough to fight the West Wind, and hearty enough to almost defeat him, but most importantly, to still have your act together after seeing my true form, imagine what great a terror you could be as an immortal. No wonder they've been massacring your lookalikes by the dozen, in the hope of crushing you while you're still mortal." Polyope sat up with a harrowing grin. "Isn't it amazing that they couldn't find you?"

I stared at her, my brain overheating, the absurdity of the topic flinging me back to when my childish mind failed to grasp hard concepts. Like when Cassia's father explained to my four year-old self why people couldn't lay eggs.

Instead, here I was, twenty-five and being told that assorted deities, for some preposterous reason, wanted me wed or dead.

"But I want nothing to do with immortality!" I blurted out, in the throes of deepening disbelief. "I was born to be Mistress of the Granary, where I would work the earth until I go into it. I'm no threat to anyone, let alone to gods!"

Both deities stared at me for nerve-fraying moments.

Even with Polyope having a humanoid and very expressive

face, it was Adamantus I felt I could read. I sensed that confusion, again, that uncertainty.

Polyope's jarring tongue-click tore my attention back to her. "A likely story. As if anyone would choose mortality over immortality. But *even* if you were daft enough to think so now, you could always change your mind. If not you, your descendants would. Especially if they're fathered by a god, like Erthamos intended. Better to cut down the threat at its roots, so to speak."

"Then these gods—are going to keep killing if they can't locate me?"

"No. They will move to killing far more than your lookalikes."

"*Why?*"

"To smoke you out, of course. And when they can't..."

She cackled, as if it amused her people were getting slaughtered at the whim of her fellow gods. As I was sure it did.

I heaved up to my feet, enraged, frenzied. "You mean everyone, my family, could be killed unless I show myself and get brutally murdered?"

Adamantus' grip tightened on his bident. The grip that could squeeze diamonds out of coals, that must have crushed armies and populations whole. It felt as if he was—disturbed.

I couldn't begin to imagine what Death found disturbing.

"Even if it's all a ruse, and I'm its target, I cannot pay the price of ending it," he muttered. "I would be playing into their hands, but I will not let the others achieve their goal. Yet, they are not above decimating a whole region in their frustration. That would unbalance everything immeasurably more."

I gaped at him, realizing he was talking to himself, yet understanding none of his incensed, internal debate.

Suddenly coming out of it, his smoldering gaze slammed into me, making me shudder. "Whatever the cost, you will remain here until my purpose is served. I can see to it that no more harm befalls anyone in your land. Not on this hunt's account."

"How?" I cried.

"I can make sure it's known that Erthamos found the one they've been looking for—and lost her, to another god. While they try to figure out who took you, and what they did with you, it should ensure your people's safety, until this situation is resolved."

He'd said "can" not "will." His help was conditional, to something he wanted in return.

Both me and my people were at Death's nonexistent mercy.

"So, you are part of the camp that wants to use the demigods?" I rasped, disappointment crushing down on me. "You brought me here to make your bid?"

"Quite the opposite." Adamantus sat forward, one talon twisting his jeweled rings as if in agitation. "All I desire is to find the culprits."

Skepticism sprouted several heads within me. "What do you get out of that?"

He rose like the dark wave of inevitability that he was, stood across from me. "Reinstating stability in the world, fixing the skewed death rates they've created for me, and preventing a divine war that could send us all back to the Dark Age of the titans."

"How would killing demigods cause *that*?" I scoffed.

"Because power vacuums are dangerous, could even prove catastrophic. And those not in the fight to fill it, want to recruit me. Even those who are would do the same, to throw off suspicion. My refusal to play anyone's game made sure I have no allies in the Heavenly Court, even among those who despise the conflict. I am in need of a misdirection, as well as help investigating."

My head whirled, everything he'd said, so dangerously sincere, going straight over it.

"And this is why I brought you here. Because, whatever your own purpose, you're the one who can help me."

I burst out cackling like Polyope had in the maze—until I realized he meant it.

I stopped, spluttering. "You think I can help? *You?* With any of that?"

He gave a grave nod. "It must be why I saw you."

At its mention, the encounter flashed into being, long enough to juxtapose itself against this waking version. "The dream?"

"It wasn't a dream."

"What was it then?"

"That isn't relevant now. The only thing of importance is that you give me an answer."

"An answer to what? How do you think I can help you?"

"Those details depend on your willingness to join any effort of mine." As the word "mine" rang in my ears, he was within touching distance without me realizing he'd moved. "But you must be capable of serving my purposes, are what I could use to end this crisis. This has to be why the Fates showed you to me."

My heart clenched, bitterness flooding my mouth.

So this was why he'd been looking for me. The Fates were responsible for all this. The Lord of the Dead had a problem he needed taken care of, and they'd offered me to him as an instrument to use. He wanted nothing to do with me except as a hammer to level a few nails.

Feeling stupidly, precariously close to tears, I muttered, "What if I don't agree?"

"You already did when you came to me." Adamantus reached out a hand, as if to touch me like he had in that dream that hadn't been a dream. My heart was almost bursting when he withdrew it. "Whether we like it or not, we are now at the center of this conflict. It is in our separate and best interests to work together. Now, give me your answer."

He was doing it again. Pretending to give me a choice. After he'd just claimed I'd already given him my consent. And my wearing-thin sanity couldn't take it anymore.

I needed anything to make me feel I wasn't absolutely disempowered. I needed *something.*

Suddenly, I knew what it was.

"I'll give you an answer if you drop this," I demanded, waving around him.

Adamantus merely stared at me, head tilted in puzzlement as he had in my dream.

"Unmask," I ordered.

"I wear no mask," he dismissed.

I felt ready to breathe fire and destroy his aggravatingly opulent ensemble.

"I know you have a face!" Flushed, trembling with futility and fury, I jabbed a finger at his skull. "Show it to me!"

"Even if I had a face, why would you risk seeing it? Aren't you afraid it might drive you insane? Or make you drop dead? Maybe it's how I reap souls, showing my real face to mortals."

"No, it's not, or you wouldn't have said all that. It's you who doesn't want anyone to see your face. But I won't consent to do anything with you until you *look me in the eye!*"

"Miss Spica, I don't need your consent to proceed with my plans."

"You need me!" I pounded on my chest, hard enough to bruise it. "You just said so. If you want to get to the bottom of whatever this is, you need my help."

One talon-tipped hand waved me away, bejeweled rings catching the eerie light of Polyope's abode. "If you are that contrary, I will use your cousin."

The flames of wrath roared within my burning gut. "That's not going to happen. You will not come near her. She can't handle any of this."

"Moments ago, you thought you couldn't either. So what makes you a better option?"

"Because I was bred for it!" I snapped, all the trials of the Mistresses of the Granary, of my mother and grandmother, flowing through me like our rivers. "I am of the fertile earth! You bury me in snow, set me aflame or sow me with salt, and I rise again. I am of life, and life *always* finds a way!"

He expanded, at least a foot, bore down on me. "You're doing it again. Forgetting where you are, and who I am."

But I hadn't, not for a second. And it was far too late for me to cower and plead. I wouldn't do it, anyway. If I was to be pitched head first into hell for aggravating Death, so be it.

An oak tree didn't cower before those who would chop it down, and neither would I.

"Show. Me. Your. *Face!*" I hissed, saliva spraying between my clenched teeth.

An ominous rumble filled the room, spreading its dread inside my marrow, like a realms-shaking earthquake.

I'd done it. Like I had Erthamos, I'd provoked Death into disregarding whatever value I had to him.

Just as I thought he'd rip my soul out, a thunder clap blasted through my every cell.

"*Fine.*"

13

BENEATH THE MASK

Adamantus' single word of towering exasperation echoed in the chamber, an unrelenting pressure that threatened to rupture my ear drums.

But I didn't care. Nothing mattered but what was happening before my eyes.

As his teeth tore apart, the flames in his sockets burst out, spreading over him, like he'd been doused in alcohol and set aflame. Then hellfire engulfed him.

And within the inferno, I could see his face begin to change.

Like he was wax melting and being remolded in the same instant, his shape changed in jarring snaps with each violent jolt of his head. The sound of an already-fading roaring reached me, like I was hearing him from the other end of an endless cave.

I watched with open-mouthed anticipation as his antlers retreated into the unfurling dark hair, and the skull caved inwards, until a reformed bone structure emerged.

He moaned, like I did when I stretched after grueling field-work under the scorching sun. Out of intense release and relief. The sound wasn't amplified as before, but I felt it resonate within me even harder. I shuddered as he moaned again, louder, keeping his head bent and the transformation hidden from my feverish eyes.

Then he finally raised his face.

My heart almost toppled me over, at his feet. The bruise it had sustained against my ribs felt permanent.

In all the curiosities and marvels I'd encountered in my years of travel, nothing had hooked my gaze and anchored my soul like the scorching intensity of his eyes. Unearthly violet in their center and eternity indigo at the edges, they were a shade of purple no mortal artist could dream of, and no divine hand could recreate.

It took all my willpower to unlatch my eyes from his, before I passed out. For I wanted—no, *needed* to see the rest of him.

My stunned focus revved back to life to devour him whole.

And as a whole, he was what the idealized sculptures and paintings of gods, emperors, and heroes had attempted to emulate—and failed. Miserably.

Unlike his depictions, as a bearded, burly middle-aged man, he was the epitome of sleek vigor, clean-shaven with a tantalizing umbra over his rugged yet refined jaw. His perfect, polished skin was the palest blue-grey of marble, a stark contrast to his vital halo of ink-blue curls that undulated to his shoulders, and framed his chiseled face like black soil did bleached bone.

Then came his features. The imposing mount of his forehead, the warning arch of his eyebrows, the commanding slash of his cheekbones, the imperious stroke of his nose, the spectacular sculpture of his lips and the hypnotic slant of his eyes.

Whoever had carved his long, hewn, melancholy face, had been a master of the sublime.

When I could finally talk, I bit out, "I commend whoever tailored your person-suit."

He cocked his head, unblinking stare blank with befuddlement. "That has got to be the strangest compliment in the history of language."

"It should soften the landing," I said with sour sweetness—and swung my fist into his divine jaw.

My knuckles met his face with a bone-shattering crack, and for a millisecond I felt triumphant.

Then pain shot up my hand like it had been skewered.

I staggered back, clutching my hand as I shouted and swore to vent out the flare of agony.

Raucous laughter beat down on me. I would have preferred he backhanded my soul out of my body.

Shredding any expression of weakness between grinding teeth, I forced my eyes open, and glowered up at him. But Adamantus displayed no sign of amusement, his blue-tinted lips a compressed line. It was Polyope who was dementedly cackling.

I shook out my hand, growling and stomping my foot when that only intensified my pain and rage. "*Gah!* What is your face made of?"

"Diamonds," he deadpanned.

Whether he was being serious or sarcastic didn't matter. It made me want to attack again. The fire of helplessness and fury had consumed me. And now he had a face for me to direct everything at, I wanted to pummel it, come what may.

Only I couldn't. Unlike Erthamos, his face showed no sign of my resounding punch. While I wouldn't be hitting him, or anything else for a long time. All I could do now was grunt and heave to suppress the urge to scream and cry.

I'd bashed my fists into countless faces, beefy mortals and supernatural creatures alike. I'd even battered the wind-incarnate. And I'd suffered nothing like those white-hot nails being hammered within my bones.

The unknown, debilitating sensations amplified the drowning feeling I'd been struggling against, pushing my head further below the surface of this nightmarish situation.

Standing here, betwixt two entities feared by all to the extent the living wouldn't utter their names, I was beyond defenseless. And now I was also incapacitated.

Calmly, gracefully, Adamantus reached for my hand.

I jerked away from him, practically spitting, "Back off!"

It was stupidly risky to continue antagonizing him, but I couldn't help it. I'd been prepared from birth to govern a whole sub-continent. It had been engrained in me to face overwhelming odds and threats with dogged bravery. Even if I'd never anticipated those would one day be gods, I couldn't change who I was, or how I responded to their menace.

Toes and teeth clenched and my whole body vibrating, I waited with heavy, unsteady breaths for him to revert into his monstrous form, to lift me by the neck and pierce my eye as his caresses had threatened.

But the only change in him was a grimness tingeing his entrancing eyes as he drawled, "Or what? You'll break your other hand on my face?"

That unclenched my jaw, dropping it. "It's broken?"

He gave a smooth nod. "You hit me with all your considerable strength. It's a wonder your arm didn't snap in half. You must be even sturdier than I thought."

"Did it hurt?" I asked through trembling lips.

Faster than lightning, he caught my pain-wracked forearm and hauled me closer. His pale, taloned grip tightened, until he wrung a whimper of pathetic feebleness from my depths. Numbness followed, an actual respite from the agony. But I knew trying to wrench away would dislocate my arm—or rip it in two.

"Next time you disrespect me, I will rip your spine out through your mouth," he murmured, terrifyingly calm, twin sun eyes so bright, mine watered. "Understood?"

His cold breath frosted my face, spreading an immobilizing chill through me. Like I was a waterfall frozen in the last move I had made.

Fragile as I felt, I refused to yield. If he was diamond, then I was steel. Not the hardest material the earth had formed, but stubborn enough to maintain my stance for longer. It was too soon for me to break.

Instead of giving him the groveling response he must fully expect, I went with my next best thought as I sweated under his inexorable gaze.

"Do you blink?" I panted, licking working, cracked lips. "You haven't blinked once yet."

Adamantus' lids fell shut as he exhaled with a low rumble. They opened as he released me with a shove.

Stumbling back, the blood he'd trapped flooded my arm with redoubled agony, breaking the dam of my overwhelmed state. Beyond enforcing an invulnerable front, I sobbed, holding my swelling arm to my chest, fist curled against my will, deformed.

But despite the hot tears that poured down my heaving face, I kept my head high, not looking away from his eyes as he brooded down at me. If I couldn't help weeping, I'd at least have the decency to appear frustrated rather than defeated.

"All right, I believe that's enough posturing for today," Polyope said, rising lazily to reach a clawed hand to his shoulder. "Why don't we return to the issue at hand..." She paused to snicker. "...as broken as it is now."

He raised *his* hand, blocking her touch, still focused on me. Even with his horrific threat, anger had yet to show itself, but something akin to hurt flickered in his eyes, like a dying flame.

After sizing me up one last time, he turned away, the swishing of his sumptuous cape the lone sound in the suffocating silence.

"W—Where are you going?"

Ignoring me, he headed to the inky pool we'd transported through, the hounds at his heels.

"Hey!" I yelled, sounding hoarse and congested. "I'm talking to you!"

Only Cressida stopped, her dark-gold eyes shining, as if asking if I was coming.

Sparing me a glance over his shoulder, Adamantus muttered, "If only you were this eager to talk earlier."

Before my stuttering breath allowed me to answer, the dark

waters swallowed him and his two hounds whole, without a single ripple as evidence of their presence.

Left behind, Cressida rushed back with a questioning bark, floppy ears flying. At her approach, the stiff foundation of bravado keeping me upright this whole time collapsed.

My knees hit the floor with a crack, but I could only feel her cold, metallic tongue licking at my face, miming a real dog's concern. And I finally broke down, sobbing uncontrollably.

It hadn't been long, but I already missed my family and pets to a lethal degree. I longed for the life that filled my home, all our animals and manageable threats, the system I knew inside out and the existence void of surprises.

Throwing my left, intact arm around Cressida, I rested my face against her head, letting tears soak the gold fibers of her fur as the dark currents of fragility and desperation claimed me.

Not only was I in Death's domain, but I had to do his bidding to keep his shadow from falling on those I held dear, and his cold touch from claiming their lives prematurely.

The crackling and scraping of bones, like those when Adamantus had shifted out of his Horned God form, rose at my back. I didn't dare look behind me, not when the last time had almost distorted my mind like dry corn popping in flames.

A hand stroked my hair. "It's all right."

"Piss off," I mumbled, no bark or bite left in my voice.

Polyope's laughter swept around, until I felt her stop before me. Two fingers found my chin, sharp nails dangerously close to vulnerable vessels, and tipped my face up.

Thankfully, she hadn't reverted to that madness-inducing state, or the stomach-turning fused-triplet one. She remained a lone, humanoid version, just smaller, coming down to my level. Her exotic, dark eyes and surprisingly youthful face smiled sympathetically down at me, her flowing, rippling hair framing her moonstone-skin.

She grinned when I glared up at her. "As amusing as your lack of self-preservation is, I think you've depleted yourself. You're past due for a bath and some food and rest. You'll feel better after that, I promise."

"Chloë?" I rasped.

"Is being watched over by my nymphs."

Hugging Cressida tighter, I sniffled. "What's going to happen to us?"

"For now, nothing." Hands smaller than mine pulled at me, slipping the hound out of my embrace with a yelp of surprise. Lodging them under my armpits, she lifted me to my feet as if I didn't weigh two-hundred pounds but two. "The conversation is on hold until you both calm down."

"He's going to throw me in the hell-pit," I blubbered, rubbing at my eyes with my good hand. "Why did I do that? Why did I do any of this?"

"I'm still pondering that. But I suppose it was partly out of love for your cousin."

I sobbed harder, inhaling the dripping snot. "Then my efforts have only doomed her along with me."

"Why do you think that?"

"Because I attacked Death Incarnate, the god of this realm, after I spat the offer he extended to me back in his face?" I massaged the part of my arm he'd held, still feeling the press of his fingers in a ghostly grip. "He's going to slit my throat over those bloody waters, or feed me my own fingers, or something I can't even envision."

"Adamantus is many things, but he's not petty," Polyope said, resuming stroking my hair. "If he was, no matter your value to him, he would have split you from mouth to groin and left you to bleed out for eternity."

"Thank you for that visual." I dared meet her eyes now that we were on the same level, teeth chattering with thawing stress. "What will he do now?"

"He'll go back to reviewing the latest death reports, or over-seeing the judgements of the vile and violent arrivals."

"I meant to me!"

"He won't do anything, if you don't 'disrespect' him again. He did let you off with only a warning."

"He said he'd fillet me alive!" I grumbled weakly.

Polyope's disbelieving amusement trilled over her dark lips. "And you're taking exception to that? When he let you get away with what no entity ever had?"

"I assume 'disrespecting' him includes not obeying his every whim, correct?"

She waved dismissively. "You will have to participate in his plans of your own free will. That is Adamantus' way."

"Oh, yes, he always gives that illusion. But I don't really have a choice. I got the impression he'll withhold helping my family and people if I don't 'participate in his plans'."

"Adamantus doesn't deal in prevarications. If this was what he meant, he would have left you in no doubt. My advice? Next time you see him, be on your best behavior—or pretend some, since you don't seem to have any." She wrapped a lock of my hair around her fingers, its steady texture contrasting against the shifting gradient of her skin. "I'd rather you didn't force him to make good on his threat to make you choke on your spine. Someone who could withstand me without clawing their own eyes out is too interesting to waste that pointlessly."

"About that, why do you have that effect?" I tried to remember what I'd glimpsed of her, but all I could recall was the fit she had created. "And does...does he do that too?"

Hand on my back, she led me towards the dark pool. "Don't worry about that for now."

"Telling me not to worry just makes it worse!"

That seemed to increase her delight with this whole situation. "Any new revelations will have to wait. There's no need to tax your mind any further, even if its resilience is impressive."

"What resilience? You almost fried it."

"Almost being the key word. I *always* drive anything sentient irretrievably mad—if not on purpose. Not like Theoneus is so fond of doing." It didn't sound like she disapproved of such a dreadful act. "Though he did that even as a mortal. When I first sensed his presence it was when he made a man peel off his own face and eat it."

As repulsive as that image was, the name Theoneus distracted me, being vaguely familiar. I thought I'd heard it when I'd visited the Orestian royal family.

"Who is he?"

"One of the two new gods—though he feels much older. You might meet him if you agree to join our efforts."

The word "our" entered and exited my awareness as I grumbled, "So he can finish searing my brain?"

Polyope chortled. "If you don't bother him too much, the most he'll do is dull your senses and inhibitions. He's a funny boy that way. I sometimes wonder if he's one of my descendants as well as Eurycrius'."

I stared at her, the random topic further testing the alleged resilience of my mind.

At the edge of the pool, Polyope petted my head, like I was no different to her than Cressida. "Truly, dear, you need no less than two hours in a blistering bath. You reek of all those disgusting scents mortal bodies squeeze out. It's a wonder Adamantus didn't turn you inside out for that alone."

Then she pushed me in.

14

RIVER OF BLOOD

All my life, I'd acquired cuts and bruises, but never fractures.

What broke others and left them scarred or disabled only inflicted wounds that healed and marks that faded.

But my hand now suffered all I'd ever been spared.

Chloë hissed in sympathetic pain as she examined my scabbing, misshapen knuckles. "The only time I saw something this bad was when a boy got pushed in the street and a carriage ran over his hand."

Slumped against the pillows, I groaned tiredly, spastic fingers in a half-curl. A mere twitch sparked such pain it made me sweat. Straightening them felt like sticking them in a furnace.

Gently, she set my hand down, then reached for the silver tray that had been left for us. It was packed with what we'd come to expect of guest-spoiling treats. This time it was a gilded teapot filled with cardamom tea, and crystal bowls heaped with nut-filled nougat, cubes of baklava, and piles of lokum.

Hungry enough to wipe out the whole offering, I reached with my good hand to a bowl and somehow bumped my broken one.

My strangled cry wrung an exclamation from Chloë. "I still can't believe you punched a god!"

"Which one?" I grumbled, stuffing lokum in my mouth, scalp and back drenched in sweat. "I've punched two, so far."

She rolled her eyes up as if heavenwards, a useless gesture when in the Underworld. "You know who I meant."

"You can speak his name, you know?" I mumbled around chewing the crunchy, syrupy golden spheres. "And you can stop asking why again, and again."

"I ask again because you still didn't explain what he did to provoke such a—uh, suicidal reaction."

"Aside from him keeping us here, you mean?"

Pouring two cups of the bitter-scented amber tea that complemented the confections' sweetness, she looked around the beyond-sumptuous quarters I'd been assigned. "Could be much worse. If only all captives had such cushy spaces."

I twisted my lips at her as I took the crystal teacup with my left hand. "A pretty prison is still a prison."

"Are we really prisoners?" she said with that baffling optimism, pigtails for once undone, and hair arranged in soft curls around her shoulders. "From what the lampades told me, we're being hidden from what had been killing the girls back home."

She'd been getting a little too friendly with Polyope's nymphs, who'd been tending to her every need since Adamantus had handed her over to them. And since Polyope had tossed me to them to scour, they'd been doing everything for me, too.

The one thing I appreciated was the tons of delicacies and sweets they brought me. The baths that melted the grime of a lifetime away weren't bad either. It was when they progressed to brushing my hair into hairstyles I'd never thought possible, and dressing me in nightgowns that seemed to be spun from luxury and light that things started getting too much for me. And no matter how much I thanked them and tried to dismiss them, saying I could manage even if I had two broken hands, they had one answer. It was Polyope's wishes.

The constant fussing was driving me insane. That and the relentless luxury. But mostly it was Adamantus' absence.

It had been three days since he'd walked away from me, judging by the amount of meals and baths. But my hand had yet to start healing. It just grew more swollen, the purple bruise that had engulfed it darkening to one of the shades that permeated his majestic cloak of shadows.

Meanwhile Chloë's injury, what she didn't seem to remember, had healed without a trace. She had been "tended to," no doubt at Adamantus' command. He clearly didn't think I deserved the same mercy, was leaving me to suffer the full consequences of my fist-fracturing blasphemy.

"If I didn't believe we're safe here before," Chloë said as she sipped delicately. "The treatment we're still getting after you attacked Orcus proves it."

"Adamantus," I murmured, his shifting form replaying behind my eyelids, that entrancing contortion when the fearful became familiar, but retained enough otherworldly traits to not register as human. "Orcus must be a name given to him by the living."

She raised her brows, face half-covered by her cup. "I've never heard that name before."

"Don't think anyone alive has." Until me. "Must have faded from collective memory eons ago, replaced by titles and euphemisms so you wouldn't risk attracting his attention."

Looking unconvinced, she still nodded. "Makes sense."

Adamantus' unblinking eyes returned to the forefront of my thoughts. Their width and slant as they nestled under those spectacular wings of intimidation. That hue that would make amethysts, violets and wild indigos dull in comparison. What, if grown and extracted, would cost a thousand times more than ultramarine blue pigment and imperial purple dye combined.

But I had yet to reconcile him with the entity I'd been bewitched by in dreams.

Perhaps it was because he now had a face I could be angry at.

One that was more man than somber symbol. The source of foreboding and fear to all but me.

Now I had come out of our face-to-face, or rather face-to-fist meeting with bloated, bleeding fingers and extravagant surroundings I had no use for. Was that all I would get from finding what I'd been searching for in exhausting dreams? It couldn't be. It wasn't what I had roamed the night for, or what I'd descended to his domain to get.

It wasn't why he'd lured me into his grasp .

But what exactly did he want from me?

"I should have let him explain before I hit him," I murmured into my cup.

"Cora?" Chloë prompted, eyes wide in watchful worry.

Realizing I'd said this out loud, I shook my head. "Nothing. I wasn't in my right mind. Nothing further to explain."

After that, I avoided her gaze and continued stuffing my face.

There was no version of this ending with me running out of the Gates of the Underworld with her over my shoulder, a hero of a new folktale about outwitting Death. And if I proved too difficult to keep or to use, she would pay for my boneheaded actions.

But escape wasn't even a concern anymore. Not after what those monstrous deities revealed. The stakes of this terrible situation were far larger than I could have imagined.

Yet, now I'd had time to think about it, I wasn't as helpless as I'd thought.

The Lord of the Underworld needed me. If that wasn't power, I didn't know what was.

And from that position of power, I would bargain.

Mind made up, I pretended I was too tired and needed to sleep. I waited until Chloë left me to her quarters, unstuck my body from the bed and changed into another nightgown. A deep-green satin one that didn't let most of them hang out like the rest. Nothing else was provided for me to wear, with my own clothes long gone. Burned, according to the lampades.

At the door, no fuss was required this time, as it opened upon my approach. I had borrowed one of the amethysts that allowed the lampades to go and come as they pleased.

Leaving Blackglass Hall was also easy, since I had memorized our initial path. The one thing that slowed me down was the luminescent Nightwine fountain. But I was too sated and quenched, I could resist its temptation.

Once I had descended the quartz steps to the green water's level, the aptly named River of Memory, it wasn't much later that I found plentiful signs of life.

Or, signs of afterlife.

Souls milled about in the distance, bright, semi-translucent and moving with weightless grace. Following them led me away from the banks, and into the last thing I'd once expected to find in the land of the dead. What I'd glimpsed during our journey here, and from the tower. A city.

Arranged in circular levels that grew larger and more intricate , the riverside settlement had ancient structures that blended with modern architecture, from every culture and region I'd ever seen. Apart from what looked like domiciles, they also mimicked everything else found in mortal cities, from temples and public buildings, to shops and restaurants.

Taking my chances, I blocked someone's path, part of me still tensing up for a collision.

Surprise registered too late for her to not go right through me, and I got the reaction I aimed for. The full attention of this soul, along with that of dozens more.

She broke the silence first. "Are you...lost?"

Not wanting to admit that, I said, "I only need directions."

Faded coloring notwithstanding, there was still enough of an echo of humanity in her to inform behavior. The soul, a Northlander judging by her wide-set eyes, and long, pale hair, glanced nervously around, then back at me. "To...uh, where?"

"I want to know where Adamantus is."

Confusion grew across many faces, as well as her own.

Of course, subjects didn't refer to their rulers by their names, and he was King of the Dead, after all. Though they probably didn't know his. He gave it only on demand, it seemed, and I bet no one, living or dead, had ever dared ask him anything. No one but me.

But patience was far from my wounded grasp, especially when the deep unease of this place made my shattered fingers clench further. "Take me to your lord and master."

She cringed at my snap. "Th—that's not something within our—our reach."

That I could still inspire wariness, even from those who had nothing left to fear, should have been a confidence boost, especially now I was about to barter with him. But it only made me feel worse. For those souls who could still experience intimidation, and still dreaded Death.

"Someone here has to be able to point me in his direction." I gestured at my ruined fist. "I have several broken bones I need to pick with him."

Identical expressions spread across the gathering crowd, too faint to decipher, maybe falling somewhere between surprise and realization.

The Northlander soul finally nodded. "I can show you where he is." She pointed across the river. "He's on the other side."

Relieved, I followed as she led me into one of those rib-bone barges and spoke to the glassy ferryman. But any relief evaporated as the other souls piled in after us. They blurred as they huddled together, their dim glow a sickening buzz. Their unblinking stares remained fixed on me as we sailed down the river, heightening my unease.

I turned to my guiding soul. "Why are they all here?"

"They want to see what will happen."

Being in the presence of the conscious dead was uncomfortable to begin with. Being watched this closely, just so they could be entertained when their ruler reprimanded me, was increasingly disturbing.

"Is boredom biting you this hard down here?"

"When we're made aware of it," she said, the implication clearly blaming me for upsetting their balance. "What brought you here intact?"

Intact. Now there was a fun alternative to "alive".

"He brought me here for his own purposes. It's what I need to discuss with him."

The soul looked past me to our audience before she said, "I'm sure you do."

If I had a standard comparison for afterlife behavior, I could tell if I was right to feel suspicious. But it wasn't like they could harm me. And then, why would they?

My self-reassuring efforts dissipated as distant wails scraped the air. The ferryman had turned into an enclosed space with curved walls and visible ceiling. Tributaries poured into the river, darkening and thickening it, slowing us down between basins lit by the same foxfire-green flames as Polyope's maze of teeth.

The similarity forced me to relive the brain-searing terror. And that was before the stench swarmed my senses and the canal emptied us into a boiling whirlpool, each spin belching up screeches from its center.

A far older memory clawed at me, when I was stationed in the military camps in the north of Orestia to be educated in their methods, and they fed me their infamous black soup. That was what this river smelled like.

A bubbling vat of blood.

I tried to stand, to demand that the ferryman took me back. But the coppery heat and reek were too strong, as was the current that captured the barge, sucking us into its rotation.

"What is this place?" I shouted. "Where are you taking me?"

There was no response. I sought the Northlander out, but could no longer recognize her. The souls had blended together, and their arms were sticking out of their cluster, reaching for me.

Unable to escape, I suffered their touch, what was closer to

Erthamos' contained wind than to a living being's, intangible to my flesh, but a pressure that intensified with every shove.

"What are you doing?" I shrieked.

"Putting you back where you belong!" they chorused.

The force of their combined wills slammed into me like a wave, tipping me over the edge, my scream joining those that awaited me below.

Flailing in the fetid vortex, I tumbled into its spinning center, eyes bulging as the gap above shrank, and the bone-barge sailed away. I could see nothing but the spiral's bottomless center, hear nothing over the symphony of suffering that pierced my marrow.

I plummeted, with the slowness of my numbing senses, like I were sinking through leagues of blood, nothing to grab onto, just waves of tumultuous torment.

Nothing was left in me as I fell. I was void of thoughts or feelings or sensations as I plunged past endless levels, each narrower, like a funnel of despair.

Then at one point, my free-fall ended, with a hard yet moist slam.

No amount of tolerance I'd amassed, towards the abhorrent and atrocious, could have prepared me for what I landed in. A field of clotting blood mixed with noxious secretions, slimy filth and rotting flesh.

Gagging, I heaved up, and only then deciphered the abominations that writhed within the expanse of shambles.

Beneath my feet, two men had been fused face-to-face, arms and legs penetrating each other, constantly ripping their sealed flesh apart, only for it to meld even as it ruptured.

Then they saw me through their merged eyes and lurched to reach for me, squirming like a dying centipede.

Though I realized they were too uncoordinated to chase after me, their wriggling form and their suffocating screams still sent me crashing down, held hostage by the horrific existence they spent their eternity in.

Whatever I landed on moved, dragging its large, sludgy body to block the melded pair.

A slug-like mass of rippling human flesh undulated toward me, filling the blood-soaked air with squelching noises. Its once-human faces were distorted, features melted into each other, mouths ripping on cacophonous pleas for help.

Crawling back on my elbows, I kicked at it, only to bump into another pleading monstrosity, this one taken apart and reassembled in twisted shapes. Shrieking my horror and disgust, I finally scrambled up again.

But there was nowhere to go. Everywhere I turned, the ruined forms slithered towards me, mutilated arms reaching out of the contortions, begging screeches deafening me.

At one point, something scurried out of the thrashing remains with a clacking noise that shot me with revulsion to my core. And that was before I realized it could move, would reach me.

I backed away, only to slide on the sweltering muck, landing hard on my shattered hand. Paralyzed by pain, lungs filling with decay, all I hoped for was to puke my guts out, then pass out. I wanted to be unaware when I died.

But I wasn't allowed either mercy. This hellish place only offered me the hopelessness it emanated, shackling me, keeping me stuck watching as the creation of a gruesome mind clambered towards me sideways. The stretched torso of a man forming its center mass, a dozen eyeballs were mounted on a braid of ligaments and veins, and as many limbs fastened to the sides. Human carcasses in crustacean design.

Man-eating monsters and magical pests were no stranger to me. They were akin to animals and belonging to breeds. They made sense, had known weaknesses, and could have their actions predicted and counteracted. What I understood had never scared me.

No part of my life experience applied here, as what reached

for me, its endless teeth on its destroyed necks, was beyond comprehension.

But the moment half a dozen hands with peeling flesh and exposed bones grabbed me, I was roused from the grave of defeat.

I wouldn't be this literally damned thing's meal!

Just as I started plucking out bleeding eyes and kicking in rotten teeth, a sheet of solid lightning hit the abomination, charring it.

Gaping, all my hair standing on end in the discharge, I watched its blackened mass land beside me, pierced by the lethal prongs of a silver bident.

❧   15   ❧

THE SPIRAL OF SUFFERING

"**W**hat was it your ancestors were fond of saying? *'The difference between a hero and a madman is how far one goes?'*"

Steps manifested above me, appearing one after the other as Adamantus descended, majestic, unmasked—and furious.

An irate gesture dislodged his bident from the smoldering carcass beside me, summoning it back to his grip. He still came to kick the deformed monster away before looming over me, unblinking eyes staining the air around them that uncanny purple.

"Well?" A taloned hand grasped my injured arm, lifting me up, uncaring as I twisted in pain. "What's your excuse this time?"

When I couldn't say anything, mind blanked by agony, he dragged me with him up his newly-forged stairs.

Not even my morbid curiosity chanced a glance over my shoulder at the levels we passed on our ascent. What I'd been forced to see at the bottom was more than enough.

But the foulness was lessening the higher we got. The moment I could breathe again without gagging, I felt compelled to answer his rhetorical question.

"The distance between madness and courage is a mere leap," I said,

voice as shaky as I felt. "Could be a dialectal difference, as it's mostly the same phrase."

He slid his fingers to my elbow for a punishing squeeze. "And how far do you think you're jumping, now you've done the same thing twice?"

Barely biting down on a cry, I gritted, "I wasn't trying to escape. I wanted to talk to you."

"Why couldn't you just call me from the safety of your quarters?"

"Oh sure, next time I'll whistle or ring a little bell to get an audience with Death!" I spat, only for a coughing fit to overcome me.

He said nothing to that, and I focused on not passing out until we climbed out of the spiraling pit.

At our exit, he flung a hand out, in what felt like exasperation, and split the bloody river. Its gory waters thundered apart to tower above us, a macabre passage of roiling suffering, until we reached the bank of the River of Memory.

Tearing my arm from his grasp, I didn't care about the intensifying pain or the invading memories as I dunked myself in its water. I now welcomed the horrible images flashing past my consciousness, as long as I got to wash that grisly place off of me. In fact, the suffocation of dying moments were pleasant by comparison, seemed to smother the unbearable experience, muting its horror.

Adamantus hovered at the edge, waiting patiently until I climbed out before he summoned a smaller barge.

It was only after the screams no longer rang in my head and the blood didn't coat my tongue that I finally asked, "What the hell was that?"

Without turning to me where he stood unaffected by the ferry's undulations, he ran a stiff hand through his hair. "Exactly that. Hell."

"That—that was the Chasm?"

"No. The 'Chasm' is something few humans earn access into.

It's a prison for those far worse than the ones you saw in the Spiral of Suffering."

"There are worse punishments than what I saw?"

"Infinitely so."

Thoughts stuttering, refusing to imagine anything worse, I dropped my hand into the river, fingers cutting through the jade surface. It continued fading fragments from today, allowing the most horrifying sights to drift off from my mind's eye, hopefully into my subconscious.

"Are they all like that?" I finally choked.

"In the Spiral? No, each level houses its own brand of criminal, with their own measured punishment." He half-turned, a cruel, smug smirk curling his dark, sculpted lips. "You just landed in the most creative tier."

Had he said this to me through the skull of the Horned God, I wouldn't have felt half of the roiling emotions I did watching his face. His striking, humanoid face, cast in the cold tones of precious materials, and the solemn symmetry not even grandmaster painters could capture.

This face transformed the state of—everything.

What had been firmly detached from reality, improbable enough to warrant fantasies, was gone. Adamantus, along with his chthonic court, felt too real now to romanticize.

As I pondered my new perspective, the ferryman took us across from Blackglass Hall and through a canal that delved into multiple structures hewn from smoky quartz.

The towers were linked by bridges that we sailed underneath. From their countless windows, I heard voices coming and going as if in conversations, and saw creatures moving around with purpose in their gaits.

I looked up at Adamantus, curiosity revving back to life. "Is this a workplace of some sort?"

"This is the business center of the Underworld." He turned fully now, sending a thrill skittering inside my taxed chest. "It's located conveniently close to the city of Psychepolis, where my psychopomps, spirits and lesser gods reside, along with some hand-picked souls. Tending to this domain and its constantly growing population is a literally endless task."

"Just like working the earth."

Eyes widening, he inclined his head, making locks of gleaming ink swish over his marble-pale face. "Is it?"

My hands, even the broken one, tingled at the sight.

Gritting my teeth, I nodded. "Managing farmlands is an ongoing cycle that can never be broken. It's all about juggling time constraints and supplying demands that are never sated, exhausting a fraction of the population to nourish the rest."

The slanting wings of his eyebrows dipped, his free hand rising to his jaw in contemplation, his every move and gesture elegance incarnate. "I never thought of the similarity between my domain and yours."

I huffed a harsh breath. "That's probably where the similarities begin—and end. For instance, there are limits to what we can do to our criminals. From what I've seen, limits aren't even a concept to you."

"You were never meant to see that part of my domain. I would have announced your presence to my subjects if I imagined you were going to attempt roaming it again."

"And I would have considered your kind coercions if I suspected refusing you would get me tossed head first into Hell."

"Refuse me three times and your eyes will end up on the back of your head."

Though I couldn't tell if he was tacking onto my joke or being serious, I smirked at him. "Couldn't I just get an extra pair, so I can watch my back?"

"If you had four eyes, how would you decide which to see through?"

"Like this." I shut one eye at a time in quick succession.

His broad chest and shoulders as well as his dark lips jerked, briefly.

Was this amusement? Did he have a sense of humor? And I just tickled it?

Before I could investigate further, the ferryman stopped by an entryway in what appeared to be the central tower.

Adamantus disembarked in his favorite insubstantial fashion. Once he helped me out, his hand didn't leave my elbow, my uninjured one this time, as we ascended past souls and other creatures who skittered out of our way at his approach.

Our journey ended in a corridor with multi-faceted arches, and for some reason, I felt the shimmering door at the end led to one of his personal places.

As soon as I stepped inside, I knew I was right. It was an office, his, ten times as spacious as my room, and a hundred times more opulent. It would have been that even without the cases and vitrines arranged along mirrored floors and in between metallic furniture, teeming with a dizzying display of mind-boggling wealth. I could again see wars being fought over any item of those bejeweled weapons and artifacts, while one of those timeless scrolls and tomes could probably change human history.

He gestured for me to make myself comfortable, and I flopped onto the chair across from his desk, what looked fashioned from onyx.

Coming to tower over me, he rested a hip against its curved edge, one leg hanging off the floor, a gleaming leather boot and a silk pant leg, both in charcoal, peeping through his cloak. The cloak I only noticed now was no longer the ornate one shrouded in shifting shadows, but a modern one, with metallic sheen and embroidery, if still in another shade of purple.

The casual stance made him even more sophisticated. Along with his fiery scent enveloping me, and his arresting face brooding down at me, it made me gulp down gathering drool.

The hellhounds followed us in from only-he-knew-where, circling me as their master watched me. Thankful for their distraction, I welcomed them with coddling coos. They accepted my touch to varying degrees, the silver wolf remaining the least friendly.

And still, Adamantus watched me. I felt he was counting my breaths, my pores.

Needing to interrupt his fraying focus, I blurted out, "So how do you decide who gets what punishment in the Spiral?"

As if rousing himself, he shook his head and straightened. "I employ judges and juries to sanction each soul, and only sit in on the greater cases." A few measured steps brought him looming over me again, his eyes flaring brighter. "Is that among your duties up there?"

"It will be someday." Needing a stronger diversion, I retraced the moments that led to that torturous experience. "Why did the souls push me into the Spiral?"

"They could have thought you had escaped it." Not taking his eyes off mine, he delved a tranquil hand beneath his cloak. My heart forgot its rhythm. He only produced a crisp-white pocket square. With practiced ease, he wiped the charred blood off his bident. Tossing the silk scrap away, it burst into flames and disappeared midair. "Most probably that you were yet another foolish mortal venturing into my domain for a quest, or what I usually get, an avaricious one attempting to steal from me."

I flicked a hand at the splendor all around. "You can't have a place like this, then be surprised you're attracting thieves."

He let out a snort, lips barely twitching, so I couldn't tell if it was amusement or affront. "My latest favorites are not what they come for. They seek what they can use to prove to others that they can defy even me."

"Like?"

A cutting glare hit me right in the chest, though I couldn't be its target. "The last meathead demigod with unusual strength attempted to steal my hounds."

Wondering if he considered me another such demigod, I goggled at him. "All of them?"

"They were fused at the time, so yes."

My eyes snapped even wider. "Fused?"

Adamantus snapped his fingers, a sharp, startling sound like wood fracturing. "Merge!"

In an obedient hurry, the metallic hounds collided. I cringed in anticipation, but the clang of hard metal never came.

Liquifying at the edges, like they were being melted down by a smith's roaring furnace, they melded together mid-leap and grew tenfold, barks comparatively louder, and vibrating every item in the room, and every bone in my ribcage.

In seconds, a green-tinted, three-headed monstrosity draped us in its shadow.

"Oh—wow!" I croaked as all heads lowered to my level with glowing eyes, each set of jaws big enough to chomp off my head in one bite.

Deciding it was best to treat them as I had till now, as I treated all large, aggressive dogs, I offered my injured hand to the middle head, the one with Cressida's droopy ears.

"Hey, girl. Remember me?"

A gust of wind from her enormous snout dried my hair and coated me in gooseflesh. Then she opened her mouth, baring spearhead teeth.

So she didn't remember me in this form? And Adamantus wasn't reprimanding her. Maybe I did provoke him into considering me too problematic to use, and he would let his composite hellhound dispose of me.

As Cressida's gargantuan head lunged, a last thought streaked through my mind. That it was better to meet my end between the jaws of an animal, however it had come into being, than at the hands of another person or a monstrosity.

But the shredding bite never came, just a large slab of cold metal that licked my front, bunching up my flesh along with that flimsy nightgown until it raised me to my feet.

Swaying, I stared at the tongue that had slurped me right out of my chair. It was lolling in perfect mimicry of pleasant panting.

So she did remember me, and Adamantus didn't want to be rid of me. Yet.

As I wondered when and how he would, I realized why he had forged his three-headed hellhound from those breeds—to combine their traits.

No wonder the fellow "meathead demigod" had tried to steal this magnificent beast. It would have been the ultimate prize, not to mention a personal triumph over Death, depriving him of his personally-created perfect canine.

But though their combination was his ideal pet, I preferred Cressida myself.

Letting my tension go, I hugged her huge head. "Good girl! Darling girl!"

Adamantus shifted behind me, a current of delicious darkness rushing over me. "She's grown quite familiar with you."

I shot him a smug smile over my shoulder. "I have a way with animals."

He merely quirked an eyebrow at me. "Again, you do realize they're not real animals? Just the creations of transformative magic?"

I shrugged. "They don't know that. It'd be pretty cruel to tell them otherwise."

His gaze grew pensive as he regarded them, before he settled it back on me. "As the living are well aware, there is no shortage of cruelty here."

"There isn't any up there either." Content to turn my back to them, I faced him again. "Imagine my surprise when I found a reflection of the mortal world down here. So why are there cities here? Where did they come from?"

"The same place my hellhounds came from." He tapped his temple with a sharp nail. "I couldn't have the real thing, so I built my own."

16

THE LIFETIME LIBRARY

In every culture I'd explored and studied, depictions of the afterlife ranged from vaguely blissful to hopelessly bleak. Paradises were exclusive spots for the heroic or noble. Median spaces were dull and mundane like those they were meant for. And the parts dubbed 'hell' were close to what I'd witnessed.

But never did it occur to me that any afterlife would be this structured, this detailed. Or that the Lord of the Underworld would be into construction and development.

"You made cities for the dead?" I exclaimed.

A tranquil nod. "There are also towns and villages on the edges, for those who don't like their views cluttered by buildings, and their existence cramped with people."

"But why? What's the point of all that down here?"

"It keeps the souls busy, mimicking what they left behind in terms of business, hobbies, and excuses for social interaction. It also makes it simpler to categorize people, put them to work in what I need done around here."

Smokey tendrils of outrage curled through my hazy mind. "You're *enslaving* the souls?"

His brow almost collided in what looked like offense. "There's no need for that, especially in regards to those in search of fulfillment or familiarity."

"What does that mean? Who are 'those'?"

"Engineers, masons, smiths, as well as artists, teachers, accountants, or anyone else with a purpose or passion towards any endeavor. These are given purpose. Not many are content to spend eternity idle."

"I thought that's what we all looked forward to, the great rest after a life of work."

Something akin to self-satisfaction curled his blue-tinted mouth. "That's how it was before I myself grew sick of the barren landscape I'd been dealt, and undid it by mirroring the cornerstones of life, with spaces for activity, interaction and progress."

Far too many questions sprouted at that revelation, but what had me wriggling on a hook was the dumbest. "You're telling me that, even in death, boredom and restlessness still exist?"

"Anything cursed with consciousness will always suffer such irksome emotions, though they affect the dead differently."

This had to be one of the worst things I could have discovered about what awaited us all at the end.

I threw my hands up, and my injured one punished me for my carelessness. But damn it! He'd just knocked down a major pillar I'd leaned on all my life.

"So, there is no bliss, or peace, or actual end to existence?"

"There is always oblivion, if you'd like to be thrown into the Void," he offered calmly. "Even then, I can't guarantee those trapped there aren't aware of their state, and are perpetually driven insane by the nothingness."

The last drops of energy condensed into cold sweat, running down my face and back. I felt weaker than when I'd visited accursed locations that had starved me with subpar meals in girl-sized portions, never mind that I was two-meters tall.

I shook my head helplessly. "Then what's the point?"

"Of what?"

"Of life? Or death? Does any of it even matter? Is there any purpose to all this...?"

Stopping, I tried to reel in my agitation. This wasn't the time to get sucked back into the crisis I'd had upon my grandmother's death. She had long become dirt, the body nourished by the land and the cattle that grazed upon it, in turn fertilizing the earth and pushing out crops. *That* was our purpose, to be part of the circle of—

It was no use. All these convictions meant nothing anymore. Now I felt I'd lost Nonna all over again. Her purpose and passion had been shepherding life, and in this place where nothing lived, she must have gone into the Void. She would now be suffering the most unthinkable fate the industrious and purposeful could, for eternity...

I couldn't remember how to breathe, would suffocate, like when Erthamos ripped the air out of me...

A cold shock jolted me, made me gulp down a shrieking breath.

I blinked up through tears at Adamantus. He'd gripped my arms, his frown simmering beneath the midnight-blue hair that had fallen across his brow, its shadow no match for the brilliance of his eyes.

"If there was no purpose to all this," he ground out. "I would have created a one-way tunnel from the Gates to Oblivion ages ago and saved myself the effort."

I dragged an angry hand across my wet eyes. "What's that purpose then?"

He let go of me abruptly, stepping back, making me sway. "The meaning of Life and Death is a too-complex subject to discuss at the moment."

I gritted my teeth. "Then when?"

"At my own discretion, if ever. Now it's time we discussed your own—purpose here."

The way his eyes flared as he stressed the word "purpose" drenched me in dread.

Before I could splutter out a question, he clasped my hand. "Come with me."

Lightheaded yet lead-footed, but getting so used to having my hand in his, I dragged myself after him. He headed to a bookcase at the end of his expansive office, waving it away to reveal a hidden doorway.

As the hellhound rushed through after us, Cressida's massive snout pushed at my back. I turned to find her head lowered, eyes looking up at me entreatingly.

After that near-meltdown, I had no effort to spare for inhibitions. Acting on childish instinct, I slipped my hand from Adamantus', and jumped onto their back. I braced myself as they stood on all fours, then settled my weight.

Adamantus had stopped to watch us, his eyes bathing him in jeweled light, his lips quirked to one side.

"Comfortable?" he murmured.

I sighed as I flopped across Cressida's head. "Amazingly so. I always loved hard surfaces, but now I realize I need even harder..."

His eyes flared, making me almost swallow my tongue. He'd said he was made of diamonds, the hardest substance of all. And now all I could think was lying over him...

He raised one eyebrow, as if reading my thoughts. I both dreaded and wished he'd say something.

Instead, with one last laden look, he turned and led the way into a greater hall with soaring ceilings that seemed to go on forever, and felt like a museum.

After my heart remembered its lifelong job, I took in my new surroundings.

For as far as I could see, it was lined with statues of men and women, all modeling clothes from various cultures and time periods, but taken to a divine level in complexity and luxury. Like the collections of jewels I'd glimpsed in his displays, the costumes grew more striking as we moved further into that mind-boggling wardrobe. But it was their inconceivable materials that called to me, tempting me to touch. And touch I did.

As the hellhound passed by a statue of a woman frozen mid-dance, I grazed my fingertips along her sheer, shimmering gown, a net spun from diamonds. Past her, a man was wearing a cloak that was fully gem-encrusted, and next to him was one modeling a coat and boots tailored from what appeared to be dragon-hide. A series of male figures after them wore a variety of outfits made from unusual leather, some from creatures I couldn't even parse.

Then I passed a gown that hung off the swaying figure of a woman, and realized it wasn't a cleverly dyed satin or even a gilded fabric. Upon touch I knew it was made from pure gold, somehow spun into a soft, supple cloth.

Though I'd never cared about fashion, and spent my life in pants, shirts and suspenders, I let out a shamefully wistful sigh as I let the magical material slip through my fingers.

"Where did you get these? Don't tell me you made them, too!"

He turned with that same eyebrow raised. "Why not? You think these are harder to create than a hellhound and cities?"

As I started to explain I couldn't imagine him at a sewing machine, and saw him modeling unique creations, not tailoring them, he shook his head with an almost teasing twist to his lips.

"But I can't do everything myself, now can I? In this instance, I didn't. I got those from challenges and competitions I issued to master designers, tailors, smiths and the odd sorcerer." He mirrored my urge, dragging his hand across the irresistible material. "The lack of limitations here unbridles their imaginations."

"Limitations like what? Forging any material they can conjure, uncaring about expense, and risking no injuries?"

His eyes flashed as he inclined his head and resumed walking. "Among other things."

Our trek went on for miles through the fantastical fashion show, and I would have welcomed it being much longer. But regretfully, we finally came to an end at another circular door centering an expanse of hewn-stone stairs.

For some reason, when he waved it open, it didn't give way soundlessly under the brunt of his magic. Heavy scraping shook the ground beneath my feet as it unveiled an interior so bright it had me fooled for an eye-searing moment that I was back under the sun.

And in a way, I was. The fiery ball hovering high above, its rays gleaming off mile-high bookcases sculpted from abalone walls, did shine like the sun. Around it revolved a set of planets, each made from a precious stone or metal. A celestial simulation like the one I'd seen in the Trimorphium, only far superior with that spellbinding central figure.

Apart from that, it was a faithful approximation of our place in the cosmos. The favorite model of astronomers, high priests, or even the agriculturalists and meteorologists who worked under my mother, helping us keep an accurate calendar to plan sowing, reaping and storing.

As the hellhound passed beneath it, light reflected off their alloy in a blinding flash. When the sting faded, I saw where he had brought me.

What appeared to be a realm-sized library.

Beneath me, the hellhound shrank and split apart. I found myself draped over a normal-sized Cressida, almost crushing her, and her bark of protest had me scrambling off her.

Head spinning, I stumbled after my deadly guide as he descended yet more teeth-gnashingly steep stairs.

The bookcases on every side were the size of buildings in width. In height, I couldn't decipher if they did end. From the ones close enough to see, there were no symbols or alphabets on shelves or tomes to determine how they were arranged, just stretches of shining spines.

At the bottom of one endless flight, we approached a circular desk with a hollow center, where three souls sat, each busy copying with gilded pens from floating tablets onto ancient hardback tomes.

The one facing us was an elderly woman with a thick, pale braid, beak-like nose and half-moon eyes—a face I saw plenty of in the northeast near Opona. To her left was a middle-aged woman with dark, curly hair, a deeper skin-tone, bulbous nose and thicker body, typical of someone from the lands south of Cahraman. Lastly was a girl no older than fourteen, with a hard Orestian profile and thick brows pulled into a frown of concentration.

Upon his approach, they all dropped what they were doing to rise, greeting him with bowed heads.

"Sire," said the old woman, eyes still downcast. "We have updated the records."

"Any new changes in pattern?" he asked.

"No, sire," said the woman to the left, flipping through the pages she had inscribed. "Apart from the pattern change in that particular region, it remains random everywhere else."

Adamantus approached their desk, making them all stiffen. I got that pang again, seeing this fearful behavior from those already dead. "Anything else you've gleaned from the data?"

"Only that it's still the same in one aspect," said the girl. "Whoever is doing this is powerful enough to avoid being registered under Cause of Death."

Adamantus hummed thoughtfully, then pointed at the girl. "Show me the statistical records."

Within a blink, she phased through the desk and ran ahead to fulfill his command.

"Who are they?" I asked as we followed. "Where are we?"

"The Lifetime Library. This particular section is the Hall of Death Records, where every passing is recorded and shelved by cause and circumstance under specific categories." He jabbed his thumb over his shoulder. "They are my Lifetime Librarians. Efrosinia, the eldest, is in charge of managing natural causes. Satiah investigates and categorizes accidental or violent deaths."

"And the girl?"

"Zenobia registers and researches unusual or supernatural deaths. I'm not sure if that subject staves off her boredom, or if it is helping her deal with how she ended up here."

As if her age wasn't upsetting enough. That she might have died in a way similar to all the girls who'd been mistaken for me, sank my mood further into misery. Now her updates might reveal that more lookalikes had entered the Underworld after I had.

My feet dragged heavier on the softly-glowing ground, the tightening shackles of helplessness digging into my flesh.

It wasn't like I hadn't heard of or seen untimely deaths. Children still succumbed to fevers and infections. Some were born weak, or died in accidents. But usually, after one passed a certain age, especially in my part of the world, they were strong enough to live a full life. Anything after that was marked tragic. Like her death must have been.

Watching her lead us between the enormous rows of bookshelves, I couldn't help but wonder how her family felt. It was dangerously close to the heart-stabbing thoughts of my mother, whom I'd left behind without a word. My only consolation was that Cassia knew part of what had happened, and my record of wrestling and beating the odds might give them some comfort.

My slack-jawed trudge suddenly ended in a collision. Into the wall of Adamantus' body.

He *was* as hard as diamonds.

He steadied me with another brooding glance, the strangeness of his coloring clearer under the false sun, and his effect on me even more potent.

It wasn't the menace he emanated, or the chokehold of fight-or-flight Death Himself ought to inspire in me, like all others.

The feelings he wrenched from me were beyond my ability to subdue.

After everything that had happened since he'd appeared to me, I still only wanted to stroke his unearthly skin, to roll locks of his uncanny hair between my fingers. As I had done before he'd unmasked, after a near-death encounter with a demented goddess left me in a haze of disinhibition, I wanted to quash restraint and suspicion, and give curiosity and desire free rein.

I wanted to touch him, all over.

Had I been this overwhelmed before he'd discarded his Horned God form?

I guessed I had been, but it *was* getting worse. If I wasn't careful, I'd turn into that stock flustered maiden character I'd always mocked, especially for being so easily lured to her death.

Except he hadn't lured me to my ugly demise. Not yet, anyway. And I'd followed him into the unseen depths all living creatures dreaded, for a cause nobler than sating my own yearnings. I'd come for answers, not to lose my wits every time Adamantus watched me with that unblinking absorption meant for eclipses.

My head spun, tearing me out of his fever-inducing focus.

But my lightheadedness wasn't purely in my head. The space around us was distorting, a staircase spiraling down toward us.

Glowing gaze capturing mine again, he drawled, dark and ominous, "You realize you haven't given me your answer yet? When you said you would when I showed you my face and looked you in the eye?"

He again appeared to be giving me a choice. But he knew I had none. I was far too deep in his deadly domain, in this lethal mystery, to look back. I could only continue forward.

I still gave him my best challenging look. "And you realize you haven't given me an actual offer worthy of an answer? Or was it another command?"

"When I give you a command, you will not mistake it for anything requiring your consent."

"Then, since this wasn't a command, it was an offer. To 'join any effort of yours.' And where I come from, offers are discussed, detailed, negotiated, and met with counteroffers. So yours doesn't even qualify as one. The Horned God, Lord of the Underworld or King of the Dead you may be, but I'm *still* not giving you carte blanche."

His lips tugged, and I was certain this time. This *was* amusement. "I thought you'd be braver than that, Miss Cora Spica of the Granary."

"Braver than socking Death Himself in his diamond jaw? What more can I do to prove my bravery? Crack my skull head-butting you?"

His lips twitched this time. Triumph spurted in my chest.

"I would advise against it, since I need you intact. But it's strange to see you so fearful and demanding assurances and guarantees before you leap."

"Try another one. You're not goading me into proving myself by leaping blind."

"It's even stranger to witness your caution now, after you threw yourself off a waterfall of death throes, and into the lowest rung of Hell."

"First, I was *pushed* into Hell. By souls who wanted to ingratiate themselves to their lord and master. Probably because they want you to build them a park or a theater or something. Second, even Hell has nothing on gods who've been killing 'my kind' out of paranoia. Or boredom. Or some other twisted motivation. Third, you still haven't told me what you need from me. So, you're not getting any answer until you do."

"It seems dispensing with the horns is making you forget again who you're talking to."

"It seems you're the one forgetting what I did with those horns when you had them on."

He made this rumbling sound again, and my already unsteady legs almost buckled. "You know you're going to submit in the end."

"Seems you're having a dialectal problem again," I almost gasped. "It's consent, not submit."

Something dreadful crept in the depths of those stunning eyes as he led me up the first step. "We'll see."

With a snap of his fingers, the staircase shot off the floor, spiraling us up so fast, everything beneath us receded.

THE EARTH'S TOOTH

Clinging to the railing like a raft in a storm, my eyes bugged as we spun up through the endless library at a speed that rivaled Pardalus' ascent.

I somehow remained upright against my body's wishes as level after level zoomed past, displaying realms-full of book spines and scroll casings, categorized by gradations of every color in this existence, and shapes from many others.

But it was when we reached a section that rotated, like interlocking mill wheels, that my balance had enough.

Unable to turn my head to face Adamantus, I mumbled, "We better stop soon or I'm going to hurl all over your fancy boots."

"We'll need to find a solution for your fragile humanity."

With everything I had dedicated to holding myself up, I could only stick my tongue out at him. Otherwise, I would have treated him to the assortment of vulgar gestures I'd picked up in my travels across the continent, with my broken hand for good measure. That would have shown him "fragile."

But I was feeling my intestines slithering up my esophagus, creating a suffocating bulge in my throat. And since he wasn't impressed I'd held on till now anyway, I allowed myself to sit down until the staircase came to a blessed halt.

As I stepped onto steady ground again, I thanked every god whose name I could still remember. Zenobia floated ahead, unfazed by either the dizzying journey, or when more sky-scraping bookcases shot into the scene and almost overturned me.

On wobbling legs, I squinted against the dazzling brightness until a wave of Adamantus' hand dimmed it. Our fuzzy surroundings slowly solidified, and I discovered we weren't alone. Many souls and the odd corporeal being seemed to spring into existence, removing or shelving books or inscribing tablets at tables.

As we passed them, I noticed there were now dividers between sections. Enormous columns made of unfamiliar materials, some with shifting colors, some filled with morphing shapes and some translucent, as if only half-existing in this realm.

Zenobia headed toward shelvings by a more peculiar column, but Adamantus stopped her. "I would see the collated case records instead."

Nodding at once, the girl rushed away, shrinking into the distance, followed by the hounds. Adamantus stood staring after her, back to me.

Still unsteady, and not about to ask that he turned to me, I approached the strange column.

Unlike the previous dividers, this one looked unworked, its near-perfect smoothness natural. It was yellowed near a base that had to be thirty feet in diameter, its color brightening to off-white as it curved up to a sharp end I had to crane my neck all the way back to see.

This only hit me with another wave of queasiness so hard, I fell against it to steady myself. The material beneath my palm and face was as cool and had the same color and consistency as porcelain, if that could be made feet in thickness.

Straightening, I ran my dry tongue over the dips in my molars. I felt I should know what this was...

A tooth. It was a *tooth*.

But unlike the teeth in Polyope's maze, this one was at least a hundred feet tall!

Something I'd never felt, never imagined, overtook me. Startled by the detonation of ferocious, primal emotions, I ripped my hand off it, staggering back violently.

I would have crashed on my back if something hadn't hooked around my waist. Head lolling back and bursting with the cacophony of sensations, I scrambled for a hold. Staring blankly into depths that had no space or time, I clung to something hard and soft, lethal and vital. Devastating, destined.

Then from the abyss of eternity something else, as pervasive and precious filled my ears, my being.

A heartbeat.

It was incredulity that finally lurched me out of my stupor, and against the inexorable arm wrapped around me, reuniting me with my awareness, and Adamantus' crackling gaze.

"What is it?"

For long moments, I was mute, focusing on the sensations of being pressed into his unyielding hardness beneath the silk and cashmere. Feeling the dig of his nails into my back, and the graze of his gold medallion against my forearm. Yet it was what I picked up from what lay beneath my ear that sent my senses haywire.

He pulled me back so he could look into my eyes, something like concern furrowing his brow, and intensifying his already denuding focus. "Did you drink from the River of Woe or the River of Memories? I don't know what effect their water has on the living."

"Water" was not what I would dub boiling blood, or liquified death throes. But they certainly weren't why I still clung to Death like he was my lifeline.

My eyes fell to the cobalt-blue vest I was still crumpling in my fist, and the navy coat over it and the slate-grey shirt beneath it, only then realizing—*he'd taken off his cloak!*

Entranced by the momentous event, I stared at the marble

skin two undone diamond buttons revealed, wondering if what I'd heard beneath it, beneath his indestructible flesh and bone had been real.

Too confused by the avalanche of sensations, from when I'd touched the tooth, and when I'd heard his heartbeat, I stepped away, my own heart booming.

"I drank from the River of Memory," I rasped. "But it only made me hallucinate a bit. I just got lightheaded after that trip up here. A side effect of my 'fragile humanity.'"

He shook his head, frown deepening. "That was something else. You stared into nothingness, even as you clutched at me and moaned, for a full ten minutes."

It had felt like moments to me.

More rattled, I still waved it away. "I'm fine, all things considered." Before he could persist, I pointed at the gigantic fang towering over us. "What did you get that from? None of the mythological beasts I've ever heard about is anywhere that big."

His eyes told me he was letting this go at his own discretion. Then he shrugged. "I got it from the same thing that made the Bone Gate you glimpsed at the entrance to the Underworld." I glared at him, and he added, "What you stood on before I found you."

"The *earth*?" I shouted, voice cracking. "Are you telling me the earth has teeth?"

"Endless rows of them," I started to splutter, and Adamantus only steered me away. "This was one of the few loose teeth I found intact. The rest had been unearthed and repurposed."

"Repurposed?" I choked, unable to wrap my mind around the concept. "Into what?"

"Monuments and palaces on Anactoron, I believe. At least, that's what I think they did with her remains. I try not to enter the Heavenly Court, but the situation we both have found ourselves in has left me no choice. "

Her remains? *Her?*

"But your peculiar reaction further proves you have a role to play in this conflict."

"You're telling me that—" I pointed a shaky arm to the earth-tooth. "—has anything to do with why I'm here?"

He made no answer, and I could barely breathe until we reached a spread of silvery tables, where he pulled back a chair for me.

Head spinning at this vacillation between gentleman and boogeyman, I slumped into it and over the table. Adamantus remained standing, back rod-straight, perfectly still. If it weren't for the slight tug of expression at his features, he could have been mistaken for one of his clothed sculptures. Especially now he'd dispensed with his antlers and cloak and stood before me in extravagant yet modern clothing. The last thing I would have expected him to wear.

But no matter how hard I stared, I couldn't spot any signs of life.

Had I hallucinated the heartbeat?

"Do you breathe?" I suddenly asked, watching his chest.

His head snapped towards me, shaking a loose lock of hair over his face. "I don't know."

"How do you not know?"

Unsure whether it was to prove a point, or provide some normalcy for my sake, he blinked. "It's not something I've considered before."

I kicked out the chair next to me. "Well, I'm not going to ask if you get tired, but don't just keep standing. It's making me nervous."

Without any argument, he set his bident against a shelf, and settled beside me. He didn't even adjust the chair, sat in the angle my kick had left it, almost facing me.

He sat with enviable composure, back effortlessly erect, palms on parallel knees. The very opposite of how I sat, knees spread far apart, bad arm thrown over the back of the chair, and good one flung on the table.

We watched each other in silence.

Contrary to most, I was used to being stared at. Gawking at my size and strength had been ever-present since infancy. But as I grew older and traveled outside my region, distaste had overtaken novelty. Men with smaller statures, which almost all were, had been especially vile, appeasing their fragile egos by despising everything that made me myself. I had been mocked, reviled, and even raged at, because I was the opposite of any feminine ideal. In a world that treated women like chattel, by just existing, a nonconforming, physically-towering woman preparing to take the reins of power and responsibility, I was a living act of defiance, and a maddening threat to the status quo.

But here was someone who looked down on me, and everyone in existence, in every conceivable way. And while I raked my eyes over his indulgent image at every opportunity, the embodiment of unadulterated grandeur, he stared at me with such abrading intensity, as if he couldn't make sense of what he saw before him.

I'd never cared how men looked at me. Actually I reveled in exaggerating what made them bristle with antagonism and spittle with disgust. Never have I wanted any man's eyes on me to fill with anything but intimidation and antipathy.

But right now, the focus that had been squeezing unknown reactions from me, from agitation to arousal, made me suffer something else I never had. Awkwardness. Worse. Self-consciousness. It made defensiveness, yet another foreign sensation, rise up within me, displacing the exhaustion of my trials and the weakness of my mortal limitations.

"What?" I snarled. "What is it now? You going to tell me to sit properly or not meet your gaze?"

Adamantus' brows rose. "I beg your pardon?"

"I know you're judging me. I don't care what you are, or how dumb you think I'm being, but you won't make me feel bad about how I behave or what I am."

"I would ask if you were talking to me, but there's no one else here."

A growl escaped my lips. "What's the point of playing dumb? You won't stop staring at me like I'm something repulsive you can't tear your eyes away from, a carcass vultures are picking at, or a massive spider."

"Why would either of those repulse me? I have far more abhorrent things residing in my realm. You've seen a sample. None are worth my attention in any form."

He had a point.

I still remained confrontational. "Then why are you looking at me like that?"

"Like what?"

"Like you've never seen anything like me and it's bothering you."

"Because I haven't, and it is."

I blinked at him. I was used to wrapped-in-civility insults and cowardly cruelties. Even those who loved me, rarely spoke in total frankness. People never said what was truly on their minds, good or bad.

But he, when he chose to say anything, hit me with the unadorned content of his thoughts. I should have known it would take Death to finally gift me with killer candor.

He tilted his head as he always did, as if seeing me from another angle would help him fathom what I was or what I said. The effect with that face, that hair, tingled in my spine, making me angrier.

"I don't know what to make of you. Neither do I truly understand why the Fates showed you to me."

"You said it was because I'm the one who can help you in this situation." Or rather, the instrument he would use. The realization that had crushed my nebulous, ridiculous hopes for the figure I'd sleepwalked to. I didn't want to rehash the letdown. "We already discussed this."

"Not as I would have wanted. But there is no invasive company this time to stop me from broaching this subject."

"What subject?"

"Our first meeting."

Aggravation gone up in smoke, curiosity overwhelmed me in its place. "Oh?"

"I was in the Dreamfields, the sub-court of Codeinus, god of sleep, when I saw you. I thought you were someone's dream at first, but you kept walking towards me. So I spoke to you, and you spoke back."

And it seemed I had sealed my fate when I had. A fate I would have welcomed, if it hadn't turned out I was just a tool to him, a pawn.

"You acted in a way no one ever had before. You looked at me, in the form everyone dreaded, and smiled." He sat forward, arm resting on the table, bejeweled rings and taloned nails glints of superiority and lethality. "Why?"

I considered saying it had been just a dream to me, and we mortals did the strangest things while dreaming. But I couldn't. I always told the truth anyway.

I exhaled. "Because I didn't fear you. I knew what you were. And all I wanted was to get close to you."

Something I couldn't grasp unfurled in the depths of his eyes as he sat forward. "Why would you want to get close to me?"

I shrugged, helpless to explain it even to myself. "All I know is that I spent ages trying to find you. I may not have known it was you, but I knew you were what I was meant to find at the end."

"What did you want from me?" His pupils expanded, hell pits even more harrowing than the Spiral. "What *do* you want?"

Breath fled my lungs in a startled gasp. "Nothing!"

"No one seeks me unless they want something forbidden or nefarious." His irises pulsed, his sudden vehemence shocking, a flame melting the wax of my flesh. "State your purpose."

I struggled up before I slipped off the seat in a boneless pile.

"I have no purpose. None but helping my family and people and stopping the murders!"

"Don't lie to me." His timbre was low, like a storm reverberating in the distance, and far worse than if he had shouted. "It will only compound your punishment."

I stared at him, mind stalling. He still had the face of Adamantus, but felt more alien than when he'd donned his nightmarish form. This was not the Horned God, this wasn't even Death. This was the God of the Underworld who dealt unimaginable, eternal torment.

Strangely, I still didn't fear him. But feeling his threat directed at me, and worse, his suspicion, was more distressing than when I'd smashed my fist into his face.

Shaking with disappointment, I whispered, "I'm not lying."

"You are. You forget who I am, again. How do you think I judge souls? I see their intentions. I can't see yours, and it's even more proof you're hiding something. Something devastating in its significance. *That* I feel."

"This is ridiculous," I protested. "You're the Lord of the Dead, and I'm still alive."

"I read mortals, dead or alive."

My comeback hiccuped in my throat, and I shook my head. "Then how are you not reading me?"

"That's what I'm asking you—what makes you opaque to my powers? And that's what you'll tell me."

"I have nothing to tell you. And don't say I'm lying again. I'm not. Otherwise, I would have bartered for whatever I allegedly want from you by now."

"You did. You already mentioned negotiations and counteroffers."

I heaved up to my feet, shouting, "That was about what *you* want from me!"

His infernal gaze pinned me for a fraught moment. I had no doubt it could reduce me to ash on the spot.

"You said you spent ages trying to find me," he said, eyes

reverting to their usual intensity as abruptly as he changed the subject. I was under no illusion he'd dropped it. "It was a while for you?"

Steeling my jaw so my lips wouldn't tremble, I gritted, "Years."

He scanned my face as if seeing me for the first time. "You walked those woods for years, looking for me?

"It wasn't like I had any control over it, since I was sleep-walking. But I assure you, if it was up to me, I'd take it all back." The banked flames flared for a moment as I collided with his menace head-on. Lips twisting, I couldn't help sounding bitter. "I take it you only saw me that one time?"

He nodded, the ruthless god tucked away, and the suave Adamantus back in residence.

"I don't get it. How can you think I have an ulterior motive, when according to you, it was the Fates that made sure our paths crossed?"

He raised a tranquil eyebrow. "You mean you don't know how capricious the Fates are?"

"But all this is happening because *you* believed they were guiding you to something you need. Someone. Me."

"And I already told you, I have my doubts about their intentions. They would as easily lead me to a solution as they would a trap."

"What trap? You're Death Incarnate! What do you have to fear from the Fates and their games? They only mess up mortal lives."

"Immortal messes are proportionately worse. Mine, on the other hand—existence itself can't afford them." He shrugged one prodigious shoulder, the navy cashmere coat's golden embroidery catching the sourceless light. "But I am still working with the assumption that my initial assessment was right, and you are what I need to resolve my problems."

Feeling deflated as I never had before, I sat down, exhaling raggedly. "About that, *were* you going to tell me what you want from me, before I—" I pointed to my hand.

His gaze panned to my mangled fist before he shifted in his seat, lips moving, and...

Zenobia appeared in front of us with the hounds in tow.

I called the accursed Fates every foul name I knew in ten languages. It seemed part of their game was to withhold answers from me as long as possible.

Resigned, I was wondering where Adamantus' ordered collation was, when Zenobia leaned over the table, touching its center. A hardback tome as long as my forearm and as thick as my fist manifested, bound in green leather and engraved with a gilded script.

"Here it is, Sire," Zenobia said, not meeting either of our eyes. "Every region's reports, collated into one Mortem Codex."

Adamantus flicked a majestic hand at her in dismissal. "And evacuate this whole section."

No thank you, not even an acknowledgement of her efforts. Seemed giving souls purpose was mainly for his convenience, after all.

After Zenobia disappeared, he slid the book in front of me with a wave of his hand. I couldn't even approximate the script of its title, until he flicked a finger and it seamlessly shifted into a familiar one—Standard Imperial Campanian, the lingua franca of the south. The book declared itself *Deaths of Divine Descendants*.

Before I reached to open it, another finger flick wrenched it open, pages fluttering past to stop at one that faded into view.

The title at the top was *Mortal Deaths Associated With Divine Descendants Deaths*. The murders committed in the search for me.

Beneath was a table split into Name of the Departed, Time, Location and Method of Death. The Cause of Death column was blank.

It was the dates my eyes clung to first. It was all this month.

The locations were in Lower Campania, climbing up and trickling down to the Granary. A tightening noose.

At the bottom of the page, the names I recognized started. Among them were the dead girls that had been found in my area. Who I had found.

The latest report was dated to what must be this morning at home. They had killed another lookalike. Another relative. Nera.

According to Polyope, they would soon start killing indiscriminately. And now I understood what Adamantus had muttered to himself that day, it wasn't beyond them to decimate the region's whole population in frustration and wrath. If he didn't stop them.

When I dared to check the previous pages, it got progressively worse.

The entries went beyond my region, and the current month. Names upon names, hundreds, thousands, all my relatives one way or the other, maybe some siblings I didn't know about, and now never would. The same method of murdered all, some with long, involved descriptions, some with pithy and even worse ones. "Sweated out the entire blood supply" and "Chest cavity collapsed as if built on poor foundations" made me flash back to the moment I'd seen Theodosia.

Skin clammy and organs retreating against my spine, I sat back.

I couldn't look anymore, not without imagining every member of my extended family among those names, along with myself.

He flicked the codex closed. "These are the full records of those who'd been murdered related to our case. But in murders, the reports *always* come with the murderers' name. None of those recorded a culprit. As Zenobia said, it is someone powerful enough to hide their tracks from even me."

"That's why you insisted it was an old and powerful god," I choked, still unable to believe an actual god is responsible for this murder spree.

"Or gods." He exhaled, maybe pretending to breathe for my sake. To me, it only signaled I was about to get worse news.

I was right. He sat further forward, eyes crackling over my face. "This is where you get the answers you claim to want. Whatever your purpose, whatever else you know, and whoever you've allied yourself with, know this. Once I share *my* purpose with you, you will have given me your implicit consent. And there will be no going back for you."

I shook my head, no longer making sense of what this confounding god said.

He gripped my face like he had after he'd extracted me from Polyope's maze, one talon scraping softly under my eyelashes. "Do you understand my terms? That, for both of us, this is the point of no return?"

Hating my melting reaction even now, I tore his hand off me in exasperation. "Oh, just get on with it already."

His gaze simmered all over me, before he nodded. "So be it, then. The deal is sealed."

I just made a deal with Death. How very cliché.

Though maybe not. I doubt anyone in history had accepted his terms with such irreverent impatience. I must reserve the unprecedented spot of being the one who knocked down the hand of Death and told him to hurry the hell up.

"Sealed with what?" I scoffed, delirious at the absurdity of it all. "A kiss?"

That rumbling purr shot straight to my core again as he went still, gaze falling to my cracked, unsteady lips. They combusted under his focus, and what it told me he wanted, whether that was real or in my mind.

"Is this the compensation you require?"

I wanted to hurl myself at him, tackle him to the ground and bite off those dark, lush lips. But it would only make my situation here infinitely worse.

Bringing the mad urge under control, I rasped, "Hold that thought. For now, I want a contract. And advance payment.

What you promised to do to protect my land from your fellow gods—oops, the *other* gods, since you're oh-so-unique. I want your *word*."

I shouldn't antagonize him, at least until he gave it to me. But whatever little control I ever had on my tongue was gone.

As if I'd said nothing, he continued watching me as he started talking. "Around three months ago, I began to get reports of one demographic dying in droves. Any child or descendant of a god was targeted and killed untraceably. Since gods aren't privy to the identity of other gods' offspring like me, unless they become famous, the murders started with such a hero. They then used his heart in a divination to find another with divine blood. And so the search and elimination continue to this day. The only time it failed was with you." When I only gaped at him, he exhaled, as if exasperated. "But I couldn't find a single reason for the mystery of the ongoing eradication of demigods, until I was summoned to the Heavenly Court by the council of gods."

"Did they think you had an answer?"

"They completely ignored the issue, as they had a greater problem at hand. And that's the part I believe you're not privy to."

"You thought I was privy to anything you said so far?" A deadly glare made me exhale in defeat. "Fine, your Irrational Majesty. What could the gods possibly consider a bigger problem than someone killing off their progeny?"

"Only the biggest calamity to happen since the war with the titans. Eurycrius, king of the gods, has gone missing."

He paused, no doubt to let me take this revelation in. As if that was something I could process.

When I said nothing, he continued, "From what I can tell, most demigods are being killed as a secondary precaution against any bids for his throne. But the primary target has been his offspring. Now only one remains. You. Eurycrius' last living mortal daughter."

DAUGHTER OF EURYCRIUS

Deep down, far past the layers of disbelief, cynicism and rationalization, I knew this.

And I knew just when I knew. That day, in Eurycrius' temple, with Prunella's body torn open at his feet, and my mother standing between me and his altar.

The way she'd looked at his effigy, then at me, and the terror in her eyes—the knowledge had burrowed into my mind. But with everything that had been happening, I'd refused to acknowledge it, had buried it.

Now it had been unearthed. Like the earth's teeth, there was no hiding it anymore.

For generations, women in my bloodline had lied about gods siring their children, to maintain power and block male relatives from using the law to take what was rightfully ours.

When it was her turn, my mother had told everyone my father was Consus, a local agricultural deity. I'd never believed it, had always thought my father must have been some foreign man she'd taken a fancy to, but Mistresses of the Granary needed heirs, never husbands. That explanation had appealed to me, because I needed to be rational about everything.

But rationality had expired since I'd walked to Death in the woods and reached for his hand. I'd already been forced to believe that, since our first Spica ancestor made that claim, only my mother had told the truth. That I was a demigod.

Now it had taken Death Incarnate to tell me there was more to the story, and that my mother had lied still. A lie as devastating as the god who sired me.

Eurycrius. King of the Gods.

No wonder she'd hidden the truth from everyone, starting with me...

I threw up. There was no gagging build-up to all the sweets and drinks that gushed up my throat and sprayed out my mouth. I barely had a fraction of a second to aim away from him and the book.

When I managed to lift my head again, the sour taste of bile coating my tongue and teeth, I found the library had gone dark, leaving us in a dusky glow.

"Are you done?" he said, calm, almost resigned.

I nodded as I wiped my hand across my mouth, grimacing, at how filthy and disheveled I felt, especially compared to his pristine perfection. "How? How did you find out? A few days ago you didn't know who I was, or even where or when."

"Polyope. She deciphered you after you lost consciousness in her Maze. It was then she called to me, to come collect you."

"So you didn't come to my rescue that time! Good to know I only owe you my life twice, not three times."

"With your recklessness, even had you been a cat, you would have owed me a dozen lives already." A beat, then he gritted, "I would have come then, too, if her Maze and Trimorphium weren't the only two places in the Underworld I don't monitor, in courtesy to her, as an older goddess."

My snort was spectacular with all my rawness and congestion. "I hope you don't say that in front of her. No woman, even a hellish goddess untold millennia old, likes to be reminded of her age, especially by a younger man, and one she fancies, no less."

His glare must have made other gods piss themselves. It only made me smirk at him. "You know that, right? But then, who wouldn't fancy you?"

He blinked, as if surprised, or even baffled.

What I saw was gone in less than a second, I doubted I did. "At least you're no longer pretending you don't know who you really are. Good. You were playing a very dangerous game."

"I never pretended. I only found out the truth when I came here. First believing I was actually a demigod—demigoddess—then now, realizing which god is my father. I believe it only because it all makes sense. It's *your* conviction that's making me doubt it a bit. I now understand many things you said to me, and it's clear you have a completely false assumption of who I am."

"And who *are* you, Miss Coralia Spica of the Granary?"

"Just exactly *that*. You can look into my maternal lineage, my own travels across the continent to gain experience with the world I'd deal with as the next Mistress of the Granary. I'm too well documented, too tried and tested and true, it's laughable to have me in the same sentence as forbidden and nefarious."

He leveled me with a probing stare, and I realized what was different about him. He was frustrated, and now I knew why. Being opaque to him must be driving him mad. It was probably why he felt the most transparent since I'd nagged him into showing me his face, the most like a person.

"You shouldn't have needed a divination in the first place, being that conspicuous," he finally drawled. "So how do you think it did not work in your case? How weren't you found and killed off weeks ago?"

I frowned as the realization fully solidified. "How indeed."

"I don't have any patience for games." Adamantus rapped the table, a mere tap for him, but still sent me flying back in my chair.

Pitching my weight forward hard, before I crashed back on the floor, my midsection met the table with a rib-bruising bump.

Caution evaporating with the last wisp of sanity, I yelled,

"Neither do I. I expected Death to be 'braver than that.' But you've been needling me with snide insinuations like every man who'd ever questioned my right to my land, and I've had enough." I slammed both hands on the table, broken one and all, incensed when he only seemed exasperated. "*What exactly are you accusing me of?*"

In a cutting blur, he shot up to his full intimating height. I instinctively reached for something to throw, useless as it would be. I had nothing but the book.

It hit him, sharp-corner-first, in the chest.

Had he been anything mortal, with the force of my pitch, it would have lodged in his heart like an axe. I knew it wouldn't injure him, but I still hadn't expected what happened.

The tome exploded against his luxurious cobalt vest, the pages bursting in blue-hot flames, and raining ashes on the ground.

I stared at him, one thought filling my mind. *What if they don't have other copies!*

In less than a blink, he was in my face, eyes radiating a glare that rivaled a hundred hearths.

As I squeezed my eyes shut, thinking he'd at least break the other hand that had assaulted him, his cold one wrapped around my neck. He slid me along the floor until my back hit a bookcase. Bleeding infernal shadows, he bore down on me until every single inch of his diamond-hardness was a hairbreadth from plastering mine.

"You want to know what I'm accusing you of, Miss Coralia Spica of the Granary?" His mind-altering scent flooded my lungs as he traced my ear with his frigid breath, and poured his enthralling voice straight into my brain. "What I'll punish you for once you serve your purpose? That you dare plot against me. But I'll fashion a new torment for your other charge. What you've been trying to do ever since you came to me in the woods. You will pay an eternal price for attempting to seduce Death."

19

FALSE STARS

Suffocation was a harrowing experience. But at his hands, it somehow—wasn't.

It was—arousing, debilitatingly so. My body was suddenly on fire, my nipples hard, my core molten. I knew he wouldn't kill me. Not yet. And though he'd just told me he'd torment me unto eternity for it, I couldn't help writhing against him, and not in panic or a plea for my breath.

I snatched a feel of his hardness against my thigh and his rumble filled the library, the realm. Before I could really lose my mind, and clamp his hips in my legs, he released the pressure on my neck with a harsh imprecation in a language I didn't understand.

After he stepped away, and I could talk again, I gasped, "You're out of your death-dealing mind, you know that? I just thought someone should tell you."

The shadowy torment blurring his outline, what must have sent hordes hurtling off cliffs to escape it, receded into his clothes. His polished boots set a hypnotic rhythm as he paced in front of me.

"I have been doing nothing since I first glimpsed you, but search for a reason why I had. With everything else considered, the only logical explanation is that you have been sent as a distraction."

I tried to push away from the shelves, and only ended up arching against their support. "And am I succeeding? Am I distracting you?"

A literal-Death glare took in my unintentionally suggestive pose. I didn't scramble to straighten. It was probably suicidal, but I might be damned already. Might as well get the most out of my last days as a corporeal being.

Gaze fixing mine, he continued talking, as if to himself like last time. "At first I thought the mortal murders in your area were a false lead for me to pursue, instead of weaving the loose threads I've been pulling at. Then I discovered you were at the center of that storm, unscathed. Then I realized who you are. Putting it together with how you've been with me from that first time, I could only reach one conclusion. A god, or several gods have recruited you. You are a spy sent to sabotage and seduce me."

That had me jackknifing away from the shelves. "Wait! You think I'm working for other gods? If I was, why risk destroying myself before I 'served my purpose?'—only to fall into the hands of the one I'd conspired against, for eternity? I would have died here twice already!"

He made a bitter sound as he walked back to me. "You knew I'd come to your rescue."

"How would I have known that?" I cried. "When you your-self told me if I disobeyed you, I was on my own with the horrors of your domain."

"Oh, you knew," he murmured, his tone suddenly dipping into shocking sensuality as his eyes dragged actual heat down my nightgown.

If I didn't know better, I'd think he meant I was influencing him. Me, Cora Spica, who only ever repulsed every sort of man, was seducing Death.

I would have laughed if my throat wasn't too raw. And if the implications of his suspicions weren't too horrific.

"You think I'm working for the gods slaughtering my people?" I clenched my fist, clashing with the gaze that made the living and the dead cower. "You think I'm in on a plot that's terrorizing my land? And you must consider all this talk about saving them 'misdirection.'"

"Who knows what deal you struck in return. Everyone wants something."

"And what do you want?" I rasped, my throat swelling along with everything inside me.

His gaze scraped down my face and neck, raked over my heaving breasts, making me feel as if he'd already touched me, fondled me.

"I want the old order to be restored. That can't happen until I find all the missing parts." In another blur, his lips were back hovering over my ear. "And the first gap to fill is you."

My feverish mind supplied me with a dozen dares for all the gaps he could fill for me.

It was insane, but my inhibitions were exhausted. By the Spiral's ordeal, by that encounter with the earth-tooth, by the revelations about my lineage, and that was only today. But mostly by exposure to this maddening god. Death Incarnate one moment, sophisticated savior the next, now irresistible predator. And with every form and face, he unearthed raging cravings I never thought I could experience.

Now, with him so close, the scent I was coming to crave, besieged me, blanked my mind.

It was nothing like mortal men, who stank of either sweat, cologne or insecurity, or all of them. From the first time I'd smelled him, his scent was unique, hints of forged, *male* metal. Like he was one of those bronze sculptures worshippers stroked for favors, but that had just been struck by lightning.

And instead of reeking with rage, like all men before him had under the brunt of my challenge, his aroma simmered with control, sizzled with curiosity.

If people only knew what Adamantus was like, in either monstrous or humanoid form, they would be rubbing his groin instead of Lyceus', and not for love or fertility favors, but for the pleasure. I wondered if anyone had dared approach enough to...

Stars above, being knocked about had rattled my senses so hard, it seemed to have reversed my blood flow permanently from my head to my loins.

Here I was, moments from being flung back into the Spiral of Suffering by a god who believed me to be a spy, and all I could think about was if anyone had ever stuck their hand between his legs. And if I'd get the chance to.

There were no tales about women seduced by Death or demigods fathered by him, aside from motifs dubbed Death and the Maiden. Allegories for winter and spring that got popular enough to take on lives of their own across the centuries. And here I was, starting to imagine myself in her place, and to believe his every word and action, even now as he accused me of treason, mirrored my own inconvenient attraction.

Worst part was, I could see where he was coming from. Conspiracies were everywhere in his world. The gods never stopped scheming against each other. After an eternity of wrestling with their ruthless cunning, I'd be paranoid, too.

A talon that could shred steel traced my carotid, hard enough to only tickle. "So, what are you?"

I shuddered, knees on the verge of buckling. "You already asked me who and when am I. What exactly do *you* think I am?"

"I considered that you're a convenient mole planted to throw me off this mystery—but you are no pawn. Then I thought you're an accomplice in this conspiracy, and you probably are. But you're too versatile and unpredictable to be only that. Now I'm leaning towards you being a maverick, an opportunist, playing all sides, riding the tide of the events. You are making an independent bid of your own now you've captured my attention, and learned of my need."

My abdominals clenched hard, expelling my breath as the

word "need" coincided with his talon-tip trailing between my breasts, eyes now cascading silken menace.

"That's a fiction to rival the ancient tragedies," I gasped. "I'd read such a novel."

"It's far more plausible than any other explanation." A razor-sharp talon rested at the top of my nightgown. "You have much to gain by eliminating your endless siblings and cousins, and by courting my favor."

I wrenched away from him, staggered to the table and collapsed at my chair. "Where are you getting all these ludicrous ideas?

He was above me in a blink, his lips twisted in a cruel smirk. "I have far worse ones."

"Why? What have I done to make you suspect me of such atrocious motives and actions?"

He gave me an incredulous look. "You have the temerity to pretend you don't know? Again?"

"I don't, damn it! Just tell me why you think I deserve these accusations."

"You are Eurycrius' daughter," he gritted, a flare of fury in his eyes for the first time. "The ultimate depraved, heartless, treacherous bastard. You must be capable of anything."

I gaped up at him.

With just those few words, he'd struck the foundations of my being down.

All my life I'd felt I was nothing like my mother, from looks to temperament. That I had to be wholly my father's daughter. Now I knew who that father was, that knowledge took on terrifying dimensions.

But no. Whatever I inherited from him, it had no bearing on who I was raised to be. Who I *choose* to be.

One talon trailed down my hair to my shoulder. "So, how did it feel to read all the names of the innocents you helped murder?"

"You're out of your mind!" I yelled. "I am nothing like my father. Nothing!"

I tried to heave up. But he kept me down, one hand on my chair, the other on the table, caging me between his power-laden arms. He stared down at me, as if trying to probe me, decipher me, for what felt like an hour.

He finally broke the filled-with-my-panting silence. "Whatever they offered you, I can top it. I haven't made deals with mortals in a long while, but if giving you a dragon's hoard of wealth is what it would take to end this then so be it. If it's anything else, name it. I have far more at my disposal than all the gods combined."

"Yeah, good for you. Ruling the dead seems to be a very lucrative business."

His gaze singed my lips, literally. A spark of heat enough to sting but not to harm. It sent molten fire roaring to my core.

He leaned down closer, his voice almost a whisper. "Tell me what you want."

I barely caught back a scream. *You!*

Instead, I gasped, "I already told you. And if, after everything that had happened, everything I'd done in the last few days that could have led to my death, every random time you've come to my rescue, you still think this is all a convoluted plan and I'm an ingenious spy, then there's nothing I can do to convince you otherwise."

The flames arcing from his eyes hit lower this time, my left nipple, right over my heart. The treacherous thing would have catapulted from my chest to throw itself at his feet if it could.

"You said yourself I was hard to find," I cried, furious. If only he was hurting me, I could withstand pain. But I was helpless against his sensual torment. And I wasn't even sure this was what he meant, or if he thought he was intimidating me, and it was me who was aroused by anything he was or did.

He inclined his head, and his hair slid over my shoulder,

sending another gust of arousal thundering through me. "Your point?"

"If I had been in on the plot to kill my lookalikes as a new twist in the mystery to keep you occupied, would I have pursued Erthamos to save Chloë? You felt me because I was *dying*. Would I have risked you being a few seconds too late, just to lure you to me? If you do, then you really don't know anything about mortals. Funny, really, when you're the one who sees them in the throes of terror at losing their lives, and see the lengths they'd go to to prolong them."

The lash of heat hit me right over my midsection this time. I spasmed with the pleasure that forked between my legs to my toes so hard, I almost squeaked.

He shrugged smoothly, his voice alone almost pushing me over the edge. "There are mortals who are reckless, who take insane challenges and dares, and risk their lives constantly. You're evidently one of them."

"Didn't I tell you you know nothing of the mortals you judge?" I spat, on the verge of head-butting him and cracking open my own skull. "Such foolhardy mortals are never in demand as spies—or seducers. Their traits are the very opposite of what those jobs require."

I lunged up, grabbed his lapels, shoving my face into his, making him look me in the eye. "I wish it was that simple, and I had a deal with another god. If I did, I would have jumped on your counteroffer. I'd rather have you as a patron, or recruiter or whatever. No matter your vices, I know you don't lie, like they do. I also wish I had my own agenda, since you've already offered to give me anything I want, and Death always keeps his promises. But I don't want you to give me anything but my family and people's safety. I can't have any more people dying on my account. Please." I let go of him, slumped back in the chair, deflating on an exhalation. "Apart from that, about why I hadn't been killed, I'm just as confused as you are."

The fire finally died down and his eyes returned to pure

hypnotic purple.

Straightening, releasing me from the terrifying yet coveted prison of his suspicion and nearness, he gave a terse nod. "I believe you. And I apologize."

My mouth dropped open, my whole body slackened. "W-what did you say?"

As always, he took it at face value. "I said I believe you. And I apologize."

"I heard...I just can't believe... Is this a trick?"

"I have no use for tricks."

So this was real? Death was apologizing to me?

If I were the fluttering maiden kind, this would be when I'd swoon.

"D-did you just read me?"

His lips thinned. "You remain the only mortal impenetrable to me."

I barely stopped myself from telling him how penetrable I was, to only him.

He really must stop giving me ammunition for lewd suggestions!

He might not read my intentions, but he must be reading my condition. It must be why he put distance between us now, giving me his back.

I had no idea what he was thinking, and what he'd do. Where I would, or could go from here. I still knew nothing, of the situation, of what he needed from me.

I almost fell off my chair when he suddenly turned around. "You have no theories on how someone as conspicuous as you, who has toured your realm for years, for the firsthand experience needed as your region's future leader, went unnoticed? When they are looking for someone with your basic traits, too? You should have been the primary target."

So he'd researched me since I'd last seen him. He probably now had my every move documented in a book in this library. And he'd still suspected me.

Though maybe my life did give him fodder for suspicion. A girl touring the continent alone at twelve could be suspected of being "capable of anything." I *had* seen and weathered everything my world had to offer.

So far, all my experiences hadn't done much for me in his domain.

He came to tower over me again, this time devoid of sensual intimidation. Which I found myself ridiculously wishing back. In spite of everything, my body was still on fire.

I cleared my throat, swallowing a lump of lust and disappointment. "Maybe they know where and who I am, and they are killing my lookalikes as a diversion to you like you said? Or as a message? But to whom? Eurycrius isn't there anymore."

"Or perhaps they're just playing with their kill, closing in on you, making you lose your mind with fear, before finishing you off."

Wasn't that just comforting.

"That still doesn't make sense. The gods don't have that kind of patience." He ran a frustrated hand through his hair. "Even Polyope has heard of you, through her Silver Sisters no doubt. Your world must be full of whispers of this singular, golden Campanian girl who embodies Spring and Summer combined, who braves the wilderness of a ruthless world alone, who saves caravans and leads revolutions, who towers over men, and shoves their entitlements down their throats."

Was this how he saw me?

I'd never had a wish or taste for flattery. But this was far more than that. It was real, but put in such a way that made gratification flush through me from head to toe. Coming from him it felt like the ultimate recognition.

But was this discomfort trilling inside me—shyness? What other inconceivable things would this god make me feel?

Fidgeting under his earnest gaze, I said, "I doubt they'd be describing me in such poetic terms."

Interest gleamed across his face. "How would they describe you then?"

I couldn't help the smug leer. "Big, blonde, beastly bitch."

His lips tugged. "Nowhere as bad as what I've been called. I've lost count of the slurs."

"Same, though you have entire civilizations-worth of euphemistic titles, too."

"I wouldn't call Lord of Maggots, and all variations of Evil and Destroyer of All Good Things, euphemistic. I can't remember a time when all of existence didn't loathe me."

"I'm sure there are a few death cults that love you."

"Nothing says love like butchering your own children at the handful of altars that were built for me," he sneered, dripping with disgust.

"And the cannibalism. Why did they do that?"

"Based on the assumption that I devour souls after my underling maggots consume the bodies. No wonder I'm always being depicted as an adversary to the 'Good God King' in endless plays, about how I tried to usurp him and was flung down here as punishment."

Sensationalist tales that got popular in the west then spread via stage productions did seem to affect public opinion rather quickly, not to mention permanently.

"So, you never tried to take the Heavenly Court?"

He rumbled a sound packed with eons of annoyance. "If I did, would I be looking for your father, against the obvious wishes of most other gods?"

My father. A fact that still refused to sink in, no matter how much sense it made. How right it felt.

I emptied my aching chest forcibly. "They don't want him back, do they?"

"And they don't want me to look for him." A hum like a swarm of wasps rose with the displeasure darkening his pale skin and emptying his eyes. "I made certain of that when they asked me to take his empty throne."

20

AN INFERNAL PROPOSAL

Against my sore face's wishes, my brows shot to my hairline. The hammers knocking inside my head quickened as I tried envisioning such a bizarre situation.

For the favored and powerful deities to petition Death to exchange his silver bident for Eurycrius' golden spear was unthinkable.

The hum filling the air had risen to a worrying buzz until I broke his stiff posture and blank stare by blurting out, "They want you to be the new King of Heaven? What about the Underworld? You'd be the king of both?"

I couldn't even begin to imagine that extent of power.

He shook his head, as if to return fully to the moment. "I don't believe they intend for it to be permanent, that I'd act as regent until a new Head God is installed."

"Installed how? By election?"

"Or by conquest."

War preceded conquest. The war he'd said could hurl us back to the Dark Ages.

"So Eurycrius doesn't have an heir?"

"No use in having designated successors when you don't die. It's why his mortal offspring are being eliminated now."

"I still don't get why gods would resort to mass murder! How is the average semi-divine mortal a threat, or a contender for succeeding the King of Heaven? Demigods of note were few and far between. Those who achieved divinity even less."

"A god with Eurycrius' blood was deified recently. Divine bastards are all over your world, and if more are deified, especially his blood, sooner or later, it would upset the balance of power, and whoever replaced Eurycrius wouldn't sit on the throne for long. I am talking centuries, but being immortal, the gods plan far ahead. That's my theory so far. But to me, that part of the mystery has been secondary. Their reasoning can come to make sense after I find out what the circumstances of Eurycrius' disappearance are, and who is involved directly in the murders, and how many camps there are in this conflict."

"You mentioned two camps before," I said, remembering that fateful encounter at Polyope's. "But that was in respect to their position on demigods. What are the camps when it comes to their position on his disappearance? The ones that really want you to take power versus those fighting over the Throne of Heaven?"

He nodded. "Somewhere in between are those attempting to distract me from investigating, for their own reasons. And till now, I am uncertain who belongs to which camp."

After that, he fell silent, hands clasped behind his wide, tapered-to-slim-waist-and-hips back, head tilted upwards and eyes staring, probably into eternity.

The morose storm of his expression, the singular slashes of his bone structure, these almost-alive midnight-blue waves, and those simmering with endless eyes, made me wish I knew how to paint.

I'd commit this scene before me to a canvas, in a painting that invoked the dark sensuality of Arborean art, those indulgent, shadow-filled depictions of shameless decadence. If I could only capture a smidgeon of his grandeur, fanatics of exquisite art would tear each other apart for the chance to acquire any item I used in the painting, would die for the chance to bid on *The Melancholy of Death* by Coralia Spica.

Poetic imagery and hyperbole always seemed to frolic in my mind in his presence. If I wasn't careful, I might start writing sonnets to his praise, or create a new Death religion.

He opened his eyes suddenly, beckoning me. "Come."

I scrambled to follow him, and for some reason, the plummeting trip on the twisting staircase was a lot more bearable than the ride up.

Once on stable ground, the hounds ran out of the Hall of Records to join us. We exited from a back entrance leading to a snaking, sloping path of iridescent black marble. After the library's brightness, the nighttime tone of the false sky was gloomy. On either side of us roads lead away to a settlement in the distance, what must be the city he'd mentioned, Psychepolis. With its own architecture and sky, it mimicked the watercolor gradients of dusk and dawn.

Only when he slowed to gaze upward did I notice the source of the ambience.

Countless stars blinked down at us from an unmeasurable expanse of purples and blues.

After blinking at them in disbelief for long moments, I realized what they were. Far away as they were, I knew only the most coveted rock of all could sparkle that brightly, what he claimed to be made of. This overarching tapestry above us was spread in diamonds like our night sky was scattered with stars. A simulation the Lord of the Dead had created for his dread region.

I tore my gaze down from the twinkling gems, and found Adamantus watching me. "This is—astounding."

"Is it? It's only a simulation. The Upperworld has no idea how spoiled it is. It gets to see stars every night. We just have this."

It felt strange how he said "we." Did he consider the denizens of the Underworld his people?

"So, did you source out in creating this, too?" I asked.

"The jewelers and artists among the souls were particularly helpful—and involved."

"That must have really been the project or a lifetime—uh...an afterlifetime."

"They seem to appreciate it when I give them the means they never had in life, to chase their imaginations. It also pays to keep them busy."

"Do they cause trouble for you when idle? Is that why you're doing all this?"

His eyes flashed. "You think anyone or anything can give me trouble here?"

"Point taken." I wrestled with my raging reaction for a while before I said, "But how do people get the Underworld so wrong? This sunless, starless splendor you reign over is nothing anyone imagined. I'd seen countless depictions during my voyages, from Arbore to Orestia to Opona and even as far south as Zargoun. And it's always monotonous, idyllic fields for the noble, bleak wastelands for the not-so-noble, and hellish land-scapes for the criminals—which are the only things we got sort of right."

"That's how it used to be."

"Until you got sick of it? "

He looked into the distance. "It can get maddeningly dull to simply exist for eons."

For some reason I didn't feel he was talking about the souls.

Chest suddenly heavy with trapped breath, I felt the stupid urge to tease him, to lighten the moment. "I didn't think Death could empathize with mortals in any way."

He shrugged. "I just found it to be a horrible existence, either lingering in an idyll until you fade, or languishing in bleak-ness, until you also dissipate. It's no different than a ghost haunting their place of death. There had to be a reason it was called an 'afterlife', where one could continue living in the here-after. Otherwise they would all go straight for the Void."

That was a depressing possibility I did not want to entertain. His astonishing version was a far superior fate.

He gestured towards the diamond-strewn expanse above. "This is due to spread to the rest of the 'skies' here, once I've gotten to the bottom of this ordeal. I will also go about creating a series of moon phases."

"Made of what? Pearls?"

"Now there's an idea. Come, we still have much to discuss."

After a while of resuming our path, the unthinkable spread out on either side of the path.

Endless rows of fruit trees grew along neat curves, lined with bushes.

Life growing in the land of the dead.

Or at least that was what it appeared to be. There wasn't a hint of green, everything in metallic shades. The only colors were found on those glass-like trees with fruits that belonged in artisanal bowls in manors and palaces.

"Are these *alive?*"

He nodded as he waved, and a round, red fruit ripped off its branch. As it hurtled to fall into his palm I recognized it as a pomegranate. Big enough to fill his hands, he dug his thumbnails into the top, and ripped it in half. I wondered if he'd offer me one. He didn't. Thankfully. Nausea was still hovering at the edge of my senses. But he *could* have offered.

I waved around. "How is all this growing here?"

"These are magical plants I've found in other realms, and select locations in the Upperworld that can grow without sunlight. There have been quite a few disappointments, but once I acclimatized them to this environment, they aren't too bad."

"I never even considered the Underworld *could* sustain life, being the land of the dead and all," I said, my mind dragging back to Nonna, and I decided to ask. It wouldn't be worse than socking him in the jaw. "My grandmother—she would have wanted to continue her afterlife where any form of life grew."

He went silent for a while. "She is."

All my nerves loosened, forcing me to grab his coat with my functioning hand before I pooled at his feet. "How-how is she?"

"Now that I have all the information, she reminds me of you. And like you, she's—thriving. But I will not show her to you."

"*Why?*"

"You are reckless enough in your efforts to save the living. I won't put it to the test what lengths you would go to for the dead." I opened my mouth to object, and a talon beneath my chin closed it. "That's my final ruling."

As much as I wanted to destroy my other hand on his divine face, I actually thought he was right. I didn't want Nonna to see me here either, and to worry about me. It was enough, for now, to know she had a better afterlife than I'd ever imagined possible.

As we continued walking, I soon forgot everything, caught by the infernal starlight shining on the ruby-like seeds and his smooth tongue flexibly gathering them in mouthfuls.

I wanted to know how long and versatile that tongue was.

Mid-chew, he caught me watching. "Isn't the food I offer to your liking?"

Chagrined that he'd mistaken my ravenous stare for a desire for sustenance, I scoffed. "You call sweets, bakeries, and drinks food?"

"Isn't that what's considered luxurious where you're from?"

"Yes, but you can't live off luxury alone, otherwise it becomes ordinary. That, and it would make you sick."

"Sick?" He frowned. "I would have known if my underlings brought you anything expired or diseased."

"Not that kind of sick."

"What other kind is there?"

"You know, when you eat too much of something rich and it upsets your stomach...?"

Just what am I trying to do, explaining mortal indigestion to an all-powerful deity?

I eyed his beyond-perfect form. "What do you usually eat? Do you even eat, or are you pantomiming human behavior now for my own ease?"

"I eat when I feel like it. Like now. And I can eat anything."

Outside the peculiar groves, the landscape changed in a distorting wave after we passed what felt like an invisible threshold. Behind us, I no longer found the urban and suburban parts of the Nether Court but more dizzying stretches of space, blurred at the edges, almost like they were beyond my perception.

Between one blink and the next, it was as if I had fallen through a trapdoor to another realm. As instantaneous as Polyope's black pool, I cut to a warmly-lit chamber.

Teetering for moments, I blinked at the indulgent interior that greeted me once again. But it was far tamer and much smaller than his previous study, and without an abundance of precious materials and articles. Closer to what I'd see in a king's quarters in the land of the living, but with just enough strangeness to make magic's presence known.

The fireplace between the black leather couch and the in-built bookcase was carved from one block of obsidian, and its flames were white outlined with burgundy. A floor-to-ceiling peaked window in front of an ebony desk gave me a glimpse of what lay far below; the soul-city with only the parts that scraped the sky visible.

Stepping back, I nearly tripped over Platinus as he scratched his large ear. "Where are we now?"

"A favorite place of mine."

Before I scoffed *"That wasn't helpful!"*, his words sank in.

He'd brought me to a favorite place of his!

Better still, he was rummaging through the desk, giving me the chance to ogle him at leisure.

It still hadn't sunk in, how he styled himself in private. The last thing I'd expected him to favor was the modern, industrial-era garb of the wealthy. Tailored suits, vivid vests, gold buttons from his cuffs to his coats, decadent materials and embroidery, and leather boots with more shine than a black cat in the sun.

In opposition to the rulers who emulated divine depictions, Adamantus mimicked the aesthetics of mortal power. Did the other gods do this?

If they did, I'm certain it wouldn't suit them like it did him. But then anything suited him. He made anything he wore the epitome of godly grandeur or manly finesse. I wouldn't be surprised if he was the one who inspired mortal fashion.

Throbbing head dropped back on the couch I collapsed on, I found the ceiling less dizzying to observe than his pale, dark perfection.

It was fully, exquisitely painted, a flat view of the sun system that hovered in the Hall of Death Records, surrounded by constellations. A richer, updated version than what I saw in temples, with stars outlining legendary objects and beings. And they were all moving in their celestial orbits.

But I didn't feel awe this time, not with the definite pattern that had emerged.

It made heart-aching sense, that the one god deprived of the sky would yearn for it, as I did for my home.

It was beyond strange to find any similarities between us. Or feel any sympathy for this unstoppable force of nature.

Suddenly I noticed what I'd been staring at. One glitch that upset the entire scene.

Not one to keep opinions to myself, I called out, "Hey, one of your undead artists made a mistake."

"Impossible," he denied immediately.

I pointed at it. "The constellation of the Golden Sickle has an extra star at its sharp tip. It doesn't exist."

Adamantus ceased his rummaging and the room brightened so abruptly I squinted and teared up.

I smelled him before I saw him, now like singed copper.

When I dared peel my eyes open, he was in front of me, looking up where I'd pointed. "This is one of the oldest things I had commissioned. Royal astronomers from civilizations far earlier than yours were consulted on this."

I smirked. "I know humanity loves to romanticize the past, but our ancestors got a lot of things wrong. Wars were fought over whether the sun orbited around us or vice versa."

A sarcastic huff told me he was aware of that conflict. "Lyceus will be proud to tell you that the world does, in fact, revolve around him."

"Is the sun god as pretty and full of himself as he appears?"

"You'll see for yourself, if this conversation goes as I hope."

"And you'll tell me what it is you hope at last?"

"In good time," he said as he strode back to his desk.

"I hope that happens before I grow old. Not all of us can afford to squander time like you." Hunger rising from its sickened slumber, for food this time, I eyed the tempting fruit on his desk, surrounded by similar clusters of blood-red gems. "So, while I'm waiting for you to feel like telling me, you might as well serve me a sample of *your* favorite delicacies."

He produced a large scroll, waved the drawer closed, then looked at me across the space. "That might not be the best request."

"Why not?"

Maintaining eye contact, he raised the gem cluster to his mouth. His pearly teeth unleashed a cacophony of crunching crystal that had me doubled-over with visceral, imagined pain. Horror never hit this hard when I caught monsters disemboweling still-living victims, but watching him chew what would need an iron hammer to break had my gums aching and my mind offering up visions of broken teeth, a bleeding, mutilated mouth and a cut-up tongue.

That lasted seconds, before I was entranced as he walked back to me, watching the bones and muscles of his jaw shift to grate the fragments like it were candy. A sculpture in tantalizing motion.

Unblinking, he swallowed his mouthful of crystal and dropped the rest in my lap. "This is why."

Disbelieving laughter escaped me like a cough. "So, you have a titanium jaw. That's why it ruined my hand."

"*You* broke it on *my* face."

I wrinkled my nose at him. "Oh, don't act like it hurt you."

"It did," he deadpanned. "It hurt my feelings."

"You have feelings?"

His expression darkened, that bleakness tingeing it. "I'm feeling quite annoyed at the moment."

That seemed to be the extent of his emotional range so far.

"Anyway, I wouldn't have bothered, if I'd known how hard you are..." And it was impossible not to take that thought to its conclusion, straight to the hardness I'd grazed against.

His eyes simmered as they followed my tongue licking tingling lips, flooding my mind with images of having both on him.

Shaking his head, as if to clear it, he crossed his arms and tilted his chin up at me. "What would you have done instead?"

I gave it a moment's thought, before I waved. "I would have done it anyway."

He huffed, and this time I had no doubt. This was definitely a chuckle.

To stop myself from giving in to all the insane urges streaking in my mind and body, I stared at the assorted gems of the ornate rings on his dark-taloned hand. It was the star-sapphire I focused on. In my travels, I'd seen it only on the high-ranking officials of religious or magical institutions. In the northwest or the southeast though, it was viewed as a sign of black magic.

Endlessly gazing into the starburst center of the gem, I felt him move toward me. Sudden movements had always had me in defensive mode. But with him there was no point. And then my survival instincts never activated in his presence. They remained dormant, now. In fact, they would do so curled in his lap if they could. It was insane, yet still true, and there was nothing I could do about it. Death was my own personal safe haven.

"What are you thinking of?"

That I want to tear you out of those maddening layers of opulent trappings, and pull you on top of me.

But since I had no idea if he'd still consider this a seduction attempt punishable by a brand-new eternal torment, I said another thing that had been on my mind since I'd first seen him. "That I rarely met a man taller than me."

"I am not a man."

This wasn't the first time he'd said something like this, with the same tone, what I couldn't tell was hauteur or resignation. "You sure look like one to me."

"Is that all it takes to be considered something?"

"It usually is. If it looks like a dog, barks like a dog..."

His gaze flitted to his hounds. "Shapeshifters exist."

"Unless they're hostile, I would consider them what they prefer to look like. Your hellhounds are dogs and I don't care how they were made. We're all made, one way or another, anyway."

Adamantus' face emptied. And it was only then I discovered how expressive he had been. Even when he'd been in Horned God form.

My heart kicked me in the ribs at his abrupt change. "A-Adamantus? Are you having another paranoid episode?"

He shook his head slowly, seeming to reanimate again. "I just think it's time I tell you my purpose. To reiterate, once I do..."

"It's the point of no return. As if I can forget that." I made a hurrying gesture. "To make myself redundant, too, tell me already!"

Those spectacular lips pursed, and I saw in his crackling eyes that he was considering punishing me again. Before I succumbed and begged him to, he said, "I will help your family and land. But you will remain here until my will is done."

Memories of my mother, Cassia, and everyone who would die if he didn't stop it, dragged its claws across the tender flesh of my lungs. Before I'd known about the danger to them, I'd intended to barter my acceptance for his favor in something else. But I was far beyond bargaining with him. I was the one who needed him, who would do anything to secure his aid.

"Whatever it is you want, you can have it. As long as you help them, I'll do whatever you need."

"*Whatever* I need?" he murmured, the devastating sensuality back like an inexorable undercurrent.

"Anything," I wheezed, blood chilling as I suddenly felt I was selling him my very soul.

Not that I had a choice. I was actually lucky he was willing to buy it at this price. Death didn't save lives. He was doing this for me by going against his very purpose, and by subverting what he was.

He led me with a hand on my elbow to his desk where he spread the scroll to reveal a highly detailed illustration of something akin to a family tree. He gestured for me to peruse it.

All the gods were mapped out, each with a symbol by their name. Except, the levels weren't markers of descent. They were categorized based on something other than their relationship to one another.

Eurycrius, King of Heaven, had a lightning bolt by his name, Nerios. King of the Seas, had a trident, Lyceus, the sun, Telephassa the crescent moon, and Orcus the bident, then the domains became more abstract. Almagera, Eurycrius' queen, presided over the home, health and fertility, of great importance to me and mine. Eglaia was next, goddess of beauty and also fertility. Beneath her was her replacement as goddess of love, Altagratia, who'd married Eglaia's son, Amatius, god of desire. Now *that* was a story people didn't get sick of telling.

The names went on, but down the list there were names I didn't recognize on the fringes, including a married pair dubbed

Theoneus & Aristagnë, their symbols grapes and an octopus respectively.

Polyope had mentioned a Theoneus before. That latest deified demigod, and the new god of madness. The one who made people eat their faces.

Grimacing at the visual, I turned to Adamantus. "What am I looking at exactly?"

"The Hierarchy of Divinity." He pointed to indicate the columns were on the same level. "Gods are categorized based on the size of their domain, which dictates their influence and might. This is the balance that needs to be maintained so as not to cause a power vacuum. One which Eurycrius' disappearance had now created."

The memory of him saying those could prove catastrophic hit me with belated understanding. I rechecked the names, finding all celestial gods on the same level as gods of the waters, saltwater for Nerios and freshwater for his wife, Naia, followed by a gap, then Orcus.

"When I refused to take Eurycrius' place, leaving the Throne of Heaven empty for further strife, I angered the Council."

"They can do that? Be angry at you?"

Instead of answering, he held out his hand. I hadn't given him mine since I'd punched him. And I'd been missing his touch so much it was ridiculous how eagerly I reached for it.

He shook his head. "The other one."

This time I hesitated. I was reluctant to let him get a closer look at my "human fragility." But he needed me intact. I needed me intact. I gave him my mangled hand.

The moment he engulfed it between his palms, the pain increased until it was unbearable, as my broken bones twisted and crackled. Just as I thought this was his belated punishment for daring to hit him, the pain vanished.

He removed one hand, kept it in the other, and before my eyes, the swelling receded, the bruising faded back to my tanned olive-tone, and my bones were rearranged..

I'd only thought he'd examine it, then get me healed. I hadn't imagined he'd do it himself. How had he done it? Death could heal?

My swirling thoughts sloshed as his bewitching gaze burned into mine, and his fingers closed around my fully healed hand. My heart rammed against my chest, awaiting the worst.

Then in a solemn voice as fathomless as the Void, he said, "I need you to be my bride, and the Queen of the Underworld."

21

HIERARCHY OF DIVINITY

Whiplash scattered the words tumbling out on my swelling tongue, suddenly too big to fit in my mouth. "Bride say and queen did you?"

Good thing was, he got what I was trying to say. "Yes, you heard me correctly."

"Th-that's my purpose here? You want me to *marry* you?"

And I burst out laughing, hysterically, painfully. I hiccuped and snorted and blubbered.

All the while, Adamantus' brooding eyes dimmed, his mouth thinned, and the sharp angles of his jaw and cheekbones jutted like cut diamonds, emphasizing his inhumanity.

Tears were running down my trembling face, and I was in stitches when he finally dropped my hand. He watched me struggling to bring my fit under control until I straightened, wiping my wet face.

Expression draped in unsettling blankness, he pointed to the scroll. I rushed to look. After I'd just laughed Death in the face, after he apparently proposed to me, I'd better not push my luck. A talon underlined the empty space by his name as Orcus.

"I was told that to maintain that balance, I owed them a new major god. A wife."

The finality of that statement, weighed down by his distaste, made me bristle for some reason. "But you don't want one, evidently."

"Of course not."

"That's why you want me for that role? I'd be easy to get rid of?"

"You will only *pose* as my bride."

"As in, you want them to just *believe* you got married?"

"Exactly."

"And that will keep them satisfied until when? When they notice the power balance hasn't changed at all?"

He rapped his knuckles against the top of the chart. "Until we find your father."

"Then what?"

"Then everything goes back to the way it was." He lifted his hands and the scroll rolled before sinking into the desk. "Eurycrius is reinstated, the death rates even out to their usual causes, and I send you and Chloris back home."

I held off on correcting her name, because his empty eyes unnerved me like never before, and I was still unable to grasp what I'd signed up for.

Mind whirling, my gaze fell on the blank space bordering his name, and I found myself wondering aloud. "How come there has never been a Queen of the Underworld? All major gods and goddesses have had consorts, not to mention countless lovers, but I never heard of any sordid tales involving you."

"If this is a joke, you're going to need to rework it for me to find it funny."

A biting quip about him not having a sense of humor was crushed between my teeth under the weight of his glare. In this new state, I might end up losing the toe I stepped out of line.

"It's not a joke. I was asking why, outside of the Death and the Maiden motif artists are fond of, you have not been known to either bed or wed a woman?"

His nails unsheathed to the length of his fingers, gouging the desk's onyx surface. I removed my fingers lest I lose them. Figure distorting, darkness rose from him, blurring his outline and blocking the window and snuffing the light as he grew to further tower over me.

The shadow of Death covered me. All I could do was stare up at his magnificent horror, all I could see were the blazing cuts of his eyes.

"No one, not even another deity, can stand my presence for longer than they need to." A hand, bone-white now, stuck out of the swirl of darkness, no nail beds, just long fingers that tapered off into lethal tips, pointing at himself. "By just being, I inspire the most horrific sensations and volatile of actions from the living, and no matter what I provide for them, the dead avoid me. And you ask why no woman, human, fairy, nymph or goddess, has been able to come near me, let alone chosen to be here, by my side, for eternity?"

From his reaction, it seemed it was his turn to misunderstand my intent. But whereas I had considered him a man belittling me, he saw a mortal mocking him.

Times like this, it paid to be stubborn as a mule. Whether it was bravery or insanity, I dug my heels into the earth and raised my chin to look at the mass of wrath and torment he'd become. "It's a valid question. People know they'll get burned by the sun god, but Lyceus isn't short of dalliances. How many men and women died horribly because they turned his head?"

"Because no matter the risk of getting burned, people love anything that gives them light, be it the sun, the stars, the moon or lightning," he hissed, voice now a knell of doom that reverberated its desolation within me. "They will venture into the seas, disregarding the risk of drowning, attempt to fly even when they would crash, eat poisonous plants because of their beauty, or pursue beasts to tame or fight. They'll even engage in all manner of war and risk willingly. But when it comes to bypassing all that to meet me directly? Only the troubled or deranged will seek me out."

Did all that mean what I thought it meant?

I let out a shuddering breath, the shocking revelation humming in my bones, and vibrating my insides with disbelief and anticipation.

Mouth so dry, my tongue stuck to the roof of my mouth, I rasped, "You know, if you lost the morbid Horned God facade or the horrific sight I'm looking at now, you'd have far less trouble."

"Meaning?"

"Meaning, if people saw you the way I do, they would willingly dive off cliffs, not to fly or swim, but for a glimpse of you. Myself, I've been debating risking eternal torment for one—under the exasperating layers of your buttoned-up fineries, of course."

A thunderclap burst from within him.

The deafening noise recurred a few more times, each growing shorter and faster.

It sounded like what people heard before lightning struck, stampedes arrived and grounds caved in. Instead of running away, I remained still, too caught up in my thirst for answers to flee.

The noise increased but grew lighter, less dissonant until it shrank into a familiar sound along with his form as he returned to being Adamantus.

It wasn't a furious, chthonic growl, or a warning of impending disaster. What shook his shoulders and bared his teeth was—*laughter*.

The false proposal had dropped my jaw, but what I was witnessing threatened to permanently unhinge it.

I'd conquered many a difficult task, but making the God of the Underworld laugh was not among what I thought I'd accomplish.

But here he was, devastation in humanoid form, laughing at my own suggestive proposal.

And I had never even imagined such beauty as Death laughing.

I was on the verge of swooning, or charging him when he finally sobered, and shook his head. "It's not about the phantasmic form I've been taking the past while. Even when I appeared to them as I am now, I have made battle-hardened heroes shit themselves with a mere glance." The flash of a grin held too much pleasure to be a complaint. "That fact is what most made me suspect you weren't who you appeared to be."

Chagrined that he hadn't addressed my blatant flirtation, I gritted, "And now?"

"I still need an answer for why you seem so undisturbed."

"I don't know. Whatever it is that people feel in your presence, the terror, the helplessness, the finality, I understand, but don't experience."

"So, I'm supposed to believe you have been overlooked by the furious divine, *and* are immune to my effect, by chance?"

"Ask the Fates, they put you in my path."

A cold chuckle crackled past his sharp, pearly teeth. "I would if I could."

"What do you mean? Don't they live here?"

"They do, but you can only speak to them if they want you to." It must have been evident on my face that I needed further details, since he continued, "There is a known entrance to their part of the realm, but if anyone attempts to enter it they'll find themselves looping back to where they started."

I hoped it wasn't Polyope's maze of madness. "Aren't you their king?"

"The Fates answer to no god, but we are at the mercy of their whims as much as anything else."

The way he offered up that fact, with the apathetic sigh of efforts long given up, dipped me into ice-cold realization. Even gods had something they were powerless against. So, where did that leave me in the pecking order? Was I even on it?

I echoed his resigned sigh. "If they arranged our first meeting, there had to be a good reason for it. They couldn't be leading you into a trap using me, of all things!"

"Yes, they could," he said, not missing a beat.

"But how could I be a trap for you?"

"You know why."

I inhaled sharply at the unmistakable heat that enveloped me whole, even when his expression went cold. Had I wanted his acknowledgement of my flirtation? Here it was.

I had literally courted Death. And he was letting me know I had succeeded.

And he wasn't happy about it.

Apprehension should be the dominant emotion now. Everyone knew what happened to mortal women who roused a god's greed.

And this wasn't any god. He wasn't Eurycrius who raped and seduced women daily, it seemed. Or Lyceus who beds women, and men, and anything that breathes for a pastime.

This was Death Incarnate.

And he'd just told me he'd never had a sexual encounter in all of his existence.

So I hadn't either, had resigned myself to my own efforts, and that the only time I'd be with a man would be to have an heir. But I'd had ten years of frustration. He'd had ten millennia, or way more. Even worse, he'd never been in physical contact with anything alive.

I was the first living being to ever touch him.

The pragmatic side of me told me not to pursue something so potentially disastrous. Yet the growing, gambling side I had kept smothered all these years, only offered up reckless, hedonistic urgings.

Eyeing him now, it would be easier to convince myself the sun was red than to deny the raging desire he'd ignited in me, in all of his forms. So, I'd preempt him, take the initiative, to have some semblance of control in this situation.

For the duration of this mission, I would silence the part of me that prioritized everything but my own desires, and indulge myself. If he let me, I wanted to glut myself with him before it ended, and I went back to my world. I had never felt anything like that for any man, and I wasn't wasting my one chance at experiencing the

Adamantus phased through the desk to lean against it, arms crossed, sleeves riding up his sinewy forearms, focus denuding. "How long have you been awake?"

My long, contemplative silence must have given the impression that I was about to crash.

He really couldn't read me at all. Not even the way people read each other's expressions and cues. It would be another thing I'd work on now I seemed to have the time.

For now, I said, "I don't know. What time is it? How do you tell time in this place?"

"By the level of activity in Codeinus' part of the realm. Once the River of Dreams slows and the manifestations of dreams decrease, the 'day' begins."

Codeinus was a figure I'd seen depicted among abstract concepts rather than gods. Always as a floating, lilac being dragging a cloak over fields of poppies. Whether he was the god of sleep and all that came with it, or specifically the god of dreams, differed by account.

"Wait, other gods can have places here?"

"Where do you think Polyope sleeps?"

"You sleep?"

"Fortunately, I would have gone mad a long time ago otherwise." He tapped his fingertips on his forearms, dragging my attention to the way the gemstones caught the firelight, and the taut, defined muscles from the elbow-down. My gums tingled.

"The Nether Court is like any other court. I can't operate a domain in which countless souls, spirits and creatures reside without outsourcing effort. Some are directly reporting to me, such as the psychopomps and the judges. Others like the nymphs report to Polyope. She and Codeinus have their own sub-courts, so to speak, where they can now be the patron god of one of my soul-cities and employ those in it, so I don't have to keep finding ways to keep them busy."

That was a lot more structured than I had even imagined. And to think, from all our information in the living world, it had always been just shadowy, dangerous Orcus, who sat on his dark throne, judging all souls, with only three eternally boring destinations to send them to.

"Psychopomps, judges, archivists, cities, libraries, and lesser gods, and keeping them all neat and running. That's a good system."

"It better be, I've been perfecting it for the Fates know how long," he griped, looking at the window over his shoulder. "And I'm still a long way from done."

"How come no one knows anything about this place?" I asked. "Where did all the misinformation come from?"

"Because I want it that way. It may act as a deterrent. I also don't want it known that I had decided to throw everything away and start from scratch."

"Funny, that's what my ancestors did."

He tilted his head towards me, urging me to continue.

"Just before the collapse of the Campanian Empire, my ancestor had a revelation that made him sell everything and pack up to flee south. His family found so much unused fertile land, bought it for cheap, and spent ages in its reclamation. Three generations down, it all came to fruition, and cities and towns were built around the farms and vineyards, and the title of Master of the Granary was born." I sighed wistfully, homesickness assailing me more than ever. "In time, I'll be the eighth Mistress in a row."

"Likely the only one to truly be the child of a god—though I imagine that explanation lost all credibility. Especially as your stronghold has gotten more valuable over the decades. How long do you think before the greed and jealousy of male usurpers puts that status quo at risk?"

"What?"

"When those who covet your birthright delegitimize it with that worn-out excuse that women shouldn't inherit or rule," he emphasized.

"What are you riling me up for?" I snarled, prickling at the thought of men like Chloë's father. "I worry enough about that."

His smile emerged again, unsettling me in every way. Had I ever wished he'd show a sense of humor? A severe or reserved Adamantus had already fried my restraint. A wicked one? Total annihilation.

"What if I ensure that your bloodline survives, and your claim to the land is secured by divine decree?"

My heart almost kicked me flat on my face. This was exactly what I'd wanted to bargain with him for, before I prioritized my family's and people's survival.

"Why would you do that?"

"So you will in turn ensure my goal is met, no matter the cost."

"I already said I'd do anything."

A worrying gleam danced in his eyes, blue flames flickering, before he waved. "I thought you'd appreciate the extra incentive, but if you'd rather not have it…"

I lunged at him, grabbing his forearms, his cool hardness a balm to my overheated flesh. "No, no. I would certainly rather have it. Definitely. Absolutely. So—what can you do to guarantee my family and people's roots grow deeper?"

His sardonic smile reached his eyes. This was progressing at a dangerous speed. "I can bestow a 'blessing' and you return with gold bars declaring you and your own to be vital to the land. I'll ensure more fertility and health to both land and population to prove your worth."

"How would you do that?"

"By strong-arming the gods of disease to avoid half their usual crops and people, and installing consequences for whoever tries to threaten your way of life, eliminating conspirators in divine-wrath-type deaths." Devious delight crinkled his eyes in anticipation of the fun to be had with unscrupulous mortals. "The hand raised against you will rot with instantaneous gangrene."

"Could I have them locked in pig stalls to be eaten untraceably?" I grinned up at him, remembering Chloë's vile father and brother.

"Whatever you wish." He returned my bloodthirsty smile as he extended his hand, not in offering like before, but to be clasped in binding agreement. "So, Miss Spica, do we have a deal?"

"I thought we had a deal already. You said it was sealed."

"There was nothing to seal then. I was only testing you to see how far you'd go."

"And did I pass your test?"

"You decimated it, and every expectation I ever had. So, Miss Spica, will you be my Queen?"

A quake went through my being at the words. Even when I knew it would be in pretense.

But just pretending with him, for the Fates knew how long, until Eurycrius was found, was beyond anything I had dared dream in my life.

This could go wrong in a thousand ways, all leading to my demise at least, or that and my land's. But without him, I would have been long dead, pointlessly. If I met my end here, one way or another, it would mean my family survived, and our land thrived. For I knew he'd keep his word.

"I will be your Queen, My Liege." I curtsied and fluttered my lashes, to acknowledge the sham status of our agreement, even as my whole being quaked.

He kept his hand extended, and I pressed my palm against his and the long fingers wrapped around mine. He drew me to him until our bodies touched. Crimson-edged, white-hot flames flared to life all over us—then vanished just as suddenly.

"*Now* our deal is sealed."

And now I have truly made a deal with Death. I had to be

insane, since I was deliriously excited to plunge into this role, and into his domain. And if I played my cards right, his bed.

He let me go, slowly, reluctantly. But the moment he stepped away, it was as if the gravity of the situation descended on his shoulders again. Any levity left his expression as he said, "We'll need to plan how to present you to other gods, without risking recognition."

I perked up, fantasies from my pile of repression resurfacing, starting with the desire for mischief. "You mean I might need a secret identity?"

"It's doubtful that you will avoid vicious questioning and suspicion, so it's vital that we create you a doubtless life." Adamantus reached out to tuck a loose ringlet behind my ear, eyes brooding again as his nails scraped up along my cheekbone, releasing sparks like iron on gravel over my skin, and a lightning storm of want in my core. "But the killers will be in the Celestial Court and they cannot suspect who you are. Your form will need to be altered with a disguise simple enough to be maintained. The question is, which part of you is the most distinctive?"

"You tell me. You're the Eventual King, the Receiver of Many, who's seen every face to exist once their eyes shut for good. Who better than you to make the comparison?"

In a flutter of my lashes, he had come dangerously close, violet gaze casting its mesmerizing light on my face.

Talons grazed my jaw as his fingertips reached my chin, up-tilting it. "No other face has ever or would ever warrant this close an inspection, let alone inscribing in my memory."

My blood frothed like sea-foam in a storm, my whims rising and crashing in its waves, my heartbeat the echoing of its thunder. It was no use. I was going to climb and kiss him. I just had to get business out of the way first.

"I have a few ideas that could repel suspicion," I murmured, leaning into him.

"What do you have in mind?"

You. And bedding you. And having you bed me. Come what may.

Out loud I said, "What are my limits?" I couldn't help grinning at the ideas taking shape. "What can I get away with?"

"I'll trust you to know that yourself." Adamantus was so close I could feel his cool breath on my lips. "Get some rest. We'll have much to do when you wake."

"But I haven't sealed our deal yet. You did it your way, now I do it mine."

Before I could leap and take his lips, he shoved me.

I flopped back with a yell and landed on my bed before I could register the portal I'd fallen through.

Either he still suspected me of trying to seduce him, or it was difficult for him, after eons of separateness, to have someone as tactile as I was pawing him at every chance. Even though he seemed helpless to stop touching me, too. Or he could have a whole list of reasons I was too spent to think about now.

Whatever it was, I wouldn't rest until I sated my curiosity for every way he differed from the men who were incomparable to him, the men I would never want, and my insatiability for that being like no other.

I was not going to masquerade as Death's bride, without getting all I could from my pretend-infernal husband.

BRIDE OF DEATH

If I must die,
I will encounter darkness as a bride,
And hug it in mine arms.

William Shakespeare, *Measure For Measure*

22

BEHIND THE CURTAIN

An hour away from debuting as the Bride of Death, I wasn't complete.

I had yet to choose what to wear for my meeting with the gods.

A week ago, that statement would have made me roll on the ground with laughter. Today, it was my reality. Death was looming over my shoulder, waiting patiently for me to finish so he'd take me to Anactoron, to present me to the Council of Gods as his bride.

I wasn't ready. Neither in an emotional nor practical sense.

But I couldn't afford to succumb to anxiety, had to focus on what I could do something about. Hence, my ongoing quest for the gown to suit the momentous occasion.

If I couldn't find one in his vault of miraculous apparel it would be my fault. He'd given me free rein to choose whatever I wanted for my role. But the souls who'd made them, spurred on by their new lack of limitations, had indulged their imaginations too much. The garments were more art-pieces than gowns. But I was determined to enjoy this for what it was, starting with my disguise. Right after I found the perfect gown.

Polyope had chosen what I was wearing now, a flowing satin

dress in blacks and greys. But that would suit one of her priestesses. Today I was here as the future Goddess of the Underworld. That, and the shapeless thing did me no favors.

Grimacing at my reflection, I told him that. At once, he said he'd choose something, and his reflection behind me receded.

My gaze clung to his image, one hand in his black pants pocket, the other holding the etched glass fracturing the nightwine's glow. His inky hair had been parted over his left eye, sharpening his angular profile. His preferred attire of modern, three-piece formalwear, what always ended up with the coat discarded, had been traded for a long spider-silk coat with embroidered shoulders. All in purples, of course.

The styling made him appear colder somehow, the approachable touches of messy curls cascading past his shoulders, and rolled-up sleeves gone. And it only made him hotter.

Groaning, I tore my gaze away and turned to inspect my new reflection once more.

Even with the minor alterations, I looked unrecognizable. My hair had been darkened from the sun-streaked blonde of an aging goldenrod to the cool, lustrous brown of brewed coffee. It also now fell past my waist in loose waves, having been unfurled from the usual frizzing curls. The other small yet impactful change were my eyes, now mirroring the blue-amber of the charm Polyope had given me to lock the illusion.

I tapped at the choker that held it, too unused to jewelry of any kind, let alone a large gem against my throat. "Is it too late to ask for horns?"

"What creature are you supposed to be again?" Adamantus answered, his voice not raised like mine, but felt as if it had poured into my ear.

"We could say they're a trait I developed in my tenure as Polyope's priestess."

"Is that known to happen, clergy being mutated by their patron gods?" he said as he strolled among the modeling sculptures.

I snorted a laugh. "Never thought of it as a mutation."

"What else would you call it?"

"A blessing."

The idea must have entertained him, as he chuckled. "Horns would be a blessing?"

"You're the last person to disapprove of the idea, Your Infernal Majesty, the Horned God."

"I'm not a person." Whether this bristly insistence was born of superiority or semantics, I had no chance to object before he added, "And infernal is also inaccurate. Only one part of the Underworld is on fire."

"Many people, especially in the east, think it's one eternal blaze."

"Yes, a good method for keeping children in line is to tell them I'll be stoking them over hot coals. Which I do, if only when they grow up into criminals, and only in the Spiral." He returned with something my own reflection blocked. "This would be a perfect choice."

I turned, and almost gasped. A waterfall of molten gold seemed to pour continuously from his offered hand.

It was the dress I'd sighed over the first time I'd been here. This priceless creation queens or sorceresses couldn't dream of touching, let alone swanning about in.

"Not to your liking?" he asked.

I shook my head, eager to accept that marvel. I did gasp at the sensation, cool, impossibly smooth and undulating down in soothing loops, but never once disturbing its imperial design or the details along the plunging neckline.

"Put it on," he urged.

I contemplated doing so on the spot, but I wasn't wasting the first time I undressed before him on a dress fitting in the middle of his divine wardrobe.

I went behind one of the sculptures, but the material was almost alive, slithering out of my hands, making it impossible to bunch it up to slip over my head. I would have tried harder if I hadn't already decided it was too tame for the occasion.

I came around and handed it back. "It's breathtaking, but still not right…"

Just then, a glittering column of vivid, sapphire-blue behind him called to me.

I ran to it, a clinging creation totally worked in gems, with no back and a net waist of alternating, triangular gaps, all held up by sheer straps that crossed at the neck. This made a bold statement. I snatched it off its sculpture and bolted around it.

With it on, I thought it maybe too bold. It showed a major cleavage, and backless design plunged low over my buttocks.

But the future of my land depended on this ruse succeeding. And if I was meant to pull the wool over the searing eyes of the divine, the first impression needed to be indelible. I had to look the part of the perfect foil for the God of the Underworld, the vibrancy to his darkness, the disinhibition to his control. And in the gown, I looked exactly that.

When I came out, Adamantus's gaze devoured me whole.

But he said nothing until we got back to his office, then rumbled, "I still think the gold one was better."

"It might have rusted if I wore it," I joked.

"Self-deprecation doesn't suit you." His glower told me I was testing his patience. "And gold doesn't rust, that's half the reason it's precious."

"What's the other half?"

In a blink he was a foot away, tantalizingly dragging his tongue over his pearly teeth.

To keep my wits about me, I tried to remember what those were capable of. It didn't work. All I could imagine was them nibbling my most tender flesh.

Clamping down on the untimely images, I laughed. "You eat it!"

His lips took on a smug tilt. "Yes."

"Unbelievable. What are you, a dragon?"

"Judging by your desire for horns, I assume that's an envious comparison."

"In some cultures he is a dragon!"

I whirled around at the gleeful voice, found Polyope emerging from one of her blackwater pools that served as her portals. Her skin looked like polished moonstone, and her hair midnight arranged in a crescent behind her head, like the horns of her torchbearers.

She was wearing another charcoal dress that undulated with her every move, while a matching sparkling cape was fused to silver bracelets, so when she raised her arms to greet us she invoked a gigantic bat.

"Why are you still here, Adamantus? You're late. And I told you I'd bring her once you broke the news."

"The gods can wait." He refilled his glass, and sipped calmly. "And I need to be certain everything is in order before I make my entrance. Have you both gotten your story straight?"

"Down to the letter." I worried my bottom lip. "I just hope the gods will buy it that you married a mortal."

"It isn't unheard of for gods to marry mortals that they deify upon death, or demigods spawned by someone else." I could see the amused smirk behind the glass. "Though, our newest god has made an interesting choice in his partner. But he's a unique case, and so is his wife." He gestured with his glass to the liquor cabinet behind him filled with fantastical bottles. "These were a gift from him, for looking the other way while he took his girl out of my river."

"He made the bottles or what's inside them?"

"Both, I believe. Theoneus was deified as the god of inebriation, madness and transformative experiences, if not transformation as a whole. I've been told his presence is almost as unsettling as my own, that he can drive people mad just by smiling at them."

That sounded a tad less horrific than making them eat their faces.

"Causing madness is fun, experiencing it not so much, right Cora?" Polyope wiggled her eyebrows at me. "Which has me wondering how his girl enjoys him."

"Aristagnë is no mere girl," Adamantus reminded her. "Otherwise she wouldn't have held his interest, and you wouldn't have tried to pawn her for yourself."

"Then what is she?" I asked.

He downed the last of his drink, what he still wouldn't let me sample. "A sea monster."

I recalled the Hierarchy of Divinity, where Aristagnë was symbolized by an octopus. "What kind?"

"The kind that had to pretend to be human. The last time I saw them was when the Council of Gods were gathered like today. But they were voting on making her a minor goddess. Many voted against her."

"But not you?"

"It was my vote that broke the tie. I thought it'd be idiotic to refuse him a reasonable request. Not when he's not above driving whole cities insane out of spite, and ruining my statistics by skyrocketing the rates of slaughter and suicide."

I coughed a laugh. "For a moment there I thought you were championing true love. Phew."

"I do what needs to be done, unlike the other gods who let their whims guide them. In this case, I got something quite novel to me. Gratitude." He showed me a large black pearl ring on his left small finger. "This was among the gifts she sent upon her veneration as Goddess of the Unseen Deep."

"What were the others?"

"Some of my newest installations in the Lifetime Library, such as a giant starfish, and ruins from a long-sunken city. As well as some things that aren't as easy to display."

"Like what?"

"The fossilized remains of a giant squid locked in battle with a gargantuan shark."

"Ugh. Why would they consider those gifts?"

"Theoneus and his wife share what I've been told is a 'sick sense of humor.'"

"You don't think it is?"

He frowned in brief consideration. "I don't know if I can judge what a sense of humor is."

"Because dead men tell no jokes and you're surrounded by them?"

I winced at my thoughtless quip when he said, "Because I've never been in a situation welcoming enough to foster it."

Sympathy flooded my chest. No one had ever wanted to see him, not even those who suffered through drawn-out deaths. No flesh-and-blood creature would come near him, except the perverts who killed in his name if he gave them the chance. They were humorless monsters, anyway.

I grabbed his forearm. "You do have a sense of humor, a wicked one. Take it from me."

His eyes, which had been almost human the past few days, flashed. "You'll have to explain this fully—later."

"Save the newlywed simpering for the Council of Blowhards." Polyope reminded us of her large presence. "Go on then. We'll be right behind you."

Adamantus retrieved the bident he'd leaned on a sculpture before leveling her with a withering glare that made temperature plummet. "If you do anything to disrupt how this needs to go, I will lock you out for the next age. Am I clear?"

"Try having a little faith in someone else for a change," she tutted, petting my head like I was a cat. "And do make Eglaia claw at the walls, for me?"

"I always do, but certainly not for you." His descent into the black pool was joined by a seamless shift back to his alternate form. The last to dip into darkness were the Horned God's antlers.

Why would he keep that form among the gods?

23

THROUGH THE MIRROR

Polyope steered me beyond the entrance of her domain, sliding my heels over the pitch-black ground, and towards another bone stairway.

I had been bombarding her with questions ever since she transported me here. She had been answering in her strange way. But I'd been gleaning information nonetheless.

"And what did you mean by Adamantus..."

Her nails dug into my arm, almost breaking skin. "Dear, never mention that name in front of anyone. He is Orcus to everyone."

Ugh. He'd already told me that. I had to be more careful. "Yes, of course. So why does he make Eglaia uncomfortable?"

"The divine despise those who resist them, and dread those who are immune to them. It will be easier to explain once you see her for yourself."

See her. Gods above and below—and around. I was going to be surrounded by them!

If I'd been nervous before, now I was starting to feel like the side character in a tragedy. I could just see it. A hundred years from now, some tone-deaf mistress of a composer would play an infinitely stupid take on my role, what would undoubtably end in being incinerated by a god's wrath.

Belated stress swirled within me, combining the broken bodies of my lookalikes, all the near-death experiences I'd amassed within less than ten days, and the absolute—otherness that Polyope, and even Adamantus, had shown me. Sometimes, when I was in bed, and I realized again where I was, who Adamantus was...

Adamantus. When he was around, he affected me like a siren song. In his presence, I could take all this in my stride. I could only see the reality of this terrifying situation when I left his side.

When I'd said that, he'd thought I was only talking about meeting the gods, had told me to be myself. He'd meant fearless like I'd been with him. But those gods weren't him.

It was far too late to get cold feet. One crack in my facade would have all the lurking predators leaping at the chance to gouge my neck. Not mere opportunists, bruised egos and blood-thirsty beasts. Gods. What we all revered and feared. Who could annihilate me with a snap of their fingers if I angered them. And many would no doubt despise me on principle.

There was nothing to do but forget my human sensibilities and limitations completely, and behave with all the swagger of my character, and the entitlement of the Bride of Death.

Now all I had to do was pull this off.

Throughout the climb, I debated the likelihood of leaving the Underworld bearing Adamantus's gifts to my people, with minimal damage. I had decided the odds were slim by the time the lampades met us atop the first flight, holding unlit torches.

Focusing on my breathing, I slowed my ascent as the nymphs dispersed around us.

The last to leave was Chloë. She lifted the veil of a Silver Sister and caught my hand between hers fervently. "Be careful."

I pulled her into a fierce hug. "Don't worry about me. Just

contact our mothers, at least tell mine where I am before winter hits, if it hasn't already."

Reluctant to let go, she addressed Polyope while avoiding her. "You have a cult in our city, we met a priestess of yours. It shouldn't turn too many heads if another returns to meet the Mistress of the Granary. I can talk to her then."

Adamantus had done what he'd said he'd do. But he'd also insisted if Chloë returned home, after we'd both been presumed dead, the killer gods would suspect they'd been duped, and she'd be in danger all over again.

"Until this issue is dealt with, Cassia Granturco is my mother's heir, *not your brother.*" I grabbed her hand, her quaking infecting me. "No matter what, hide until this over...don't come back here without your body, all right?"

She nodded shakily, then with a cry, jumped to hang around my neck, burying her streaming face in my chest. My eyes were stinging, and I was clinging back to her when one of the Lampades came to pull her away. Slipping through my fingers, she retreated with unsteady feet and trembling lips with the lampades to where Polyope's followers would keep her safe.

I bit my lip over the need to snatch her back, or find a way to follow them, and escape the Underworld. Even if I could, I had no idea what Adamantus would do if I reneged on our deal. I didn't want to imagine it.

But there was no escape for me. Now I needed to see this through.

I couldn't be more ready, anyway. In the past days, after we'd learned Chloë would be sent off to pose as an acolyte, we'd finalized the identity of Death's Bride. Polyope had encouraged us to be creative, but within reason. I needed to make sense, both in regards to being her priestess, and to how my "engagement" to Adamantus came to be.

While the persona we'd created pushed a little beyond the limits, one thing I'd learned as the object of speculation and censure, was that people asked far less questions if you were too strange, or unsettling. They usually filled any gaps with worst assumptions, and left me alone. I hoped it would be the same with gods.

We arrived at a towering, three-paned mirror, the tallest in the center and reflecting a layout I couldn't see behind me.

Here Polyope granted me water buffalo-like horns, and wrapped my now-dark hair around them like they were sharp, curving side-buns. It gave me a silhouette that resembled her horned nymphs, and the crescentic curve crowning her.

I finally took the first full look at myself. What I saw before me was the last thing I'd ever expected I'd one day look like. Apart from the changes, I looked—outrageous. Gone was Cora Spica who spent her life in pants and shirts, sweaty and unkempt, and in her place was the Bride of Death, sophisticated and savage.

The sapphire dress cascaded with sparkles with my least movement, and the gaps at my waist nipped it, widening my hips even more, while the crossed straps hoisted my breasts up into a generous cleavage. Diamond-studded sandals added six inches to my height, making me almost seven feet. Last touches were silver lines that enveloped my eyelids and extended in wings, and dark-blue lipstick, matching Adamantus's lips.

Then I noticed that I remained in the center mirror, but Polyope appeared in all three, second and third forms facing sideways. I could only wonder what those versions of her saw or did, if they were manifestations of her or if what spoke to me was a combined personality of all three. And if they were really three entities, I didn't even want to know how they came to be fused. Or how it felt to live trapped within someone else's body.

It was not the best time to ponder those gut-churning beings when I had to deal with far more of them.

Matching grins appeared from different angles, and three voices chorused, "Ready to dive into the deep?"

"Haven't I already done so?"

The central form unfolded the spiderwebbed veil over my

face. "Darling, you've only scraped the surface of our existence. As for—Orcus, you've seen nothing of what he's capable of, can't imagine the power he wields. You better be careful with that one, dear. "

Seizing the opportunity, I asked, "Has he always been like that?"

"Like what?"

"So…" I dug around for a proper description. "I don't know, stoic? Detached?" Even if he wasn't with me, he seemed separate from everything and everyone. And I felt it had nothing with what he'd told me, about any being fearing him. There were workarounds if he'd really wanted to have connections. "I would chalk it up to him being a god, but the world has no shortage of gods that express everything from rage to base urges." I pointed to her with my unlit torch. "Like you! I can't believe I'm saying this, but you're much more—personable, somehow."

Polyope's tripled voice cackled in an eerie harmony. "You're thinking about him in the wrong way."

"And what is the right way to think of him?"

"Unlike any humanoid being you've encountered, even myself."

I already thought of him in ways unlike anyone or anything, bewitched by his stark strangeness and the quiet danger he embodied as conscious death.

"I've existed for eons, interacted with people of all sorts long before my fall from favor. He has never had that." Against reason, and positioning, three pairs of hands were set on my head, shoulders, and waist, a contortion that unlocked a visceral unease I could do without right now. "I know how to behave, and I do have senses and feelings that were given to mortals at their inception, because I predate you."

I suppressed shudders at the sight of her fractured form. "And death doesn't predate the rise of humanity and its offshoots like the fey and whatnot?"

"It does. He doesn't."

"That makes no sense."

The middle head flew back in thunderous amusement. "You're still not getting it."

"Then explain it better."

The mirror-glass distorted softly, liquifying like the silvery surface of a moonlit lake, and I saw past our reflections. Glimpses of what awaited me, bright and beautiful figures strolled into view, all gathering to the center.

The gods were arriving.

"He isn't a person, he's a *personification*," she said callously. "Entities like him can't be expected to behave like those who were, at their conception, people detached from their purpose."

That was an uncomfortably familiar sentiment, considering I was born to fulfill a purpose. "Oh."

"Mhm." Polyope patted my back with four hands. "Keep that in mind when you're around him, dear."

"I assure you, I need no reminding of who brought me here."

"Not who, what," she emphasized. "You need to understand that he's not a man, he just looks like one."

Invisible, iron knuckles punched me between the breasts, making it painful to breathe in.

"Looks like most of them have arrived." Polyope blithely pointed with three hands, as if she hadn't just made me doubt everything, starting by my very senses.

Shaking off this latest blow, I stared ahead, found the mirror had become more of a window, showing the space they mingled in.

"Are you ready to make your entrance?"

Gritting my teeth, I nodded. "As I'll ever be."

Exhaling, I raised the torch. It burst into flames as I crossed the threshold and passed through the mirror and into Anactoron, the realm of gods.

24

THE CELESTIAL COURT

Paths stretched into the unfocused distance, and my surroundings were a blur of sound and color that splintered into vibrant sources, attaining more detail as I ventured further in.

As if encased in a glass orb, the haziness around me was shattered by a sudden increase in pressure. The smothering overlay scattered into all directions, and unveiled the overwhelming setting I had stepped into.

Walls of jaw-dropping, neck-breaking scale enclosed the curving space, made of living mother-of-pearl that swirled softly like condensed daybreak clouds. No matter how hard I looked, I couldn't make out a ceiling, just the clearest patch of night sky. A view not even the highest mountain peak could have afforded me.

As we progressed inside, entire sections disappeared and others appeared, taking and bringing mile-high doors and columns with them. Approximating it with the grandiose homes of the mortal elite, I gathered this was just the foyer, especially when a hallway yawned open, its arch sharpening as we closed in on it.

"Is this it?" I whispered. The floor I treaded changed hue and pattern with each footfall, like stepping into a still lake and disrupting its reflection of the sky.

"It's what your little eyes can perceive," said all three of her heads.

"Can you...describe what you see to me?"

All three of her laughed fondly, like I had done something stupidly quaint. A dog barking at a stuffed animal.

As we passed beneath the arch, I tried to gather my wits before we emerged.

Not that it would have mattered. Neither did it matter if I had nerves of steel. The sensations that swarmed me as I entered the gathering of the gods had them crumbling like sandstone.

Pillars of frozen light held the imperceptible roof and the open levels whose balconies overspilled into waterfalls of flowing, glassy material. The base structures were made of the same living nacre that greeted us, and structures grew up from it. Tables packed with foods both familiar and strange, fountains of wine like the nightwine in Blackglass Hall and statues that morphed before my eyes from one shape and pose to another.

Further in, my perspective tilted until I could inexplicably see too far, then in a blink I was looking down another waterfall, but it was one that gushed off the edge and into nothingness.

The realm of heaven overlooked a knee-buckling view of the world of mortals below, far smaller and smoother than what I'd glimpsed while freezing atop a pegasus. It threatened to make the adjusted breakfast Adamantus had sent us come back out, and made my head swim, ready to tip me over to land headfirst into the Deep Red Sea.

Polyope dragged me away and we walked deeper until, past a certain point, the veil of limitation lifted, and the cause of this escalating pressure appeared one by one in snaps of fractured light.

God by god took form before my overworked eyes, like they had each gone through a prism and reassembled in varying combinations of color and brightness. It went on until the sheer amount of them had me bug-eyed and curve-backed like a scared cat.

"I can't do this," I wheezed, recognizing just one so far based on iconography alone. "I didn't think—I didn't know —Adamantus—"

"Isn't here," Polyope chorused, a clash of tones with each mouth voicing a different reaction; shock, anger and concern.

Attention scattered, I didn't make note of those approaching us until they were too close to ignore, their edges blurred, details and distinctions lost to the strengthening glow and the effects of its heat.

One bright piece separated itself from the vibrant mass, and took the distinct form of a woman, gaining more details as she approached.

"Feeling brave today, Polyope?"

A wall painting come to life, the Holy Mother herself, Queen of Heaven stood before me. Almagera's short cylindrical crown sat on dark-green ringlets, her bright skin the yellow of a ripening lemon, and her gown layers of peacock feathers.

It was hard not to be awed by her presence, as her influence meant so much to my people, a beacon of comfort and plenty. Except the hostility she greeted us with was nothing like the serene, motherly image I'd grown accustomed to.

The other gods that materialized were no better. They all regarded me like I was a centipede they caught scurrying too close to their toes, with irritation at best and revulsion at worst. It was hard to tell if this was due to my unwelcome mortal presence, or if it was specifically due to my getup, that Polyope's worshippers were just as reviled here as they were in the world below.

I decided to go with the former. "If you're all this put-off by mortals, then why do you like going out of your way to fuck us so much?"

A laugh cracked the heated silence, diffusing the tension long enough for me to breathe out the trapped air in my chest.

Several deities practically leaped out of the way for the one making her way through, and I felt the shift in power before she stepped forward. "I never understood that mindset. I enjoy my mortal men, even when they make the chase tedious, and I have no problem admitting that."

Nine-feet tall, with a mass of glowing curls in shades of luminescent white at the roots and growing out in silver and steel-blue ringlets, the goddess had vibrant cerulean skin and white, round eyes. She stood draped in a one-shouldered, high-waisted white gown that wholly glittered like crystalized snow. Most of all, she had a halo!

The ring of moonlight encased her hair, intensity matching her pale eyes, monochrome until she looked down at me, irises and pupils shades of blue-grey.

I'd never been the best worshipper, save for going through the holidays, rituals and functions required of us, and those partaken in for fun. Neither apathy nor disinterest was to be found while I gaped up at her, struck dumb by her simultaneously intense yet enticing aura.

Others were hard to look at, but her I could gaze at until I forgot everything that had ever bothered me.

"You're the Moon," I realized with childlike glee. "Hello."

Telephassa beamed down at me. "Polyope, what's one of your little bats doing here?"

"Yes," Almagera said venomously. "What nerve do you have showing up now and bringing one of your demented witches? Is she going to do tricks for us or use one of your paths to find *him?*"

An armored being joined us, his hair and beard the color of dried blood, his ruddy skin the warning glow of red-hot pokers. "She's not here to help, she's here to gloat." Machaius, god of war and the forge, unsheathed a sword so sharp its edges could split hairs. "Maybe if we mangle her bat-bitch she'll remember to piss off."

"Touch her, and you'll feel every death I've collected under your name," the Horned God's deep, menacingly cool voice thrummed through the room.

The crowd parted with forceful speed and scattered like a broken chain-link. As if wrenched apart, they all made way for the living ink-splatter that was Adamantus's aura, the smokey tendrils encasing him like the starless night did the moon.

Here he was, the universal image set to heed warnings and beware danger. The morbid combination of a giant skeletal monster whose very presence distorted its surroundings, and the sharp outlines of unstoppable power, striking obvious unease into other deities.

No matter the brightness of heaven's courtiers, and the beloved and revered aspects they embodied for life back home, I wanted to avoid them all and cling to him like a limpet.

Two feet taller than usual, Adamantus approached with the menacing hum that rose with his anger, loud enough to hurt my ears. His head was now a helmeted version of the demonic stag skull, the antlers ending in knife-sharp points.

His presence seemed to absorb the sickening amounts of radiation they emitted, because my drowsiness lifted, making it easier to process the situation. Namely that Polyope was as unwelcome among most gods as she was among most mortals, and that distaste had extended towards me now for daring to prioritize her.

This was going to end with them all using my head as a kick-ball, and there was nothing I could do to stop it.

Would being blasted out of existence by an angry god count as dying in a blaze of glory?

For now, they all gave us a wide berth as Adamantus pulled me to his side, the grip of his large hand spanning from my waist to my hip. I'd never been touched this intimately, yet instead of winding me up further, I felt myself relax, ready to stick my sweating self to him in the hopes that I'd disappear.

"Orcus, what is this?" Almagera demanded.

"What does it look like?" Polyope snapped in threefold. "I

did what none of you bothered to do. I found him what we need to maintain the power balance until Eurycrius is found."

Telephassa's white brows rose as she let out a disbelieving laugh. "Are you telling me that this entire time you could have done something about this and didn't?"

"It's probably because she was hoping he'd pick her, so she could usurp him afterwards," someone shouted from the back.

The shadow of Polyope's three-pronged top rose over us. "That's the last thing I want, and you know it."

Sending her a smirk of disbelief, Telephassa then bent over, hands on her knees to reach my level, and whispered, "Are you being blackmailed or bewitched? Give me a signal and I'll get you out of here safely."

Everyone really believed no woman would come near him of her own free will. But then until me, that had always been the case.

My arms found their way around Adamantus, reassuring him otherwise, clinging to the safety of his familiarity, the neutralizing effect he had on the others' overpowering presence, as well as selling our announcement.

Waves of shock passed over our spectators, going from being disdainful of my presence alongside Polyope, to giving me their full, stunned attention. They didn't need clear faces to express, they projected their feelings just as they did their power.

It wasn't every day I made powerful beings question their own eyes. Inspiring that was enough to anchor me to the moment and the mission—and get back at those who'd instantly wished me harm.

"Impossible to care about blackmail or be bewitched for a seasoned practitioner of black magic such as myself," I said, smiling at Telephassa.

Emerging from the side, instantly recognizable from the white-hot curls and sunshine skin, his details and outlines drawn in bright white, Lyceus the sun god mirrored Telephassa. "So, you expect us to believe you're here willingly?"

"Why wouldn't I be?"

To say he was stunning would be an understatement. Aside from him truly exuding the heat and brilliance of sunlight, his face was arranged in the golden ratio of obsessive artists dedicated to him. Lyceus's smile spread easily into a smarmy smirk and I saw just enough of him in the skintight clothes to count his muscles.

Standing before the gods of the sun and the moon, I now understood why women and men leaped off the deep end, foolishly thinking they'd jumped high enough to grasp at what lit up our lives. Whatever happened when they landed didn't matter, just getting to experience their attention, let alone their desire, their favor, or even their love, would be worth it.

What was I thinking? What was this place doing to me?

Lyceus heightened how small I felt, bending to look down at me condescendingly. "What could you possibly be getting out of this?"

When Adamantus clutched my hip, I knew I had to do it now. Shatter all restraint, all intimidation and fear, and become the character I was playing.

Locking gazes with Lyceus through the sheer veil, I dragged my palm down the front of Adamantus's coat, from his collarbone to his crotch, feeling him hard and long beneath my sweaty grip.

"Don't tell me you're not dying to know what's under all this." I leered at Lyceus. "I know I am."

Adamantus's fingers spasmed over my buttock, and that low grumble vibrated out of his skull, coating me in gooseflesh, and sending liquid heat rushing between my thighs.

I couldn't believe it. Here I was, among gods, *hostile* gods, and not even that was extinguishing the arousal he ignited within me.

"You do realize that he goes around looking like this for a reason." Lyceus gestured to Adamantus's head. "You really don't want to know what might be under there. He could have a spiked club between his legs for all you know."

"And that's a bad thing?" I looked up at Adamantus, the maddened urge making it even easier to step into the flesh of my character as I rubbed against him, none of it an act. "If this is why you still insist on waiting till our marriage-bed, then I promise you I can't wait to see, and touch and taste—all you've got."

"Is that so?" he finally spoke, when he'd been content to observe so far, clasping me to his side harder, his rumble deep and devastating.

I reached up for his helmeted skull and antlers, caressed them like that first day. But this time I wasn't exploring, I was pleasuring myself and servicing him. "I went out of my way to qualify as a priestess for Polyope, made my way up the ranks to have access to the darkest of magic so I can find a way to summon and seduce you, and you think I'll give up now?"

As Adamantus lifted me off the floor, to bring me closer to my sensual task, Lyceus's grin shattered.

Telephassa laughed again. "By all the stars in the sky, it sure looks like everyone's efforts were pointless."

"What do you mean?" Polyope asked, just as Almagera and another woman yelled objections.

"You think we're just going to approve deifying that piece of deranged trash Polyope brought you?" Machaius shouted and Adamantus put me down on my feet as his shadows pulsed and his bident sparked. It was amazing how the most vicious of gods balked, a whine tingeing his tone when he added, "Not without a fair effort from everyone involved."

Adamantus maintained his deadly, detached air. "Involved in what?"

"You told us the last time you were here to choose brides for you, and we have done so." A goddess appeared by Machaius. At first I couldn't quite see what she looked like. Not because of the emanating power straining my human eyes, but from how fast and seamless her shifting appearances were.

As she approached, she developed definite features, hair

growing large, dark waves of dark-blue, cheekbones high and sharp, body the hearty shape of well-fed and active women back home, and eyes turning violet—

Eglaia. It had to be her. The goddess of desire seemed to be she reflecting the only features I'd grown enamored with.

"There is no more need for your suitors, as I have chosen my bride," Adamantus said, voice now ominous.

"Not without consulting the rest of us!" Eglaia's offense roused shouts of agreement from the rest. "We're picking a new major god. One who will have crucial influence and power to keep us balanced, and you will honor the gravity of this situation by choosing one of them."

This meeting had turned from an announcement of the woman who'd accepted Death's proposal, and a chance to ogle and malign her, to an ambush with rival brides.

I could think of only one feasible way out of this.

"Why not make this fun for everyone?" I said, loud enough for everyone to hear. "Bring out your candidates and have them compete against me for his hand, if they dare."

25

PROSPERA OF MEROPIS

Antlered and expressionless as his head was, I could sense one emotion above all others exuding from Adamantus. Concern?

That must be the closest thing he could feel to anxiety, about his plan not going as planned.

This mission had hinged on their belief that they were misdirecting him from investigating their king's disappearance. If they had accepted me as his bride, he would have been expected to be distracted by his new wife and the process of deifying her, for the time needed to erase their tracks or bury evidence.

But if their collective chose a bride, they might force her on Adamantus, and it would be them who distracted him, and planted a real spy in the Underworld. He might never find Eurycrius, or find out which gods mass murdered my kind.

He needed to examine each major player in the fate of the world, while they were distracted. How better to achieve that, than making them focus on having their chosen brides become his queen?

When my offer got no response beyond blank stares, I gave them a nudge.

"That's what I thought," I said, forcing my voice steady, and injecting it with maximum provocation. "If that's all, then we'll be on our way."

As he turned us both away, I could have sworn I heard an amused huff come from Adamantus.

"Where do you think you're going?" Eglaia demanded, having acquired more detailed features, long, pale fingers, sharp, dark nails, blued lips and eyelids that accentuated the piercing violet of her irises.

"To continue my tour of the Underworld." I bowed only to Telephassa, aiming to rile up the other goddesses. "It was an experience being in your presence. I can't say the same for everyone else."

Telephassa's dazzling smile grew further. "I never thought I'd say this, but, good job, Polyope."

Oh, to go home and say "I had the Moon's blessing to marry Death", and that it wasn't a metaphor of any sort.

I snuck a glance at Polyope and found her faces all set in a neutral stare. "I didn't realize I needed your approval on anything."

Something above my perception was exchanged between them, raising the pressure in the air to suffocating levels. Any higher and I would start leaking like a squeezed tomato.

Out of line or not, I disregarded whatever protocols applied to Polyope's underlings when I tugged on her shapeless gown. "As fun as this has been, I'd like to leave before the brightness here turns my eyes into boiled eggs."

A shrill noise tightened the hinges of my jaw so hard, I almost ground my own teeth to dust. The sharp, trailing end of a screech magnified and its bass pressurized my flesh.

"*No!*"

Fingers spastic over the lapels of Adamantus's coat I watched with a booming heart as Eglaia leapt out of her previous form, towering over by six feet, all of her the shades of a pink dahlia.

"Have mortals stopped warning their children against hubris?" she raged, her voice like waves crashing against me, body and mind. "Or do you really want to see how I can punish your gall?"

It was too tempting to mouth off to someone like her. And witnessing the effect I inspired emboldened me further.

Adamantus dug his nails into my hip bone as I stepped away. "What are you doing?"

"One of the few joys I had on earth—fucking with the elite," I murmured, before Eglaia got my full volume in goading abandon. "Aww, what are you going to do? Make me fall in mad lust with a merman and drown myself for him?"

"I'll do far worse than that, you hideous roach!" Blindingly bright, she lunged for me, arm raised, clawed hand as large as my torso.

Before it came down and hacked me to pieces, Adamantus's bident shot forward with a rupturing speed. Its prongs stabbed right beneath Eglaia's collarbones. As she shrieked, he waved, and the bident slammed her down, impaling her to the strange medium of the ground..

As she screeched loud enough to bring down the heavens, she morphed through dozens of forms. But resisting was a mistake. Her attempts to phase through the metal only pinned her harder. And it wasn't only that. Shadows started to slither beneath her skin, to wrap around her throat until they started to bleed from her eyes and belch from her mouth. It was then I realized his bident must be a manifestation or conduit of Adamantus's power. The power I could now feel pulsating ominously.

Heavy, muffled pounding filled the room, like the floor concealed a gargantuan heart. Shrinking, Eglaia retched to its beat, her vibrancy dulling, body blurring between colors and shapes until they began to cancel each other out.

"Did you not hear me?" Adamantus said calmly as his power literally rocked Anactoron. "Touch her and you feel all the agony that has been wrought in your name."

Vicious satisfaction rushed through me as I watched the

goddess who intended to shred me gag and heave. Even if it wasn't a feat of my own strength, it was done for me.

With a tranquil flick of his fingers, Adamantus ripped the bident out of her, leaving her to collapse and Machaius to rush to her side. Just as the thought of revenge seemed to cross his burning-red face, the warning glint of the prongs in Lyceus's light made him back down.

Polyope brought all six of her hands together in a jarring clap. "Any other objections?"

Almagera, keeping her distance still, reiterated, "Yes, the suitors we chose for him, who are no doubt better and more trustworthy options than whatever this..." she trailed off, eyeing me. "What are you?"

Seizing the moment for my dramatic reveal, I lifted my veil, showcasing the silver eyeliner, navy lipstick, hair-wrapped buffalo horns, and winked up at them. "I'm Prospera of Meropis, and I must say meeting you all has been a displeasure."

There was something bizarrely pleasing about how much Machaius looked ready to backhand me through a wall. "Is there a shortage of sense as well as tact in your homeland?"

I gave a spectacular snort. "If you were the basis for sense and tact then the empires that prioritized you would still be here."

"Careful," Adamantus grumbled for my ears only. "His temper is as bad as his wife's, he might try something stupid."

"So, you're saying I can easily goad him into stabbing himself on your staff?"

If he were anyone else, I would have sworn I heard him stifle a laugh.

"Is this situation a joke to you, Orcus?" Almagera said viciously. "My husband—the King of Heaven!—is missing. You refused to act as his regent, and when we ask you to substitute that slight by choosing a queen, you don't even consult us?"

"A joke?" he hummed distractedly. "I wasn't aware I had a sense of humor."

That made her bristle. "Since the one you chose volunteered, you will be presented with our offered brides. And for it to be fair, they will compete for your hand."

I shrugged. "It's their funeral. Literally. I've caused enough deaths worth inspecting to get a glimpse at him. Anyone who hasn't put in the blood, sweat and tears of others into this effort has no business claiming him!"

"Oh, I see what this is," Lyceus said knowingly, addressing Polyope. "She's insane."

"Is that your excuse for everything these days, Lyceus?"

Ignoring only gestured at her tripled form. "What did you do to her? Did you wait until she was desperate for her prayers to be answered, then appeared to her like *that*?"

Everyone's reactions to Polyope had me overrun with curiosity. Was it because she was the favored god of dark magic practitioners? But these gods had never cared what humans did to each other. All they cared about was their worship.

No, this felt strangely personal. All the talk about her usurping Adamantus or Eurycrius had to come from somewhere. What had she done?

"Appeared to me like what?" I asked.

Taken aback, Lyceus gestured between Adamantus and Polyope's unsettling appearances. "Don't you see how they look? How is this not making you wet yourself with fear?"

"If that keeps happening to you in their presence, then I suggest you find the reason why," I said, wiggling my brows. "Perhaps you should seek out your own oracle at Ecapodia?"

As Lyceus grew brighter in affront, Adamantus made that advancing-doom noise. It emboldened me further.

"So, where are my competitors?" I asked Almagera, rubbing my hands together. "Line them up, and we can settle this out the old fashioned way and be done here and now."

"And what way is that?" Lyceus asked, light back to his previous levels.

"Well, first you gut a boar and spray its blood all over the ground, then you battle for its intestines and tusks and use them to—"

"Are you a maenad?" Lyceus cut me off, lips curled back in distaste. "Is that what this is? One of that new god's pranks?"

"Theoneus has yet to meet my priestess, but I am sure he'll have the sense to appreciate her," Polyope said icily. "Not that you had any sense to begin with."

His outline and hair flared like salt had been flung into his white-hot flames. "Tell me, which one of us is now stuck in the dark for all eternity?"

"That's enough!" Almagera interrupted. "Leave us. We will regroup when we have had time to prepare for this unexpected occurrence." In a twirl of peacock feathers, she aimed an accusatory finger our way. "Until then, Orcus, if you marry this brain-damaged idiot before she competes against our picks, then I'll make sure no one votes for her deification."

Adamantus waved her off. "Whatever you need to hear to end this distasteful event faster."

Deities dispersed in a mind-bending kaleidoscope of colors and sensations, warping reality around their collective exit. Only the major gods of the Council lingered.

"Meropis eh?" Telephassa mused. "Now all of this makes sense."

Lyceus's fiery focus remained on me. "How so?"

"The fumes from a volcano drive mortals mad," she explained, in the vein of a quaint fact, akin to owls being nocturnal. "One can only guess how that population developed over centuries of breathing that toxic air."

I tried not to look surprised by that fact.

Meropis was an island at the end of the world and, consequently, the subject of much hyperbole. People had depicted it as everything from a sinister land of unspeakable sights to the target of parody, playing off centuries of fear-mongering for laughs.

It was why me and Chloë chose it for Prospera's birth place.

People knew so little about it, I could make any claim and no one could challenge it.

Lyceus threw a jab at Polyope over his shoulder. "Explains why they'd be dedicated to you."

"We can't all play our cards right every time," her middle head said.

"I don't need to play when I can seek the outcome through my oracles," Lyceus sneered. "It's your magic that's far less reliable."

Polyope had existed for me less than any other deity, but I despised how they talked to her. From what I understood, whatever she'd done, she was being punished for it for eternity. But that wasn't enough for them, was it?

With an airy voice and vacant expression, I went for the throat. "I wonder, if you have access to such crucial information, why not have the Oracle of Ectapodia divine His Celestial Majesty's whereabouts?"

"It's never that simple nor clear." Lyceus rounded on me, sizzling and crackling. "If that were the case, I'd have found him immediately."

Sweat poured from my hairline and into my good-natured smile, but I didn't even twitch. I'd worked the fields since I was a child, and fallen into hell. He'd have to do far worse than that to overwhelm me. But it would also get him impaled on Adamantus's bident.

Intoxicated by having Death at my back, by the whole experience, I taunted, "Would you have? I don't know how he's received on the mainland, but we hear nothing but worrisome tales about him where I'm from. I wouldn't miss him if he were someone I had to defer to. Would you?"

I kept a sharp eye out for the reactions of those who remained. They ranged from irritation to suspicion to dismay, save for Eglaia, who looked ready to make another ill-advised lunge for my throat.

"Easy for you to say, the balance of power that runs the world isn't your priority," Lyceus hissed. "What are you again? I can sense that you're not entirely human."

"That's what I've been wondering as well," Telephassa added, features pinched with scrutiny. "I can't get a clear impression, it's almost like I'm seeing you through a dirty window."

Their examination made every injury I'd ever suffered and healed ache again, and the scars on my back tighten, emphasizing the shape of the brand. It was as if they were nullifying its protective power, before they waved me and the effort to read me away.

"Polyope must have cobbled her together from the mangled corpses of the girls sacrificed to her," Eglaia spat, even when unable to remain upright unaided. "It makes no sense otherwise."

"You're welcome to do better. I'm sure as the goddess of passionate unions this should be easy for you. *Unless!*" Her second and third mouths lagged, echoing the doubtful addition. "Unless you still can't understand what he wants."

"What I want is right before you, but since you've determined to politicize my marriage, you've only just complicated this matter for yourselves." Adamantus' rumble silenced all adjoining questions with a sharp finality. "We're done here."

When he released me, I felt the steadying, cooling effect leave with his grip. The loss of his touch didn't last, as his palm slid across my lower back on its way to take my hand.

A portal opened beneath our feet, starting our descent back into the Underworld. As the gap closed after us, I caught Lyceus, Almagera and Eglaia whispering together. But the last thing I glimpsed was Telephassa waving at me.

❧ 26 ☙

HEAVENLY METAL

Halfway down, Adamantus turned into himself.

His silence was killing me. Ever since we left Anactoron, I'd been ready for him to grab me by the neck and singe me with his displeasure. While part of me really wished he would, the other was mortified. I hadn't stuck to his script.

But then it wasn't my fault the gods had changed the play.

"You're a menace."

I found myself flushing like he'd just complimented me. "Why, thank you."

A rumble shook the in-between, and I braced myself for his —annoyance, since I'd yet to see him angry. Just as I wondered if it could collapse the fabric of this space, I realized I'd heard that thunder once before. It was his laughter.

He was laughing!

I was so surprised, I missed a step. He caught me mid-trip as if I weighed nothing.

As I pulled away, needing to see his expression, I found his too-sharp, pearly teeth on display. "You're not angry!"

Regretfully, he put me back on my feet, sobering. "Because you stepped out of the lines I drew for you? I should have

237

expected all of them would have reason to reject my choice. I never shared space with them longer than I need to, I tend to forget how, manipulative and power-hungry and—petty they are. My plan no longer worked, so you improvised." His eyes suddenly blazed. "You improvised so expertly, so seamlessly, I had to consider you've been doing the same when you convinced me you were not a spy."

My heart almost stopped. "Actually, now I think about it, you have every right to think so."

The flame in his eyes subsided. "I don't. Even if I did, it would change nothing. We have a deal." Before I blurted out some objection I hadn't even formulated, he shook his head, the flames back, but dancing in mirth. "I never thought of riling them up for my own amusement. Now I've seen how easy it is, it should make Council meetings much more bearable."

"So I didn't mess up anything?"

"While this didn't go as I'd envisioned, the reactions you ignited have given me a lot to consider."

"Mind telling me what you uncovered while you watched us all make fools of ourselves? I was too busy to make any notes, what with keeping my wits about me in the presence of gods."

He scowled. "You've been in the presence of a god for some time now."

I shook my head. "It's not the same. You don't feel like they do."

He fell silent until I thought he wouldn't talk again, until he suddenly said, his voice somber. "How do I feel?"

Too many thoughts, feelings—and answers bombarded me at this simple question.

I chose the easy way out, for now. "You feel like—you."

That seemed to satisfy him. But my head whirled as I realized I was on the cusp of treading an unknown path, and as I asked myself the same question.

How do I feel?

As the future Mistress of the Granary, I had no time for frivolous feelings. I was to be responsible for maintaining and nour-ishing millions. I was raised to take charge, be stoic and practical to an extreme. No matter who sired or even preceded me, a woman in power was a precarious position, and any sign of vulnerability broke the dam of disrespect and degradation.

The luxuries of smaller duties were not within my reach, and I had no need for them. I was above the need for base emotions like insecurity, flightiness and desire, shamelessly shared by others deemed weaker than myself.

Except I did have all those feelings. I was a living woman just like any other with blood pumping to my head, heart and between my legs. Right now I couldn't tell which was being prioritized. And they were all craving Death.

I watched him as we descended side by side. With his complexion muted by the ambience like a lifelike charcoal portrait, he looked almost human.

But I had to remember he wasn't human. According to Poly-ope, he wasn't even a man, only a personification of one.

As if to save me from my turmoil, he looked down at me. "About your performance, it was supremely—effective."

"Because it wasn't a performance. Prospera only gave the excuse to say and do exactly what I wanted to."

"Including the parts where you touched me?"

"Especially those parts." Suddenly, I was unable to not touch him anymore. I slid a trembling hand beneath his coat, felt his chest like cool, chiseled granite through his silk shirt. "Adamantus..."

He turned to me, and I surged into him, letting my torch clatter down the stairs, undoing his diamond buttons, shaking so much I tore off two. But I needed to reach his skin. Needed it on my burning flesh. He didn't bend to me, so I kissed right over the heartbeat I was now certain existed.

He rumbled something in some ancient language as his hand closed over my nape. I cried out as that sound, that touch sent a gush of arousal coursing though me. Blind, out of my mind, I hooked a leg over his hip and ground against him, desperate for release...

"Children, kindly keep your hands to yourselves until we return." Polyope passed by us, a separate, foggy path like lilac glass paving itself beneath her many feet as she wandered off into an unseen outskirt of the Underworld. "We can discuss how antagonizing the Heavenly Court excites you after we plan for 'Prospera' battling others for your cold hand."

It was like being doused in hell again followed by falling through the ice of a frozen lake.

I stumbled away from Adamantus, but didn't raise my eyes to his as he steadied me. I could only stare at his chest. His heaving chest.

Before I could look up, say or ask him something, he turned around and resumed his descent. I followed on legs that felt like elastic with embarrassment and frustration.

He finally spoke when we reached the Bloodstained Shore and took the docked barge.

"I'm not keen on the thought of you competing against their candidates, but I'll admit it's an efficient way to further distract and observe them."

"You think I can't handle them?"

"It's not the women they'll choose that I'm worried about."

He fell silent again as we passed the Bone Gate, sailed down the River of Memory, then through the soul city of Psychepolis.

At least the city provided some distraction as canals took us on a tour that defied physics and engineering. Buildings clustered in arcs overhead, housing countless abodes, while even more souls and chthonic spirits passed us in roads criss-crossing over the river, going about their days in an imitation of urban life.

Wonders of the world had passed me by in business visits, my missions on behalf of the Granary leaving me no space for tourism. Even on the occasions where I had gracious hosts eager to educate me on their culture, I never got to see breathtaking views.

After spanning the world in my travels, I haven't seen anything worth seeing in a foreign land, until Adamantus took my hand and led me into his Underworld.

"I still can't believe this place is real."

"Some days, neither can I."

I whipped my head up, realizing I'd talked out loud, and that he'd answered.

"It's just...for me 'dead' was a rigid reality. An unchanging eternity I'd spend in blissful disconnection from anything that summed up feeling alive." I realized I was rambling, but I couldn't stop. The whole night had taken a toll I was just now feeling. "Here feels like a continuation."

"Since an afterlife implies as much, I had to allow some semblance of living to exist here."

"I also still can't believe you did all that."

"I mostly orchestrated it. But I never experienced life up close for long enough. It always strives to escape me, even when I'm just there to observe. The duty of designing this continued existence had to be delegated to those who experienced it."

"So, there's a committee dedicated to maintaining the after-life experience?"

He nodded, distracted. What was he remembering here? Whatever it was, I was thankful he didn't mention that I'd accosted him.

I accosted Death!

He suddenly met my chagrined gaze. "You enjoy being feared, I can tell as much. But do you find joy in it always?"

"It's never a downside in my case, not unless I've scared off an animal I wanted to pet. Fear is respect among people. It untangles complications and shields others on your behalf."

"But fear can lead to resentment, which can unbalance respect, if there's enough cause to defeat you instead of defer to you."

"You're thinking of Eurycrius?"

"Among other things." He leaned forward, elbows on knees, hands together between them. "The fear you inspire won't always be personal, but depends on what you represent. Yet all it takes for power to go from inevitable to uncertain is enough determination in the right person."

I groaned internally at the thought of every relative and stranger who coveted my destiny. "So, you're saying it won't be enough to return with your 'blessing' to scare opportunists off?"

"I'm saying whoever is targeting you, is probably behind Eurycrius's disappearance. There's a god or gods who had enough drive to do that, but are threatened by your existence." He tapped his metallic nails on his bejeweled rings. "Who among those we spoke with has the most motive?"

"You said it could be personal or not, so suspects can shift from his wife to any ambitious major god. But they all seemed too invested in distracting you. So the question is who's behind this, and who's joining the ruse to appease them."

He shook his head. "The question is why none of them sensed you're what they're looking for."

And it suddenly hit me. "Was that why you chose me to play this role? You put me in front of them hoping whoever the culprit is, they'd recognize me and try to kill me?"

"It would have solved the mystery."

I flung my torch at him. "You—bastard!"

The tungsten cone bounced off his unbothered face, devious as the moment we had struck our deal. "Surely, you knew the risks when you shook my hand."

And to think I made a fool of myself back there, and had been thinking all those sappy, addled thoughts about how isolated and untouched he was!

But there was no denying that I had known what I'd been signing up for.

"You could have warned me of the possibility beforehand!" I fumed.

"For what purpose? Considering how untraceable Erthamos and I found you, it was unlikely they'd have felt different in your presence. And then you went out of your way to provoke almost all of them, until Eglaia did attempt to kill you."

"So what if she is the culprit?"

"Even if she is, she didn't recognize you for what you are. She tried to kill Prospera, not Cora. Besides, I quite enjoyed your act. Filling you with pointless fear would have robbed us of such entertainment."

Not quite calmed, I scowled at him. "Glad I entertained you."

He nodded, his irises becoming like burning amethysts. "Everything you do commands my attention, it's hard not to enjoy it. You're distracting without being a detriment to the investigation. If anything, you've invigorated me."

Unexpectedly, the blatant honesty of his reasoning had extinguished my rage. "Careful, that almost sounds like a compliment."

His inquisitive head-tilt, coupled with that unblinking stare, brought to mind a large cat. "Why wouldn't it be?"

At a loss, no longer knowing how to feel or what to think about this confounding god, I cleared my throat. "So, what you're saying is, you want me to continue being a menace?"

Adamantus rose as the ferryman slowed our flow, a pillar of darkness against the vibrancy of the downtown area. The barge docked by a marble building that evoked banks.

"Whatever we need to get to the bottom of this, do as you see fit."

"No reins?"

He reached down and pulled me up, and I saw it in his dimmed eyes. The memory of those feverish moments. He hadn't been unaffected.

But he only said, "No reins, no limits."

What I'd always wanted to hear.

Inside the building, my assumptions were proven right. It

acted as some sort of depository for precious items. Souls puttered about, measuring, documenting and polishing objects. The further back we went through the aisles, the higher the exhibits seemed to rise in value.

A spirit met us by a massive, circular vault door, with pointed ears, black eyes and limestone skin. "Sire, Polyope informed us of your arrival. How may we serve you?"

Adamantus presented me to him. "Our guest just challenged a few gods. We need to find her a weapon that can withstand their antics."

Residual smugness from unpunished hubris made me forget everything as I smirked. "They started."

A wave of his bident opened the vault. "Yes, but they can finish you."

"But you won't let them, right?"

That went unanswered as the treasurer spirit rushed ahead asking Adamantus questions to narrow down what he could provide me. Adamantus dismissed him, telling him I had to make my own choice.

Variety greeted me beneath the mirrored ceiling, its matching floor multiplying the white firelight that bathed the armory.

Blades of every shape lined the walls, along with projectile weapons and armor. I hadn't even known so many kinds existed

I spun through the center, arms out to embrace the selection. "What is all this?"

He twirled his bident as if to mimic my impromptu dance. "A boastful collection, some acquired in my travels in the Upperworld, others the winners of competitions for my weaponmakers here. Some are lent out when souls reenact battles."

"Now there's an interesting way to pass the time." I hungrily examined the displays, my senseless want for material goods validated through usefulness. Whatever I chose had a purpose, and it wouldn't hurt for it to be as decadent as a king's ceremonial sword. "Was your staff the result of a challenge?"

Adamantus halted his play, earlier distraction briefly returning.

"No," he said after some thought.

"Who made it then?"

"I don't know."

That struck me as particularly odd. "How do you not know where your symbol of power came from?"

He brought its end down hard, echoing throughout the vault. "It wasn't always mine."

Letting that sleeping dog lie, I spun again, trading the wall of blades for the side covered in armor. Everything from shinguards to helmets was mounted too high for me to reach.

An antique Orestian armor called to me from the far right, white-gold and seemed to suit my build. Tempting as it was, no specific weapon came with it, and I had to choose that first.

Adamantus joined me at my next stop, the wall of assorted long-distance weaponry. "What are you adept at using?"

"Anything I can make use of in the moment." I leaped up to pluck a longbow, pulled its bowstring in his direction. "I just realized I can use you as target practice."

"You already did. With a fist, a book, and a torch. Which actually proves your claim. If I was anyone else, you would have pulverized or killed me."

"That's why you're perfect!" He raised one eyebrow. "As a target I mean, being invulnerable."

"For which purpose? Shooting accuracy, or venting?"

My lips split from ear to ear at that. "Both, actually. What have you got to lose? Both will make me a better contender. And you want me to win, right?"

He pursed his lips, and just as I thought I'd pushed my luck too far, he nodded. "One shot. Let's see what you've got."

Unable to believe Death Incarnate had agreed to let me shoot him, I pounced on the opportunity before he decided to toss me back to the Upperworld, and close the investigation, come what may, just to get rid of my aggravation.

I released the string to test its power, experimented with the weight of the bow, then chose an arrow and tried its balance. He stood there at the other end of the vault, waiting, both hands in his pockets.

Suddenly, I was angry. Incensed. And I wanted to hurt him. For everything that I felt, that he made me feel. For everything that had happened. For everything that he was.

I let the arrow fly.

It hit him right where his heart beat, but apparently didn't exist. It exploded, but not in a burst of that blue-hot fire. Into a thousand splinters.

His eyes widened, and there was the tiniest hint of a jerk.

Did that actually hurt him? Or was he just surprised his fire didn't manifest?

Or maybe, he was just unable to believe that I got him in the heart on the first try?

He lowered his gaze so I couldn't read him. When he raised his eyes, they were pulsating, but his face was impassive. "Seems you don't need to practice, after all." A beat. "About the motivations the other gods might have, has anyone struck you as particularly suspicious?"

"Eglaia!" I said at once.

He shook his head. "I can't imagine a reason for her to rise against Eurycrius."

"That would make her a prime candidate for a seamless crime. That's the case in some popular detective novels." I returned the bow, still feeling the rebound in my arm, and his jerk in my nerves. "Who's your main suspect?"

"Not exactly a suspect, but Almagera is the one who'd take the most issue with your father, and his bastards. But what would set her off after all these lifetimes?"

"Or what she hopes to achieve with him gone, if we're following your theory of fearfulness inspiring some to defeat rather than defer to you." I took another look around, now put off by the surplus of choice. "How can I pick something when I don't know what to expect?"

"You have no preferences?"

"Everything here has its downsides, especially in limited use or even mobility. Is there anything a little multi-purpose, and easy to keep on me?"

Using his bident, he unhooked a coiled whip from its mount. It fell in his hand, and he offered it to me. "How about this?"

His fingertips stroked my palm in the exchange of hands, raising all the hair along my arm. Standing back, he observed me with an expectant stare.

Mystified, I tested the bluish-silver material by a few tugs. "What is this?"

"Orichalcum."

My jaw dropped. Orichalcum was a metamorphic metal, a staple of fables whose existence remained unproven. "This stuff actually exists? I thought it was a myth!"

"It's as real as where we just were, considering it's mined from heavenly mountains." He jerked his head towards the weapon. "Give it a try."

Not wasting a second, I cracked the whip and felt it stiffen into a staff. On a second swing, it went limp. "How am I supposed to carry this?"

In response, the whip recoiled, feeling like an obedient serpent in my grasp, alive and itching to move, and when I trusted it to, it coiled up my arm, wrapping itself around my forearm like a bracelet. "Oh, this will work nicely," I exclaimed, instantly enamored. "I'll still need something sharp though."

He halted my reach for his bident, grasping my hand between us. "Not this. Only the God of the Underworld can wield this weapon."

Mesmerized by his intensity, by his nearness, all over again, I forgot to explain that I had been joking as I sighed. "Pity. I wanted a chance to play with your staff."

That innuendo was unmeant, mostly, but there was no sign it

stuck the landing. Until his pupils dilated, and my breath escaped me.

He broke the silence first when leading me out of the vault. "I believe Polyope has something as adaptable as this whip."

I nodded, struck mute by the feel of his hand grasping mine. And though I was more confused than I had ever been in my life, I knew one thing.

Whatever awaited me in the next phase of this plan, I would face it with the tumult of emotions he had ignited within me.

THE HOLY GUESTS

"This isn't what I was angling for," I groaned, slouching against a serpentine column, watching the Horned God pacing his throne room.

At my frustrated lament, Adamantus stopped beneath an emerald chandelier, antlers casting grasping shadows across the green marble floor. His obsidian throne was at his back, with three, massive circular windows pouring bluish light that reflected off his giant, merged hellhound.

My offer to fight his bridal candidates was inadvertently bringing all interested parties to the Nether Court. It was under the pretext of keeping us all under "one roof" for fear of cheating or a secret elopement, and to organize a competition that would take place in their respective chosen spaces. That required the temporary installation of Godsgates. From what I understood those were portals fixed towards one location, to avoid suspicious activity. Or sabotage.

He'd chosen to receive the gods in Athanasia, the first soul-city he'd built, because it had the only throne room in the Underworld. With him being a hands-on ruler, he never used it, except in the rare cases when he, not his judges, sentenced souls.

But he had to keep it formal with the gods, would sit on his throne to be presented their candidates, my rivals for his hand.

"Why do they have to come here?" I groaned again.

As usual, he answered my rhetoric question. "If I'm to watch them all closely to gather evidence and clues, then yes, I need them all in one place."

"Yes, but why couldn't this one place have been Anactoron?" For some reason I hated that they'd be here. I felt—protective of the Underworld somehow.

"That's the last place we both should be. It's either this, or they figure out what I've been up to."

"Would that be so bad?" I pushed off the column and shook out my ankles. It was bad enough that I was made to wear sandals, but now I had to keep up the illusion of Prospera for hours at a time. "What could they do even if they found out?"

Adamantus leveled me with an eyeless stare, the skull expressionless beyond the frozen menace of its exposed bone and teeth. "Think of what brought us all to this moment and say that again. Whatever they did to your father, they can do to me."

That made me stop in my tracks. "But you're the most powerful god in existence!"

He huffed. "I thought mortals believed that was Eurycrius."

"Not if power is based on the size of your domain. You're the only one with a steadily growing one."

He only inclined his head, as if to acknowledge my deduction. "Even so, if many unite to combine their powers, they can overpower even me. And if they do, it won't only be a power vacuum. No one but me can control my domain, and if it went ungoverned, it would spill onto the other realms. It would be total chaos."

I gaped at him. Sometime I forgot the stakes here. I didn't even think they'd sunk in yet.

He started pacing again. "But I wouldn't put it past them to not calculate the consequences in their power hunger. They didn't when they usurped the titans that now reside in my

Chasm. It had been mere luck that the realms hadn't been destroyed."

"I totally forgot about the titans," I admitted, biting my lip. "What were they like?"

"Certainly stronger than the gods, which only proves my point."

"I meant, were they similar entities, or—I don't know, ever harder for a mortal to be around?"

It seemed he wasn't going to answer until he said, "Ask Polyope."

"Why not you?"

"Because I wasn't there."

"What do you mean you weren't there? Things didn't die back then?"

"Death existed." He gestured to his body. "This aspect of it didn't."

I couldn't grasp what that meant. Just like I hadn't when Polyope called him a personification.

"So, when and how were you born exactly?" I probed.

"I wasn't born. The conditions for how I came into being are...nebulous at best."

"You don't know?"

He shook his head.

"How?"

"Do you remember being born, Coralia? I've waded through the River of Memory, through the experiences my souls leave behind, to simplify their continued existence. The earliest memories I've glimpsed rarely precede the age at which mortals begin to fully speak."

I nodded. "I don't remember much before four years-old." Nothing actually preceded the memory of being branded with the *acanthomatia*. "What were you like as a child?"

"I wasn't."

Something about the way he expressed this hit me like a

hammer on a gong, painfully resonating within my head as levels of its meaning layered themselves.

Gods had been born, so had their predecessors the titans. So they'd grown up, had been children once. The only things that hadn't been were vague entities, primordial beings we had no clear idea of, but personified for the sake of art and simplicity.

To think that he was among those things, having sprung into being out of the primordial void, filled me with unfathomable—horror? Or was it sadness?

Fighting off imagining him as a prehistoric monster, I forced myself to get back to the moment, to think of the most mundane things to ask. "Do you have any siblings?"

"None that I'm aware of."

That meant none of the gods were related to him. He was detached on every level of existence.

Polyope's explanation made more sense in the worst way. She hadn't been de-personifying him. He truly was the furthest thing from any living being I'd ever encountered.

Somehow, that didn't deter me. It just strengthened my urge to creep over the threshold between the known and the unknowable. And nothing was more unseen than what awaited us all when we closed our eyes for the last time.

If the gods of the world had us during our lives, the Starless King would have us for eternity.

And here he stood before me, willing to give me answer that no being before me had ever had. No realizations, no matter how world-shaking, would make me end this topic prematurely.

I stopped before him, tilted my head way up. He'd made himself bigger to match the gods' preferred size. "Did you always look the way you do as Adamantus?"

"More or less. I can change superficial aspects of my humanoid appearance, hair length, beard, nails, such things. Any greater effort ends in a total transformation, like I appear now."

Stepping closer, I rose on my limiting sandals, aiming to peer into the Horned God's sockets. "Why go to such an effort at all?

I always thought these depictions were humans being creative, but why did you choose to go from a man like any other god to this?"

"Because I am not a man." He sighed. "I shouldn't be perceived as one when I am no such thing."

"Is this out of principle or preference?" I reached up for the skull, just as I had in the throes of delirium, and again on Anactoron. "Because I still can't tell if it's because you see us as 'roaches' like the rest, or you disagree with them interacting with us at all?"

He shrugged. "It is pointless to appear as I do to you, when the living refuse to interact with me as they do the others. They want to scream at the sight of me? I'll give them a good reason to scream."

"That's depressing." I softly caressed the angles of the skull, the sensation closer to ivory than bone. "Giving the people what they expect at your own expense."

"It's what I exist for." He caught my hand before I could reach for the antlers. Thumb pressed into my palm, fingers reaching my forearm, he watched me. "What is it with you? None of this makes any sense. Why are you unaffected by me? And unnoticed by the others?"

"I somehow think those two things are unrelated."

"How so?"

"The way I feel about you feels independent of anything else. But if you really want a logical reason, all I can think of is maybe I see no point in fearing you. If you want to kill me you'll do it, and there will be nothing I could do about it."

His grip on my hand tightened, a pressure that popped my wrist. "Are you telling me that you're like this with me because you've rationalized yourself out of a deep-set primal instinct that drives people to insane measures and unimaginable atrocities?"

"I don't know why I'm like this with you. I'm only giving you a possible explanation."

"If you are claiming to be braver than the brutal, hard-hearted warriors that kill with no remorse, and the fearsome sorcerers who tried to achieve immortality, then I hope for your sake it's true."

I grabbed his massive hand when he removed it, brought it to my face. The tips of his nails grazed my cheek and chin, sharpness dangerously close to my throat. But that wasn't what made my breath quicken or my legs tremble. No matter what I told myself, or even after what he'd just told me, I wanted him, fully. I needed to be with him, to feel him, all over me and inside me, in any form he chose to take.

His hand wrapped around my neck as he bent to let me cling to his antlers, that rumble that liquefied me reverberating inside his skull, sounding almost pained. "You need to focus, Cora. Whatever my guests have in store won't be easy."

"It certainly won't be!"

At Polyope's triple exclamation, I snatched my hands off him and almost jumped back.

She had just shot out of one of her pools, her middle body bearing a lapis lazuli box with gold fastenings. "We should have checked if you had any powers before presenting you to them."

I lowered my veil to hide the flush that exploded across my face.

Still feeling his gaze on me, I squeezed my legs to subdue the pounding between them as I almost croaked, "Did demigods beyond Alcaeus the Great have powers? Even then he just had great strength."

"My children were all great sorcerers," Polyope said proudly as she approached at an uncanny speed, given she was a trio of nine foot-tall bodies fused at their backs.

No matter how many times I saw her, it never ceased to disturb me. Her structure was hard enough to look at, but the scale she chose only made it worse.

But now I had gotten an answer from Adamantus about the origin of the Horned God, I wanted to know the reasoning behind her eerie appearance. Perhaps it would tell me why the gods were so hostile to her presence, and why humanity had turned against her. I might get the chance to find out, after all this was resolved.

"Any power a demigod inherits needs a boost, usually consuming something made for us. In your children's case, it was your breastmilk." I marveled at the difference in his voice as he addressed her, how he'd gone from obliging to fed up. "It was why I attempted to steal a golden apple from Almagera's gardens, but I didn't have time before they started threatening you both."

"That's why you were late?" I exclaimed. "I thought it was for the dramatic entrance."

As if at the mention of entrances, the gates of the throne room creaked open and the overwhelming sensation of divine auras heralded their arrival.

Gritting my teeth, I psyched myself into Prospera's role. Here went nothing.

Adamantus climbed the steps to his obsidian throne, his giant hellhound rushing to sit guard beside him. He sat down and leaned forward with a forearm on one knee as the shadows of torment rose to swirl around him, looking every inch the all-powerful, ruthless god who granted no mercies.

Entering first was Almagera, nine feet of luminescent lemony skin in a mantle made of peacock feathers over her green gown, her verdant hair bound up and centered by a brass cylindrical crown.

Without even attempting a greeting, Almagera snapped, "Orcus, would you take off that horrible disguise?"

So even other gods had no idea he shapeshifted into this form, that it was no helmet?

He only said, "No."

The instant intensity of her offense drew white-hot outlines around her features. It seemed the gods would remain easy to rile up. What was it like to rarely, if ever, be told "*no*", for a denial to hit you like a cannonball?

From witnessing the tantrums of those possessing control over all but themselves, I knew I wouldn't want to see a god's outburst. But my pettiness rivaled my reason. I really wished to see Adamantus causing Almagera a meltdown.

Striding behind her was a green-skinned dryad, a piece of home that was welcome for all of five seconds, until she gave me the ugliest glare.

Adamantus might bemoan the reactions he received from all others, but I knew he derived some pleasure from his effect.

It didn't take long for him to prove my point as Almagera repeated her demand, harsher this time. He only sat back in a goading pose.

This time Almagera climbed up to his throne, yelling, "Take it off this instant!"

Shadowy streams burst from all around him and snapped around her reaching arms like a black squid. "What part of 'no' do you not understand?"

She struggled against her bindings, persistent to unmask him, and they pulsed the bright purple shining from his eyes. She tripped backwards and down the steps with a gasp that threatened to burst my eardrums.

Hands pressed over her midsection, she cried, "What is that?"

"A taste of what your rage reaps—death by starvation," he hissed, as calmly vicious as a viper.

The dryad came to her goddess's side, avoiding looking at him by aiming her scowl at Polyope and I.

Offense had begun to stir until I remembered I wasn't Cora of Granaria now, a child of golden fields and green pastures, but Prospera, black-magic priestess of a reviled goddess.

The bident manifested into his palm, and he aimed its prongs at them. "What did you bring me?"

Almagera gathered herself, dropping her confrontational attitude. "This is Perilla, one of my groundskeepers on Anactoron."

Perilla was the color of honeydew, with pointed ears, leafy-green hair, and eyes in shades of yellow-green, with no whites. Her clothes left little to the imagination, a tight strapless band across her pert breasts and a short skirt with slits at the sides showing off her tiny waist and slim hips.

The way she posed and kept slowly rubbing her hands up and down her legs while staring blankly in his direction was meant to monopolize his attention.

She had it, but not quite in the intended way. "It is unclear what you expect me to do with a tree nymph."

In response, Perilla rose to his throne and *climbed into his lap*.

I was ready to fling my torch at her.

Straddling him with her arms around his neck, Perilla sensually mumbled, "I can do lots of things to you and for you. I'll give you a taste of life you won't be able to find anywhere else."

He set his hands on her hips and pulled her close, making her go so stiff she could have been shifting back into a tree. "Leaning too hard on the lustful nymph angle, aren't you?" Then he threw her off him and down onto Almagera. "If you want to seduce me, you need to do a better job of hiding your disgust."

Almagera was furious, at either of them or both. I was buzzing with petty delight.

"See, this is why Eurycrius never kept to your bed!" Lyceus chose that moment to enter, aglow with his sunlit skin and his white, wavy hair on its ends like rays, eyes and outlines matching in luminosity. His white tunic was molded to his body and its neckline at his navel.

Compared to the brightness level of the room, Lyceus was painful to look at, like staring into the midday sun. He had briefly blocked out the woman he brought, who only became noticeable when he dimmed.

Throughout approaching the throne, he kept his bright eyes in my direction, his smile as dazzling as Telephassa's. A great departure from how he'd behaved before.

Lyceus set his foot on the bottom step and casually leaned

forward, arm on his knee. "Good day, Orcus. Do you have days here?"

"Not quite." Adamantus uncurled his hand towards the bride. "I hope yours knows how to behave herself."

Lyceus's bright smile grew, arm out to present her as she curtsied. "I bring you my granddaughter Aethusa, a princess of the Summer Court in Faerie."

Aethusa was a toned-down version of her grandfather, with white-blonde hair, pale, pearlescent skin and light grey eyes, her ears ending in sharper points than Perilla, with a rounded face and curvaceous body.

After bowing to Adamantus, and wrinkling her nose at me like I was a pile of dung, she stood with her head turned up, aiming her eyes at the window above the throne.

When it became clear she wasn't going to say anything, Adamantus snapped his fingers. "NEXT!"

The doors were kicked all the way open by the divine gust of Machaius and Eglaia. Their combined, intense red and pink gradients forced me to squeeze my eyes shut until their voices were too close to ignore.

Machaius was in full war regalia, and Eglaia quickly retook the shape and coloring of the woman she'd displayed to me last time.

"Might as well cut the others out now," Machaius announced, arm around the armored woman next to him. "Here stands our daughter, Formeta, goddess of battle tactics, the only woman in existence who will match your effect on the world."

My smile fell off my face and I nearly dropped my torch.

❧ 28 ❧

SIX OF BRIDES

A goddess. They'd brought a goddess to compete against me.

Why hadn't I anticipated this? Had I gotten that high off the fumes of my own confidence?

My thoughts tangled as my stunned gaze panned over my divine "rival".

Formeta was entirely in greyscale, the darkest parts being her tightly-braided hair and the breastplate of her armor. And I could feel the dread she both inspired and fed off of in her worshippers.

"How bad is this?" I whispered to Polyope. "What are my chances?"

"They'll be less about her and more about what task you'll both be given." One of Polyope's heads bent to whisper back, the way a girl would tell her best friend the latest gossip. "Unless they change their minds at the last minute, you won't be required to wrestle her as you initially planned."

"That's good?"

"Not quite." Her left-side head joined her right one at my level. "We might have to resort to an extreme preventative measure."

"What is that?"

"Adamantus may not have gotten one of Almagera's golden apples, but I can find you something just as good to boost whatever latent powers you have."

"Do it!"

"Are you sure?" her middle head asked. "It might have permanent effects."

Returning home with even greater strength and resilience or even glowing eyes sounded like the least of my worries right now. "You want me to win or not?"

Polyope's three heads grinned down at me. "Always an impatient little beast. Fine, I'll get it."

Feeling my blood fizzing with agitation, and at the hope that I'd have something to level the playing field, I turned my attention back to Adamantus.

Either this was him being detached from the risk this posed to me, or he was aiming to frustrate the gods before him, he seemed totally unimpressed with the offered goddess.

"And why is that?" Machaius was cut off from answering by Adamantus pointing his bident in their direction, making Eglaia flinch. "Not you. Her. Tell me why you are my ideal match."

Formeta made no move, she just emanated a sharp-edged fog that displayed hazy scenes of battle, and the cacophony of clanging metal and horrified screams.

"I inspire the leading cause of mass deaths," she said proudly. "No other woman could appreciate your role in existence more than myself."

He might be expressionless and blending into the darkness of his throne and shadows, but I could sense from the way he tapped his nails that he was displeased, if not rolling his eyes inside that skull.

Instead of replying, he pointed to the one attempting to hide behind Eglaia. "You brought a human?"

Formeta's face scrunched up in offense at being ignored, and she lurched forward, ready to repeat the mistake of heckling him. Machaius clamped a steadying hand on her shoulder, allowing Eglaia to push her bride forward.

"I bring you the loveliest of my subjects, Rhoxane," Eglaia said smugly. "Granddaughter to the witch-queen of Zhadugar. A beauty who could cause wars and blasphemy if she hadn't chosen to dedicate her life to my service."

At the mention of Zhadugar, my attention snapped to the trembling sorceress dwarfed by her company. I'd been there during my eventful political visit to Cahraman. Before I'd ended up leading Sunstone's citizens in a revolution against their magical despot, I'd tried my best to get eliminated from King Cyaxares's bridal competition.

When I'd still ended in the top five contestants, we'd visited Marzeya as part of the eliminations tests. The witch-queen, an ancient and demented hag who delighted in traumatizing her visitors, had flung the obnoxious Princess Fairuza of Arbore into ghoul-infested caves to teach her a lesson. Mean as it may sound, I wouldn't have cared if Ada, the only one I'd found worth befriending, hadn't been swept along, and I'd forced the then-prince to take me along for the rescue. Good thing, too, since while he'd fought off a horde of ghouls, one had caught the girls on their way out. I'd ended up breaking its neck.

The head of that very ghoul was now among my travel-trophies back home.

Rousing myself from the memories, I focused on Rhoxane. Swathed in rosy silk, with a curtain of dark hair held back by the diadem of an Orestian priestess, she had no resemblance to Marzeya. In fact, she looked like an Orestian version of Ada, with similar heavy-lidded eyes and an open face, even if her tan color was significantly paler, either from origin, or health.

She was also the most reluctant to be here, looking ready to pass out on the spot.

Pity, along with transferred fondness for the friend she resembled, softened my view of her, especially when she struggled to speak and failed.

"Is this the best you could find for the Bride of Death?" Adamantus rose from his seat like a towering wave of doom. "I am not impressed."

"You don't have to be." Lyceus, still blinding to look at, winked at him. "You are bound to marry the one who wins the competition."

A thunderous clap made even the gods flinch. It summoned a dozen souls, phasing through the walls to attend to each "guest".

Adamantus reached the bottom of the steps in a blur of shadows. "My souls will take you to your rooms, and call you when dinner is served. Do not attempt to tour my domain without my permission, or you could end up falling into the Spiral, or maybe the Chasm. If you do, no effort will be made to retrieve you."

His threat was clear, and the gods took objection to it. Their complaints clashed as they milled around him. That made the hellhound burst into motion, legs slamming down on either side of him, heads snarling and growling in all directions.

Almagera's dryad, Lyceus's faerie princess, and Eglaia's sorceress-priestess all but fainted. Formeta only got angrier and unsheathed her broadsword.

Fueled by the combined rage and pride of her parents, she swung at Cressida's head. "You will show us some respect!"

Fury burst in my head, painting my vision red. Metal or not, an animal was not getting attacked on my watch!

I charged across the room, and blocked her sword with my torch.

Formeta's outrage grew, darkening her grey cheeks. "Get out of my way."

A war-goddess had her personal weapon denting my makeshift one, aiming all her powerful rage at me, and instead of retreating, all sense fled as the thrill-seeking side of me awoke.

"Why?" I taunted. "So you could hit a guard-dog for doing its job like some colossal brat in the throes of a tantrum?"

She increased her pressure, sword cleaving through the

bronze of my torch. I bent backwards to avoid buckling under her strength, snatching a glance at the rest of the scene.

Adamantus watching in the background, hellhound barking on top of us, gods around us, cheering Formeta on as she spat, "You seem to have death wish, and I'll be glad to grant it!"

I waited until she was putting a bone-breaking force into her pressure, then slid to the side. The sudden loss of my resistance sent her crashing right below Cressida where I planned, who snapped her up in her jaws.

Machaius shouted, Eglaia screeched. That only made Cressida start chewing their daughter, wringing war-drum roars from her trapped body.

"Good girl!" I cooed at her as I sought Adamantus's gaze across the space. He hadn't taken his eyes off me, so I winked at him. How invigorating was that?

His amusement rumbled through the air, the realm. He seemed quite entertained.

The heads of Argentus and Platinus swooped down when the gods attempted to attack Cressida, forcing them to retreat.

Lyceus was the only one who'd hung back, going from exchanging strange looks with Polyope to watching me with interest. "You really are insane, aren't you?"

"I think I'll be the judge of that!" announced a new voice in a loud, infectious tone that had me perking up.

A tiger prowled through the gate, making way for the young man that sauntered towards us with a purple aura outlining him, altering the view around him.

Unlike Adamantus's shadows, which centered him like a beacon in the darkness, this one amplified what he passed through until it became hard to focus.

Lightheadedness overtook me as he arrived, rendering me too unsteady and slow to register what was before me.

Bull horns grew out of his long, curly, reddish brown hair, which fell to the middle of his back and covered more than his clothes did. As if he had just come from a day at sea, he only wore a short, tight, white skirt, and had all of his dark olive-skin on display, his sinewy body swaying hypnotically with each step, mirroring the walk of the giant cat before him.

Once within our perimeter, I knew who this was. Theoneus, the last demigod to be deified before Eurycrius went missing.

Theoneus's face split in a delighted grin, golden eyes sparkling, arms out to embrace whoever he collided with. "Has anyone seen my wife? I lost her somewhere near an underwater volcano beneath Iacoot."

For some reason, I decided to grant him a greeting hug. "There are volcanoes underwater?"

Without warning, he lifted me off my feet. Popping my back, he swung me around before setting me stumbling back against Adamantus. "Oooh! You are stiff!"

"Excuse me?"

Theoneus gestured with expressive fingers, crimson sparks dancing between them. "You are stiff, too wound up, too serious. You need to relax."

"I am relaxed."

"Mhm, and Margarita is a bear."

Margarita, the tiger, just watched us with matching clear, yellow eyes.

"What are you doing here?" Almagera asked him.

Hands up, he shimmied his shoulders. "You think I'd let you have a party down here, without me?"

Almagera completely missed his humor. "This isn't a party, Theoneus. We have brought five brides in our effort to appoint the Queen of the Underworld."

"Which is a waste of time, if you ask me." He flashed his fangs, electrifying the air. "But I'm here to witness the disastrous fallout of whatever you've all got planned."

Machaius rounded on him, growing larger to aid his intimidation. "Either participate or leave."

Theoneus's grin sharpened with a mischievous edge, before

he put two fingers in his lips and let rip a whistle that sent every soul around scurrying.

Aethusa and Perilla leaped aside with shouts as a third pointy-eared woman seemed to appear out of nowhere.

Theoneus laughed. "Lyssa, change of plans!"

Barefoot in a thin, rumpled raspberry dress, Lyssa was the color of honey, with hair wilder than Theoneus's own, wine-dark curls larger but firmer. Her deep, dark, energetic eyes scanned the room like a predator.

As they landed on me, she hustled over, giddy. "Hello, Sister, raise any dead lately?"

Veil or not, I tried to keep my eyebrows still, surprise crashing into realization. Was teaching mortals necromancy the reason Polyope was so reviled?

"Unfortunately, that was an ability I didn't train for."

"Shame." Lyssa leered at the nearest soul. "You can always claim you can bend the truth by snatching one of these."

"Theoneus, what is this?" Eglaia's appearance had become more detailed, her profile strong and angular, the planes of her jaw and cheekbones cutting.

"My main maenad, Lyssa. We traveled together before I ended up down here for the first time," he explained cheerfully, as if his death had been a chance for some brief tourism of the Underworld. "My wife was going to bring a caecilia, but they're hard to catch. If she succeeds, consider my maenad a placeholder."

"That's not how this works!" Almagera objected, fuming at him. "Either you take this seriously, or you leave!"

"You don't give the orders here!" Adamantus's impatience shook the throne room. "Six is enough. Go to your assigned quarters. I'll see you when I'm done."

The hounds dropped Formeta onto her father as they stepped over us, shrinking to follow him out of a portal in the nearest wall.

Theoneus and his tigress followed immediately, with Polyope and I in tow, followed by the chaperone souls and their charges.

Lyssa cartwheeled to catch up, coming to skip alongside me. "Have you ever cannibalized someone?"

Taken aback, I quickly responded as Prospera would. "Does it count as cannibalism if we're not considered the same species in their laws?"

Theoneus shot me a pleased look over his shoulder and Lyssa matched his mood with a wheezing laugh.

"I like you," she declared, before addressing Polyope. "Do you accept maenads as acolytes or is it only chthonic nymphs?"

Theoneus let out an exaggerated gasp, slapping his hands over his heart. "Have I not been enough for you, you traitor?"

Lyssa waved him away. "You're one god. She's three-in-one and lets you eat people."

"I never said you couldn't eat those you and the others rip apart, just that making wine from their blood was impractical," he argued good-naturedly. Might as well have been discussing fermenting mushrooms rather than people. "Also, aside from the thrill of the taboo, I doubt human meat is worth the effort."

"I feel it would be very gamey," I said, partaking in the macabre humor, even if I doubted it was only that. "Wouldn't it, Mistress?"

"Cannibalism is not encouraged in my cults," Polyope said in unison. "It's a practice born out of offshoots who don't quite practice what I passed down. I don't appreciate the sacrificing of goats either."

Lyssa pouted. "How disenchanting! I was looking forward to inviting some of your followers to a frenzy, to see how they could elevate the celebrations."

"We still can," Theoneus said with a scheming smile. "We've yet to host one on burial grounds. Perhaps some necromancy could have the undead join us."

That made me envision plague-era art, all favoring the depiction of dancing skeletons.

It was becoming clear they weren't behaving this way to bait the others like I had, but genuinely thought this way. They definitely weren't here to compete, but to seek disastrous entertainment. And I couldn't blame them. This was out of mythological tragicomedy. If only I weren't the leading female role.

Adamantus had dipped out of sight, leaving the souls to guide the gods to their quarters at Blackglass Hall.

Theoneus refused their escort, and busied himself with sampling from the nightwine fountain, while Lyssa took off in a no-doubt ill-advised direction, cackling like a lunatic.

As their voices trailed off, Polyope and I headed for Adamantus's main office, past the diamond-studded sky, and into the study where I was once again caught by the inaccurate constellation on the ceiling.

"Tell me you find it odd, too," I said to her. "There's an extra star at the end that isn't there in real life."

Adamantus groaned from behind his desk, now free of the nightmarish disguise with his hound split apart. "If you look at any charts older than a millennium, it was there."

"So, a star just blinked out of existence?"

"Stranger things have happened," Polyope said distractedly. "But I do remember that star."

Adamantus tapped his nails on his desk. "You can discuss astronomy later. Did you give her your gift?"

Polyope offered me the lapis lazuli box she'd been holding. "Use it carefully."

The lid flew open, revealing a weapon unlike any I'd seen before. Platinum with a crosshatch handle and gold borders, its blade was a thick corkscrew that ended in a sharp point.

"A tridagger, representing my three forms," she said proudly. "It contains two other shapes besides the default."

Awed, I carefully lifted it to examine its craftsmanship in the firelight. "How do I use it?"

"You're a clever girl, I'm sure you'll figure it out."

I played around with the tridagger, swiping it through the air to get a feel for what methods of attack it was best suited for. "Very helpful, as if I'm going to have the mind to parse how this thing works when Formeta is running me through with her sword—"

The tridagger unraveled with a burst, spinning out into a longsword.

Since I'd decided to give up most of my earthbound restraints within the Underworld, I let out a shriek of excitement as I went through all the moves and poses of sword fighting.

"What's the third form? Do I just keep swinging about in the dark until it—there it is."

The longsword rounded, narrowed and lengthened, its end hitting the floor with a piercing thunk, becoming a pole.

"I am going to have a lot of fun with this." I whooped as I raised my face to her central one. "Thank you."

Each face bore a different but connected expression—surprise, fondness and delight. "Thank me by wreaking havoc in my name."

I bowed with a flourish and the tridagger retracted into its spiraling state.

When I straightened, she was gone and Adamantus stood in the center of the study, beneath the sun on the ceiling, half-lit by the fireplace, the other half cast in shadow.

Unblinking, glowing eyes staring at me, he said, "If you die in this mission, she may be tempted to reanimate you and keep you as a pet."

"Is it the necromancy? The reason why everyone has turned on her?"

An intake of breath prepared me for similar revelations to his own, but he decided against it. "It's not my story to tell."

Interest piqued further, I edged closer until I was a touch away. "So, it's more than that."

"We're not here to discuss her past, but the future we need to prevent."

"That's already been discussed. But after finding out I'm competing against a war goddess of all beings, I need an extra incentive to stick out my neck for your investigation."

"I've already done my part in protecting your people from the gods' wrath. And you will be returning with an unchallenged ownership of your farmlands, and whatever riches you desire to expand your efforts and alleviate any struggles. What more would you like?"

He wasn't angered, or even annoyed, but tense, as if expecting me to pull out of the deal, even when he knew I couldn't.

"A substitute to the answers you're now withholding."

A pause weighed by consideration, then he relaxed. "What would you like to know?"

There were a thousand questions I had about this place, about his motive for being so invested in the mystery, about his history and experiences. But the woman in me wanted to know one thing...

"What do you see when you look at Eglaia?"

The center of his eyes brightened like stars, and my heart raced its own beats, my blood gushing with molten fire. My every nerve revved in anticipation of climbing him, wrapping myself around him, and taking those lips I'd craved since the first time I'd seen them, and...

"Nothing."

Taken aback, I felt as if he'd backhanded me. "Nothing?"

His gaze flitted from my body to my face as he nodded. "Her status as the most beautiful woman depends on reflecting what the viewer considers ideal. I always saw her base form, a featureless figure, and it unsettles her far more than when another woman is worshipped in her stead."

"Oh, that's what Polyope meant by her having no power over you."

A smirk broke over his masterpiece face, sinister with self-satisfaction. "It does make her claw at walls."

Disappointment trickled into my lungs, snuffing out the flame that had been lit from that first day I'd seen him in the woods. Every conclusion I'd arrived at had been wrong, all along. Even as I craved the delirious experience of bedding him, the god everyone dreaded, the man no one had dared touch, no one but me—he didn't reciprocate.

His insistence on not being viewed as a man, Polyope referring to him as a personification, and him being unaffected by the goddess of desire herself, seeing nothing instead of anything that resembled me, all came together in a neat, silent rejection.

But what had I expected, really? He was Death, and I'd always wondered what the myths of Death and the Maiden were all about, how he could want a mortal woman. Now I'd gotten my answer. He couldn't.

Swallowing the lump in my throat, I found him looking at my orichalcum bracelet.

Deciding to change the subject, to close it, I forced a grin on my face. "I still can't believe this is real, and not just fool's gold for treasure hunters."

His dark lips curled like he relished the thought. "The reason the adventurers hardly find their fabled treasures is because I have beaten them to it."

"Hoarding all the wealth like a dragon. I despise you," I said with no bite.

"I'm not wealthy, I'm rich in natural resources. After all, it is all mined from beneath the earth, so I have a greater claim to it all than anyone else does."

"Except for the earth itself. Which has teeth." If I wasn't having Death, at least I'd have answers. So I asked, "Why does it have teeth?"

"Because it used to be alive."

Many eerie ideas came to mind, only to be smothered by my own existence as someone who relied on the earth's consistent growth. "And it isn't now?"

"The best way I could describe its status now is brain-dead."

"Not even comatose?"

The blueness that circled his eyes as if in kohl, and darkened the hollows of his cheekbones intensified as if in weariness. "It breathes, it functions, but the consciousness it once had is gone."

"What happened?"

"You better not know, or you will never look at your lands the same way ever again."

I tsked. "You know you're just making me want to know even more, right?"

"I guarantee you there are many truths about existence beside myself that are better off unknown."

Including himself among the prehistoric mysteries only fueled the flames of my curiosity.

I narrowed my eyes at him. "Are you trying to scare me off?"

"I'm doing the opposite by not telling you," he said tersely. "It is best that you keep your distance from such things before they ruin your view of your world."

"Because I have such a rosy and sheltered perception of it?" I tapped the tridagger against his chest, close enough to breathe his air. "What are you hiding?"

If I could believe my senses anymore, and I didn't, I would have thought something akin to dread hardened his features. "Nothing you need to know."

Too late to backtrack, I trudged ahead, following my gut on why he was so tight-lipped about everything. "You don't have to worry about scaring me, I'm not afraid of you."

Burning purple flared from his eyes and mouth. *"You should be."*

The floor disappeared from beneath me and I fell out of his study and back into my bed.

❦ 29 ❧

THE MUSE OF CAPRICE

Much to the dismay of the visiting gods, dinner was held in a grand hall in the soul city of Athanasia, with stationed tables spread in food and drink, forcing them to mingle among the resident dead. None save for Theoneus made rounds on all the attendees, unnerving most with his enthusiasm.

Adamantus lurked on the periphery, daring anyone to approach him. None did. I certainly didn't.

Since he'd tossed me back in my room after he'd told me about his nonexistent response to Eglaia, I couldn't stop overthinking it. Even after I'd told myself I'd forget about it, I'd been retreading every moment we'd shared. Every touch, every spark, the constant charge between us, every time I'd felt him holding back, every instance when I'd been certain my arousal was a reflection of his own desire. Not to mention all these years I'd roamed searching for him.

I'd already decided it had all been in my mind. A necessary attachment to the one man I'd allowed myself to feel anything for, because ironically, he was the one who'd meant me no harm. Along with the lure of the unknown and the impossible, and the

novelty of being with someone far stronger, far more self-suffi-
cient, yet also burdened with a destiny he couldn't escape even if
he wanted to. It all combined with knowing I had no physical
intimacy to look forward to in my life, just like my mother, that
I'd live the life of a mother to all, but a lover to none.

I had wanted it to be him, the man I'd take into my bed, my
body, and I'd wanted to give him what no one else had ever
wanted to. My trust, my welcome, my pleasure to see him, to be
with him.

I supposed it didn't matter anymore. I'd tried, I'd offered, but
he wasn't interested. Maybe he couldn't be. As he and Polyope
insisted.

Now I had to focus on what lay ahead, this competition, and
what would come after it, after I went home.

But first, I'd *eat*.

Veil hanging on my shoulders as a shawl, tridagger hanging
from my hip and orichalcum whip around my forearm, I prowled
around feeling armed and dangerous, filling my plate with whatever caught my eye. I stuffed my face with grape-leaf dolma,
tomato rice, breaded meatballs and fried eggplants, all smelling
of the herbs, spices, garlic and onion that reminded me of home.

The change in cuisine from the spoiling selection of sweets
and desserts to Campanian and Orestian dishes had me sneaking
looks at our host, wondering that he'd acted on my prior
complaints. In spite of myself, a warmth spread through me that
I couldn't pass as heartburn.

Halfway through my third helping, dipping my bread into the
seasoned olive oil, I felt the unwelcome proximity of a hostile
aura.

"We never got to discuss much at our introduction,"
Almagera greeted, syrupy sweet, dryad by her side. "What are
you, because it isn't wholly mortal."

Talking as I chewed loudly, I recited the fiction that had had
Chloë and me in hysterics as we'd come up with it. "I'm not. My

father was a satyr, and my mother is Tabliope, Muse of Improvisation."

Disgust flared her bristling outline. "Of all things, why is there a Muse of Improvisation now? Wasn't a Muse of Alchemy bad enough?"

"You'd be surprised how inspired you need to be in a tight spot," I shrugged, licking the oil off my fingers, eliciting more sparks of revulsion.

"That certainly explains why you'd volunteer to be in Polyope's service," Perilla said in condescension. "You make haphazard decisions and end up paying the price for life."

Perilla reeked of peppermint oil, but her green coloring made me long for the hills I lived among, the vibrancy of their hues after morning rain in the spring. It was a shame she was as venomous as her mistress.

Maintaining a light tone, I bared my teeth at her. "Didn't we all volunteer to be here, sweet nymph?"

"Yes, but you seem to miss the point of us being here," Almagera snapped.

I raised my eyebrows. "Which is?"

"To choose a worthy queen," Perilla said, nose in the air.

"You really think that could be you?" I tutted at her, before looking at Almagera. "Thinking you could make a living tree Queen of the Dead is like believing a cow could run a farm."

The noises of offense Almagera made were highly entertaining.

It really did break my heart on some level that she was so unbearable. The goddess we valued the most back home, not just as the Queen of Heaven, but the fertility we relied on to maintain our population, health and agriculture, ought to have been more motherly.

An ache spread to my extremities, like I had fallen from a cliff and bruised my whole body. I missed my mother. I hoped Chloë informed her of our situations, assuring her that I wasn't dead.

Perilla, meanwhile, continued being as nasty as her scent. "Your mother seems to have been a great role model for you. So what is her main area of expertise? Improvising with satyrs?"

It may have not been my actual mother in mention, but in this moment, I was ready to chase her like the one I claimed to be sired by. Only I wouldn't be discouraged once she took the form of a tree, I would sharpen my axe and take great pleasure in delivering each swing.

I sighed. "I guess it's impossible to explain last minute gambles to a tree."

Lyceus had arrived with his champion. "You gamble much, Sister Prospera?"

If the presence of a dryad stoked my homesickness, then Lyceus's approach made it roar like the bonfires I missed.

"If I find it worth the time, yes."

Initially painful to observe like the sun, his light was welcome, bringing to mind how I'd rise every morning at daybreak and watch as its rays poured through leaves and painted buildings and mountains.

He may have also toned down his brightness, because I could see everything from the shape of his triangular jaw to the pleasing smoothness of his features, perfectly symmetrical.

Noticing how I was eyeing him, he responded with a suggestive smile. "I didn't think you could appreciate beauty, when you are so content to wed what lurks in the shadows with good reason."

I snorted. "Enjoy your own reflection that much, Your Brightness?"

Lyceus licked his lips as he wagged his brows. "From time to time, yes."

"Quite sad though, to be a god with so many options and stuck with your own hand."

"On the contrary, I think everyone should love themselves first before anyone else," he purred.

"Then what would be the point of love at all if we were all

content with ourselves?" Eglaia objected, her sorceress sticking close as they joined us.

"You wouldn't understand," Lyceus told Eglaia.

"I am in charge of such matters, no one would understand them better than myself!" Eglaia retorted.

Stars in heaven, they really did have the mental strength of a spoiled brat. No wonder they reacted with such heat and hate to slights in all their stories.

But the goddess of desire and beauty was what broke my restraint long enough to sneak a glance at Adamantus, who was caught by Theoneus's energetic gesturing.

If he saw nothing, then what was I supposed to do with her still reflecting back a female version of him?

It made me livid. At her, for holding a mirror to people's inconvenient desires, baring their weaknesses and obsessions and shame to them, leaving them no place to hide from the painful truth.

With the memory when she'd almost killed me for much less replaying in my mind, I still looked up at her and smirked. "It would be hard to enjoy your own appearance when you change it so often. Do you know what you look like, I wonder? Does it get tiring or even depressing to not exist when no one is regarding you?"

Almagera and her dryad backed away as Eglaia drew near, her proximity alone reversing my blood flow to my most sensitive spots. "What would you even begin to know of beauty when your sect of lunatics revel in the macabre?"

Another glance caught Adamantus looking back at me, having approached to observe our small gathering.

His nearness seemed to negate her effect on me, and I glared up at her. "Beauty born from the dark and deadly might be rare, but that's what gives it such great power. You of all people should take pride in the catastrophic endings your influence has caused, all in the name of beauty, love, and desire."

In diplomatic settings, people who lost arguments, changed

the subject. Eglaia was no different. "What did you say your mother was? There's a muse for gambling?"

"Improvisation. She's among the younger, lesser crop of muses of cartography, tragicomedy, mathematics and prose," I listed off.

"They'll just deify anyone these days, won't they," Eglaia sneered.

Glee fled the weakening shackles of my reserve as I sighed with disgust. "Tedious, isn't it? Why does lust need a deity? Men and beasts will fuck regardless of divine influence, be it by mounting their own or each other."

It flew over a number of heads, but the rest expressed the desired amount of discomfort and disgust. Ironic, truly, considering what Eglaia herself was known to do to people who offended her, using her power over their desires to make them commit the unthinkable.

"Absolutely tactless, to speak like this in such company," Aethusa, Lyceus's fey granddaughter, finally spoke.

"What use is tact when we're here to run right into the arms of certain death?"

When I sought him out again, I found Adamantus gone.

His primary company for the evening, Theoneus, joined us by jumping onto the nearby table, rattling the silverware and the guests, before dropping down, crystal water jug and matching goblet in hand, idly kicking his legs. That was when I took note of the size he presented himself in. None of the other gods appeared in anything shorter than seven-feet, yet he hadn't bothered.

Even stranger, the lulling energy he exuded was far more commanding than Eglaia's.

"What are we whispering about?" he asked jovially, pouring a glass.

The water left the spout and landed in the goblet as blood-red wine.

"Nothing that concerns you," Almagera snapped.

Perilla, on the other hand, gravitated towards him.

He dropped his head back to face Almagera. "Aww, somebody's in a bad mood."

"Mind your tone with me," Almagera warned.

"Or what, you'll spank me?" he pouted.

I let out a stifled giggle.

Almagera grew, citrus-yellow light washing over us. "Don't make me have you thrown off of Anactoron. Eurycrius isn't here to vouch for you anymore."

In my mind, I added several underlines beneath her name on the list of suspects.

Theoneus twisted at the middle, half-facing her as his reddish aura pulsed to the loud heartbeat that settled between my ears, spreading a drowsing flush.

"I think you're taking this way too seriously," he said to her, voice all-encompassing, but soft and soothing, unlike Adamantus's commanding rumble.

Almagera reached a clawed hand for his neck, a dark swirl growing in her palm that reeked of poison. An inch from him, she froze and his pulsations grew faster and brighter. For the life of me I couldn't tell where his voice was coming from, but it made my muscles loosen, plate slipping from my weakened grasp and clattering by my feet.

"You could use a nap," he told her. "It might make you less cranky."

Entranced, Almagera's hard outlines softened as she shrunk and turned away, descending from our platform with Perilla right behind her.

Facing us, he had taken on a stronger reddish-purple tint, but his eyes remained yellow.

It didn't take long for the others to show signs of being affected, Rhoxane peeking from behind her goddess, Aethusa approaching him with a glazed look in her eyes, and even Machaius's war-goddess daughter had joined us.

When the souls congregated, that was when I knew it wasn't purely out of whatever lust he inspired in his near-nakedness, nor the shameless splay of his legs, as he leaned back on his elbows to survey us.

He was doing something, but I couldn't place what exactly.

Eglaia picked up on it first. "Stop it."

"Stop what?" he hummed innocently, batting his long lashes at us from over the rim of his goblet.

"Let the boy have his fun," Lyceus cut in. "There's only so much we can do to entertain ourselves here."

"His brand of entertainment is turning people into rabid animals," Eglaia spat venomously.

"Bold complaint coming from you," I found myself saying. "You punish people by making them go mad with lust over the worst things."

"That's for those who deserve it, not that you would understand the limits of what is right or wrong." Eglaia bearing the female version of Adamantus's face made her distaste hit harder. "Aren't you here because your mother mated with a satyr?"

The strange disinhibition the youngest god inspired loosened my tongue to a risky degree, as I felt the furious urge to correct her that I was here because their king had chosen my mother.

Enough remaining sense rerouted me back to my purpose. "And all I have to show for it are these horns," I whined, sticking my foot up, eager to kick her in the chest. "I could have had hooves but I got stuck with these oversensitive feet instead."

The lone being unaffected by Theoneus, Eglaia smacked my foot away and left to join her husband in overlooking the city.

Rhoxane lingered, hands over her midsection, like she feared I'd spontaneously disembowel her.

"What's the matter, darling?" Theoneus beckoned her with curling fingers. "Come here."

Bewitched, she approached with dilated eyes and a half-open mouth.

If it hadn't been for the inexplicable calmness he instilled in me, seeing a god about to toy with a defenseless mortal would have had me stepping between them.

Instead, he offered her his goblet then poured me one. "Here, drink up. You'll need it with her breathing down your neck."

Rhoxane took it, but something stopped her before she could sip. Panic had entered her eyes, and her arm trembled, sloshing the wine down her hand.

"It's not poisoned," he assured her. "Almagera is the one you have to watch out for in that case."

She squeaked, eyes darting around for an escape.

"Oh, do you prefer it white?" A snap of his fingers changed the drink of red to the color of his eyes.

Unblinking, he sat forward, sending waves of sedating warmth my way. "What's the matter, little witches, is my token not good enough for you both?"

Rhoxane trembled. "I—I can't. I shouldn't."

My head felt heavy, eyelids on the verge of closing, and no fight against the urge to drop.

"Why?" The space around him distorted, just as it had when he arrived, colors blending together and tinted by his aura. "You're both hurting my feelings. I'm not the one you should be worried about."

Some of the drowsiness evaporated to make way for pursuing that hint. "Then who?"

He quirked an unimpressed brow at me. I took that as a sign that he wanted me to drink first and downed the whole glass. It was sweet and smelled of peaches, something I haven't had in years.

He gestured for Rhoxane to drink up. "See? If I meant you any harm, I'd be obvious about it."

Polyope approached, coating him in her massive shadow. "I think that's enough for now. The girls are going to need their minds clear for their challenges."

Instantaneously, the spell broke. I lurched forward with a gasp, like I had been underwater.

Sobbing, Rhoxane dropped the goblet and bolted from the vicinity. I was caught between pitying her and wanting to smash the jug over his head.

"What was that about?" I snarled.

"I was being friendly, something there seems to be a shortage of in this level of existence." He laughed. "I felt you two were in the greatest need of some relaxation, especially her, she looks ready to pop."

Polyope set two of her hands on his shoulders, and another two on his head, petting the space between his horns like she was calming an agitated dog. "Theoneus, now's not the time to play with people's feelings. I'd like a moment alone with my priestess."

Groaning in reluctance, he stood and stretched. "You're all no fun."

"You can arrange your fun after the first test is done," she told him. "Now go collect your maenad, she's terrorizing the souls."

Shooting me a wink, Theoneus obeyed. He leaped off and headed down into the city, swinging his hips and shoulders to the music.

I breathed hot air out through my nose. "How did you do that? He refused to listen to anyone else."

"He's a simple, if unsettling, being. Treat him kindly and he'll respond in kind. You antagonize him like the other elder gods do and he will find a way to pull on your puppet strings." Crowding me, view of anyone nearby blocked, Polyope dropped a pomegranate before me. "Quick, eat some because there's been a change of plans."

I dug my thumbnails into its top and split it with one tug, scattering some seeds onto the black table, shining like rubies. "What's going on?"

"Adamantus just learned that the gods are so impatient that they want to start the competition now."

"WHAT?" I picked the fallen seeds and tossed them into my mouth. "I'm not prepared for this."

I remembered too late that this was from Adamantus's orchard, where the fruits grew with metallic rings and had crystalline flesh, but the seeds crunched between my teeth, spilling sparkling juice.

So, they were edible for me all along.

"I doubt anyone beyond Formeta is prepared—that's enough for today."

I made a grab for the fruit, but she left me with one half. "Don't you want me to, I don't know, get boosted?"

"This is ambrosia, eat too much of it too fast and it will burn you up," she hissed, second and third heads on the lookout. "Eat only a small amount of seeds before each exertion, do you understand?"

I crunched the last of the seeds in my mouth and nodded.

"Good." She caught me by the scruff of the neck like a kitten and lifted me out to where they had gathered in the city square.

Coping with being made to feel small and weightless would have to wait for another day, because when she dropped me back on my feet between Rhoxane and Perilla, I found Adamantus ready to pierce Machaius with his bident.

"Don't raise your voice in my home." His order reverberated throughout the ground, quaking it. "I told you it's not happening today."

"Why not?" Machaius argued. "Let the Godsgate open and for us to be done with this already. You think we have time to hang around this mausoleum for eternity like you do?"

Lyceus stepped between them to mediate. "Here's an idea. How about we start with someone other than Machaius, a tamer task to be fair to the girls?"

After considering it, Adamantus lowered his staff and turned his head all the way around, making the onlookers fidget. He paused in my direction. I stared back, still feeling the pinpricks of pomegranate juice crackle along my tongue.

"We'll begin with Almagera's task," he decided. "Her Gods-gate will open here."

GODSGATE

Preparation was a luxury in a life determined to pull the rug out from under me.

But whatever awaited me on the other side of this test could be dealt with. I was born and bred to handle whatever came my way. I could and would handle this.

I kept telling myself this, over and over, as the circular Godsgate solidified before me and my competitor. It was made of green wood bursting with curling vines and flowers that filled the air with sweet scents. It creaked open, flooding us with daylight and open air, and homesickness alone had me stepping through without looking back.

Once I stepped onto the white garden path, the border of the gate dissipated and left me enveloped by precious greenery. Laid out in exquisite gardens that would put royal estates to shame, Almagera's holy grounds were orchards upon hedges upon bushes bursting with produce and flora that stretched for fields bordered by forests. It was a sampler of every plant life known to man and I wanted to kick off my sandals and run through them, never to return.

The urge to bolt like a startled deer would never be an option, but releasing my feet from their stiff binding did a lot to ease my nerves. Leaving the sandals by the gate, I headed out, taking in deep breaths of fresh air.

It might have been the weeks of deprivation, but pressing my bare soles down on the sun-warmed path, then stepping onto the lush grass was an ecstatic experience.

Perilla approached, sunlight passing through her green skin, illuminating its insides. "What are you doing?"

I groaned, turning my face to the sky and stretching out my arms, like I could grasp at the sun, channel it through me and into the earth I dug my toes into. "I envy you, you know."

"Why?"

"You can just dig your roots in and become part of all this, and understand it in a way I never could."

"If you love this so much, what are you doing working for the Ghost Queen?" she asked with more confusion than mockery.

"What makes you think I had a choice?" I wiggled in place, grinding my soles further into the earth, and felt it pulse up my legs, threatening to buckle my knees.

That was new.

I tried it again and it crackled against my skin then shot up my calves, the same jarring buzz as slamming my elbow.

An experimental step forward felt the same charge, not just beneath me but around me, a slow recovery from the pins-and-needles of full-body numbness.

Deciding it must be the aftereffects of what Theoneus's drink, I asked Perilla, "What about you, did you have a choice in being here?"

The peppermint scent intensified, reminding me of the winters I spent up north, where they delighted in candy and drinks made of it. "It's an honor to be chosen."

"That's not what I asked," I said as I set out, searching for our task.

Peacocks marked our start, strutting around a table overlooked by citrus groves in the open emerald grass.

Polished greenwood that shone in the light filtering through the leaves above, the table bore six clear-glass bottles.

"Is this it?" I picked up the third bottle from the right, checking the viscosity and clarity. "What even is this?"

Almagera's voice rang from above. *"Four are poison, two are not."*

"You better not be expecting me to drink this," I grumbled, uncorking it for a sniff.

The scent that tickled my nose was all-too-familiar. Wintergreen oil, what I helped massage on my mother's joints in the winter. Drinking this would definitely kill me.

"They are for you to use wisely," Almagera said, way too happily for my liking.

"Use for what?" Perilla asked.

Something moved nearby, rustling among the trees.

Keeping an eye out in that direction, I checked the other bottle. It was watery, and suspiciously odorless. Laurel water, a favored poison of Arborean courtiers and widows.

Both tucked into my belt, I continued my inspection while Perilla remained staring over my head. "Do you hear that?"

The pungency of the vinegar in the third bottle yanked a sneeze from my overworked nose. "Are there animals here?"

"None that I can sense."

Gut feelings weren't uncharted territory to me. People had animal instincts trained out of them, through social necessities of politeness and politics, to ignore warning signs.

Even if my senses had been dulled by years of socialization, I still relied on the reactions of the creatures around me.

Eagle-eyed, I watched Perilla for signs of overt-confidence, because her mistress wasn't above helping her cheat. The good thing was, she looked just as wary as I felt. Whatever this was, she wasn't in on it.

The very same something rummaged closer.

I felt the ground shake and jumped right as a giant tendril shot out from between the trees.

It hit the table with a shattering force, spraying splinters everywhere.

Staggering back, I grabbed Perilla. "DUCK!"

Another tendril, larger than the first, burst through the left. It split the trees apart, knocking lemons everywhere in its haste to grab at us.

I threw us back to dodge it and she scrambled away the instant we hit the ground, gathering the fallen bottles.

Perilla wasted no time bouncing back up, running with the remaining bottles.

Up after her, I knotted my skirt up by my hip to expand my mobility. "Almagera! What are we supposed to do here?"

"Where did all that confidence go?" she taunted. *"You were self-assured enough to mouth off to us. I couldn't punish you for your insolence in Polyope's presence, but she's not here to help you now!"*

When I got home I was defacing every idol of hers I came across! I was going to use the wooden ones as kindling, I was going to bury the stone ones in the stables and hang my washcloths on her face!

We didn't get far uphill when another, much larger bristled tentacle burst out in front of us.

There was no outrunning it, and Perilla and I shared the same conclusion of jumping onto it when it swung to crush us.

I dropped to embrace it, arms and legs clinging to the sides as it whooshed us up and over the trees. "Do you have any idea what this is?" I yelled at her. "Because I don't and it's my job to know!"

Her feet transformed into roots that gripped the surface. "You think I'd tell you if I did?"

The force of the movement, and the resulting wind nipping at my skin, made it too hard to maintain my hold.

For a splendid second, it paused in its rise and allowed me a view of the holy gardens. The vibrant variety of green, shades reflecting the golden sun in velvety grass, glossy trees, matte bushes and gleaming dots of fruit scattered across the grounds.

The moment was brought crashing down with the tentacle and my intestines tied themselves around my spine.

There wasn't anything I could do against the long swing down and the wind that had me floating up, hovering airborne with panic as I clawed for the rough surface of the tendril.

I couldn't land like this! It would break every connecting bone in my body, especially my neck!

A blinding gleam off the metal on my arm flashed a hare-brained idea past my eyes and into my head.

Focusing on the orichalcum whip, it snaked down my arm and formed a handle in my palm. When I fell past the treetops, I cracked the whip at a bough and swung all the way up and onto it, hugging the trunk as I landed.

Whatever this plant monster was, it stemmed from some-where further in, and that base would be the best place to work on killing it.

The giant tentacle had landed with a crash that rattled the trees, and Perilla yelped in pain. Taking hold of the whip, I jumped down, having it dangle me two feet above the ground so I'd land on my feet.

My feet picked up on the pulsation from earlier, but it was stronger on the forest floor. Pursuing that strengthening sensa-tion took me further in, where the crackling that electrified my soles grew, pointing me on the right track.

Inexplicably, I knew where to go, taking a twisting path through the trees to evade the other tendrils until I caught their source.

A massive stump-like structure formed the base, a giant earthy squid embedded into the middle of the woods. It was unlike any plant I'd witnessed before, appearing less like a full being and the remnant of something that had once been even larger, and scarier. Like whatever grew the gigantic tooth in the Hall of Death Records.

This thing better not have many hearts like a squid, because I wouldn't know where to start stabbing.

Not that it would have given me the chance to chop at it. The smaller tendrils shot after me, one catching me around the waist and hoisting me up so fast I blacked out for an instant.

Head swirling, I kicked idly in the air as Perilla and the largest extremity crashed right in, the force breaking her roots and sending her flying hard into a tree.

"Perilla!" I tried to reach the bottles in my belt, hoping the laurel water affected it the way it did those of us with blood. "Perilla, give me the poisons!"

"Do you think I'm stupid? I know you picked the useless ones and now I'm going to win!"

I pounded onto the captor holding me up. "This isn't about winning, this is about making it out of here alive! Now help me down and hand me the bottles!"

"You really are crazy if you think I'll do that."

Up and unfazed, she uncorked two bottles with her teeth and flung one at the stump and the other at an advancing tendril.

Neither did anything but enrage the central stump.

Extremities flailing harder, it pitched me through the trees. My back slammed against a trunk, knocking the air out of me with a cough that almost expelled my lungs. I slid down and landed hard on my tailbone.

Perilla cursed and screamed at the forest monster from the nearby distance, a desperate edge to her shouts. She'd used up all her bottles with no results.

That left what I had, and if there was one right answer among them it was the vinegar. Back home, invasive plants got sprayed with a mixture of water and vinegar, so the only liquid that could do any kind of damage now was its concentrated form.

I just had to get close enough.

Summoning the whip again, I flung it at the mid-height bough and climbed up the side as it recoiled. Now I was close enough to observe and plot.

Perilla's attempt to escape was blocked by the largest part

swinging back at her. Out of fear, or to evade detection, she stood still and morphed into a large mint plant.

This tactic may have worked on those with eyes to be deceived, but this was as connected to the dirt as she was.

She was uprooted with a brutal tug that exploded her pain through the air like a thunderclap. Back as a nymph, she struggled in its hold, babbling and blubbering with her wits shattered.

Another time, I would have made the back-breaking effort to spare her along with myself. But it didn't matter how much fondness I carried for her kind, or how I valued being fair back home. I wasn't here as a future leader and embodiment of the good green earth whose gifts we relied on.

I was here to win. That meant I couldn't risk myself for her safety.

The tendrils tightened around her, squeezing out a shrill scream before it crushed her with a loud, wooden snap.

Hanging limp in its grasp, Perilla's body echoed the broken corpses of the girls mistaken for me.

Leaping off the bough, I dove straight for the glowing center of the stump.

As I feared, a tendril followed me and wrapped around my leg. I dangled for the second it took to tug me up and back before it moved to slam me against the ground.

The breaking fall was close, and I was on level with the stump. I ripped the bottle of vinegar from my belt and flung it hard enough to dislocate my arm with a furious scream.

The bottle burst upon impact and filled the air with the sour, acidic stench of vinegar as the stump absorbed it.

Throes of agony rang between the scrape of metal on gravel and the creak of a rusting hinge, and the tendrils unbound me, retreating into the dark as I tumbled down.

A FRACTURED FANTASY

I crawled through the Godsgate on my elbows, whole body smarting from the killer landing.

Returning to the dimness that pulsed with the gods' combined radiation was too much for me to adjust to now. I flopped down, huffing out shallow breaths as my heated flesh melted against the cool ground.

"There you are." Polyope lifted me to my feet, side-hugging me to the groove between two of her bodies.

Groaning pitifully, everything hurting, I rested my head against her in an angle that allowed me to witness their reactions.

Eglaia and Machaius' warm colors blended together through my bleary eyes, Theoneus was nowhere to be seen, and my competitors lurked on the sidelines with the growing crowd of souls.

Adamantus was out of my line of sight, but I sensed him watching me.

Almagera saved me the effort of moving my head by blocking my view.

I rolled my eyes up to her furious face. "What?"

"It appears I went too easy on you."

"Easy?" I wheezed. "Perilla died!"

"Yes, I made a mistake in choosing her."

If my whole body didn't feel bruised, I would have had more to say about how terrible she was, or even keep up the unfazed facade of Prospera by agreeing with her.

"She died for you, in a test you made. Where is all the motherly warmth and lover-of-life aspect you are so beloved for?"

"It might have slipped your broken mind but it is an honor to give your life to your god." Almagera turned to leave. "She will be planted in my gardens for her sacrifice, whereas you will end up a scarecrow when the next challenge proves greater than my own."

"That's a very bizarre way to admit defeat," I called after her.

A slow-clap preceded Lyceus taking her place before me. "That was fast."

"Can't take your time when you're about to be crushed," I mumbled.

He was oddly pleased with this outcome, beaming at me with luminance my aching head couldn't handle. "Regardless, I must say I'm impressed. I can't wait to see how the rest of this competition goes."

"Why? Are you going to fight me yourself for Orcus's hand?"

Lyceus threw back his head as he laughed, a jovial, musical sound that somehow lessened my headache. "If I saw what you find desirable in him, I might. But I find you far more interesting now."

Aethusa appeared at his side, complaining about something I didn't care to decipher. Lyceus ignored her in favor of reaching for me. "Allow me."

Witnessing him in all his sunlit splendor, radiating timeless beauty and charm that had beguiled countless others, I had little resistance left to view him through unaffected, methodical eyes.

It was easy to see why he was the favored subject of artists, not just for his patronage, but the wonder he inspired.

When he took my hand, I felt most of the pain fade with my

shaking exhalation, and the blurred corners of my vision began to clear.

A cat on a dairy farm wouldn't be this pleased with himself. "How's that feel?"

"Eh."

That earned me another laugh, an open, easy release to revel in.

However enamored I might have been by him now, a treacherous part of me compared his laugh to the ones I'd wrung out of Adamantus. The sheer unexpectedness, the break of tension and power of knowing that no one else had ever seen him that way.

Polyope patted my cheek, hand encompassing my head. "That's enough exertion for today."

I made no complaints when my feet left the floor and I was carried out of the room by the back of my dress.

The heated gaze I felt following me out wasn't Lyceus's.

OUT OF MY disguise and ruined clothes, I drifted in and out of sleep as my hair dried from the bath I'd napped in.

Perilla's demise shouldn't come as a shock to me. Plenty had died under the orders of their unfeeling authorities, but somehow I expected better of the gods. They had all the faults of those they ruled over, but they were meant to be better.

Though that may have been the modern view I was raised in, where devotion to a leader or deity was invested in their morality rather than their purpose. The same went for cultural heroes, who performed feats I grew up reenacting with wooden weapons and quotes from fictionalized accounts.

The hooks of sleep unlatched from my edges when Adamantus came through my door.

I rose on my elbows, damp, curling hair falling off my face. "Come to tell me I did a good job?"

"No." The Horned God peeled off him as he unclasped his

cloak and dropped it and his bident by the tea table. "It is too early to celebrate, this is but the first stage."

I watched him roll up his sleeves with grateful distraction. "Who's celebrating? I'm just asking for a little praise."

Adamantus had moved on to unbuttoning the top of his shirt, and my eyes stuck themselves to his clavicles as he settled by me. "You did better than I expected."

"Meaning you expected me to not come back out?"

His agreement was in the way he moved on to his waistcoat, avoidant and tense.

I followed his careful fingers as they undid another layer of his expensive garb, mouth drying. "What are you doing?"

"For hours I've felt like my skin was shrinking, and one wrong move would have me bursting at the seams," he said, sounding hoarse, breathless. "I couldn't show any signs of discomfort among them."

I edged closer, itching to reward myself by indulging in pushing the waistcoat off his shoulders. "So, you came to me to express your discomfort?"

"Yes," he agreed quickly. "You are my partner in this ruse, aren't you?"

"I'm your pawn," I corrected, too tired to put any heat into it.

He shook his head, exhaling heavily through his nose. "A pawn is expendable and oblivious, like Almagera's nymph. You are neither."

"And yet, you can't tell me 'good job'?"

"This isn't a job. This is a task that is proving to be harder to keep control of as it goes on," he said, voice grating with mounting frustration. "This was meant to end the minute I presented you as the only one I could ever think of. Now they are here, inviting themselves into my home where they are initiating these tests without briefing me. Forcing my hand while I try to examine each of them for any hint that they are behind what brought us both here to begin with."

His breathing grew louder, hands unsteady as he continued to rid himself of his waistcoat, nails clacking against the golden buttons. "But I couldn't. I couldn't observe them since they sprung the first test on me. Having to wait to see how you fared in it—I could barely contain my rage, let alone detach myself enough to watch for their reactions."

There were many ways I'd expected him to behave, but none this human.

"You were worried about me," I realized.

"Of course I'm worried. This whole plot hinges on you besting their candidates, and I thought I'd find a lead based on their reactions to you winning this round, but that's not what I was thinking of." Adamantus gripped my face, fingers through my hair, thumb pressing into the hollow of my cheekbone. "*What is happening to me?*"

There were plenty of good answers. Pent up anger towards the other gods for cornering him into this situation. Territorial rage from them infringing on his space to hold their competition. Worry over his investigation falling through by my failure and the demand he marry the winner.

But this. Coming to my room to openly vent his inability to focus, expressing my fate as the reason without blaming me for his distraction. He truly had been worried about me.

"How do you feel?" I asked him, my own voice shaky with wonder.

His cool breath shuddered over my face. "I don't know what it is to name it."

"Describe it to me."

"Like I swallowed a wasp's nest—" He caught my hand and pressed it to his chest, and I gasped at the powerful hammering of his heart. "It won't stop."

This had to be a dream. But unlike our fateful introduction, this was no answer to a nebulous fantasy, that ended with him out of reach and me with even more questions. This negated his every belief of himself. This destroyed all talk of personifications. This validated where my singular urge to touch him and be touched by him came from. From this. This capacity for feeling he hadn't known existed, couldn't recognize or handle when it assailed him.

Testing his limits, I slid my hand under his half-open shirt, feeling the hard muscle of his chest. His heart pounded against my palm like the pulse of a star.

A fuse was lit within me, sparked by the detonations within my own chest, consuming all reservations from his earlier actions and claims. Even if he was immune to the goddess of desire, didn't see my face when he looked at her, it didn't matter. Because it all got lost in the flare of my own wants.

"I can't think. All my instincts tell me to take revenge, to ruin this effort, to attack them all one by one and rip the answer from their stuttering, dying lips, but it would destroy everything I've built till now, and the balance..." He heaved, panic rising beneath my palm. "It would target my Underworld, you, would end everything—"

I mirrored his hold on my head, gripping his hair to pull his mouth down to mine.

It was an excruciating few seconds before he began to respond, kissing back with a fervor that knocked his teeth against mine.

Messy, uncoordinated, his fangs nipped at my lips, and his nails dug into my scalp, but I didn't care. I knew, like I'd always known, that he wouldn't hurt me. And I wanted him to lose himself inside me, needed the tension I'd been drowning in since we'd locked gazes in the woods to finally shatter.

I moaned around his cold tongue as it imitated mine, and drove inside my mouth in a frenzy, like I needed him to fill the gnawing emptiness between my legs, to pound and plunder me until he seared me with his pleasure.

Grappling at his clothes, I pushed the waistcoat from the bunching muscles of his shoulders, and he obliged me, not breaking the kiss, devouring my lips in escalating abandon as I pulled his shirt from his pants and blindly tried to open it all the way.

The way I hungered to see more of him, one would think I hadn't lived among sweaty farmers working shirtless under Lyceus's sun, or with boys who swam naked in the lakes.

But it wasn't only because it was him, it was the deprivation—of how covered up and hidden he was, how distant and strange, like the dark and unknowable gaps between the stars.

And now a glimmer of their starlight was being shed onto him. He was here, with me, present, willing to share the unfathomable with me. What he had never shared before.

Impatience got the best of me and I ripped his shirt open, scattering diamond buttons everywhere.

I got only a glimpse of a wide expanse of perfection before he crashed his lips on mine again, growling mindlessly into my mouth. His feel, his sounds, his taste—all unimagined, and beyond my imaginings. Molten readiness poured between my thighs as he went with my clumsy maneuvering and climbed on top of me, that massive manifestation of darkness I'd craved from the first moment I'd glimpsed him.

Ruined shirt half down his arms, I roamed shaking hands across his back, feeling the sharp angles of his shoulder-blades and digging my fingers into the ridges between his thick, sculpted muscles.

Rumbling incessantly, Adamantus pressed between my legs, and I felt him hard, long and daunting against my thigh.

Exhilaration shuddered through me.

There it was. There it all was. Proof that I hadn't made any of it up in my head.

I hooked a leg over his hips, pulling him further to grind against, seeking out the friction for us both.

His delirious rumbles echoed down my throat, and I shook like I was gearing up to explode. But I wanted, needed to do so with him driving deep within me.

I reached between us to touch him as I had while taunting

the gods. I found him, through his pants, too thick even my hand spanned only half of him. My core pounded as I squeezed his length and moaned, "Adamantus—I want you inside me..."

He flew off me.

I sat up, dazed.

Here was a sight to commit to memory long after I'd left here.

Gone was the untouchable and inscrutable Lord of the Dead, and here was Adamantus with his mussed-by-my-fingers hair, torn-by-me shirt and swollen-from-my-kisses lips. His pale, blue-tinted skin bore a faint shimmer, like a fine coating of perspiration on a spring morning, or granules of broken glass amidst the sand they came from.

He looked positively wrecked, and I was the one who'd done that to him.

"What?" I croaked, voice a covetous, frustrated rasp. "Why'd you stop?"

There was no response. He just watched me with dilated pupils, black holes consuming the purple fire, expression unreadable, not quite present.

Worry cooled my excited flush. "Are you still with me?"

Only when I reached for his face did he snap out of it. In a blink, he was back on his feet, gripping his bident.

I tried following him, head spinning with the crash from the heights. "Adam—"

"You don't want this," he rasped, and disappeared in a burst of smokey shadows.

ENTER THE KRAKEN

Throughout the second day of divine competition, my mind looped in a chaotic tangle.

It all revolved around one question in a hundred variations. Had I misread the situation? Misread him? He hadn't needed me as much as I needed him?

And if he had—*what happened?*

I had a hundred possible answers, too. Each of them made me feel worse.

That didn't stop me from losing myself in a recount of every single second over and over, of the way he'd felt under my hands, on my lips, and against my body. No period of silence passed without a flashback to those smoldering moments, how he'd given the reins to me to direct the motions, how lost he'd been in the pleasure of us—and how *alive* he'd felt.

Now I sat on a stone bench in the center of the soul city, watching as the gods and their champions played tourist, while Adamantus fulfilled his primary duty to the Underworld.

The one good thing about yesterday's outcome was that they'd all left me alone.

The moment I thought that, Lyssa the maenad dropped

down next to me, having absconded with a silver fruit bowl. "Brass coin for your thoughts?"

"How about silver for your insides?" I grouched.

Of course that had the opposite effect on her, earning me a giggle. "I like you." She sat astride the bench, raising the fruit bowl. "Wanna see how many grapes I can fit in my mouth?"

She didn't wait for my response, already starting to shove the red grapes in her cheeks. I couldn't do much besides count them for her.

We'd reached twelve grapes when I caught Rhoxane looking lost nearby.

I whistled at her. "Hey! Over here!"

She jumped like a skittish deer then watched us warily.

"Yes, you. Come here."

Stiff with cautiousness, she approached. "Hello?"

I patted the space beside me. "We don't bite."

Judging by the look she gave us both, she firmly expected us to do much worse.

"What are you doing here then, if you're so scaredy?"

"Oh, I'm—I don't—I didn't mean to offend. I'm just—" She glanced around, playing with her hands. "Am I truly the only one mortified about being in the Underworld while alive?"

"I doubt it, but we're all here for a reason. What's yours?"

"My mistress chose me for this."

"We get that, but everyone here is hoping to get something out of winning."

"I doubt I'll win," she admitted, choking up.

Pity rose back up for her. I caught a handful of her rose-pink skirt and pulled her to sit by me. "Honestly, of all the people at her disposal, why did Eglaia choose you?"

"My grandmother may have offended her, and to spare us all she now decides what to do with me."

"I met your grandmother," I said distastefully.

"You did? How?"

"On a trip to Zhadugar to learn about their brand of black

magic," I lied smoothly. "Not surprised Marzeya managed to piss off Eglaia, considering how much she likes to play god herself as she did with us."

Rhoxane cringed. "I'm sorry about her."

"It's not me she owes an apology to, but my friend. She ended up tossing her in a cave full of ghouls." I gently tucked a lock of her dark hair behind her ear. "You remind me of her."

Her eyes grew shiny as her lower lip trembled. "Is she...here?"

"No, she's alive and where I left her." In a mountaintop palace, preparing to be the next Queen of Cahraman.

"Oh, good."

She toed off her shoes, resting her swollen feet on their heels. It was then that I noticed the rest of her was retaining a fair amount of water, bloated in a way that would require a medic to check.

Rhoxane wiped at her eyes, sniffling. "So, what are you both here for then?"

"The benefits of becoming so scary no one dares cross me again, or at least getting His Infernal Majesty to pull strings for me," I said, a vague account of the truth.

Lyssa swallowed all of her squirrel's mouthful. Rhoxane reached for her throat as Lyssa's own stretched to accommodate the grapes. "I've come to create chaos."

"What does that mean?"

"It means her god brought her to make the others angry," I explained.

"Why would he do that?"

"You met him yesterday, he's not exactly on the same track as the rest. Isn't he, Lyssa?"

Lyssa nodded, now chomping on a strange fruit with a pink skin and white, seed-studded inside. "His wife was the one meant to be bringing Orcus a bride. Until she does, I'm here."

Nearby, the sound of bubbling water surged, followed by souls gasping and chattering. The gods emerged from between the stone buildings, following the commotion.

Lyssa scrambled up, juice spilling down her jaw as she sputtered through a full mouth. *"Shivhew!"*

She's here?

I pulled Rhoxane up with me, hoping to offer some comfort by linking my arm with hers. "This I've got to see."

Shoes in her hand, she hobbled alongside me, legs much shorter and thighs no doubt rubbing together in a way she was unused to, otherwise she'd have adjusted her stance. "Do we have to look?"

We began our descent on a sloping street, following Lyssa as she cartwheeled down.

"Aren't you curious to see what he married?"

"No. I'd rather go back to being utterly clueless about these matters and unnoticed by all gods," she whimpered. "Nothing good ever comes from catching their attention."

I wanted to ask more about her experience, but we'd arrived at the basin my bedside waterfall poured into—and it was writhing with giant, green tentacles!

At first, I saw them as the same creature that had crushed Perilla, but the hooked teeth and suckers on their undersides removed all association.

Flailing over our heads, the tentacles began to shrink. They'd fully sunk back into the calming water when a large, bony hand with webbed fingers reached out.

Theoneus came sprinting down, arms out. "My love!"

He splashed in, caught the hand and pulled the rest of her out.

What stepped out of the water to drape over him was a woman with shining, pale cyan skin and rust-red hair down past her hips.

Straightening, she held him in place with her webbed hands before devouring his mouth.

Never had I seen a kiss truly look like a tongue was being shoved down someone's throat until now. Judging by the pleased hums and petting, Theoneus was enjoying being mauled by a sea creature that had just appeared to us as a kraken.

Adamantus chose that moment to arrive, breaking apart their shameless display.

Almost too quick to notice, he had glanced my way before giving his full attention to the amorous couple.

"Nice of you to finally join us, Aristagnë." He gestured to the water. "Is your champion joining us?"

"No, sir. After a lot of chasing and consideration, I felt it would be cruel to bring you something that would always long for the sea," she said, unnerved by him. "Sorry for the fruitless wait."

Lyssa bumped her shoulder against mine. "Looks like it's you and me against whatever Theoneus cooked up."

That was a better alternative to whatever deep-sea monstrosity Aristagnë would have brought for us. I guessed.

Fully out of the water, her body morphed, coating her in a backless, shimmering dress made of sea-green scales, the sides baring the large gills bordering her chest.

Up close, she seemed familiar to me, but the large, glassy eyes and mouth full of small, sharp teeth made it hard to envision her as human. There were smaller gills on either side of her throat, and the skin of her face and topside of her arms and legs glittered faintly.

The spellbinding beauty was interrupted when she recognized Almagera.

Her eyes bulged and her jaw unhinged to extend outwards in a hair-raising screech. "What is she doing here?"

Whether it made sense or not, I was taking the reaction of the younger gods as another hint that Almagera could be behind her husband's disappearance.

"I'm here because unlike you, I was efficient and successful in setting forth a candidate for queen!" Almagera bit back.

"Oh, and where is this successful candidate? Because it

certainly isn't Formeta or—" She stopped when her eyes landed on me.

She swore loudly, stomping her webbed foot. "Now why didn't I think of bringing one of those?"

Polyope came up behind me, hands resting on my shoulders. "Good thing you hadn't, because this one is mine, as they all should be."

Aristagnë seemed less unpleasantly surprised to find Polyope among the welcoming party. "Why did I think Telephassa was among the competitors?"

"Telephassa, among others, will start joining us here," Adamantus said. "They heard how exciting the first round was and would like to observe the rest of the competition."

I couldn't hold back my frustration with him. "Did informing us of that slip your mind?".

"Yes."

Fists clenched, I dared him to look at me properly. "Don't you think I have a right to know if I'm going to have an audience?"

Shadows splattering the air around him like squid ink, he was in my face, towering over me with a stifling atmosphere and eyes like gas lamps in the dark. "If I had deemed it important, I would have informed you. You need to busy yourself with worries such as surviving the next round."

For the first time in a while, I was more than a little intimidated by him.

Was he angered by what had happened between us the night before? Did he consider I'd tried to seduce him again? This time using an unprecedented moment of weakness that he'd come confessing to me? Was that what this was all about?

"Who's going next?" Almagera asked.

Adamantus pointed at Theoneus without taking his eyes off me.

Not missing a beat, Theoneus whooped as he led his wife, and by extension everyone else away from the lake and to another area of the city where the amphitheater was. The location of the next round of the competition.

"Where's the pomegranate?" I whispered to Polyope.

She took out a half from her pocket. I took a quick, crunching bite of a cluster of seeds before we followed the rest of the crowd.

Laid out in ringed levels, the amphitheater was filled to the brim with souls, and the odd, colorful presence of a god not among those competing.

Telephassa's moonlight halo centered her among the audience, luring my attention as I made my way to the starting point. She waved at me, prompting me to smile, until Adamantus descended to sit at the front, fingers threaded with expectant ease over his lap.

The second Godsgate manifested on the stage, a verdigris garden-gate coated in ivy and grape vines twining around the small bars in its window.

Wiping my sweaty palms down my leather pants, I exhaled my apprehension.

Theoneus leaped before us, bowing us in. "In you go!"

His excitement did not bode well for me.

Without a parting look to anyone, starting by Adamantus, I steeled myself and crossed the threshold.

A grey, misty wasteland met us on the other side. Endless miles of pale, dusty sand, with dead trees scattered across the distance, and the sound of ocean waves from an indiscernible direction. The sky above was dim, yet cloudless, and the sun nowhere to be found, like it were the early hours of the morning.

"What are we supposed to do here?"

Lyssa twirled, taking in the surroundings. "No idea."

"So, you've never been wherever this is? Are we just meant to find our way out of here?" I tried to find any clue for what it was we were meant to do here. "This can't be it."

She pointed ahead. "What about that?"

A hooded, humanoid silhouette had appeared, and it was fast approaching.

I untwisted my tridagger into longsword form, and readied myself to meet it with a cutting swing.

Lyssa beat me to the contact by running straight at it, nails grown into claws, until it threw off the hood and let out a world-shaking shriek.

White-hot knives stabbed through my ears and brought me to my knees.

I clutched at my pounding head, heaving wetly as I felt my skull shrink and crack beneath a piercing crown of mounting pressure.

Crying, I pounded my fist to misdirect some pain, but the ground tipped beneath me. I rolled back down the sudden slope, writhing with explosive agony as its shrieking continued.

Jaw locked, I was able to pry my twitching eyelids open. Burn holes opened in the sky as its edges melted into unsteady gradients, ranging from the yellow-purple-blue fade of heated steel to fractured, highly-contrasting shades that hurt to witness.

Getting back onto my knees was a persistent struggle, with the ground dipping beneath my weight like warm dough.

"Lyssa?" I choked.

There was no answer, and I threw myself back and up, rising onto staggering legs that felt the ground see-saw and melt under my weight with every other step.

The landscape had devolved into a nauseating mix of eye-searing colors and distorted angles, like my eyes had been traded for thick, singed glass.

My aching head swam with pond water that poured out my every orifice. The shriek moved away, but remained a single, ongoing, piercing note. A long, hot needle going through one ear and out the other.

Either I was going deaf, or the volume of its glass-shattering screams had dulled, because no distance had grown between us.

Blood pooled in my mouth, diluted by my saliva, and I lifted my heavy head upright to meet the screecher.

An upright black-armored crab sat on the shoulders of the creature, pincers twitching like crackling fire. Its armored underside split apart, and out poured intense purple light that shrunk my skull, squeezing my eyeballs until they were on the verge of bursting.

The light flashed over and over, speed increasing, lightning-bright, like I was blinking rapidly at the burning summer sun. Instead of leaving fading blotches that lingered behind my eyelids, it burned me.

A furnace had been lit within me, cooking my insides, melting my skin like it were wax while I helplessly watched it peel off in layers, leaving the meat and blood vessels beneath exposed to cruel air.

Any hope of screaming left along with my mouth, my nose no more than nostril slits that breathed in the charring flesh and muscle.

The tightening crown of pain worsened, a net of screws drilling into the bone, spreading the intense vibration down my body so I jerked and flailed, screams of anguish smothered by my sealed skin.

Mid-shake, I caught my undamaged hair out the corner of my eye. If I was falling apart, why hadn't it burned in the heat?

The purple light blinked off and what remained behind was a larger version of the screecher, an even scarier sight to behold.

This was a delusion. It had to be. The monster feeding off my mind, and deteriorating it in the process. How did I fight something like this?

The screecher stretched its pincers, sharp tips ready to impale me.

Awareness in embers, I couldn't think, only act. I raised my trembling, skinless arm, and aimed the blade of the tridagger to my face, and sliced my mouth back open.

Gaping wound overflowing with blood, I screamed at the top of my lungs.

In the split second its shock afforded me, I threw myself forward and plunged the blade into its open face. Cracks spread along its form, releasing white rays that grew until it shattered into a million pieces, and I fell into infinite, blinding whiteness.

THE SCREECHER

Falling through the Godgate felt like I had drunk a barrel of wine.

I was welcomed back in by Adamantus holding Theoneus off the ground by his throat.

Theoneus was unbothered by his stranglehold, his high-pitched, choking snickering filling the amphitheater. "You have to admit it was clever."

Adamantus's booming roar shook the whole city. "I am going to make you regret the day you left my domain!"

"I was doing you a favor, Orcus." Theoneus's wheezing giggles only increased. "Only a strong mind can survive one of those. You need that, don't you?"

"Get fucked, bastard," I howled, stumbling towards them.

Adamantus slammed Theoneus down, blurring over to me, grabbing my face to drag my lower lids down with his thumbs.

"Wha're y'doin'?" I slurred.

"Miraculously, your sanity is intact." He released me, facing the audience. "The show's over."

The souls scattered, leaving only the attending gods along with those on the stage.

Swaying, I attempted to raise my shaking arm to point accusingly at Theoneus. "Hey," I addressed his wife. "Slap him for me, would you?"

Taken aback, she giggled. "Why not do it yourself?"

"Rather not break my hand today."

Aristagnë eyed her grinning lunatic of a husband. "It might not hurt as much as you'd like."

"Don't care. Just hit him."

Her laughter increased even as she slapped him so hard it flung his head back with an alarming crack.

Theoneus reset himself with a low groan, then gave her a devilish grin. "Harder."

In any other case, I would have found this funny. But his fun was had at my expense, so him eluding any satisfactory backlash by enjoying it was not helping.

"Of course, you're the type of bastard that gets off on pain," I seethed. "Let me guess, you spent your wedding night whipping him bloody."

"Actually, she just made real good use of those teeth." Giddy, he angled her face our way and pulled down her jaw to display her too-many, small, razor-sharp teeth. "I spent my whole life wondering what's missing, until I had pain joining the build-up to a climax so good I—"

Polyope spared me by knocking on his head. "Considering you're one of the lucky few that functions that way, you're just going to make everyone upset for not finding reprieve in agony."

"I don't know, would he still find it fun if it wasn't his loving wife roughing him up?" I raised my fist, no doubt failing at being anything but twitchy with exhaustion. "How about I stick a rusted shovel up your ass?"

Regret hit instantaneously, as my attempt at a threat just made Theoneus's eyes roll back as he let out an obscene moan that made his wife flush a darker shade of cyan.

"Oh, fuck you," I huffed, sagging against Polyope. "Get me out of here before I do something I'll regret."

Halting her giggles, Aristagnë narrowed her large eyes. "Do I know you?"

"Doubtful."

"I swear, I know you from somewhere," she insisted, pupils narrowing. "You feel very familiar to me. Did we meet before you joined your priesthood?"

The odd thing was, I felt something familiar about her too. But aside from me having no recollections of chatting with sea monsters, it was impossible to tell who I was in this disguise...

...wasn't it?

"I was born into this life," I said.

Not quite convinced, she hummed, neck-gills flaring. "It's just...*your voice*. It's so distinctive."

Nervousness raised my pitch, attempting to mask whatever characteristic traits shaped my speech. "Is it, really?"

Adamantus's tendency to remain unblinking was peculiar, but Aristagnë's stare read firmly as predatory, setting me in her unnerving sights. "Yes."

Polyope saved me the trouble by removing me from the scene, and breezing out of the amphitheater until Telephassa blocked our way.

"It's a good thing I never liked this idea, because if I was competing I would have wanted to snatch you for myself," she said to me.

"Do you have to have your eye on all that I have?" Polyope hissed in trifold. "It's too late for you to join, so back off."

Telephassa raised her hands, shoulders shaking with barely-restrained chuckling. "My, someone's touchy. I just wanted to compliment the little phantasm, considering we haven't had much to smile at lately."

"You'd be touchy if you cared about what hung in the balance." Polyope grew even larger, lifting me further up so I sat in her arms like a child. "Any reason why you're making no efforts to find Eurycrius?"

Telephassa circled us, emitting a magnetic force that tugged at my skin and thinner bones. "What would you have me do, rip the world apart in search of someone who doesn't want to be found?"

"It's the least you can do to show your worry."

"Why would I be worried?" Telephassa came too close, her pull increasing to an extent I felt in my gums, like it was about to rip out my teeth. "He either comes back or he doesn't. The Fates know Lyceus would make a better King of Heaven."

Lyceus.

"As interesting as this is, I'd like to bathe now," I said from between them. "You can just put me down and continue with your spat."

Polyope set me down and shooed me with four of her arms. "I'll pick you up tomorrow."

I wasted no time getting as far away as possible from Telephassa's pressurized atmosphere.

Disoriented and rattled by what I'd just escaped, I got lost and wandered through the city until I collapsed by the river.

Staring at the water for what felt like hours, I tried to keep my mind from replaying what it felt under the screecher's mercy, or connect it to the similar experience I had in Polyope's maze.

The pebbles crunched beneath his boots as he came down beside me on his haunches. "Are you all right?"

"Piss off, you antlered bastard."

He only hailed down a passing barge and waited for me with an offered hand.

Groaning internally, I let him pull me into the barge and rested against the opposite end, facing him.

When we sailed away from where I could sense the visiting gods, I found myself rasping, "What happened?"

"Theoneus thinks testing the limits of the mind is humorous."

"Not him. I understand him." I worried my bottom lip, remembering how his teeth had felt against it. "What I don't get is you."

"I imagine it's difficult to make sense of anything after what he just put you through."

"Oh, I'm very much present, just worn out." I crossed my arms, tapping my fingers onto them. "Quit dodging the question and tell me what on earth happened in my room."

"We're not on earth."

"Adam."

He jerked at my sharpened tone. "I came to my senses before I could do anything I'd regret."

Offense struck like a slap. "Think Theoneus trying to rip my brain apart hurt less than that."

"That's not what I intended."

"Then what did you intend?"

"I don't know." His fists clenched over his knees, veins rising against his skin, like blue ink was flowing through them. "I've yet to make sense of what happened."

"You came into my room, started stripping, kissed me back, wound me up then left me high and dry without an explanation. That's what happened!" Just recounting it out loud restored the corrosive insecurity I'd rarely, if ever, allowed myself to feel.

After a pensive pause, he carefully asked, "Is that what happened, from your perspective?"

"Since we met, it felt like we were building up to that. But every time I took a step forward, you backed away, until I decided I would stop trying. Then last night, you gave me every reason to believe you wanted this too, and when I let down my guard, you bolted. So, now I'm stuck wondering if I did something wrong, or worse." I let out a shuddering breath, head pounding. "Did I force myself on you somehow? Were you just in shock?"

"No," he responded immediately, and in the same breath added, "Yes. I don't know."

Embarrassment flooded my face. "Can—can you take that off when you're talking to me? I can't have this conversation without knowing what you're feeling."

Cracks preceded his form changing, retracting the Horned God so I could make blessed eye contact.

If he had been sculpted from marble, the tension gripping him would have cracked him.

It was almost like he was wary of me.

We had sailed out of the city, and the River of Dreams took us down the middle of a settlement hewn from the iron-grey stone that reflected the purple of the water and onto him.

"What do you mean 'you don't know'?"

"I wasn't thinking clearly when I came to you," he said quietly. "I was wrapped up in my fury at this entire situation. Never had I been so overcome with stress until I watched you navigate that test."

"If you thought I'd fail that easily, then you shouldn't have invested your hopes in me."

"It wasn't about the progression of the plan. I didn't calm long after you had emerged victorious." He motioned his clawed hand towards his heart. "It ate my senses. All I could think of was you, and I couldn't grasp why when I had no reason to worry anymore."

"You really were worried about me."

"Evidently." His posture loosened with a heavy breath. "I came to you, in the hope that you'd know what was happening to me."

"You were panicking," I realized. "You've never felt that before, have you?"

"Not quite. Not in a long, long time."

This just made me want to leap overboard.

Normally, I would rather bite off my own tongue than offer an apology, but this was the rare case where I felt terrible. "I'm sorry."

His brows rose with surprise. "Why?"

"Because I got the wrong impression and acted on it, when you weren't in your right mind to begin with."

"Were you? I doubt you are the kind to be so open with your affections."

Before I asked what he meant, he stood as the barge docked by a field. He helped me disembark, and kept his hold on my hand as he led me towards a field of ghostly plants, blooming spikes bearing thousands of large, six-petaled flowers. Asphodels.

Now I remembered. This was where I'd seen him in the vision.

In all the tales of the Underworld, this was the place all neutral souls, judged neither too evil or too virtuous, were said to live out their afterlife. Until Adamantus restructured the entire Underworld to make it habitable.

When once it had been teeming with souls roaming these fields, with no hope of ever leaving or doing anything else, there was nary a soul in sight. Nothing moved but glimmers from the woods in the distance, and glassy moths that flew over the swaying fields, leaving faded trails of moonlight in the cool air.

I busied myself with examining the asphodels up close, caught by their ghostly glow, just like in our dream-encounter.

"Did you mean it?" He was right behind me, so close that my back met his chest. "What you're apologizing for, did you mean it?"

Defensiveness flared like the feathers of a hostile bird. "Why are you asking what you already know? If you think I'm going to give you the satisfaction of embarrassing me further—"

"You know that's not what I'm doing,"

I swallowed. "Then what are you doing?"

Lightly, he touched my upper arms. "Trying to make sense of what has been driving me mad since I left your room." I turned in his hold, struggling to keep a straight face. "In that moment, did you want me or was I what was within reach?"

"What are you talking about?"

"No one knows more than me about the impulsive, if not drastic and insane ways people behave when they have had a brush with death," he said, voice dripping in resignation. "Was that the reason? Or were you acting on a desire for myself of all things?"

"Both," I admitted. "I was wound up in many ways, and I thought you'd come to relieve my stress as well as your own." I rolled my shoulders, popping the stiffness along my back. "Why does it matter?"

"I left in a rush because I felt you were compromised, and that when you emerged from that haze you would begin to fear and hate me as everyone else does." He stopped, as if he had to. After moments, he began again. "The way you are with me, it is unlike anything I've ever experienced before. To lose that because of a moment of weakness would be unforgivable."

Oh. Of course. How he looked beneath the mortifying facade hardly mattered when the only heat and wetness he caused in mortals was when they were pissing themselves with fear.

"Brazen and boneheaded as you may be, I dread the day I have to return you to your life, because then I would lose your company and how I feel within it."

My heart kicked me in the ribs as I stared into his vivid eyes. I should end this conversation here. We'd apologized to each other, explained. And I should just let this go.

I couldn't.

Knowing I would plunge us both into another tumultuous level of this mess, I asked, breathlessly, "How do you feel?"

"Real."

"You are."

He shook his head. "You are the last being in existence to feel the need to stroke my ego."

"I can stroke something else if you'd like," I attempted to joke, to alleviate the crushing melancholy of those moments.

A humorless huff escaped him. "I can't do that for you, not the way gods like Lyceus can."

I stepped closer, unsure what to do with my hands. "But you want to."

His features were at war with themselves, struggling to over-shadow the growing darkness in his eyes. "I can't."

"Why not?"

"Because you want a man, and I'm not one."

I was far from in the mood to entertain anyone's horse shit today, least of all his. "Oh, then what was grinding against me? Because it certainly wasn't your bident!"

His face darkened with a blue flush that had my heart rattling in its ribcage. "That's not what I lack."

"Then what's the problem?" My hands found his chest, sliding up the silk of his shirt, the infuriating luxury he wrapped himself in, which suited him better than any living wretches he found more real than himself. "You want this."

He thumbed my shoulders as if to keep me away, or keep from pulling me to him, his breath quickening. "You don't under-stand what kind of decision you'd be making."

"Enlighten me then."

"You would need to give up your life to remain with me. Otherwise, I would not be able to let you go, not after I have known what it is like to have you." He bent to press his lips to my cheek, breathing heavily in my ear. "Is that what you want?"

Conflict shattered my single-minded pursuit, and I remem-bered what had brought me down to the Underworld. It hadn't been him, I'd come to protect Chloë and remained to protect my people. To prove myself as worth the duty I was given at birth, and would gain more of as I took charge of my land.

My whole life I'd reviled women like my aunt, who'd given up their lives for their men, who'd soon lost their luster and held them in the binds of a contract struck in shortsightedness.

"You could make me stay." I couldn't believe what I was saying. "You could keep me here."

Adamantus let go as he stepped away, touch trailing across my skin, reluctant to leave. "Then you'd grow to hate and resent me, just like everyone else, and I can't bear that happening."

As much as it pained me to admit it, he was right.

So why did I feel so injured that hadn't grabbed at my offer? Proved how much he wanted me by taking me and keeping me by his side?

Witnessing Polyope's unconfined form must have done more damage than I'd thought, and I had truly begun to lose my mind.

Or was this madness something else I'd thought I'd never experience? This emotion that compels you to destroy everything, starting yourself, for another?

What is happening to me?

Adamantus's panicked confusion came back to ring in my ear, joining my own inner voice screaming the same question.

34

TEMPTING WATERS

There was no measuring the Fates' involvement since they'd put us on a joint path. But I felt setting Eglaia's test to occur now was a cruel joke on their part.

I was sneaking pomegranate seeds behind Polyope when the god of war and the goddess of beauty and desire butted heads over who would go next. Eglaia's hypnotic pink aura then flashed, and Machaius was no longer impatient.

What must that be like, to be so persuasive that you didn't need effort or intimidation? To not withhold vulnerability from anyone, including yourself, because you knew you would get your way without sacrifice?

If only I had that privilege.

If only I knew what I wanted anymore.

Rhoxane made it clear what she wanted—to be anywhere but here. She fidgeted next to me as we headed for what awaited us on the other side of Eglaia's carved, crystalline, rose-tinted Godsgate.

Gods both major and minor now stood at the outskirts of the soul city of Athanasia, as entertained as the ghostly inhabitants themselves as they observed our reluctant approach towards our task.

I halfheartedly lifted my eyes from the shining stones of the pale brass street, to see the familiar faces at the end of the march Eglaia demanded. Like we were heading to her temple on her festival day, to kneel at her effigy and pray for her intervention.

Among the faces, I caught the combined excitement of Theoneus and Aristagnë, the unaffected eagerness of Lyssa, and Lyceus's smoldering gaze. His attention remained fixed on me, like the sun beating down my neck and trapping heat in my hair as I planted seeds in the patches.

Adamantus avoided me entirely, which was probably for the best.

Sighing dejectedly, I continued to the divine doorway awaiting us at the end of the fool's gold street.

Eglaia met us by her Godsgate, all-too-pleased with herself. "Before you go, I want you to imagine what it is that awaits you on the other side of my gate, and ask yourself if you are disciplined enough to withstand it."

There was no doubt we would be faced with her son, Amateus, essentially a bolder, male version of herself. I wasn't a sheltered priestess whose tongue would roll out in salivating pants at the sight of a beautiful naked man, but Rhoxane might.

I eyed my competitor, who appeared resigned to her fate in a way that made me question Eglaia's motives in choosing her. Did she not anticipate anything beyond presenting a great beauty to the only being unaffected by her magic? If I hadn't shared those transfiguring moments with him, I'd believe he was incapable of desire.

After all, he did see nothing in Eglaia. Unless...but what would be the point of lying?

The glassy gate opened at its leisure, bathing us in its inoffensive shine and beckoning us through with enticing scents of rose oil, jasmine blossoms and rainstorm grass.

Pity shot through me like one of Amateus's arrows when Rhoxane's shivering bumped her elbow against mine. As we crossed the threshold, I took her hand, squeezing it as we were engulfed by the rosy brilliance.

Frothing waves sloshed onto my feet and a salty breeze opened my chest, unwinding my coiled tension as the view faded in.

Ships and boats floated by the dock, the bigger ones in different styles from the Orestian trireme with its centipede-like paddles, to the Northlander longship with its symmetrical, curling ends, and even the newer, wide-bellied Arborean with its stacked sails.

"A port city," I thought aloud.

Behind me I found a familiar layout of blue-domed, white-washed buildings mounted on a mountainside that validated my guess. This must be one of the islands in the Deep Red Sea. I'd only ever visited one, Galantis, right across from my region, on a starter journey where I accompanied a relative to see how trade transactions worked.

"I don't suppose your mistress told you what we're meant to do here?" I asked Rhoxane. "Do I have to haggle with some man with unearthly beauty over some black pearls or—*Rhoxane!*"

Rhoxane was in the water, waves already up to her shoulders.

I splashed in after her, hooking my arms under hers to drag her out. "What are you doing?"

She thrashed against my grip, kicking and screaming. "Let me go! Let me get this over with!"

"You can't swim across the sea!"

"Watch me!" Her knuckles collided with my chin and my sight blacked out long enough for her to slip further into the water.

I was used to fighting dirty, but not with fragile human women. Since she started it, it was on her that I dragged her back by her hair. "Are you trying to drown yourself? Because it's a lot harder to achieve than you think it is."

Keeping a hold of her was like attempting to bathe a cat.

"I don't care! I can't swim and there are sharks, it will be quick and—and—" She broke out into sobs. "Just let me go. I can't take this anymore."

It took remembering Adamantus stabbing Eglaia with his bident to regain my calm. "Why are you doing this now?"

"Because if I don't die here, she'll keep me alive to torture me!" she cried, reluctantly facing me, tears blending with the seawater. "If I die now, I'll just go back to where we started but I'll be free."

"Free from what?" I hauled her back, throwing us onto the shoreline. "Is she going to punish you for failing?"

"She's already punishing me!" Rhoxane slumped onto the drenched sand, curled in on herself. "I wouldn't be here if she hadn't 'blessed' me to begin with, and now she's punishing me for something I had no control over."

"You can't be serious." I rose, squeezing the water from my darkened hair. "All of this because you're *pretty?* You already gave up any benefit by becoming her priestess, what more does she want?"

She cried harder. "For no god to declare me just as beautiful, if not more, even in a moment of flattery to dull my senses. Even if it's a man she has no sensible right to demand attraction from, and because of what he did to me, I can't even deny it happened."

Horror tore through me, leaving me painfully stiff as I pieced together the implications.

"You're pregnant." My voice was distant and lifeless to my own ears. "You're pregnant with her grandchild."

She squeezed her eyes shut and nodded.

"This is insane. You did nothing wrong."

"What does it matter? I broke my vows of being in her service and had her own son claiming I was more beautiful than her, it's a wonder I haven't been transformed into a hideous beast." She sniffled loudly, and pounded on her midsection. "I wish she'd just done that and left me be. That I wouldn't be forced to carry this in me until she decides what to do with me."

"What do you think she's going to do?"

"That's the worst part," she mumbled, congested. "I can't do much but think of what she's done to the others before me."

This wasn't the time for me to be shaken up over something that didn't concern me. Neither she nor her child were my problem, and she was handing me an easy win on this turn.

That was, if I could tell what we were meant to do.

"Look, if and when we get out of here, I'll figure something out," I told her, lifting her up. "Unlike you, I'm here to be Queen of the Nether Court, and queens need ladies-in-waiting, right? I could ask to keep you, and she would have nothing to say about it."

Under different circumstances, Rhoxane's bewilderment would have been comical. "Why are you so nice to me? What are you getting out of this?"

"Believe it or not, it's quite lonely being me." I pushed her onto the dock, doing a quick, cursory examination of the ships. "I could use some company."

In the meantime, I would have to figure out a true solution to her disastrous situation. One my mother could have found herself in had it not been for our culture and family...

Despite my foolish desires, it was dangerous to court the attention of a god.

I chose the Arborean ship, its many sails proving it the easiest to navigate with no crew, and easily disembarked from the dock. Rhoxane saw no point in applying herself and flopped onto the deck, like a dead fish.

A small stretch into the voyage, the waves sang, casting a rosy hue that relaxed me into drowsiness. *"You are to deliver this to my temple in Claocina."*

A ten-foot sculpture made of rose quartz twinkled onto the deck, upright and unmistakably of her, naked and in an alluring pose that emphasized her body's curves.

I waited for something to happen, for it to reveal itself to be the egg-casing of a serpent I had to wrestle into the sea, or release a swarm of venomous spiders. "That's it?"

"Do not stray from your path," Eglaia said sweetly.

Was this test just us catering to her vanity?

I suppose if anyone was going to be vain, it would be her. She did reflect our desires even before we admitted them to ourselves...

Humidity drenched me within minutes, sticking the shirt to my body like sweat and turning my grip on the wheel slippery.

"Could you talk or sing or something?" I asked Rhoxane. "It's getting hard to pay attention with something this dull, I could use the stimulation."

Light, airy notes rode along the salty breeze, mimicking serene flutes and upper-scale strings, the latter rising as a chorus of uniting voices.

"Rhoxane?"

No answer could be heard over the steady rise of sounds, a growing collection of simulated string and wind instruments that joined into a familiar piece. The sweet simplicity of the surrounding music coaxed out relaxing sighs and unwound the tension from my limbs until I draped myself over the wheel.

Stars above, I was tired. I couldn't wait till this was over and I could go home. I'd spent so long sleeping in unwelcoming spaces, surrounded by distressing company and foreign worries. Just when I'd thought that phase in my life's story had ended, I was uprooted and pitched headfirst into a world not even the maddest of mortals pursued.

Soft chants rolled in from the edges of the vocalized music, a pleasant balance of deep and high tones.

The sea breeze inflated the sails and dried strips of my hair to dance alongside my face as the ship sailed faster, bringing us closer to our destination, raising land from the calming waves.

Rolling hills rose from the evaporating sea, padded with lush, long grass and split by snaking roads bordered by towering cypresses, inviting the voyage further into the land to peek at the patches of stone pines.

Nostalgia stirred like a whirlpool, and warm memories flipped through my arrested mind like pages of a windblown book.

The greenery grew, encompassing the full stretch of what lay ahead, offering glimpses at the hilltop towns and the sun-baked cities that sprawled out from the fertile land that breathed life into them.

I was home!

Shoots sprouted along the deck, bursting from the thickening wood and growing rapidly into a mass of leaves. Vines twisted down the mast, fattening with every breath until their grip cracked the structure.

The music had intensified to an enthralling song, a multi-layered chorus that plucked on my heartstrings and inflated my chest with delirious love for the sight before me.

Exhaling a wistful cloud, I threw off the veil, kicked off my sandals and left the wheel for the ship's edge. It could dock by itself by crashing into the land, but I couldn't wait any longer.

In my haste, I barely heard Rhoxane yell, and sprinted with unbroken momentum til I leaped off the edge.

The crush of grass bedding never came to soften my landing, but something far wetter shattered apart to engulf me in burning salt.

Head underwater, cut off from the beautiful music, I stared up at the rays pouring through the transparent patch in the creasing surface.

What had just happened?

What was I doing?

I swam back up, gasping and whipping my head around for some kind of answer.

My home was nowhere within reach. The only land I could glimpse over the heavy sloshing of seawater was our destination, the coastal city of Claocina.

What had convinced me otherwise?

The heavenly tunes flowed back to me, broken up by the waves and wind, and Rhoxane screaming down from the ship.

It was sailing at a greater speed than I anticipated. I narrowly avoided it smashing into me, diving as far down as possible to circumvent it and reemerge on the other side.

Drenched and disoriented, my one clear thought was to latch onto the rope ladder as the ship passed and pull myself back aboard. Halfway up, the music returned clearer and more powerful, coming from the right-hand side.

Shaking the dripping water from my face, I squinted in its direction and the dreamlike haze trickled back in, painting over the stretches of autumn air and sea with golden wheat fields, and olive groves so close I could see the fruit ripening from green to purple.

It was calling to me. Gripping me with a homesick ache so strong it hurt.

I could just be done with all this and swim home...

Since when was anything that simple?

The beckoning tunes grew louder, expanding the view into the settlements and mounted cities overlooking the fertile grounds, vibrant topography drinking in the midday sun—

I smashed my head against the ship.

SHIPWRECK BAY

A spiderweb crack of pain spread across the side of my head.

Tangled in the rope ladder, I slumped against the wood, waiting for the smarting to settle into manageable throbbing that had the sight before me flickering.

Pressing my head against the ship to maintain the pain, I caught the source of the song.

Winged women called to me from atop a mass of rocks, with the white fronts and the dark-grey backs of an albatross, and their wings so massive they appeared to stretch for a combined fifty feet.

Sirens.

"Oh, good, you're back." Rhoxane was half-hanging above me, hair blowing in the wind. "What are we going to do now?"

I dragged myself from the sirens to her, neck and head flaring at the careless movement. "Are you seeing this?"

"Yes."

"And it's not working on you?"

She sagged, weighed down with sadness. "Hard to be tempted when you have been long claimed by hopelessness."

That explained another reason for her being Eglaia's choice.

Punishing her by using her to win a round, shooting down two birds with one arrow.

Clarity receded with the pain, and the sirens' enchanting song had grown back like a rapid glaze across a freezing pond. I had to think while I still could.

Clambering back aboard, my attention split down the middle. The bewitching tunes tugged at my edges, warring against the bruise I pressed on, so both the dreamy lull and drilling migraine made it hard to think.

The entire deck was covered in leaves and vines. I trudged through them, not finding the mind to question them.

Rhoxane tailed me, getting caught in the splatter I made shaking off the excess wetness. "What did you see?"

"My home." I aimed my right eye at her, the left one twitching under the pressure of the headache. "Are you completely immune to the siren song just by virtue of being depressed, or is it something else?"

She slouched, arms around her middle. "If you work for Eglaia, you are meant to train to resist temptation. We exist to facilitate the effects of desire for others, those who worship her. But we can't resist her direct power, or anything stemming from her." She swallowed. "Like her son."

"I'll kill him," I growled, massaging the bruised section.

"If only that were possible." Rhoxane checked behind her, at the sirens. "I wish I believed them, it would make drowning so much easier. I wouldn't fight for anything, not even the instinct to survive."

"No. Stop. Bad." I patted her head, too hard and scattered to be comforting. "We're going to get out of here alive, we just need to pass them."

"Shouldn't we have done that by now? I feel like we've been here for over an hour."

That didn't make any sense. Until I checked the ship's wheel and found it spinning to the right.

A fit of giggles broke against my body's wishes, becoming interspersed with coughs.

Rhoxane took a step back. "I know madness is a requisite for working for Polyope, but you were sensible until a second ago."

Pointing to the wheel, I laughed harder. "There's your answer for why it's taking too long. I don't know why I didn't check for a trick to begin with, because of course there is one in a task set by the expert in desire and toying with mortals."

"Prospera, I beg you, make some sense before I dive off the deck."

"We're sailing in circles!"

Once I said it, it was hard to overlook that we had been caught by the loop surrounding the sirens' stand.

Small hands together, shoulders up to her ears, she was pathetically helpless. "Can't we just turn the wheel the other way?"

"Sure, why don't we juggle oxen while we're at it? That's bound to be easier than fighting the pull of a whirlpool." I retrieved my veil and wrapped it around my head tight enough to continually aggravate my cranial pain, counteracting their effect. "No, we need a quicker, easier way out of here."

"Like what?"

"Aren't you supposed to have magic?"

"It's not what it used to be, not with Amateus's parasite feeding off me." She pressed on her gut. "But you have magic given by your goddess, don't you?"

"Not quite, no."

"Then how did you do this?"

She threw her arms out to encompass the deck, overrun with plants like it had been abandoned within, and reclaimed by, a forest.

I did this? Was this a part of the siren song, giving me the sway over nature I'd longed for since infancy? How else could I have sprouted earth-magic?

Barefooted, I felt a pulse against my soles and remembered

the thrum I felt in the holy grounds. Energy that flowed up my legs from the living earth, storing an innate understanding of the area among my unconscious thoughts. Unfelt before that day, but ever-present since.

The pomegranate! It had done what Adamantus claimed a golden apple would do, amplifying the fraction of divine power I had inherited. This was the side effect Polyope had warned against as she gave it to me.

Dealing with that fact would have to be postponed. "Can you cast a protective shield or not?"

"I can, but maintaining it would be too much."

I edged towards the edge, hand on my whip. "You just need to hold it until we leave the sirens' whirlpool."

Sarcasm felt strange coming from her, but she must have thought me dumb or mad. "How? They're the one controlling the ship, remember?"

"I get them to stop singing. Just long enough to break their hold on me and the ship."

Rhoxane remained unreceptive. "What could possibly get them to stop?"

"The same thing that works on everything else. Pissing them off!"

Obeying my thoughts, the whip cracked out, and struck the closest siren, abruptly ending their song.

A beat later, they swarmed, shrieking like giant vultures.

I sprinted for the wheel. "Rhoxane, now!"

A shield curved over me, encasing me in a boiling bubble at the last second to spare my throat from a siren's swiping talons. It bounced off the barrier, and spun back through the air and into another two sirens.

With all my strength, I gripped and turned at the wheel, fighting against what commanded its motion.

"What are we going to do now, you lunatic?" Rhoxane yelled at me. "I'm already exhausted. How are we supposed to reach the city in this lousy state?"

"We don't have to! We just need to escape their area of influence!" I cut off her stressed tirade of curses. "Trust me! If I'm wrong, you'll still get your death wish!"

"I wished for a painless death, not to be ripped apart by sea monsters!"

"The painful thing would be letting such a mediocre monster overpower me." I pushed at the wheel, straining with unmaintainable effort. "Whatever kills me better be terrifying, not tantalizing!"

"What does that even mean?"

I *couldn't* lose to something that preyed on my softer feelings. The exploitable weaknesses men would use as an excuse to usurp my birthright.

I must deny them all if I wanted to protect my people and serve my land. I must adopt a reptilian temperament, a lust to inspire fear—and *power*.

Screaming with strain, I tugged at the wheel, effort all-consuming until something moved up along my legs.

Thick vines shot up to wrap around the wheel, their weight and slithering pull fought off the obstructing force, allowing it to make a hard left turn.

Heaving, I veered the ship with a cutting angle, and sailed out of the siren stand's hold.

But they swooped down to the deck as the shield burst, their screams of fury recalling the maddening screecher.

Just as I turned, with whip and dagger unfolded into a sword —silence hit and the scene ended in the rosy light of the Godsgate.

From the fading deck, we returned onto the fool's gold street, panting from exertion.

Rhoxane collapsed before Eglaia reached us. The goddess could barely maintain her smile. "How were you so sure that you didn't need to deliver the statue?"

"Lucky guess. Can I go now?"

"No. That was not how you were supposed to achieve the

task I set for you," she said, sickly sweet yet upset. "You were meant to resist the siren song by sheer will power, not by cracking your own skull."

The skull in mention throbbed, and I let out a petulant groan. "Does it matter? I got the same result in the end."

"Of course it matters," Eglaia decreed, dripping with cheery condescension. "How can you expect to be a goddess if you can't resist temptation?"

"Is that requirement brand new?" I wondered, venomously sarcastic. "It must be, because self-control sure seems like an afterthought for most of you. You all get riled up *so* easily."

Sparing me from Eglaia's response, Polyope lifted me by the scruff of my neck like a misbehaving cat and removed me from the scene.

Theoneus and Aristagnë waved at me as I was carried over them, enviably well-matched and brimming with hidden gruesomeness. Lyssa was too busy harassing the souls to notice me, and Lyceus...

Lyceus blew me a kiss.

"What is he playing at?" I asked Polyope.

"Oh, you have just become worthy of his accursed interest," Telephassa replied.

Telephassa?

I twisted to gape up at her, dazzling and singular. She was the one carrying me!

"Where's my mistress?"

"Orcus and her retreated somewhere a little while ago," she explained in disinterest. "The prospect of having a wife must have gotten too realistic for him now that it's down to Lyceus's and Machaius's efforts to determine the winner."

So, they both couldn't bother waiting to see if I emerged in one piece?

She gently set me down on the edge of the city. "You're too good for either of them."

More than a little confused by her interaction with me, I just stared expectantly until she elaborated. "Is this what you were meant for, being targeted by prideful gods with the prize being trapped here for eternity?"

My mouth wobbled, making it hard to school my face into its usual neutral state. The way I'd almost willingly lost this round, just from being shown what I longed to return to, was pathetic at best and mortifying at worst.

Shameful as my reaction had been, it did prove Telephassa's point.

I wanted to leave here. Ridiculous as it had been for me to entertain such a thought, Adamantus hadn't given me a reason to remain.

"Why do you care?" I asked her. "Why aren't you competing in this?"

Telephassa bent over, hands on her knees, her intense lapis lazuli skin and the surrounding white-and-silver curls overworked my eyes. "I don't approve of this whole event, or the reasoning behind it. When my father, wherever he may be, tried to order me to marry I was enraged, and that sentiment carries over to anyone else being forced into such an arrangement."

"Who did he want you to marry?"

Telephassa twisted her face with distaste towards the city, where the crowd had dispersed. "Lyceus. I suppose he believed that, in the event he did decide to disappear, he would want a King and Queen of Heaven who actually reside in the heavens, unlike his beloved wife."

"Lyceus? *Isn't he your brother?*"

Neither laughter nor dismissiveness responded to my squeak of discomfort. Instead, Telephassa lips were pinched with restrained giddiness. "She didn't tell you?"

"Tell me what?"

"Lyceus is Polyope's brother."

If I were being honest, I'd never bothered to study the divine family tree due to how much it differed from land to land.

People couldn't seem to agree on who was the most important, who was sired or birthed by who, or even what their names were.

But never did I expect this.

"That never came up, no." I rubbed at my head, the blunt force trauma I'd subjected it to had receded to a dull ache. "Or maybe it did, and these bridal tasks have turned my brain into minced meat."

"I don't doubt that." Telephassa moved her enormous face closer to mine, her proximity exuding the pressure from before that had me stuck still and almost breathless. "If you need to escape unseen, I can help."

"Why?"

The glow of her white eyes dimmed to a light, bright blue. "I tend to protect women escaping marriages, or whatever 'womanly duties' the world expects from them. They can serve me, unharmed and undisturbed as my hunters, my priestesses, my moondust maidens, forever free from being bound to a man and his whims as I am."

Altruism was a lovely fantasy to indulge in as a child, but as someone who was never shielded from the horrors of existence, I knew there had to be a catch. "Ah, you're attempting to poach me from Polyope to ruin her chances at winning, and with it the respect she'd get."

Her dazzling, uniform grin—too bright to show individual teeth—appeared at that point. "Many motives can be behind one act, as they'd affect everyone involved differently."

Tempting as it was—to eschew all I'd had piled onto my shoulders and become a "moondust maiden", forever wandering the wilderness with fantastic creatures and likeminded women— it was not worth considering.

The sirens' song had unearthed my deepest desire was not to be free or to belong to Adamantus, it was always what I'd planned to do: To return home.

I glanced back at the city, debating how to go about this for now. "Could you start by poaching Eglaia's bride, Rhoxane? More than anyone, she does not want to be here or in her goddess's service."

She hummed thoughtfully, eyeing the pink pillar that signaled Eglaia's position. "How noble, pointing me towards the less fortunate."

"If she fares better under your watch, then I'll consider hiding behind your skirt instead of Polyope's," I said. "Until then, I have a duty to fulfill, or else I'll be turned into a hundred-handed monstrosity for my ungratefulness."

"That is an issue I hadn't considered, but I will see what I can do with your poor little friend." Telephassa straightened to her full height, a devious tinge to her smile. "Eglaia's rage will be delightful."

"It better be."

Telephassa manifested a silver, velvet sack and I immediately held my hands out for it. "Here, an incentive to change your mind."

I pulled at the drawstrings and found a mass of glittery silver-blue power.

Moondust.

Resisting the dumb urge to press my face in it assured me of the sirens' power, not my own weakness. "What am I supposed to do with this?"

Telephassa had already vanished, leaving me hugging the moondust and debating everything I'd undergone today.

The difficult contemplations—about the ship growing vines that obeyed my command, and the ideas Telephassa had given me to unwind this mystery—could wait.

Now, I had to stave off my exhaustion long enough to survive the next two rounds.

THE ARMOR OF AUTONOË

The enthusiasm of childish glee had returned tenfold.

It grew wings when I emerged through Machaius's Godsgate, and soared alongside the sky-high levels of onlookers clapping, cheering and pounding their fists on the seats that encircled me.

In the center of a coliseum, the sun shining off my armor, I shot up my arms and reveled in the moment.

Today I would get what I wished the last two mind-breaking tasks had been. A good, old-fashioned challenge powered by the entertaining fantasy of being a gladiator.

I was still chewing on the penultimate pomegranate seeds from the half Polyope allowed me. She'd avoided answering where they'd been at my return from the sirens' shipwreck bay by shoving it in my face last minute, leaving me to gnaw on the fruit like a hurried rat.

Before that, she'd given me a triple stink-eye over the sack of moondust. Out of pettiness and giddiness over how pretty it was, I rubbed some of the glittery powder on my body.

My interaction with Adamantus had been limited to when he'd delivered the armor to my quarters.

"Where did you get this?" I had asked, running my fingertips over the grooves of the platinum chest plate. I remembered it from the armory walls. "I've never seen one with female proportions."

"The Armor of Autonoë, one of my more prized possessions," he'd said, almost fond.

If he hadn't declared his distance, I would have considered this a sweet gesture specific towards me. Autonoë was a Princess of Tritonia, who'd fought off the Avestan Empire's attempts to colonize her island. In some parts along the Deep Red Sea, she had been venerated as a goddess of home safety, something that resonated with me greatly.

Touched, I had reached for him, but he'd stepped back out, courteous and distant. "I've heard mortals use 'good luck charms' to maximize their odds. I hope this proves to be such for you."

He'd left as the lampades rushed to fasten the protective pieces to my body.

A roar from the audience alerted me to the gods' arrival, seated around in the centermost spaces for an ideal view.

Formeta announced herself by slamming her shoulder into mine, and marched out, arms up in a triumphant pose.

So far, I hadn't been intimidated by my competitors, but Formeta was a war-goddess. A literal force to be reckoned with, able to crush me with ease. The good thing was, we weren't meant to be battling each other.

If only Polyope would let me finish the whole pomegranate.

Machaius rose, a rage-red burn in the left-side curve of the coliseum. "Today, we will witness the penultimate fight for Queen of the Underworld." Cheers erupted louder, the audience invested. "My daughter, Formeta, competes against Prospera, priestess to Polyope."

Jeers cracked the joyous unity, and the closest seats flung things my way.

There went the fun fantasy that made me take this round in good stride.

Formeta preened for the positive reception, banging her

spear on its shield. I busied myself with the crowd, scanning for familiarity as I drummed on the weapons that hung from my hips, the orichalcum whip and tridagger.

Right across from Machaius sat Polyope with Theoneus and his wife, and above them Adamantus was surrounded by several feet of shifting shadows. His section of the audience quieter, wary of his presence, and his eyes were the brightest thing for miles, fixed down at me like purple stars.

A horn blew, silencing the crowd for Machaius to announce, "Begin the beast-fight!"

In reply, the ground shook, leaping from tremors to quakes until the stretch before me cracked. The rifts grew deeper and spread further fissures as the shifting ground overthrew my balance, and rattled out my breath.

I had just untwisted the tridagger into a spear, and dug its bladed end in the arena to steady myself when broken ground exploded upward by the emergence of a gigantic worm.

Screams of fear and excitement clashed into white noise as the worm rose further up, its slimy, excrement-colored mass seeming to stretch endlessly.

It reached its peak, larger than a lighthouse, and opened its face in three flaps to screech through a hellish maw of ringed teeth that flung down gallons of muck-brown saliva.

Heart beating to the maddening rhythm of the audience's pounding, I sprinted back, trying to get out of range of the missiles of mucous.

What was I supposed to do with this? How did one fight something this big?

The worm snapped down mouth-first, faster than anything its size had any right to be, and I vaulted right out of devouring distance on the tridagger pole.

The sheer force, size and impact landed too close, catapulting my organs into my throat.

Rattled, I stumbled as far away as I could before daring to face it, spear clutched by the handle like a bat. I didn't need to look to know the worm had ripped back upright, enraged at missing.

Battle-cry piercing the air, Formeta charged with her spear and kicked off the ground so hard she embedded her footprints.

The satisfying stab of its rippled skin never came. The spearhead bounced off the underside of the worm and Formeta was knocked onto her back.

It curved back to curl down onto her, and she shot back along the sand with a rough scrape to evade its mouth.

As it circumvented her attempts to wound it, I took in measured breaths, reminding myself that this was what I'd wanted. This was better than the sirens and the screecher. This predator didn't harbor deception or delusions, just plain-faced danger.

Cautious, I approached to get a better idea of the situation. Formeta's greyscale aura pulsed as she charged again, and lunged higher than ever to slam the spear right beneath the worm's mouth.

The spear snapped in half and she tumbled down to the tune of gasps and shouts.

Before she crashed down, the worm launched its open-mouthed attack my way.

I remained stuck in my spot, scrambling to think of something quickly.

This monstrosity had impenetrable skin not even a war-goddess could break. How would something like this be defeated? How?

Spectator screams threw me into motion. Right as the worm hit, I leaped to scurry up along its face-flap and onto the beginning of its back.

Too quick to compensate for, it shot upright and flung me high into the air. I spun through the higher echelons of the coliseum, the farthest I'd ever been without something to hold onto and it scared me thoughtless.

Disorientation took hold, the force of my ascension rearranging my insides. The rising momentum gave out when I reached the end of the structure, and for one instant, I was caught between the sun above and the world beneath.

Waking life rushed back in when gravity remembered me, and I fell faster than I had flown. Right towards the worm's waiting mouth.

Awaiting the worst, I curled into a ball to avoid the massive rings of teeth.

There was only one thing I could do now.

The stench welcomed me in, light and sound fleeing past me as the worm shut its face.

Here went nothing.

I waited until I reached the darkest and smallest row of teeth and cracked the whip at the nearest protrusion.

Grasping the whip, the short distance of the steadying swing slammed me into the wet, reeking flesh between the teeth. Digestive fumes had me crying and coughing, all the while I struggled to wrap the end of the whip around my waist.

Untwisting the tridagger into the longsword, I took in a burning breath and swung at the mouth.

A cut cleaved it, striking the match for a deafening noise to blare up and out of its opening mouth.

Strained nerves escaped in a hysterical cackle, and I leaped into action before they could get the better of me.

Its insides weren't impenetrable, needing the skin for protection. The odds of the skin cutting from the inside were slim, but I was tossing the dice and leaving the rest up to chance.

I climbed up across the teeth like they were a diagonal ladder, the whip stretching between me and the anchoring tooth. Halfway across the mouth, I crouched atop one and faced the section I'd cut.

"Time to test where I lie on the scale between bravery and madness."

Kicking off the tooth, I threw myself across and swung the sword with all my might.

Roaring, I sliced my way out its throat with a splashing arc of dark blood.

Heart pounding in my ears, I almost couldn't hear the crowd. Planting my feet below the gash I'd made in its throat, I stood sideways and stuck the sword back into the wound.

Jaw locked and fingers gripping the handle, I stepped alongside the growing cut I made, the skin taking longer to break along with the cutting flesh.

Momentum picked up along the curves of its body, dragging a growing cut right below its mouth, exploiting the limits of its mobility.

Fire spread through my limbs as I moved faster, right until the blade cut a full circle and the worm's face separated from its body. I ripped through the last patch, blade scattering blood and chunks of flesh through the air and the head slid off, taking me with it.

The whip retracted from its anchoring tooth, disconnecting me from the worm's crash-landing. Not long after, I followed with my arms and elbows in, bouncing off its head to land in a painful kneel on the sand.

Last to land was the worm's headless body, hitting the arena with an earthquaking crash.

Dizziness verging on deliriousness, I inhaled from the dusty clouds it created. Coughing out the sand, I rose on unsteady legs and took in what I had just done.

The last-minute, instinctual idea, that I'd gotten in the true jaws of death, had worked.

High on the success and the roar of the crowd, I raised my arms in triumph and tried not to tip myself backwards.

"I'm going to be smug about this for the rest of my life," I mumbled tiredly.

Circling in place, I received each part of the audience until I faced Machaius. He was a hot coal in a sea of windblown grass, burning against his smaller, dimmer surroundings. I half-bowed in his direction then continued on to the rest of the coliseum, basking in the unanimous applause.

"This can't be it." Formeta marched through the split parts of the worm to round on me. "There is no possible way you could beat me."

"I didn't." I stuck out my tongue, goofy with pride. "I beat the worm."

Aiming to intimidate me of all things, she raised her sharp-edged shield. "You could not have beaten either. I am the goddess, I am the one with ages of battle and the fear it creates!"

No care left within reach, I deliriously blew a wet raspberry at her. "And none of the common sense required to kill something inhuman, it seems."

Enraged, she charged to decapitate me with the shield.

Like lightning, the silver bident cut across our distance and pierced her armor, knocking her back.

Shuddering with relief, I found Adamantus descending through the seats, splitting the audience as they rushed to evade him.

Machaius joined her from the other side and I was too tired to flee through the arena.

When Adamantus ripped his staff from Formeta's body, I expected Machaius to rush at me, strangle me with the rage that emboldened an army, but he lifted his daughter by her hair.

"You told me you were unbeatable, yet you let Polyope embarrass me in front of all these people," he yelled at her. "I will demote you for this dishonor!"

Formeta pleaded with her father to no avail. By doing the unthinkable, I had led to a goddess being humbled.

Self-satisfaction filled me with a loose-limbed warmth like I had downed a full glass of liquor. It gave me the disinhibition to grin at Adamantus proudly. "Now you can't deny how good that was."

He approached, tone echoing yet distant. "The Fates do seem to favor you for now."

Machaius's Godsgate opened by us. I didn't wait for Polyope to arrive to go back through with him behind me. "Come on, you have to admit it, I am better than you could have hoped for!"

We returned to the base of Blackglass Hall, and I had to think, hard, where my quarters was.

Adamantus followed closely, and only at my threshold did he unmask. "It is too early to celebrate."

"So you've said." I removed the armor, dropping the pieces as I made my way into my bathroom. "Doesn't mean you can't tell me 'Good job, Cora'."

The chest plate clanged onto the tiles, followed by the knee-guards and the kilt. A cramp ran along my side when I reached to turn on the tub taps and I hoped whatever Theoneus had planned tonight involved tons of food. I was going to need to eat a whole cow to make up for the exhaustion I'd accumulated.

I turned to retrieve the bottles of scented oil and collided with his chest.

Here I stood, in only a shirt and covered in blood and mucous and grime, while he was coated in layers of the richest material.

I busied myself with uncorking the bottle, unleashing the scent of lavender. "What are you doing here now?"

Adamantus tentatively reached for me, but I stepped back. "Answer me."

"I find myself back at the same place I was after your first foray through a Godsgate." He seemed startled by his own admission. "I want to maintain my distance, but I couldn't until I was certain of your safety."

"I'm walking, talking and feeling quite ravenous, so, I'm fine." I dumped the oil into the hot, rising water of the tub. "If you're so concerned, then where were you yesterday? What were you and Polyope discussing without me?"

"We were trying to pinpoint an explanation for your sudden ability to manifest plants," he said so quickly, it had to be rehearsed. "And our leads on who our culprit is."

"You know, I still don't understand what you're getting out of this?" Lathering the bathwater, I scrutinized him. "You are so far away from the problems of heaven, you avoid the other gods, and as soon as they pick who's taking the throne this conflict that threw off the power balance, and your death-rate will be over. So, what are you getting out of finding and reinstating Eurycrius?"

"I get to know where he went that manages to evade detection so seamlessly."

If this wasn't suspicious before, it certainly was now. "But why?"

The defensive deflection from before returned. "Why do you ask?"

"Because I want to know what's going on considering, as you keep reminding me, I might die from the target you've painted on my back!"

"What does my reason for the investigation have to do with your mortality?"

"Oh, you're definitely being obtuse on purpose this time." I went up to him, daring him to meet my eyes. "The least you owe me after what I've put myself through is an explanation. So, *Orcus*, what is all this really about?"

His eye twitched at the name. "I'm looking for something, and I believe that finding where Eurycrius went will help me find it."

"And that something is?"

"No matter of yours," he ground out. "By the time I pursue that, this should all be over, with you returned to your home, and Eurycrius to his throne."

Every time I thought I understood him, a dozen more mysterious threads appeared, and I couldn't decide which to pursue.

"What are your leads so far? Telephassa either seems to think that he left willingly, or Lyceus is behind this."

That made him raise his brows. "Almagera seemed the most likely candidate at first, killing her husband's bastards after centuries of tolerating their existence. But Lyceus is becoming a more viable answer. Him becoming King of Heaven would be a seamless transition, save for appointing a new weather god to take on Eurycrius's duties."

"I'll try talking to him then, he does seem interested in me lately," I suggested.

Adamantus's expression darkened like a storm cloud. "I wouldn't advise being alone with him."

"Why not?"

He reached for me again, seeming larger, casting a greater shadow over me. "If he is the one behind all this, if not a big part of it, then he can't discover who you are."

"It may have slipped your mind in the fifteen minutes since we left the arena, but I can handle myself."

"Not when it comes to men like him." He gripped my arms just as he did in the asphodel fields, overwhelming me with his indiscernible feelings as well as the conflicting ones he ignited within me. "Even if he didn't suspect you of being among his targets, there is no telling what he could attempt."

"That would be the best way to get him to talk," I argued, holding onto his forearms, the contact invigorating. "Loosening lips through a kiss has worked on men of all kinds, even the most powerful among them, why not the God of the Sun?"

"No." His grip on me tightened, just shy of bruising. "He's not worth knowing your touch."

The nerve of him, rejecting me then being jealous.

"That's not for you to decide, considering how torturous sharing my bed would be for you."

Pressing firm to my skin, his touch slid up to cup my face, fingers holding my head up to meet his face. "You think I want this, to have you shown to me as the answer to all my problems then reminded that I can never truly have you?"

My hands over his own, I steeled myself against the temptation to close the gap between us once more. "What are we supposed to do until this is over, keep avoiding each other like nothing's happened? I can't do that, I'm not one to forgive or forget, so don't tell me to keep my distance when you keep putting me in these difficult positions."

"What would you have us do then, Cora?" He stroked my face with his thumbs, so cold against my flushing skin that I could feel steam rising off me. "I told you, if I knew what it was like to have you, I would not be able to part with you, and you would hate me for it."

"I don't know," I admitted. "I don't know what's going on anymore, or what to do or even what I want beyond just you. I don't even know why, but something about your damnable existence burns all the restraint I've lived my whole life by."

"This is why I will try to maintain my distance as much as possible." Abruptly, he released me and retreated from the bathroom, throwing me a reluctant look over his shoulder. "Do what you see fit tonight, but be careful. I will not be held accountable for my actions if he harms you."

He left faster than I could follow, leaving something behind on my bed.

Gleaming softly, it was the pure-gold gown he'd offered to me, from before everything had grown irreversibly twisted.

Before I'd become a victim of uncertainty and a prey to my own desires.

37

AFTERLIFE OF THE PARTY

Wall-shaking beats and twirling lights welcomed me into Athanasia, but the smell of food was what gave me a precise path to follow.

Countless souls filled the most spacious part of the city, bewitched by the sourceless tunes as I had been by the sirens. Weary, I passed through them, unnoticed by most, until I reached long, stone tables piled with mouthwatering varieties of food.

Barefoot, I moved freer than I had in days and couldn't resist dancing my way towards my goal, the music energetic and exciting. The gold dress hung over my body like it had been poured on, with slits up to my thighs so the skirt flapped around when I twirled.

It wasn't heavy like I expected it to be once I'd wrestled it on, but covered me in a smooth, cool layer, so beautiful I couldn't stop examining my reflection. The one issue was the blue-amber choker clashing with the color, but I needed it to maintain the illusion of Prospera.

Appearances be damned, I first went for the beef ribs, devouring them with messy enthusiasm and sucking the marrow out as loudly as I wanted, shielded by the thumping drums and chatter.

Recuperating from a long, hard day of work always involved sitting down at the table with our family and head workers, passing dishes around as we gossiped, complained and exchanged news. Here I was alone, with no gazette to flip through absent-mindedly, no elders admonishing me for attacking my food like a wild beast, and no predictable complaints about the railway being constructed nearby.

If only the vision of the siren song had been true. I'd be home, conspicuously unnoticed by the demigod slaughter, with Terzia on my lap and my mother hurriedly braiding my hair so it wouldn't get dirtied by my messy eating.

Mood soured, I moved on to the fried seafood and exerted some of my tension by gnawing on octopus tentacles.

As if the sight summoned her, Theoneus's sea-creature wife appeared by me.

Aristagnë was unmissable even in the fluctuating lights, her rust-red hair and slippery cyan skin stood out as much as her green fish-scale dress. "I've been looking for you."

Continuing to chew my food, I stared at her expectantly.

She approached, stopping right across the table from me. "It took me a while, but I think I've figured out why you're so familiar."

It was going to be the usual stupid comparison to a centaur or a tall Northlander woman.

She came closer, large, glassy eyes boring through me. "Cora? Cora Spica?"

I choked on my food.

Aristagnë was immediately at my side, pounding on my back. I heaved out the chunk I'd inhaled and rounded on her with watering eyes. "Who are you?"

Disappointment dimmed her sharp smile. "Oh, I do look quite different, don't I?"

"I'll bet."

Her neck gills flared with her huffed chortle. "Cora, it's me. It's Ariane of Tritonia."

"No, you're not, piss off!" I wheezed, massaging my throat.

Princess Ariane of Tritonia was among the five finalists for the hand of the now-King Cyaxares of Cahraman. I'd last seen her at the coronation because I couldn't get out of that desert fast enough.

"No, it's me," she swore, tapping her heart. "How else would I recognize you?"

I reached for the filled goblets, tossing back half the drink to soothe my inflamed throat. "Good question. Answer it."

"Your voice," she said. "To this day, I've never heard a woman with your timbre or character."

That...was a reasonable guess. "Going by voice is a bit of a reach, isn't it?"

"There is also how you are in the face of danger," she added, giggling. "Remember when you terrorized Princess Loujaïne with the ghoul's head?"

Such a specific instant could have only been privy to someone who was there.

It really was her!

I finished my drink, it had fizzled and tasted like apricots. "Gods, I hated that bitch."

Aristagnë pulled a face, exaggerated, comical horror. "It's a good thing that trip didn't work out for me. Imagine being stuck with her as your de-facto mother-in-law?"

"I'd have punted her off the mountain within the first week." I moved on to the boiled shellfish, breaking off a crab leg to suck the meat out. "Wait. *Wait.* Were you always like this?"

"Uh, not quite, no." She ran her fingers over her gills, her webbed hands with pale palms and eerily smooth skin. "I could shift into sea animals, fully or partly, but I didn't have this much power before."

The "before" was accentuated by her looking towards her husband.

Theoneus had risen to the top of a central stage, surrounded by souls, nymphs, satyrs and the odd Underworld demon, all at his whim as he conducted the musicians.

He wore nothing but a dangerously short, sheer, embellished chiton, whose neckline stopped between his hips. I had to commend his confidence because he, for lack of a better word, dressed like a costly whore.

Ariane—Aristagnë was enjoying the view, a lecherous grin widening her grim mouth.

"I'm sensing a very long and peculiar tale behind you two."

She cackled, nodding. "You have no idea."

"Was Aristagnë the name you got when you were deified?"

The brief twitching of her irises must have been her rolling her eyes. "No, it's my name. 'Ariane' was the only version foreigners didn't completely butcher."

"Speaking of butchering foreigners, you know Rhoxane, Eglaia's bride?"

Aristagnë edged closer, large irises gleaming with interest. "The sad one? What about her?"

"She's Marzeya's granddaughter."

"No!" she gasped. "How? She seems so normal."

"It seems like she never met her grandmother. Born and raised in Orestia then given in service to Eglaia for being too pretty, whatever that means."

The meaning didn't elude her, as she cringed in sympathy. "Poor girl, earning a god's ire just for existing."

"Tell me about it, except I don't know who's after me yet. You have any experience with that?"

Quickly, she had gone between being curious about my statement to slouching with defeat. "Not directly. My father angered our ancestor and he took it out on my mother and she..."

She didn't need to say it. I'd heard enough rumors about the late Queen of Tritonia birthing a monster. The whispers varied on whether she had been one in human form, like Aristagnë had inferred about herself, or if the queen had borne the result of being mounted by a beast.

It wasn't just Eglaia who punished mortals by making them fuck the unthinkable.

Huddled together by the seafood, we chatted about the competition, events concerning our part of the world, and the one we'd first met and parted in.

Just talking to someone as myself was relieving, even if it were about an inconvenient shared experience. I hadn't realized how much I just needed to talk to someone in such a simple manner, no technical or stressful elements involved.

Soon, I found myself venting to her. I didn't care how thoughtless it may have been, but I trusted her.

"As someone who's been in the divine realm for a bit, who do you think it could be?" I asked her, now having moved on to the pasta platters, made with a home-sickening authenticity.

Aristagnë slurped her oyster out of its shell. "Before you killed that worm, I would have said Machaius. He's been feeling like he doesn't get enough respect now that wars have become less viable. But the way he got angry at his own daughter instead of you tells me that this was more for pride than power."

"And now?"

"If I could pinpoint which of Almagera's sons was most likely to succeed his father, I'd say she did all this to wipe out competition for her children with him." She glanced at where the failed competitors lurked on the peripheries of the party. "She was so against Theoneus's deification, and mine by extension. I expected her to spit poison at us when the council voted against her."

"Which of her sons do you think she'd push to become King of the Gods?"

After raising a gilded jug in askance, she then poured us both full goblets of luminescent nightwine. "The obvious answer would be Machaius himself, but if you ask me I'd say Euanemus."

"The wind god?"

"King of the Winds, who better to take over for being in charge of the weather?"

"And with the vantage point to find all the demigods and descendants and…crush their chests with sudden, great force."

Aristagnë raised her goblet. "You didn't hear any of this from me."

"One of Euanemus's sons kidnapped my cousin," I told her. "He used her to lure me after them, to trap me and force me to marry him. Any ideas about that?"

She mumbled through a mouthful of wine, then swallowed to say, "Some competitors have been saying marrying a daughter of Eurycrius would help strengthen their claim. And their offspring."

"How do you know this?"

"Whispers travel far with a sea storm," she began, aiming for a mysterious air. When I remained unamused, she gave in. "All right, Theoneus knows how how to set tongues wagging."

"That he can." I watched how the dancers descended further into uninhibited actions, underdressed, writhing, pawing at each other and scream-singing without a care for shame or tune. "Does this influence of his extend to major gods?"

"Depends on what you have in mind."

"Apart from Euanemus, my main suspect is Lyceus. I need to question him but in a subtle way."

"Subtle? You?"

I gave her a light shove. "I know how to be that, in theory. I just need some help."

"You sure you don't want to try pinning him to a wall at knifepoint?" she teased.

If only we were back on my turf, where I could manage such a thing. "Just because that's what excites your husband, doesn't mean it will work for other men." The drink grew bitter in my mouth, dulling the afterthought. "Namely a god used to getting whatever he wants."

Her mid-sip giggles created bubbles in her drink. "It's not

Theo's fault he was put together backwards. But I like him that way."

"I can see that." Despite following it up with a grouchy question, I couldn't help giving her a warm smile. "You look happy. Is that genuine or him working his magic?"

The mere suggestion tickled her, taken aback with humored surprise. "As if he could affect me that way. We wouldn't be together if I responded to him the way all others did, and likewise for him."

There was no need for a follow-up question, her rows of sharp teeth and predatory gaze told me that only the instigator of madness would readily kneel to ask for her webbed hand.

"He wasn't afraid of you, not even when you were both mortal," I said, feeling oddly choked up. "He saw past the sea-monster."

I refused to look for Adamantus in the crowd.

"No, that's not it. He saw me at my most inhuman and loved me, not in spite of it, but because of it," she said dreamily. "We share a rare understanding of what it's like to look human but be something far stranger, in a way that could have only risen from Orestian seawater and wine."

Envy was among the banned list of emotions I was meant to have immunized myself against. It was alive and well, wrestling with yearning and whimsy for what brought them together.

My pursuit of Adamantus was purely for the opportunity and experience, because I could never have anything more than that. Love and romance were for naive girls with no crushing responsibilities, or the idle, wealthy daughters of ambitious men. They were the ones who could afford to pin their hopes on a man changing their lives for the better, and be blind to all the trouble that came with them.

I had no place for a man in the life I was meant to lead, because his "worth" in the eyes of gods and mortals would eclipse my own. Because, outside my inherited post, my appeal lay in the thrill of taming and overpowering me, and when that satisfaction never came I'd only be given rage and resentment.

That was why I enjoyed being around Adamantus so much. His inhumanity was refreshing, calming and disconnected from the cruel truths of life, and even though I still represented a means-to-an-end for him, he didn't treat me as such.

He'd said that I made him feel real, the same could be said for him.

"There's definitely a lot you are leaving out, but we'll have to talk about it after I take advantage of Theoneus's mood-altering event." I nudged her, mostly to test her skin's consistency. "Can he help me with Lyceus or...?"

Excited, she shoved the last of her crab meat into her wide mouth and hustled straight for the center of the celebration. "I'll talk to him. You go track down your target."

I couldn't help being affected by her enthusiasm. "Damn, you're eager. What are you getting out of this?"

"Entertainment!" Aristagnë called, dipping into the crowd. "I expect details later!"

Was this what it was like to have friends outside of work and family? If so, then I really needed a few of those. The blunt honesty and ready supportiveness was nice to experience, and did offer a lightheartedness I rarely saw.

Throwing back the remainder of the nightwine, I smoothed back my darkened hair and began my search for the sun god.

The atmosphere shifted as I crossed the floor filled with frenzied souls, becoming unhurried despite the energy.

Weariness lingered from the last time I'd been in Theoneus's hands, as well as the lulling, dumbing influence of the sirens. I ended up swiping a bottle off a nearby table, uncorking it and guzzling down half of it to force me into loosening up.

Whatever was in it made an instant impact, unlatching the fasteners of the invisible armor I carried every waking minute. Not quite disarmed, but less on-guard as I let my body move freely through the mass of souls, head and shoulders bobbing to the beat.

Humming along to the vaguely familiar music, too distracted by my search to make out the words the singers rang off every surface, I unwound like never before.

There was no one here to impress or intimidate. Judgement for indulging in the most basic joys had no sway here, no one was going to question my ability to be serious or responsible if I had fun for five minutes.

I stood within the strange god's entrancing aura and let it wash over me, stifling the deep-set urge to resist and letting myself be swayed purely by sensation.

Musical bass vibrated through the floor and up my bones, a concentrated frequency of tremors that rocked me harder than a ship in a storm. Somehow, while I grew hazy and less coordinated, I wasn't sickened or even slightly alarmed.

Lights alternated vividness and color to the tempo of deep breaths, changing with every relieving exhalation, and the liveliest of them all was the source.

Theoneus was a roaring campfire, gathering us all in from the dark, bathing us in his lulling warmth. Unsteady red-purple rays shot through the blinding cracks in his body and shone through the crowd, creating strobing lights through the souls.

Complex thinking fought my grasp like I was fishing bare-handed, and I didn't care.

The state I danced deeper towards was somewhere between the liberation of intoxication and the mania of sleeplessness, reeling out loud, inexplicable laughs and imprecise moves.

The dancers launched into a circle dance, and I skipped right along, arms in the air, screaming at the top of my lungs and laughing as the colors flashed through them. The music's tempo grew faster, hurrying the pace and raising the energy among us, with the singers belting and howling til they went hoarse with exertion.

Awash with festivity, I forgot what I'd come to do until I caught him approaching.

Golden light trapped in the glass sculpture of a beautiful man, his hair a crown of rays so bright it lost all detail and color, and his radiance was spellbinding.

Rolling my shoulders back and leading with my hips, I waded through the dead to meet him in the direct sunlight.

SHEDDING LIGHT

There was a charge in the air, like lightning had struck between us.

A fraction of the sun danced within his outline, casting throbbing rays that centered him in the colorful dark. A lantern among fireflies.

Visionaries of the past had fallen to their knees before this sight, awestruck by the beauty and its implications. Whole civilizations had prioritized the sun, worshipped its god as the king of the rest, and viewed their kings as its descendants. Plenty probably were. That was the claim fastening the tapestries of many dynasties.

The excitable influence thickened in the air around me, an intoxicating fog that had my body listening more to the music than my thoughts.

Rather than watching till he approached, the skin-deep itch to obey the beat took me through the steps everyone took to this song's intro.

The singers' voices joined in a breathtaking chorus and I rose onto my toes, stretching to my full height, grasping at the diamond-studded, midnight-blue ceiling. The imitation of night gifted by a starless king to his deprived subjects.

Heat hit my back, and a large hand covered mine, leading me into an en-pointe turn.

Saying a smile lit up someone's face was among my favorite exaggerations. In Lyceus's case, his dazzling grin did brighten his expression. "It's not often that someone proves me wrong. I'd be furious if I weren't so taken with you."

"As the god of poetry, I would have expected you to phrase that compliment better."

"But why lie?" he purred. "Your tendency to speak your first thought tells me that you'd prefer to hear unpolished responses."

I rolled my eyes. "If I wanted to hear myself talk I'd go yell into a tunnel."

"The mouth on you." He twirled me out, throwing off my balance before pulling me back in, other hand landing on my waist. "I can't tell if you enjoy tempting trouble, or if you truly are mad."

"You tell me," I said, aiming for coy, but hitting impatient. "How have I proven you wrong?"

"When Polyope brought you to us, and you foolishly goaded us into pitting you against our choices for Orcus, I was ready to watch you fail miserably." Lyceus gave me an appreciative once-over, gripping my waist tighter. "Now, I can see why your mother is the Muse of Improvisation, for it would be a great mistake to bet against you."

Music to my ears. Even if it rode in on a false premise, my triumph reached the finish line through undeniable strain.

Ridiculous, indulgent ideas sprouted like weeds as I got closer to Lyceus.

I could pursue his interest. Prove to myself that Adamantus's rejection had only hurt my pride, and that I was only after the experience he'd denied me.

It was a wonder how people could delude themselves into believing clear untruths. I couldn't convince myself that my feelings towards Adamantus were distant, uncomplicated and situational.

No matter how much I wanted it to be true.

Pride and position in life dictated that I couldn't let my feelings get the better of me, especially ones that had no use like anger and determination. The traits men were praised for. To be weak enough to be swept away by fanciful, unrealistic ideas, like wanting to be with someone for reasons beyond personal benefit...

It scared me to even question my predestined life. Did I want to be in charge of the horn of plenty I called a homeland? Yes. Did I want Adamantus, and the reprieve I've had from my life since descending here? Yes.

But why? *Why?*

I shook out my hair, loosening the locks that snagged on my horns, and put forth my first subtle suggestion. "Does that mean you're withdrawing?"

Lyceus clucked his tongue at me chidingly. "And miss seeing how you fare with what I have planned?"

"Is that worth more than the possibility of losing to your sister?"

His eyes flared, briefly too bright to see beyond them. "If I didn't know any better, I'd say you wanted me to remain."

"I do." I looked up at him through my lashes. "Not purely for the satisfaction of beating your fairy princess."

"Then why?"

"Winning would mean I might never see the sun again." I didn't need to fake the longing and dread I felt at that prospect. "There is no sky here. No stars to gaze at, no moon to help keep track of time, and most of all—" I rose higher on my toes, neck stretched to make up for the difference in height, and reached for his ego with my lips. "No sun to light up the days, to follow across the sky as it painted it with beautiful colors, and reigned as the clearest sign of divinity one could witness. Far more consistent than lightning-strikes and sea-storms, and forever more welcome than death."

"You worship me on Meropis?"

"As the King of the Skies," I said. "There you are the same entity as the god who has gone missing. The storms he is responsible for are assigned to the wind god, Euanemus."

Focus was a task to maintain through the lulling fog, but my carefully-chosen words had hit their mark. The warmth and brightness he gave off lessened, allowing more detail to show like the smirk in his full lips and the carefree angles of his posture.

I had put him at ease.

"It won't be long until the people get what they want, a constant and dependable head god rather than a temperamental one." Swift and smooth, he spun me around, feet flying off the floor. "And you needn't leave all that light behind, least of all my own."

"It's too late to tell me that. Whether you withdraw or not, after tomorrow I either win and remain as his bride, or lose and remain here among the dead."

Threading his fingers with my own, he had slimmed into an approachable size. The shape he appeared to his lovers in, making it easier to woo them without the underlying fear of being crushed. "Orcus's hand is being forced on this matter, so, I doubt you will be a true bride or a queen in anything but name."

"Thank you for emphasizing that I'll be forever doomed to loneliness in the dark," I snarked.

His chuckle was a pleasant sound, tugging up the edges of my mouth to mirror his confident calmness. "After tomorrow, you would have fulfilled your purpose in this game, and he would have no use for you."

That was true enough, despite the differing circumstances.

"How are you so certain?" I asked. "He could very well enjoy my company, and nights in my bed."

"Don't tell me you think there's anything under that hideous figure," he joked, like it was the most ridiculous idea he'd ever heard.

I contemplated telling him that I knew what lived beneath

the mortifying facade. That I felt that body pressed against mine and touched the skin he hid under layers of extravagance.

"He's not like us on Anactoron, or even those in the seas, capable of complex thought and maintaining bodies that help us carry out and enjoy our whims and desires." Lyceus's fingers danced down from my waist to my hip, large hand placing his thumb too close to my mound to ignore. "Personifications like himself, and the gods of night, time and sleep, all they have is the consciousness needed to fulfill their purpose."

Offense prickled at my numbed edges, but the fire that fueled my defensiveness was far away. All I had left in this moment was sadness, wondering how much of Adamantus's denial of personhood was the poisonous beliefs of others.

It stirred sensations I'd kept at bay for years, along with the memories of moments I'd shrugged off to not upset my rhythm. Unprompted aggression and avoidance stained my earliest memories, adults expecting me to behave as they did, like I was unlike all other children. Not just by birthright but the parameters of my conception.

To the tune of the weeping strings filling the air, a vault in my mind had been hauled open. The beat had calmed, allowing the singer to wail out an Orestian ode to the full moon, speaking of her many faces and what we did for each side Telephassa showed us. Among the songs that were meant to play the night the West Wind kidnapped Chloë.

Here were instances that I couldn't help re-contextualizing. The way everyone treated me, not just due to being far bigger than all women and most men, but whatever otherworldly essence I carried as a demigod. Did people, starting with my own mother, never treat me with affection and softness because I wasn't quite human?

Had I been deprived of comfort and care due to the belief that I had no need for either?

Lyceus pressed us closer, his mouth to my ear. "I can spare you from that miserable fate."

I shivered, sweat further plastering the gold gown to my heavy body. "Why would you do that for me?"

"When I take my rightful place as King of Heaven, I'll need a queen that inspires as much fear and respect."

"What makes you think you'll get the throne before Almagera's son with Eurycrius?"

"I'd burn the face of the earth before I let that whore and her offspring take power," he growled, heat flaring and speeding the flow of my sweat. "She is a terrestrial goddess, earthbound, and never had any right becoming Queen of Heaven."

"What about her missing king?"

"Eurycrius was a reckless fool who fucked his way across all realms, and never learned the consequences it wrought from his wife or his offspring. It was by dumb luck that he took the throne from Ceirous," he seethed, so hot he dried out my eyes.

There it was, the admission I was here for.

"But you, if you came with me, you could be what her worshippers believe her to be." He pressed light, quick kisses from the hinge of my jaw down to my throat, creating a trail of burning spots on my skin. "You are unlike any woman I've come across, possessing so much character and potential. It would be a waste if you were deified here."

Now should be my moment to slip away, and report on what he confirmed. But the atmosphere had grown harder to resist, leaving me loose-limbed in his grip and turning my head back to let him kiss further down.

Who knew when I would be touched like this again. Besides, I still had questions.

"What would you make me into as Queen of Heaven?" I asked, feeling for a detailed plot in the usurpation. "How would you tell mortals of change in leadership, or would you have them worship you under his name?"

"I'd send visions to those in power, as I do to my oracles, announcing us as the Sun King of Heaven and his queen."

"That's not an answer. Neither is how this plan is to go

against the wishes of Almagera and her sons, and whoever else is vying for the throne." I combed my fingers through the light that formed his hair and barely felt anything. It sobered me long enough to catch a flash of purple that had my heart leaping.

"My, but you are detail-oriented."

"If I'm meant to risk angering two chthonic gods and ruin my chances by running off with you, based on an empty promise, then I'll need a very good plan." I withdrew from him, single-minded search taking me towards the direction of Adamantus's eyes.

"I'll send for you when I have everything in order."

Of course he didn't have a plan, let alone the sense to reassure me of anything. What did it matter if I suffered the consequences of his whims? I was a woman, worth nothing more than the watered-down praise he gave me, because it was enough of an honor for something like me to earn his attention.

Soon he would be asking for a roll behind the barn, like every other powerful pile of shit who needed to be kicked by a horse in the balls to reset their rotten minds.

"Either you give me a clear answer or you piss off before I tell Polyope you attempted to seduce her chosen bride."

Both hands gripped my hips, steadying me as I arched back away. "Then I'll take you with me now, see how she tries to find you when she is barred from the highest heaven where I reside."

For all the good it would do against him, I whipped out the tridagger, pressing its tip to his chest just as the prongs of Adamantus's bident trapped his throat.

DISINHIBITION

"Would you like to know what death-by-heatwave feels like?" Adamantus threatened icily, louder than the thrum of the music. "If you don't release her, I'll raise your experience to that of being burned alive."

Lyceus immediately pulled away, feigning being unbothered. "If you're worried about her maidenhood, I guarantee you she came to you tainted by her mistress's rituals."

Adamantus raised the bident over his head, ready to spear him. "Burning alive it is."

Lyceus staggered back through the crowd, not finding a last word worth the risk.

I let out a sigh of relief. "I didn't know how I was going to get him off me."

"This is why I didn't want you doing this, answers be damned." His piercing shadows softened when he faced me. "You wore the dress."

Restraints torn and abandoned, I gave him a twirl. "It's a shame this disguise keeps it from matching my hair."

Breath shuddering, he reached for my throat, the cool press of his palm silencing the burning trail left by Lyceus's lips.

The blue-amber choker slipped off and I felt my hair rise,

frizzing from the sweat I'd accumulated and the curious humidity trapped in the air.

Lingering sense had me fearing onlookers spotting me. "What are you doing?"

He ran a curled lock between his fingertips, descending closer, antlered skull breaking apart to retreat behind his face. "What I've wanted to do since I first saw you."

I swayed mindlessly to the string section, body thrumming with anticipation like it had that night. "I must have looked like a right mess, drenched nightgown and muddied feet, in the woods alone like I was haunting it for a victim."

"I told you I thought you were someone's dream," he whispered, his voice a caress that encompassed me whole. "What I didn't tell you is that when you spoke and smiled at me so fearlessly, I knew you had to be my fantasy."

His eyes were the darkest I'd ever seen them, the lights totally dimmed, leaving vivid purple rings around pupils like faraway obsidian stars.

I could see myself reflected in them.

"When you reached for me, as you do in depictions of Death, I didn't want to run. I was ready to take your hand and let you have my life," I admitted, stifled by the wine-stained fog that blurred all but him. "To this day, I don't know why you leave me so dumbstruck, thinking with anything but my head."

His long fingers cupped the back of my head, eyes torn between my forehead and my bared throat. "I can't fathom why your instincts told you to accept rather than escape my grasp."

He stared at me like a man dying of thirst, and the only thing to quench him in existence was the sweat he'd lick off my body.

"I am so despised and dreaded, the living don't dare speak my name and use blackest of magic to defy me," he rasped, face hovering over my own. "But not you."

Lungs full of liquored fumes, my chest grew too tight to gasp.

"With you, I am not Death. Why is your immunity to my

presence affecting my own, setting me aflame with sensations I can't name?"

Sense and significance filtered through the relived moments, torturous with temptation. Back in the dreamy dark when I reached back and in my bed when I got to feel him.

"For the first time, I liked what I saw," I recalled. "Without implication, meaning or thought, I saw you and felt free, and I think you could tell."

"I did," he agreed, amazed. "The Fates showed me the impossible. Unearthed a want within me that would have remained slumbering in the depths, if I hadn't desired what I saw."

"Liar." I attempted to roll my eyes chidingly, instead aimed for the sparkling ceiling. "You said you saw nothing when you looked at Eglaia."

"That hasn't been true since you came into the Dreamfields and grinned at me like I was your prey. Since then I have been bewitched."

The last threads of control snapped. I threw my arms around his neck, pulling him down to stick my hands into his inky curls.

Inexperience disregarded by impatience set our faces on a path of collision, teeth scraping together as his large hand pressed against my back. Exploration led me past his teeth and shoulders, and brought him to the bare, scarred skin unveiled by the backless gown.

Cold fingertips sought out the marks, tightening the ruined flesh til he reached the eye in the center.

Adamantus unlatched his mouth, not to distance himself, but to pant into my mouth. "What is this?"

Hooked back in by the beat and bass, I swayed my hips in a circle, raising my hair in clumsy bunches to show him. "My *acanthomatia*. Do you like it?"

Reverent care traced the details in order, following the circle of thorns to the eye with a winding touch that had me fidgeting with arousal so fierce, my bones vibrated. "Why is it on you?"

I groaned, impatient, molten, maddened. "Does it matter?"

"You tell me." Examination complete, he grabbed my waist, fingers forming another set of ribs in their tight hold. "Tell me what you want."

So light, I found myself rising on my toes, head turned up towards his. "You."

Faster than I could grasp, he spun me around and my arms found his neck, bringing him swooping down to reconnect our mouths.

In his embrace, I thrived on instinct. Hands went over and under whatever was within reach, noisily chasing his lips, their smooth slide over my own tasting of cool, precious metal, his tongue a golden spoon feeding my delirium.

While I writhed against him, his hands traveled lower until they gripped my thighs. Without interrupting our chaotic kiss, he lifted me up and shot across the festive space to press my back against the wall. Like he had that day in the Lifetime Library.

No one else existed in this moment. The world had never existed. Only he had ever been there, filling my existence. Now, he'd fill me, body and soul. All I cared about was grabbing handfuls of the hair that had tormented me with every undulation and swish, and clamping my legs around that waist I wanted to remain wrapped around forever.

The world tipped back, the shift in angle pressing his massive, diamond-hard chest further against my aching, swollen breasts.

We broke apart when my chest burned for air, and I melted against the sloping wall, panting as his mouth went for my ear. "Tell me what you like."

"I don't know," I gasped. "You're the only man I've wanted to touch me."

There was no denial of manhood this time, just a tightening grip on my thighs that was going to leave dark fingerprints.

"Do what you'd do to other women."

"You know there haven't been others," he grunted, voice so

low in my ear it made me shiver as if in a seizure, made my core convulse. "I've never felt this maddening urge before."

His sharp teeth grazed my jaw, and I breathed in shocked gasps then out in desperate pants, at his mercy as he scraped down my throat. "Your mouth. Your tongue and teeth."

His lips moved against my pulse. "How do you want them?"

Nothing precise came to mind, a nebulous mass of sensations I entertained in bed, while my fingers tirelessly sought my release. I needed him. Just needed him. Any way he wanted to give me himself, of himself.

"How about here?" Sharp fangs trapped the junction between my neck and shoulder, biting experimentally.

Torn between being sobered by the threat or further aroused by it, I grew more wound up, itching for more. Legs wrapped tighter, I rubbed against his hip, craving something deeper.

And he could feel it.

Unlatching his teeth from my stinging skin, he brought his mouth near mine, our lips an inch too far apart. "I think I know what you need."

I stared at him through heavy-lidded eyes, blood buzzing. "Yeah?"

"It was all I could think of when you wore that armor." His hold slipped under the gold dress, fingers hooked into the hem of my underwear. "How short that kilt was on your long legs as you slaughtered that beast."

Lightning-fast, he ripped the garment off my legs as he knelt between them, draping my knees over his shoulders.

My grip on his hair failed to steady me through my bucking. Tight breaths squeezed my heart out of its cage and down between my legs, pumping more blood than ever to their throbbing peak where all my needs converged, poured.

Despite him being the one kneeling before me, this was the most vulnerable I'd ever felt. Pinned and exposed, at his mercy as mortal lovers had been at the hands of gods.

Coherency fled when he bit at my inner thigh, a little harder than he did my neck. Pieces of broken thoughts were scattered to the four winds when he hoisted my legs higher, adjusting along with the wall that laid me completely flat on my back with my knees by his ears. Willingly giving control to someone who looked at me like a predator that had immobilized its prey.

Adamantus's hand came over mine in his hair, urging me to press his face down. The bone-breaking resistance I'd felt when I punched him was gone, he let me push until I felt his mouth on my slit.

Stunned at the lightning strike of sensation, I didn't know what to do besides lie back and feel his lips moved around in a loud, wet search, adding to the growing wetness that trickled down my cleft to run down my thighs.

What he did next should have been terrifying, but it had me writhing. He unhinged his jaw and sucked my mound whole into his mouth, the siphoning pressure surrounding it so suddenly, it ripped a strangled moan from my contracting throat.

He pulled off long enough to ask, "Like that?"

I lost the ability to speak, leaving me to just direct him by his hair, aiming his mouth higher until he resumed licking and sucking at the top half.

Thoughtless, purely consumed by the rising pleasure, my legs kicked aimlessly. He stroked up and down my thighs, like he was soothing a startled creature, for all the good it would do when he reintroduced his teeth.

Desperate to move, I let out a shuddering gasp at the scrape of his teeth on my tender flesh. Then he gently bit the throbbing nub at the peak, sparking a trail of wildfire up my spine that fled my dry lips in a shriek.

Pleased with himself, he flashed me a wolfish grin before he dragged his tongue through the folds and pressed the tip to the center of nerves.

It never felt like this when I touched myself. Not even close. How could I go back to my fingers after this?

In just moments of playful exploration, Adamantus had me

pressing my heels into his back as I arced my own, humping his face as I anchored myself through my death-grip on his hair.

Instead of hurting, my pull just encouraged him further, making him move faster and press firmer.

Moaning shamelessly, I writhed against his grip, nails pressing into the tops of my thighs. Alternating between the flat of his tongue and the tip, he had me sweating and on the verge of crying as he upped his tempo, bringing me to the edge.

He groaned throatily, the sound vibrating through his lips and adding an indescribable layer to the growing intensity.

The maddening sensitivity centering itself between his jaws had grown too much to handle. I lost all control, my hands flying back as I thrashed against my hard support, no care given to the knuckles I'd just slammed, or my lower back as I desperately thrusted up, chasing the piling pleasure.

With each second my skin grew too tight for my burning body. I couldn't take it anymore. One more move and I was about to burst at the seams.

A scream tore through my body as he finished me off, ecstasy shooting through my tightening muscles in violent convulsions before they melted into rivers of lava.

When the world righted itself, I collapsed in a boneless heap against the wall.

Staring ahead aimlessly, my senses slowly trickled back into my heavy, loosened limbs. Everything else took longer to make itself known, my sight last to settle.

I saw him lick his glistening lips, wet with my release, and could feel new stirrings of arousal.

The mindlessness evaporated when he bridged the gap between us, gripping my knees. "Stay with me."

"I can't." I attempted to shake my heavy head, just rolling it along the wall. "I shouldn't."

The high had begun to crash, leaving me drained.

When he touched my cheek, the last thing I saw before my

lids fell shut were his lips moving, but I heard nothing as darkness swallowed me whole.

AN ETERNITY LATER, I fluttered my lashes till the light stopped hurting, and found a face peering down at me.

It wasn't the one I wanted to wake up to.

Aristagnë's large, aquamarine eyes exhibited concern. "Theoneus overdid it, didn't he?"

Head heavy and pounding, I struggled to rise on my elbows. She slid her hands underneath them and lifted me to a sitting position. "You remember anything about last night?"

"Hmm?" I rubbed at my temples, trying not to tip over into her scaly lap.

"I got Theoneus to dull the senses and drop the inhibitions of everyone in the area, amplifying his influence enough to affect gods," she explained. "So you could question Lyceus."

"Mhm."

"Do you remember any of that? Did you do any of that or did you just hallucinate and dance?"

I jolted out of my daze, like I had missed an entire flight going down the stairs. *"Hallucinate?"*

"Yeah, he has that effect on people." She pressed her clammy, slippery-smooth hand to my forehead. "You seem fine, if a little hungover."

Did—did I imagine it all?

Throwing off the covers, I aimed to jump up, but my legs wobbled under a sudden, biting pain.

Landing back on the bed's edge, I recognized my room and that I was still wearing the gold dress. I couldn't remember leaving the party.

Aristagnë rose and pulled me up along with her. "Are you feeling good?"

"Just worn out." I raised my arms, figuring it better to ask for help than wear myself out fighting the gown. "Can you help me out of this?"

"Oh, wow! I didn't really notice it yesterday, but I've never seen anything like this." She carefully peeled it off me from the bottom up, pausing to wolf-whistle at me. "Somebody had a fun night."

"What?"

"Those are definitely not from your fight against the earth-quake worm."

Lines of healing bruises and half-moon grooves crossed my thighs, leaving behind the faint ache that had caught me off-guard.

Remembering was a punch between the ribs, leaving me breathless. Not from the fragmented feelings that flooded back in, but the disinhibition that created them.

None of it had been a hallucination. It had all been real, and that just made everything much worse than before.

If it hadn't been for Theoneus's mind-altering influence, neither of us would have given into our desires. Not after we'd agreed to maintain our distance. I would have continued pursuing Lyceus for answers, quite possibly to a risky extent.

If only there hadn't been cause to interfere and spare me from the sun god's single-mindedness. It had put Adamantus and I in the wrong place, at the wrong time.

Treacherous glimmers from our foray into the forbidden accompanied me down to my final task. After which, I'd return home burdened by what I had discovered but never claim.

SUN STRUCK

Aristagnë hadn't been exaggerating, Theoneus could mess with even divine minds. Lyceus showed no signs of remembering how we parted the night before, winking at me playfully as I lined up beside his champion, the white-haired Aethusa.

His Godsgate was emblazoned with a golden sun-shield over a cobalt-glass door, and it sat near the River of Agony, too close to the Spiral.

Screams of agony and terror wound their way up, too much to ignore as I walked through the lines of onlookers.

Almagera and Eglaia were too busy squabbling to pay attention to us, leaving Rhoxane to be pulled aside by Telephassa. I hoped something came from their talk, an offer of protection at the very least.

If Telephassa didn't find her worthy, I'd ask Polyope. She had hidden me long enough to finish the first pomegranate halve then shoved me out with a stern order. "Make him regret challenging me."

I pocketed the remaining half of the pomegranate, exerting my tension through crunching the remains of the other.

Telephassa watched as I strolled past her, far more interested in me than in Rhoxane, who avoided looking back at me, pale and possibly on the verge of being sick. Carrying that winged shithead's child must have been eating at her, not just emotionally, but physically.

Surprisingly, Machaius gave me a nod of grudging respect as I passed, Formeta nowhere to be seen. Lyssa busied her idle hands by braiding Aristagnë's hair into a complicated hairstyle, and Theoneus was talking Adamantus's ear off.

Whether he was listening to him was anyone's guess, but the way I felt his gaze on me told me I owned his attention until I crossed the threshold.

The useless introspection came to a halt as Lyceus bowed us into his test, glowing eyes and teeth projecting nothing but hollow lust my way.

"I can't wait to see what you do this time," he said to me.

Aethusa scoffed at him, brimming with offense, and I couldn't blame her.

Rolling my shoulders and stretching my neck, I readied myself for whatever gilded horror tied up this hellish competition.

The Godsgate bathed us in blinding sunshine and I followed the warmth in, weapon already drawn.

Large stone griffins took form first, bordering a gate too high and wide to ignore.

"One of us will tell you the truth and the other will lie," they said in unison. *"It is your first task to determine which of us to believe."*

"And then?" I prompted.

"After you make your choice, you will be told a riddle," said the one on the right.

"If you answer right, you get to ask one of your own," said the one on the left.

United in their vicious glee, they announced, *"If you answer wrong and I answer right, I get to eat you."*

This was not how these usually went.

I needed to think of a riddle fast. But what could these things not already know?

My competitor strolled to the front. "What happens if you can't answer my riddle?"

"I concede and let you pass," they said.

Aethusa began to look awfully pleased with herself. "It's like I'm back home."

There was no doubt the fey were fond of aggravating games full of trickery, and the oracles that fed off their connection to Lyceus did tend to speak in riddles.

I considered them, remembering similar figures from my grandmother's stories. Back when I had been small enough to lean my weight against her. When she'd pet my hair as she commentated on the tales she retold, giggling as she complained about the parts that bothered her.

In this case, it was about how no one thought to test the gate guardians by using undeniable facts.

"How do we determine which of you is lying?" I asked.

"You ask a question, but only receive one word as an answer," they said.

Aethusa didn't waste another second, demanding, "Where am I from?"

"Faerie," they both said.

She frowned at them, trying again. "Where do I hail from?"

"Faerie."

"No, where was I born?"

"Faerie."

An internal scream had her wiggling with aggravation.

She wasn't being specific enough, giving them enough space to toy with her. Her question needed to specify what court she was a princess of.

I half-turned to block Aethusa's view of me. "I can ask any question? Any at all?"

"Yes," they both agreed.

"Good." I raised my hand to the side of my face, thumb curled in. "How many fingers am I holding up?"

They remained silent. I could hear their beaks grinding under the effort to keep them shut.

I wiggled my fingers at them. "Well?"

"Seven," said the one on the right.

"Four," said the one on the left.

Nonna was going to get a laugh out of this. That was, if I finally gathered the nerve to face her ghostly form, and make Adamantus let me see her.

"Your time to choose your side has ended," they said. *"It is time to test your cleverness."*

I swallowed, wishing the task was to just wrestle one of these birds. There was a reason I had less trouble in the more physical tests rather than those that screwed with my mind.

Hands on her hips, pearlescent skin maximizing her irritated expression, Aethusa urged them impatiently. "Get on with it then."

"Toothless it devours, and devastates within hours. All bow to it, even the greatest powers and even the scents it sours."

Imagining my grandmother heckling the griffins made it easier to envision my mother leaping up to smack me upside the head. Not everything could be solved with my hands, especially in cases where they couldn't compensate for my big mouth.

I could almost hear her telling me 'the first thought may have been the best thought when it came to violence, but not when it was unnecessary'. In times like this, I needed to 'let my tongue simmer before it left the volatile heat behind my teeth' or however that grating phrase went. It had had something to do with cooking ox-tongue before the translation chopped it up.

Regardless, I bit my tongue to keep myself from spitting out the obvious answer.

Aethusa said what I was thinking. "Time."

Confident in her response, she stood before the right-side

guard and asked, "What walks on four legs in the morning, two at noon and three at night?"

Overcome with disbelief at what I'd just heard, I wheezed, "You idiot, everyone knows that one now!"

It was too late, the right-side griffin launched itself at her, and she fled its relentless pursuit with the speed of a wasp.

Once its taloned feet lifted her up and away by her shoulders, I had to reset my attention before I witnessed another pointless death.

Of course, she didn't know just how widespread that riddle had become. Time moved so slowly in Faerie, they must think we still live in the second millennium.

The remaining griffin rounded on me, repeating the riddle. *"Toothless it devours, and devastates within hours. All bow to it, even the greatest powers and the scents it sours."*

No one else was around to hear me squeak out an uncertain guess. "Disease?"

The griffin lowered its head in a single nod. *"Ask me yours in turn."*

"You sure I can't just fight you instead?" I may have sounded like I was joking, but I truly wasn't. "Or literally anything else?"

It glowered at me.

When I got out of this, I was going to tackle Lyceus and stick the tridagger where even his sunlight didn't shine. If Polyope wanted it back she was going to have to rip out of her brother's anal cavity, because that's the least she deserved for sending me into all these tasks blind.

Adamantus' greatest pains seemed to be being honest or talking about his feelings, so I was going to force him to recount everything that happened last night. That alone would be far more painful to figure out than whatever riddle I was supposed to have—

But what was more enigmatic than Death Himself, unknown to even the most powerful of gods?

A hand on each weapon, I sidled up to the griffin and asked,

"What do you call Death when the living aren't around to hear it?"

It narrowed its eyes at me. *"That's not a riddle."*

"Isn't it though?"

"It's not."

I shrugged. "Then you should have no trouble answering it."

Minutes ticked by with impatient sweat trailing down my face.

Why did taunting several gods feel less unnerving than this? Was it because Adamantus and Polyope were nearby?

"The Lord of the Nether Court's name is not to be spoken out loud."

A gate guardian using euphemistic titles for Death and his domain, and a faerie princess thinking her riddle remained obscure. These ought to be parts in a comedic play.

Or the stories I'd tell my own granddaughters if I got home intact.

"Death's secret name, do you know it or not?" I pressed.

It ruffled its head, puffing its neck feathers, but not moving its amber eyes off me.

I'd put it between a whirlpool and a kraken. It could either dare to say his name and 'risk getting Death's attention or concede and let me pass.

Wild ideas did, occasionally, pay off. The gate slid open and I bolted in, running a mile before I noticed how repetitive my surroundings had gotten.

Hedges boxed me in, with thick curves making up the corners of the emerald green walls, and their leaves smelled like apples. A far nicer labyrinth than the one I'd met Polyope in.

Sandals off and veil around my waist, I let the limited path-ways lead me through whatever waste of time this was, expecting a scare around every corner.

Though I'd made lousy guesses about the previous tests, whatever waited to chase me through here, I just hoped it wasn't Aristagnë's rumored brother. I'd be too tempted to keep the horns as a trophy and that would certainly make her regret befriending me.

Several turns later, with my head thrown back as I groaned at the sky, I walked into the first change of pace.

A blank canvas sat by a readied palette, its coils of oil paint glistening like lopsided snail shells, and a stone garden bench was the offered seat.

"What am I supposed to do with this?" I yelled at the sky.

"Paint something for me," Lyceus crooned flirtatiously.

Was this a joke?

"Riddles, paint, what's next, asking me to play the harp?"

"Can you?"

"I'd sooner use it to shoot arrows!" I dropped before the canvas, taking it as a chance to rest my feet. "What is this? A punishment for last night?"

"What are you talking about?"

There was no coyness, playful or vindictive. He sounded genuinely confused.

How much of our conversation did he remember? How much did Adamantus remember?

"What am I meant to be doing here?"

"Express yourself in a way that isn't biting wit or extreme violence," he purred. *"Put forth a piece of your soul to show that you are more than just aggression, but something sensitive or even sensual."*

Each request landed like a backhanded slap, fixating on the traits I needed as pitfalls for what I wanted. Aggression versus affection. "What does this have to do with anything?"

"We need to know what type of person you are outside of cunning and warfare, especially if we're meant to deify you as, not just a new deity, but a queen."

I gaped ahead, worrying that Theoneus's festive interference had fried my mind.

"Harder than it sounds, isn't it?"

There weren't enough cruses under his sun that I could fling at him.

"Let your tender, creative side work for a bit. Artistry can be very good for reframing certain problems, and perspective was what gods like my sister and Eurycrius lacked."

Artistry? I hadn't done anything similar since I learned how to make pottery as a child, and that was all for practical use. This was for mansion-bred brats that had a boast-worthy education, who had the time to learn indulgent hobbies like painting and musical instruments. Things that Lyceus valued as a patron god of the arts.

This was a nightmare.

There was a hint somewhere in him referencing Polyope and Eurycrius "lacking perspective", but that was a trail that could be chased another time. Now, I needed to find where the catch here was.

So, I sat, staring at the canvas and fidgeting against the earth of the labyrinth.

Roots, shoots and vines rose to wrap around the stand, border my feet, and I could almost feel them move beneath my skin as well. It should have been a disturbing sensation, but it felt more like a cramp that needed to be massaged.

So far, the side effects of the pomegranate were nothing but enhancements. I was stronger, more resilient, healing faster, and felt like nearby plant-life were part of my hair and nails.

Considering I had no competitor, I just went for it. Mixing colors on the palette as I've witnessed others do, I dragged the brush across the canvas to depict the one constant I had in life before I'd taken Adamantus's hand. Waking up at the crack of dawn, trading the creaking of grasshoppers for the twittering of birds soon to be overpowered by roosters calling for the work-day to begin.

Sunrise with its liminal shades, softly blending up until it cast its morning light over the sky. A moment of peaceful transition before the sun rose over the horizon and blocked out the remnants of night, and scattered its light through the clouds.

A toddler could have done a cleaner job, but I hadn't been asked to deliver a masterpiece.

Grass grew at my feet, vines twined up around my legs, the earth itself pounding beneath my soles like a pulse. Unquestioned bliss at the speechless connection barely had time to settle in my edges. Smoke punctured the air as the beat quickened beneath my feet.

I sensed the fire before it launched at my head.

Jumping, I barely missed the fireball that tore through the hedge and consumed my portrait in a mass of angry flames.

From both ends, my section of the maze was set ablaze, leaves shriveling up and the skeletal wooden structure beneath it quickly turning into ashes.

Aethusa emerged through the devastation, dangerously bright, her white hair raging above her screeching face as white-hot fire. A smaller, more volatile version of her grandfather, she advanced as the greenery blackened and fell apart in the swarming heat.

Clawed hands crackling, she pitched a fireball at my head. "Your winning streak ends here!"

BURNING GLASS BRIDE

I was too slow.

The fire grazed me mid-escape, singeing my hair and hands as I ran with my arms over my head. It hit the hedge, bolstering the consuming flames so it burned alongside me as I escaped further into the labyrinth.

Like her attacks, Aethusa was hot on my heels, mocking how ill-prepared I was.

"Did you think you'd won? That it was that easy?" Her sunlike shine rose over the accompanying hedge-fire, elongating my shadows ahead of me. "All you did was rid me of the competition, for I was going to be pitted against them before that three-faced bitch threw you in!"

Another fireball sailed over my head and exploded a few feet away. Reflex brought me to a slipping stop, dropping back with my toes just a hair's breadth away from the dying flames.

On the ever-widening scale between bravery and idiocy, I wasn't about to tip over the line of insanity and believe I could fight off fire. All I could do was try to get out of the labyrinth as fast as possible.

Unless this was the point.

Lyceus had lured me into a trap. This whole task had been a distraction so his prized pick could chase me through a literal maze and *burn me alive*. Whether it was premeditated to spite his sister, or out of rage from my rejection, neither mattered right now.

Just as Aethusa geared up to launch another attack, I leaped over the dying flames and ran further in, unable to think my way out of this.

There wasn't a cloud in the sky and the rising smoke wasn't accumulating fast enough to trigger rainfall. There was no water within reach, and I was one of Eurycrius's many unlucky bastards that didn't inherit his whims with the weather.

What did I have left?

The never-ending zigzag through the green walls weighed on me, the exertion pulled at my muscles and tightened the flesh around my spinning head. Committing to the speed of a bolting deer exhausted me twice as fast in the midst of the burning hedges outlining my trajectory.

The whip and the tridagger would be useless against her, if not melt upon impact. What could I do? *What do I do?*

"What's the matter?" Aethusa drawled. "Run out of bright ideas?"

The fireball burned at my back long before it could hit me. I used the momentum I had drummed up to throw myself as far as I could and flopped face down onto the ground.

I'd killed the screecher devouring my sanity, evaded the sirens using my desires against me, defeated the forest monster, and killed that earthquaking monstrosity! But I was going to meet my end at the hands of a fiery faerie? It spat in the face of everything I'd built myself up to be!

Dirt spraying out my dry, heaving lips, I rose to continue and inhaled a suffocating amount of smoke. A lovely example of man's work with nature had become a nightmare with a speed only flame could accomplish. It hurt me more than I could bear.

Beneath my hands and knees, I felt the earth stir, and tug at my limbs. Stronger than it had been in the living forest and on the ship. If only I had space between my brutal coughs to let it settle.

Aethusa landed with a blinding blast that sent me scurrying back on all fours, screaming as my burning eyes flooded through the twitching gap of their lids.

Moving was impossible. Everywhere around me had become the fiery hell many claimed Adamantus ruled over.

"It really says a lot about the other gods when their choices were lost so easily in tests they made," she tutted. "It says even more about the insect goddess that she chose something so lousy. Was it delusion or overconfidence that had her lead you like a lamb to the slaughter?"

I was not a lamb. *I was not prey.*

Yet here I was cornered like one.

This couldn't happen. Not after all of this. I refused to have Chloë released back home only to tell my mother that I had died for nothing, at the hands of this living firework!

Defiance heaved out dry breaths, fed by the urge to rip her apart—and the ground rumbled in agreement. "Come any closer and it will be the last thing you do!"

Bright face split in a manic, triumphant grin, Aethusa raised her flaming hand to strike, thinning the air with the heat that robbed my body of its sweat. "You've made this too easy, I expected some excitement."

Primitive rage emerged in a throat-tearing screech that rivaled the quaking earth. "Here's your excitement!"

An indescribable link speared up through my palms and the flames consuming my corner of the labyrinth turned bright green. There was no question, no lick of confusion in how I'd withstand the tongues of flame she wielded.

Against my warning, Aethusa towed the line. Fingers tight over the binding force under my command, I curled up my arms and brought forth her doom.

Colossal thorns burst from where she stood, breaking the dry-scorched ground to brutally impale her.

Aethusa lasted long enough for her dimming face to trade triumph for agony. No chance to scream as spines pierced her center, slim, sharp blades stabbed her from the inside out, and extinguished her fires.

Exhaustion claimed me. I crashed down before her, gasping and groaning as exertion fled with the thick smoke darkening the sky.

Pain pulsated alongside my calming heartbeat. It seemed to grow the longer I lied there, unhurried now that the main threat had been eliminated, and able to process the damage I'd taken. From my neck to my calves, everything ached. The effort of killing her, not unlike lifting an immense weight in bad form, put a snapping strain on my joints and ligaments.

Now, there was no denying the leap in power I had undergone since the last task. My ability to command green-magic had surpassed the usual sense of reinvigorating sickly plants or categorizing food from poison by instinct. We had to discuss it now that this was over, and how it could be used to cement my position back home...

Why was I still in the burning labyrinth? Why hadn't Polyope retrieved me?

In the time I sat up, a portal opened behind me. Facing her flared the bruises of strain. "What took you so long? Do you have any idea what your brother put me through?"

My grouchiness was cut short in favor of slow-setting bewilderment. Instead of Polyope's triple-form, I found Rhoxane clutching a long knife.

"Why did you have to win?" Her voice shook as much as her hands. "I wouldn't have to do this if you'd lost."

Despite the roasting air, my blood chilled. "Rhoxane. Rhoxane, what are you doing?"

"What I have to."

She advanced as the portal vanished, leaving me between her

and Aethusa's body, its remnant heat hitting my back in waves. I tried to stand, but I had no strength left, my stamina and defiance mere embers among the polluted air I choked on.

"Put the knife down," I wheezed, holding back coughs. "Just put it down and we can talk about this."

She shook her head, tears falling faster down her face. "I don't have time to talk. I have to get this over with before they realize what's happening and come for you."

Rhoxane took measured steps towards me, each punctuated with a loud sob or sniffle, but her grip steadied as she came dangerously close. The blade of her knife was long, thin and ended on a sharp point, the kind that would take one plunge to pierce right through me.

This made no sense. Why was this happening, why now?

Remaining energy gathered in my arms, and I crawled back to put as much distance between us as possible until the feeling returned past my knees. "Who's making you do this?" I wrestled with my fried nerves to think, but I could only push out precious air in a shout. "Talk to me!"

"I can't. I can't," she sobbed breathlessly. "My freedom, my life depends on doing what she couldn't. She'll free me, she'll take my child and care for it while I can start a new life, a good one. The life I'd always wanted before Eglaia cut it short and her son ruined me!"

Eglaia was behind all this?

Questioning motives and plots had no place in this moment, but it distracted me long enough to forget Rhoxane's sorcery.

Her unarmed hand danced with thickening threads of magic. With a turn of her wrist, they shot at me.

I tore the tridagger from my belt, right before the threads caught me.

Tight around my neck, waist, wrists and ankles, they followed her beckoning gesture to lift me up like puppet-strings. Held up like a cleaner reflection of Aethusa, dread consumed me faster than the fire did the leaves. I could only move my wrists, fingers curled stiff around the handle of the tridagger.

"Rhoxane, please," I begged. "I can help you—"

"Because that worked so well the first few times?" she spat, on the verge of blubbering. "There is nowhere I can hide from her if I fail."

It didn't matter that I wasn't dying as my own kill had, I could feel the internal agony of a hundred spines tearing through me. I had nothing but loathing for whatever I battled, but despite hovering at her mercy, I only felt overpowering sadness.

This shouldn't be happening, neither of us deserved to be in this position.

"I'll make it quick." Rhoxane raised her blade. "Close your eyes."

There was no other way out of this. I had no choice.

Rhoxane brought the knife down in a stabbing arc just as the dagger twisted in my palm. It made little difference that I'd blinked long enough to miss the impact, I still heard my blade slice right through her.

I hit the ground, back where I'd started, helplessly looking up at her as blood poured from her gagging mouth and the hole in her left shoulder.

Doe-eyes blank with shock, her fading wheezes the only sound for miles. Staggering back slipped the knife through her fingers. She slowly lifted her twitching head, darkening blood oozing out her slackened jaw as the tridagger slid out of her and landed between my feet.

There was no last word. No instant of understanding. No shared look of forgiveness or even misery. Rhoxane might not have even registered the last thing to ever happen to her, glassy-eyed and still, even before she'd collapsed.

Unable to hold back any longer, I gave into the wobble of my mouth and the burn in my eyes. I couldn't hold anything back or keep quiet. I forced myself onto all fours and crawled to her side, the fire-baked ground stained maroon around her, a long-dried splatter.

It wasn't tears blurring my vision, her image wavered til it settled on a distorted form. One where her stomach curved outward, high up on her midsection and large for her frame.

Rhoxane had been close to giving birth, and I killed her.

42

UP IN SMOKE

There was no telling how long I lay there, fading in and out of consciousness, until a doorway appeared by me.

Theoneus emerged, hair tied back and in flowing shorts. "This is not the sort of chaos I wanted from this competition."

Aristagnë followed, webbed hands over her mouth. "I knew Lyceus's pick would try something, but not her. What could she have even—oh." They locked eyes briefly. "Theo. Theo, she's pregnant."

"Must have been her tactic, pulling on the heartstrings to seem harmless." He knelt by us, picking up the knife. "Pretty testy form of manipulation, having to depend on your target having feelings."

"It worked on you, didn't it?" Aristagnë's wet, cold hand was welcome on my hot, peeling skin. "Cora, can you hear me?"

I tried to speak, but my throat was too dry, managing only a crackling exhalation. In response, she lifted me up by my underarms and let me slouch against her on weak legs.

In between comforting whispers, she walked me to the Godsgate, circumventing the two between us.

"Last time I had to do this, she was awake and needed me to

numb her pain." Theoneus eyed Rhoxane's knife and her swollen midsection. "Oh, well. Won't matter now if I stick it in her liver!"

Arm around my waist, she turned me in to spare me the sight of him cutting Rhoxane open. The sickening sounds were unavoidable, the hard slice of a cow being disemboweled and the squelching of her butcher's hands in her guts.

A few feet in, I realized this wasn't where I'd left for my ambushed exam, but near Subsomnia, the sub-court belonging to the god of sleep.

"Where is everyone?" I rasped, so thirsty the purple river water tempted me. "Why are we here?"

Her large, fishy eyes watched me worriedly, I could almost see her thought process reflected in them. Debating whether she should respond or not. "The spot of your send-off was kind of destroyed."

Mentions of destruction elevated my pulse, blocking all sound save for the echo of Theoneus's announcement: "It's a boy!"

It took sticking my fingers in my ears and a few long, deep breaths for the burning labyrinth to leave my mind. When I came back to myself, I found Aristagnë gone. Returned to her husband and—and the child he'd delivered. A child I'd orphaned, because there was no way his godly father would come claim him. Just as my own hadn't.

I wandered towards Subsomnia, following the sound of the River of Dreams until I noticed the stench of smoke. It hadn't chased me out the Godsgate, it came from far ahead and had a different scent beneath the burn, an unnatural tang I could taste.

Barking beckoned me to the far left, where the Dreamfields grew. I pursued the oncoming noise until I glimpsed Cressida running towards me, and right behind her were the other hounds.

They were all far darker and duller than I'd last seen them, coated in a layer of something that hid their shine. I didn't care what it was, I dragged my feet until their speed doubled, meeting me just as I dropped to my knees, weeping with my arms outstretched.

Cressida slowed to a trot and licked at my face with her cold, dry tongue. I pet her wiry, metallic fur, dusting off clouds of soot.

How did soot get down here?

Argentus and Platinus encircled us protectively as a powerful force approach. Unlike the previous instances, this presence was welcome.

Adamantus came to a stop before me, and the smell that led me here intensified to the point of being unmistakable. Scorched metal.

The accusatory demand for answers died once I raised my gaze. His Horned God form was *charred*. The bone-like substance of his false face burnt black, the material of his clothes ruined beyond recognition, whole sections of it missing, leaving him in the sleeveless remains of his undershirt and his blast-torn trousers. Every part of his skin from his neck to his feet was coated in pitch, like he'd been dug out from the remains of a volcanic eruption.

I rose as he reached for me, breathing out with relief, "Cora!"

Whatever our last interaction had ended on, I could barely remember, let alone care. I threw my weight into his chest, huddling the golden hound between our legs while the other two continued circling.

"What happened?" I mumbled into his collarbone. "Why did any of this happen? Why didn't Polyope come get me?"

"Lyceus happened." He wrapped his arms around me, pressing me against him. "Not long after you left through his Godsgate, he attacked Polyope."

"Attacked her how?"

I felt his nails graze the sides of my arms until he willed himself to relax with a grumbling exhalation. "He tried to remove one of her heads."

Delirium tickled at the edges of my consciousness, as the visualizing that caused a hiccup too close to a laugh for comfort. "Is she—Is she still intact?"

"She is. Though whether that head remains functional, that answer will have to wait for when she wakes," he said. "I had to call Codeinus to put her in dreamless sleep, along with the others I could capture."

"What did all this to you?"

Adamantus pulled back and his face slowly morphed back to what I longed to see. The charred bone made way for scorched marble, the blue of his hair dulled to a lifeless black, and every sharp angle of his face smudged by the layers of burn. His eyes, maintaining their steady violet glow, were the only unmarked part of him.

"Theoneus attempted to influence Lyceus into releasing his sister, but he resisted long enough to round on me." He combed my hair off my face, it was as brittle and dry as dead grass. "I stabbed him with my bident to subdue him, and he unleashed the fury of the Sun on us."

That was a poetic way to say that he'd exploded in a mass of fiery, white-hot rage. A magnified, disastrous version of what his granddaughter nearly did to me.

"His champion tried to burn me alive. The entire test was a trap."

"I figured as much when I couldn't find you in the agreed-upon area," he said, anger lingering in his bite. "It took eons until we tracked down where you'd gone. I'd have retrieved you myself, but I had to deal with the damage Lyceus left us."

I gulped, throat painfully dry. "What did you mean 'the ones you could capture'?"

"The gods who'd come to attend the battle for my hand. I rounded up all but two. One of which I'd never considered to suspect."

"Eglaia," I acknowledged. "She sent her champion after me. She showed up after I defeated Aethusa to kill me, and—and—"

I couldn't say it out loud. It hurt too much.

"It wasn't Eglaia."

Surprise unwound my heartstrings. "But she brought Rhoxane."

"And she's still here, along with her husband in Codeinus's dungeons, snoring loud enough to be heard in Anactoron."

It made no sense. Rhoxane was scared senseless by her goddess, never once did she slip up and say "he". "Why lie at that point about Lyceus being behind all this?"

"Because he wasn't, at least not from the beginning."

If he wasn't behind all this from the start then who was? Who did we have left that was powerful enough to orchestrate all this and escape before getting caught, while Lyceus left behind to cause an explosive distraction while I was worn out by his pick and finished off by the desperate and indebted Rhoxane? Who else could have her at a greater mercy than her own patron goddess, who wouldn't have fixed all her problems even if she'd won?

"Oh," I realized, the chill of guilt and misery settling in. "Telephassa."

Adamantus nodded. "She must have convinced Lyceus they could share the sky, become the rightful King and Queen of Heaven as celestial beings."

I couldn't remain upright anymore. Whatever had kept me up long enough to see him again had been snuffed out.

He caught me, sweeping me off my numbing feet to carry me to the River of Dreams.

In the rib-bone barge, I couldn't do anything but sag in his hold and let the fumes from the river whisk me off to blessed unconsciousness.

43

REVELATIONS

Cressida's gold nose was all I saw the next time I opened my eyes.

I lousily patted at her snout, groggy and hazy. "Gu grr," I praised her, tongue too heavy to be coherent.

Bone-tired, I sat up and found that I wasn't in my quarters, but in a much more spacious bedroom. If it could be called that. The bed alone was the size of my room, high on its platform that overlooked purple granite floors, the furniture bound in dragonhide and a pair of balcony doors. One was cracked open, allowing a soft breeze and the nearby trail of music.

No, the music was coming from another direction. Through the bedroom doors far ahead of me.

Since I was last aware, both the hellhound and I had been cleaned. Her gold form polished to perfection, and my body scrubbed of grime, damp hair and skin both rubbed with hydrating oil.

When I stood, the heat-ruined clothes announced their presence by tightening around me. I hadn't been changed out of them, and the whip and tridagger were nowhere to be found, but pomegranate half had remained in my pocket. The Fates only knew if it would have done me any good against Aethusa, but there was no use looking back at the gigantic spines that impaled her.

Cressida came to my side, high enough to lean against as I hobbled out the room.

Past the bedroom doors, she led me into a recreational space, where a large crystal harp and a matching piano played a soothing tune. Surrounding them was a bookcase built into two of the walls, and eggplant-purple couches stretched out before the large windows. At least two cities of the Nether Court skyline could be viewed from here.

Cressida stopped at the couches, where her fellow hounds sat on the opposing seats, leaving the one facing the windows empty. A dip in one of the cushions told me it had been recently vacated.

Adamantus' sudden reappearance had me leaping out of my skin. "How are you feeling?"

Lingering exhaustion had dampened my reflexes. Normally, I'd be on the defensive, ready to disarm on instinct, but I faced him with a shuddering breath. "Not too good. You?"

In the same vein as his hounds, he'd been scrubbed of all the signs of a fiery ambush. Free of the burns and the disguise, he stood in an open silk robe that matched his eyes, and grey, cotton sleep clothes that attested to him making use of that bed.

The corner of his blued mouth quirked briefly, not quite a smirk. A failed attempt at a soothing expression. "I'm not looking forward to what we need to discuss."

Loaded statements never boded well. "That you haven't gotten what you wanted out of this holy disaster?"

"That we have no more excuses to avoid being honest with one another."

From his pocket, he took out the knife Rhoxane had attacked me with. What Theoneus had used to free her child.

"The baby," I choked, on the verge of tears. "Where is he?"

"With the happy couple. Aristagnë managed to import a nymph nursemaid while Theoneus lulled him. The infant screeched like he was being tortured in the Spiral," he griped, refreshingly annoyed in this depressing circumstance. "Don't worry about him."

"What do I need to worry about now?" I made a feeble attempt at a joke. "I did my job, won your hand before their eyes and helped unearth the culprit. Time for you to drop me back home."

"We need to worry about what Telephassa's next move is, now that she doesn't care that we know it's her." He chucked her knife onto the couch. "This wasn't a screwup. She gave your would-be killer the knife her huntresses carry, and expects you to be dead. What initially hid you from her barely matters when she can recognize your energy."

"Are you saying you want to keep me here longer?"

He reached back into his pocket, jaw tightening. "What I want is the least of what matters, always has been."

"Except when it comes to whatever you need to find through Eurycrius?" I pointed out. "That's what you said, wasn't it? Why do you need to find Eurycrius so badly? What could you possibly need him for if the affairs of the terrestrial and celestial realms don't affect you at all?"

"If I know what he did to be where no gods can find him, he might lead me to what I'll been looking for as far back as I can remember." Hand back in his pocket, I felt him grow worked up over whatever was coming next. "There I could find where *he's* been since he saddled me with this underworld and vanished."

In retrospect, it explained some of the stranger things surrounding him, stemming from him, but the pieces of the puzzle took their time falling into place.

"Orcus." I gripped the back of the couch for support, struggling to spit it out. "You've been searching for the real Orcus."

Head thrown back, he blew out a long-suffering breath, angles softening with relief. "Yes."

I couldn't think. The weight of that secret had left his shoulders and landed on my head, leaving me unable to string together a solid reaction.

"Ever since he left, my one lead has been the suspicious circumstances his heavenly counterpart disappeared under." He came closer, basking in my hot breath as it left my open mouth in amazed heaves. "Long before your father left a trail of chaos behind, Orcus had taken the time to plan his vanishing act. Only he made sure that he'd leave something behind, bound to run the afterlife in his steed."

As dumbfounded as I was, this event did have a precedent. Many current gods had taken over for the titans that ruled back when the world was young and still being shaped. We still knew some of their names, and found ancient depictions of them in remnants of forgotten civilizations.

If that were the case, why did no one know this about Death? Younger cultures depicted the aesthetic change Adamantus himself created, but why not acknowledge the reason why?

"Why didn't you tell anyone, the mortals who still fear mentioning him, or the other gods who call you by his name?" I searched his face, like I was seeing it for the first time. "Who are you?"

Hollow amusement bared his teeth. "Adamantus, Lord of the Dead."

"What were you before that?"

A bitter laugh pierced me with arrows of regret. "Nothing."

"Now's not the time to be obtuse or even humble," I rasped, ears pounding.

"You know I'm neither of those things, and neither are you. Just as you question my origins, I would like a real answer as to why you have randomly manifested earth-magic. Why you've gone from the run-of-the-mill demigod to summoning agile roots and killer thorns."

Polyope had never told him, and I'd never had the chance to.

"Does that outweigh the mystery of my undetectable existence?"

"That's no-longer a mystery." He stole a glance at the bedroom. "I didn't catch it the first time, but when I cleaned your skin, I saw it. It is what hid you from all divine eyes."

Recollections of the night before outweighed envisioning him washing my hair and wiping me down. I reached behind me, scraping the bottom of the brand on my back.

"Are you talking about my *acanthomatia*?" I barely recognized my own voice, dull and distant. "It's just a brand my mother gave me to—to…"

And it hit me at last. I had no idea how it hadn't till now.

"It wasn't a brand to give me connection to the earth and boost my stamina," I choked, beyond stunned. "It was brand to hide me from Eurycrius. But it also worked on other gods!"

"It would seem so."

Cressida derailed the train of thought by leaping onto the couch behind me, her head now on its back. To ground myself, I pet her fiber fur, not taking my eyes off Adamantus.

"I don't know how that mark ended up on you, or the extent of its power, but its explanation doesn't extend to your manifesting powers," he said.

Now was my chance. "I'll answer your question if you answer mine."

He worked his jaw, tense enough to create cracks along his marble face. "As you wish."

"Adam, what were you before he made you his successor?" I took his hand, vibrating with nervousness. "Tell me, who were you?"

"I told you. Nothing." He tightened his fingers around mine, humorless, aching laughter setting an eerie tone. "Prior to Orcus' plan to abandon his post, I didn't exist."

My thoughts stalled as the implications struggled to make sense of anything but the plainest answer. "Polyope said you were a personification, you are Death. You're Death Itself while Orcus just commanded you. Is that it?"

Adamantus turned my hand up, and placed something cold and smooth in it. It was a curious element, somewhere between a precious metal and a diamond, angles gleaming with hypnotic quality and heavier than anything its size ought to be.

"What is this?"

"It's me," he stated, withdrawn, eyes darkened. "It's what Orcus sculpted me out of."

Everything came to a shrieking halt as this revelation hit me headfirst. This inexplicable fact, this great, grievous secret that he had just put in my hands, upended all that I knew before and after following him into his underworld.

"Adamantine," I rasped, trying to remember how to breathe. "You are adamantine as your hounds are silver, gold and platinum."

He lowered his head in a slight nod, silent yet emanating a maelstrom of distress. Wordlessly anticipating my undoubtedly horrible reaction to what he'd just shared with me. To the piece of him I now held, worn-out body unable to maintain its mass, and unraveling mind failing to grasp this fact.

All reactionary questions and implications shattered to innumerable pieces, glass returning to sand grains. They could all wait, but how we proceeded from here could not.

There was no doubt that being torn to shreds for inspection and explanations was the last thing he wanted. I could see the predetermined disappointment weighing down his every outline, the disheartened flicker that rendered his eyes the darkest I'd ever seen them.

Somehow, I surprised us both by cracking up. "You bastard," I cackled, high-pitched and hysterical. "When I broke my hand on you, I asked what your face was made from and you actually told me the truth."

Whether this was what I had subconsciously aimed for or not, he did relax. "That's all you have to say to me?"

Fact of the matter was, I was too drained to make any sense of this. Glancing back and forth, between him and the near-mythical stone in my grip, offered up nothing but clear disbelief.

What stood before me was not animated metal or stone, it was far too complex, too real to be in the same vein as the hellhounds. And I had felt him. Felt his breath on my own, his grip on my body and his heartbeat under my touch and my aching head.

What else could I say to him now? What could this even mean?

"Anything else will have to wait until I'm certain this moment isn't born of heatstroke." I set the piece down by Telephassa's knife, pausing to regulate my breathing as I calmed back down. "Despite that, I feel that you have held this close to your chest for so long. Why share this with me?"

Tenderness softened the edges of his tortured gaze, reinvigorating the urge to touch him and validate his namesake by own senses. "Because our time together may be coming to an end, and I can't let you go without telling you what I am."

"Infinitely expensive?"

A flash of teeth expelled all trails of confusion surrounding him. He could have told me he was the nightmarish skeleton millions believed him to be and I wouldn't feel any different. I never had, not when I reached for him in the forest of dreams.

"Neither can I let us part without telling you why I wish you'd remain." Solemn, the starlit centers of his eyes reignited once they found my own. "No amount of restraint can hold back how I feel, or fight the hold you have over me."

Back on my feet, I moved into his space, smoke still filling my chest and rendering my anticipatory breaths shallow. I reached into the ruined pants, a ready hand on my end of the bargain. "You're guilty of the same pull on my end and have been since my search ended in those woods."

Heavy charge thickened the air, far from the tortuous

destruction of the labyrinth and the bewitching fog of the sirens, but just as overpowering. Preoccupations and revelations faded into the background, plunging me back into that voyage through sleep, where nothing else mattered but reaching what called to me.

"I know now that the Fates didn't show you to me as a solution, they put you in my path to show me what I didn't know I was searching for." Sincerity steadied the depth reverberating out his elegant throat, humming in my tired bones. "I have hated every miserable minute of my existence until I met you, and I can't bear the hours that await me without you."

Rage was far from my reach, but the volume that burst forth rode on frantic, frayed feelings that had me babbling like I was possessed. "You think I'll be content, leaving what I sought out for so long? After wading through waking nightmares, scraping by the death you deal out, and losing pieces of what made me myself—I'm meant to return to life before I met you?" I pounded on my chest, rattling smoked lungs and bruised ribs. "What am I supposed to do now? I am going home changed in so many ways, with feelings and magic I was never meant to have, but you'll be as I left you."

"I'll be what you made me, forever ruined by what something like me was never meant to glimpse, let alone experience." Adamantus was close enough to kiss, a being of undeniable distance from humanity and proximity to divinity, diamond-steel be damned. "The next time I see you, you'll have finished your life a different person, while no time will have passed for me."

"That's what you think." I blurted out everything that appeared in my mouth, not a care given to sense or shame. "Before you, I'd have rather ripped out my tongue and eaten it than tell a man a single word of what I've dropped at your feet."

"Good thing I'm not a man, but a facsimile of one."

Retrospect reshaped each previous denial of manhood, what contradicted his actions and what I felt towards him and against me. The truth he'd set in my palm was the reason behind his suspicious motives and strange beliefs, and I had to do the same.

"That may have been what you started out as, just as I began life as a demigod like any other, but ended this journey as something advanced." I held out my hands in offering, pomegranate halve presented in my palms. "This is the secret behind my strangeness."

Adamantus grew stiff and stepped back, accusatory finger pointed at me. "You ate from my grove?"

"You said I needed a boost, and when you couldn't get a golden apple this was the next best thing?"

That didn't seem to matter, it just wound him up further. "The golden apples grow in your realm! They're ambrosia mortals can consume without binding them to the place they grew in!"

"Binding?" I stuttered.

"Cora." He swooped back in, hands clawed, tension sharpening his angles and baring his fangs. "I need you to be honest with me, how much of this half did you eat? A few seeds?"

"I've finished the other half," I wheezed, struggling to breathe. "Nothing else I ate here was a problem."

"Nothing else was chthonic ambrosia," he stressed. "Cora, you've consumed divine energy native to the underworld, food that sustains beings on par with and beneath me."

Cold sweat drenched me, like I had been fished out of the sea. "What does this mean?"

"It means you can never live beyond here again, not for long." Fingers around my shaking wrists, thumbs on my pulse points, he anchored me to the damning moment. "You've been mutated and bound to the earth and what lies beneath it."

Fights and fantasies crumbled under the reality of what I'd been deceived to do, a means to an end that mutated me into something between earthly and deathly. At the end of all I'd obtained and achieved, the one goal I'd descended here with had been ripped from my reach.

I could never go home.

⸻ ◆ ⸻

THE END

403

⸻ ◆ ⸻

NOTE FROM THE AUTHOR

I hope you've enjoyed THE STARLESS KING!

Reviews and word of mouth are *everything* to indie authors, so share your thoughts with others! Even a line on Amazon, Goodreads and Bookbub would be vital to my success, the book's sales, and hugely appreciated.

To know when Book II of *Into the Nether Court* releases, and keep up with exclusive content, news, updates and offers, please sign up to my VIP Mailing List.

In the meantime, check out:

My first series, FAIRYTALES OF FOLKSHORE.

My villain-romance novella THE SORCERER AND THE SWAN PRINCESS.

Thank you for reading!
Lucy

PRONUNCIATION GUIDE

<u>PEOPLE</u>

Aethusa: Ay-thoo-suh
Adamantus: Aa-deh-man-tuss
Almagera: Ull-mah-jer-ruh
Amatius: Ah-ma-tee-uss
Argentus: Are-jen-tuss
Aristagnë: Ah-riss-tag-nee
Cassia: Kass-yah
Cerelia: Sir-reel-yah
Codeinus: Koh-deen-uss
Coralia: Kor-ahl-yah
Eglaia: Ee-gla-yah
Erthamos: Ur-tha-moss
Eurycrius: Yoo-ree-kree-yuss
Formeta: Fore-may-tu
Lyceus: Lee-see-uss
Lyssa: Liss-uh
Machaius: Mah-kay-uss
Orcus: Ore-kuss
Polyope: Pol-lee-oh-pee

Prospera: Proh-spair-ah
Rhoxane: Roe-ks-an-eh
Telephassa: Teh-leh-fah-ssah
Theoneus: Thee-own-nee-uss
Zenobia: Zeh-no-bee-ya

<u>PLACES</u>

Anactoron: *Ah-naak-toh-ron*
Athanasia: *Ah-tha-nass-yuh*
Cahraman: *Quh-ruh-mahn*
Campania: *Kahm-pahn-yaa*
Crisotemia: *Kree-soh-tem-yaa*
Granaria: *Grah-naar-yaa*
Meropis: *Meh-roe-peace*
Orestia: *Oh-res-tee-yah*
Psychepolis: *Sai-kee-poh-liss*
Subsomnia: *Sub-som-nee-yuh*
Tritonia: *Tree-tone-nee-yuh*

ABOUT THE AUTHOR

With one foot in reality and the other one lodged firmly in fantasy, Lucy Tempest has been spinning tales since she learned how to speak.

Now, as an author, people can experience the worlds she creates for themselves.

Lucy lives in Florida with her family and two spoiled cats, who would make terrible familiars.

Sign up to her VIP Mailing List at *lucytempest.com/newsletter*

Join her reader group <u>Lucy Tempest's Legion</u>

And follow her on

facebook.com/LucyTempestAuthor

twitter.com/lucy_tempest

bookbub.com/authors/lucy-tempest

amazon.com/author/B071SFRD84

goodreads.com/lucy_tempest

pinterest.com/lucytempestauthor

instagram.com/lucytempestauthor

FAIRYTALES OF FOLKSHORE:

Thief of Cahraman

Prince of Cahraman

Queen of Cahraman

Beast of Rosemead

Beauty of Rosemead

Princess of Midnight

Dreamer of Briarfell

The Faerie Prince

INTO THE NETHER COURT:

The Starless King

A VILLAIN'S EVER AFTER:

The Sorcerer and the Swan Princess

www.ingramcontent.com/pod-product-compliance
Lightning Source LLC
Chambersburg PA
CBHW030355200726
48286CB00014B/1429